THE WAKEFIELD DYNASTY

GILBERT MORRIS

The
SONG
of
PRINCES

TYNDALE HOUSE PUBLISHERS, INC.
Wheaton, Illinois

Library of Congress Cataloging-in-Publication Data

Morris, Gilbert.
    The song of princes / by Gilbert Morris.
       p.   cm. — (The Wakefield dynasty ; 6)
    ISBN 0-8423-6234-7 (softcover)
    1. Great Britain—History—George II, 1727-1760—Fiction.
  I. Title. II. Series : Morris, Gilbert. Wakefield dynasty ; 6.
PS3563.08742S67 1997
813'.54—dc21   97-22665

Printed in the United States of America

03 02 01 00 99 98 97
8   7   6   5   4   3   2   1

CONTENTS

PART FOUR: A HOUSE DIVIDED—1773–1775

THE WAKEFIELD DYNASTY

6

THE MORGANS

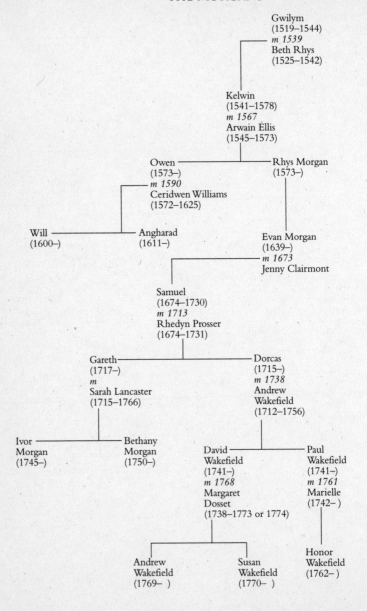

Gwilym
(1519–1544)
m 1539
Beth Rhys
(1525–1542)

Kelwin
(1541–1578)
m 1567
Arwain Ellis
(1545–1573)

Owen
(1573–)
m 1590
Ceridwen Williams
(1572–1625)

Rhys Morgan
(1573–)

Will
(1600–)

Angharad
(1611–)

Evan Morgan
(1639–)
m 1673
Jenny Clairmont

Samuel
(1674–1730)
m 1713
Rhedyn Prosser
(1674–1731)

Gareth
(1717–)
m
Sarah Lancaster
(1715–1766)

Dorcas
(1715–)
m 1738
Andrew
Wakefield
(1712–1756)

Ivor
Morgan
(1745–)

Bethany
Morgan
(1750–)

David
Wakefield
(1741–)
m 1768
Margaret
Dosset
(1738–1773 or 1774)

Paul
Wakefield
(1741–)
m 1761
Marielle
(1742–)

Andrew
Wakefield
(1769–)

Susan
Wakefield
(1770–)

Honor
Wakefield
(1762–)

WAKEFIELD DYNASTY

THE WAKEFIELDS

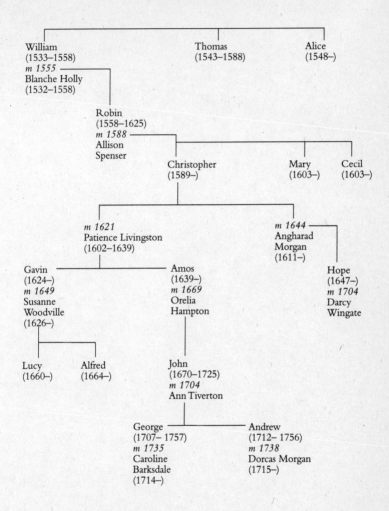

William
(1533–1558)
m 1555
Blanche Holly
(1532–1558)

Thomas
(1543–1588)

Alice
(1548–)

Robin
(1558–1625)
m 1588
Allison
Spenser

Christopher
(1589–)

Mary
(1603–)

Cecil
(1603–)

m 1621
Patience Livingston
(1602–1639)

m 1644
Angharad
Morgan
(1611–)

Gavin
(1624–)
m 1649
Susanne
Woodville
(1626–)

Amos
(1639–)
m 1669
Orelia
Hampton

Hope
(1647–)
m 1704
Darcy
Wingate

Lucy
(1660–)

Alfred
(1664–)

John
(1670–1725)
m 1704
Ann Tiverton

George
(1707– 1757)
m 1735
Caroline
Barksdale
(1714–)

Andrew
(1712– 1756)
m 1738
Dorcas Morgan
(1715–)

The Heir

of Wakefield

One

THE BAD SEED

May 1753

O h, look over in the field—the apples are ripe!"
     The speaker was a young girl of thirteen with carroty
     red hair and the unlikely name of Priscilla Bean. Her
light blue eyes gleamed as she turned to the two boys, more or
less like twin bookends, who flanked her. "Ooooh! I'd *love* to have
one of those juicy apples!"

Instantly her companions turned to look at the orchard that lay
just beyond an ancient stone wall. Their simultaneous movement
gave them an almost comic appearance, for they were identical
twins—David and Paul Wakefield.

Although often the word *identical* is used rather loosely, in
David and Paul's case, it was precisely true. At the age of twelve
they were both thin and their dark blond hair was cut at
exactly the same length, just touching their stiff white collars.
Their direct gray blue eyes and neat features hinted at future
masculine good looks—each had a broad forehead and a short
English nose, a firm mouth with a full lower lip and exceptionally fine teeth, and a pronounced chin that suggested a
trace of stubbornness. The boys were mirror images, wearing
even the same costumes: brown homespun knee breeches,
white stockings, and long-sleeved white shirts. Both wore

scuffed black leather shoes with brass buckles and carried books held together by a strap.

David Wakefield, standing to the right of Priscilla Bean, examined the orchard calmly and methodically—as he did most things. He seemed to be weighing some philosophical question, then turned toward the girl, shaking his head. "It doesn't matter how juicy those apples are, Priscilla. We're not likely to get any of them. You know what a terrible man Saul Beddows is. Remember what he did to Martin Drake last year when he caught him stealing apples?"

Priscilla frowned. "Poor Martin! He had stripes all the way from his neck to his bottom."

Paul Wakefield grinned, his eyes almost disappearing in the characteristic squint that appeared when the twins smiled. "Martin was just dumb!" he announced emphatically. "He deserved to get caught!" Then, snickering, he asked, "How do you know he had stripes on his bottom, Priscilla? Did you see them?"

Priscilla knew exactly which of the twins spoke, for David would never have been so rude. "You're just awful, Paul Wakefield! You shouldn't say such things!"

Paul, however, was paying her no attention. Twirling his books idly by the worn leather strap, he fixed his gray blue eyes speculatively on the apple tree. "It wouldn't be too hard. The ripe ones are up at the top, but old man Beddows is probably asleep. I don't see anything of him."

Knowing his twin almost as well as he knew himself, David replied quickly, "Still, he could see you from the window . . . and if you're caught, you know what a beating you'd get, Paul. Let's go."

But an air of deviltry pulled Paul's lips up at the corners. Cocking his head to one side, he grinned broadly. "Do you really want one of those apples, Priscilla?"

"Oh, you'd better not! It's too dangerous!"

Paul made up his mind instantly. "Come on, David. We can get those apples and be gone before Beddows can get to us, even if he sees us."

"No, Paul—it would be trouble, and Father and Mother wouldn't like it."

But his words fell on deaf ears. "Here, Priscilla," Paul said, "hold my books. You two stay on this side of the fence while I go get a few of those apples." Handing his books to Priscilla, he turned and advanced toward the stone wall. Carefully he observed the cottage that lay on the far side of the orchard. A thin ribbon of smoke rose from the chimney like a fragile spectre, but no one was visible outside. Paul put his hands on top of the wall and, with an agile leap, was over it. He ran to the tall apple tree, a very old one indeed, and reached for the first branch. He climbed quickly, ignoring the apples at the bottom, and soon reached the top. He plucked one juicy red apple, stuck it down his shirt, and followed with a second. He had just reached for the third when he heard a harsh shout. Glancing toward the house, he saw Saul Beddows leap off the front porch and begin to wave a gnarled walking stick furiously.

"Run!" Priscilla cried, then grabbed David's hand. "Come on!"

"We better stay with Paul."

"We've got to get away!" she urged. "I can't be caught here. My pa would whip me if he found out I'd been stealing apples."

Paul snatched a third apple and, stuffing it in his shirt, slid down the tree from branch to branch with the speed of an agile monkey. He hit the ground running, reaching the wall only a few steps ahead of Saul Beddows. Clearing it easily, he ran with all his might for the woods across the road. Behind him Saul's voice bellowed with rage, but Paul just laughed as he dodged inside the grove that lay across the road, knowing that the old man would never catch him now. He made his way through the woods, turning down a briar-covered pathway and finally reentering the road a quarter mile from Beddows's house. He waited there for a moment and soon David and Priscilla came running down the road.

"Here you are, Priscilla," Paul said, removing one of the apples from his shirt with a jaunty air. "And here's one for you, David— and one for me."

Priscilla and David took the apples, but both were reluctant. David shook his head. "I'm afraid we'll all be in trouble over this."

"You worry too much," Paul said, shrugging, then took a bite of the apple. "Hmmmm! These are good! Go on, Priscilla, have a bite." Again he laughed, saying, "Seems like Adam and Eve got in trouble with some fruit from a tree, but we won't worry about that, will we?"

Priscilla began to eat her apple, but David stared at his and then slowly shook his head and handed it back to Paul. "I wish you hadn't done it," he said. "There's sure to be trouble."

The dwelling inhabited by Methodist minister Andrew Wakefield and his wife, Dorcas, along with the twins, David and Paul, was similar to most modest homes in rural Cornwall in the year 1753. Built of native stone, its high pitched roof was covered with a thick coating of thatch. Two small windows in front admitted light, as did the single window on the second floor. On one side a massive stone chimney almost dominated the house. Creeping tendrils of vines covered the south wall and a yew tree of enormous girth served as shade and exercise for the boys.

The inside of the cottage was not pretentious: on the left, one large room used for cooking and dining, and to the right, a sitting room and a small study. In the rear were two bedrooms and a narrow stairway that led to the bedroom upstairs. The kitchen, where two women and two children sat, was low-ceilinged and dominated by a stone fireplace. Every inch was crammed with copper kettles and pots of every sort. Beside the fireplace, a butter churn held together by brass rings showed hard use, and strips of dried apples, peppers, and squash hung from the ceiling. The walls were whitewashed and, by a large window on the south side, shelves of iron and copper utensils rose from floor to ceiling.

One of the women rose from her stool by the table and moved toward a black pot that simmered over the coals in the large fireplace. "I think this stew is almost done." The speaker, Dorcas Wakefield, used her left hand to stir the soup because a childhood accident had made the fingers of her right hand curve inward and rendered them, all except the thumb, completely immobile. She was not, and never had been, a beautiful woman. But at the age of thirty-eight, she retained some trace of the prettiness that had been hers at eighteen. Her figure was more filled out, of course, but she had pleasant features: large, dark blue eyes that were still clear, and dark brown, almost black hair with not a touch of gray. Giving the stew a final stir, she replaced the lid, then returned to her stool. Looking over at the two youngsters seated at the far end of the room, she remarked, "I can't believe our children are growing up so fast, Sarah."

Sarah Morgan looked up at her treasured friend, who'd become her sister-in-law. At one time Sarah had been a Lancaster, the daughter of Sir Talbot Lancaster. When she had given up her life of ease to marry Dorcas's brother, Gareth Morgan, a poor Methodist minister, both Sir Talbot and his wife, Jane, had been astonished and horrified. It had taken several years for them to be reconciled to Sarah's choice. Tall and shapely, with blonde hair and blue gray eyes, Sarah was still a beautiful woman. Although she was the same age as Dorcas, her unlined face looked much younger. "They are growing up," she agreed, glancing at the children. "I'm glad they get along so well. Most little boys don't pay much attention to little sisters, but Ivor's doted on Bethany since the day she was born. And she idolizes him."

"They look very much like Gareth, don't they?"

It was true that both Ivor, eight, and Bethany, three, had received most of their physical traits from Gareth, their Welsh father. Both had his coal black hair, though Bethany's was long and Ivor's was clipped short. They had also received his dark blue eyes, wedge-shaped face, pronounced cheekbones, and thin figure. Sarah said with a smile, "I suppose black hair and dark eyes dominate over blonde hair and blue eyes like mine, but that's all right with me. I always thought their father was prettier than I was."

Dorcas Wakefield laughed abruptly. "Don't ever tell him that."

"It's too late. I already have," Sarah said. Although Gareth's parish was some distance away in the small town of Deerfield, they lived close enough for the families to visit often. On this occasion the Morgans had come for a visit with the Wakefields, for none other than John Wesley, the great Methodist preacher who preached revival, had come to be the Wakefields' overnight guest.

A few feet away from where the women talked, the three ministers sat in the Reverend Andrew Wakefield's tiny study. The room was so dominated by books—the walls were lined with them, every table was stacked high, and boxes on the floor were filled to overflowing—that there was barely room for the three men. The shortest of the three looked around and smiled faintly. "You were always a reader, Andrew."

The speaker, John Wesley, was fifty years old, Andrew's senior by nine years. Only five feet, six inches, John was slender, with long auburn hair that touched his shoulders. His open face with full lips and a long, thin nose had been the subject of some of his enemies' ribald comments. But this Oxford teacher, along with his brother Charles, had shaken England, their field preaching rocking the foundations of the Anglican church. The Wesleys, however, clung to the established church, hoping that the thousands of converts who flocked to their meetings would somehow be taken into its fold. However, there were such strict differences between Wesley and the established church that John almost despaired at times of seeing such a reconciliation. He leaned back now and tapped his fingers together. "I was thinking, Andrew," he said quietly, "of those days when you and I and Charles went to Savannah."

"I think of those days in America a great deal myself, Mr. Wesley." Andrew Wakefield was of average height and still as lean as he had been at the age of twenty. His dark blond hair was cut short, framing intelligent blue eyes, neat features, a broad forehead, and an expressive mouth. He smiled at Wesley, humor glinting in his eyes. "I suppose we made every mistake missionaries could possibly make."

Wesley frowned, for he did not like to be reminded of his errors, but his native humor arose and he laughed. "You're right, Andrew! We meant well, but I remember writing in my journal: 'I went to America to convert the heathens—but who will convert *me?*'"

Sitting across from Wesley was the third man, Gareth Morgan. Six feet tall and strongly built from his early years of coal mining, Gareth had black, curly hair that was roughly cut, a wedge-shaped face, and thick eyelashes, making him altogether a handsome man. He spoke now saying, "Would you like to go back to America, Mr. Wesley?"

"Indeed, I would! But there's little need of that," Wesley remarked thoughtfully. "George Whitefield has declared America his field of endeavor."

"I hear great things are happening there under Whitefield's ministry," Andrew said.

"He is the best preacher I have ever heard," Wesley said. He paused, then added, "And he also has the sweetest nature and temperament of any man I have ever known."

Gareth and Andrew exchanged glances, for they were well aware that Wesley and Whitefield had been strongly divided over doctrinal differences. They said nothing, but Wesley caught the glance and spoke up at once. "We have had our differences, George and I, on some matters of doctrine . . . but I am second to none in admiration of his character and his ability as an evangelist."

"I think you're right about George. I remember how he supported me when I was at Oxford," Andrew commented.

Gareth quickly added, "If it hadn't been for him, I think I would have quit and gone back to Wales."

The three men sat together, speaking quietly for some time, until finally Wesley said to Andrew, "How have you been able to stay within the Anglican church, Andrew? I could never understand it. They will let me speak in none of the churches in London."

Andrew shook his head. "I think they don't know much about me, Mr. Wesley. This is such a small church in a small parish. As far as I know, I preach the same gospel that you preach, but lightning strikes whenever your name is mentioned." He laughed, amused at his own words. "This life suits me well enough. I was never cut out to play a large part in the drama of this world."

"You are the Lord's servant here in Cornwall and I'm grateful to God that you have been able to retain your place in the Church of England." Wesley's words trailed off as he looked wistfully out the window. "I want no division," he continued. "I have no desire to lead anyone away from the Church of England."

Gareth waited until Wesley had finished speaking, then said, "I think it has been put in your way by God, sir. I was not there, but I have heard many times how when you were not permitted to preach inside your old church at Epworth, you went outside and preached standing on your father's tombstone."

Wesley laughed. "Yes, I did. There may have been a little arrogance in me. I'm prone to such prideful things, you know."

"Never say that, Mr. Wesley!" Andrew said quickly. He loved John and Charles Wesley with all his heart and many times had been tempted to leave the established church and become a follower of Wesley as Gareth had done. But somehow God had put it on him to stay in the church in Cornwall all these years and now he wondered aloud, "It occurs to me that someday I may have to leave the Church of England, but until I do I suppose I will remain here. The people have heard everything I know a hundred times."

"They need hear nothing but Jesus," Wesley said at once. "If they hear of him from you, Andrew, as I know they do, then they will have heard what they need to hear."

Gareth looked up as his wife opened the door. "What is it, Sarah?"

"Dinner is ready."

The three men rose at once and Wesley led the way out of the study. Entering the dining room, Andrew asked, "Where are the boys?"

"They're not home from their tutor yet," Dorcas said. "But we'll go ahead without them. I'm sure they'll be here soon enough. Mr. Wesley, will you sit here. . . ." With the five adults around the table, the room seemed even more crowded.

Dorcas had prepared an excellent meal. The table was filled with the colors and rich aromas of food: a delicately breaded baked fish, delicious stew, a platter of crisp roasted chicken basted with butter, bowls of bread-and-butter pudding spiced with currants and nutmeg, and a large bowl of chopped apples mixed with sliced pumpkin for bright color.

"You find Cornwall a hard field," Wesley remarked. "I wonder—"

The door opened suddenly and the twins came in.

"You're late!" Dorcas said firmly.

"Mr. Cummings kept us later than usual on our writing, Mother," Paul said blandly.

"David!" Seated with her brother, Ivor, on stools across the room, eating from plates placed on a box, Bethany now leaped up and ran across the room to grab David. Adults might have been confused sometimes about which twin was David and which was

Paul, but Bethany Morgan, at the age of three, never was. She seemed to know David instinctively because he had spent more time with her than his twin and showed her more consideration. Bethany clung to him, begging him, "Will you read to me?"

"After a while, Bethany," David said fondly, stooping over to give her a kiss.

"Come now, we've left you boys a bit of fish and perhaps a wing of the chicken. Can you say hello to Mr. Wesley?"

Both boys spoke obediently to the visitor, and he greeted them, saying, "As alike as two peas in a pod. How do you ever tell the difference?"

"I'm the naughty one, Mr. Wesley," Paul said with a mischievous grin. "David's the good one."

Finding this amusing, Wesley chuckled and said, "So then, all you have to do is be good, and your parents will think you're the good one?"

"Yes, sir. That's exactly what I do." Paul glanced over at David. "But David's never naughty, so he can't fool anyone."

"That's enough of that!" Dorcas said firmly. "Here, you boys, let me fix you a plate, then you can go eat over by Ivor and Bethany."

As soon as the boys had their plates, they took their places and began to eat hungrily as the adults continued their conversation. Bethany pulled her stool as close to David's as she could, asking him questions persistently, tugging at his sleeve to get his attention. The adults sat drinking tea for the next twenty minutes while the twins finished their meal. Suddenly a tremendous banging on the door made Dorcas jump nervously. "Who is that beating the door down?"

"Let me go," Andrew said. He rose, then walked to the door and opened it. "Why, Mr. Beddows—"

"Mr. Wakefield, I've come about that boy of yours!" Saul Beddows stepped inside. He was a large, burly man in his sixties whose hands were twisted slightly with arthritis, but he was still strong and hale. "I've come about the thieving that they done over at my place!"

Andrew stared at the old man, then replied quietly, "I don't understand you, sir."

"You'll understand it well enough when I tell you that one of those boys of yours stole some of my apples."

"I'd be sorry to think that my boys would do a thing like that."

"You can be sorry all you please, Pastor, but I saw him with my own eyes! I almost caught him, too."

Andrew studied Beddows's face. He knew the old man for an irascible fellow but a good, sound member of the church. A little hard to get along with, perhaps, but faithful as well as he knew how. "You're sure it was one of our boys?"

"Certain sure!"

Andrew turned at once toward the kitchen and called for the boys. When they stood next to him he said quietly, "Paul, did you take Mr. Beddows's apples?" It was significant that he asked Paul, for he could not in his wildest dreams conceive of David doing such a thing.

Paul opened his eyes wide. "No, Father! I didn't steal his apples!"

Andrew blinked and exchanged a quick glance at Dorcas, who was twisting her hands nervously. Then he turned and said, "David, did you take Mr. Beddows's apples?"

David licked his lips. He had been afraid that this would happen and now disaster lay before them! He had an active imagination and could already feel the stick on his back. He did not want to implicate his brother, but when he muttered, "No, sir . . ." guilt was written all over his face.

"*He* is the one, then!" Mr. Beddows growled. "Look at him. Guilty to the bone!"

Dorcas went over to stand beside the boys who would soon be as tall as she. As she looked at the two, somehow she seemed to know the whole history of the incident without having seen a bit of it. She turned and said, "David didn't steal your apples, Mr. Beddows."

"Why, look at him! He's guilty and he needs a bit of this stick." Beddows whipped the hickory stick through the air, making a whistling sound. "I know you'll not be letting me chastise your own sons, Reverend, but I'll think less of you if you don't do it yourself."

Andrew was miserable. He took the stick from Beddows's hand, then looked at David, who appeared more guilty than ever. "I'm sorry to have to do this, David, but—"

"I took his old apples, Father," Paul spoke up, lifting his chin and staring at the old man. "I took three of them. What of it?"

There was such daring in the boy's bearing that the adults in the room—including John Wesley—were taken aback. Paul knew a caning was coming, but he kept his chin high and he didn't show any fear.

"I see," Andrew said slowly. "Come along then . . . but first apologize to Mr. Beddows."

"I took your apples and I'm sorry you caught me," Paul said defiantly.

"Paul!" Dorcas responded, horrified. "That's no proper way to speak to Mr. Beddows."

But Paul Wakefield's lips were tightly pressed together and he followed his father outside. Soon the sound of the cane falling on the boy filtered back as the adults stood there. "I've never seen anything quite like this," John Wesley said, somewhat astonished. "I'm afraid your son is rather self-willed, Sister."

"He does have a strong will."

"It must be broken," Wesley said gently. "I had a strong will myself, and God had to deal with me firmly. I will pray for Paul."

"Thank you, sir," Dorcas said quietly.

Later, when the two boys were in their room, David said, "I told you you shouldn't have done it, Paul."

Paul, who was still stinging from the caning his father had administered, merely smirked. "It was fun! I'm going back there some night and get a whole sackful!"

The caning Paul received left no impression on him. The next day, as his father was leaving with Reverend Wesley to preach at a village some distance away, Paul received another admonition. Putting his hand on Paul's shoulder, Andrew said, "I'm sorry I had to use that stick on you, Paul. I got no pleasure from it."

Paul looked his father in the eye and said, "Why, Father, don't worry about that one moment. It wasn't your fault. It was mine."

Andrew studied this son of his and said thoughtfully, "I know it was only three apples and it doesn't seem like much to you—just a mischievous prank of boyhood. I had my share of that when I was your age."

"Did you, Father?" Paul said, smiling and interested. "What did you do?"

Andrew laughed. "I'll tell you another time. All boys do things like that."

"David doesn't," Paul said, tilting his head to one side. "I don't think he's ever gotten a caning in his life, but I've gotten enough for both of us, I suppose."

"Don't be comparing yourself to your brother. God made you both," Andrew said gently. It had pained him to apply the stick to his son and now he struggled to convey some of his concern. "We've had so many talks, Paul, and I know you think I'm a demanding father, but I worry about you. It was only three apples, but it was a willful thing to refuse to apologize to Mr. Beddows. That was what bothered me. You seem to have no sense of doing wrong."

"Well, as you say, Father, it was only three apples. He has thousands of them."

"But they were *his* apples," Andrew said. And then, seeing the stubbornness appear on Paul's face, he said quickly, "Well, we'll say no more about it. I must be gone. I will be back late tonight and Mr. Wesley is going on."

"Preach them a good sermon, Father."

Andrew could not help smiling. There was a charm in this rebellious son when he cared to show it. "Thank you, Son," he said. "I'll do the best I can." He wanted to hug the boy, but Paul was not receptive to such things, as a rule. Since Wesley was waiting, Andrew got his hat and coat and, after bidding his wife and David good-bye, he left. Wesley and Andrew were traveling by horseback, for the distance was too far to walk. Andrew waved back at his family and as the two rode on, Wesley said, "I admire your family. You have a fine wife, Andrew. A gentle woman. And that one boy of yours, he reminds me of George Whitefield. Such a gentle spirit! The other," he added thoughtfully, "he's different."

"I would appreciate it, Mr. Wesley, if you would pray for Paul."

"Certainly. You may count on my prayers."

When the two men reached the village where the meeting was to be held, they were greeted by the head of the group there, a tall, angular man named Johnson. As soon as the two ministers dismounted, he took their horses, saying anxiously, "Mr. Wesley, I think it might be best if we postpone the meeting."

"What's the trouble, Mr. Johnson?"

"Well, sir, there's a lot of roughs in the neighborhood. They've been talking about how they're going to . . . well, they say they're going to hurt you and Reverend Wakefield if you hold the meeting."

"Never take counsel of your fears, Brother," Wesley said cheer-fully. He had met mobs before, many times in his career. It had become a part of the world of Methodism. The preachers Wesley sent out were often struck with rotten vegetables or dead cats and sometimes were beaten and often thrown into local rivers and creeks. Wesley, however, showed no concern, nor did Andrew Wakefield. The two men continued toward the field where the meeting was to be held and began at once. As usual, Wesley liked hymns before he preached, and soon the dale was filled with songs, some of them written by none other than his brother Charles.

After the singing was over, Wesley, in his Anglican vestments, took his place on a rise of ground and began to speak to the crowd of ninety to a hundred people. He had become a marvelous outdoor preacher, having learned it from George Whitefield. Although he had not Whitefield's powerful voice nor the magnetism of the younger evangelist, still he was outstanding. The sermon was half over when Andrew suddenly heard a rumbling and glanced to his left to see what seemed to be a mob of some fifteen or twenty poorly dressed and rough-looking men. Some of them carried clubs.

"Shut your mouth, Wesley!" shouted one of them, a tall, burly man who seemed to be the leader.

"We are here to preach the gospel of Jesus. We mean harm to no man," Wesley said calmly.

"Well, I mean harm to you, Preacher! Leave off now! Mind what I tell you!"

Wesley began to reason with the men, but it was useless. They had been drinking, Andrew observed, and after listening restlessly to Wesley's words, the leader shouted, "Give 'em a taste of what's comin' to 'em!" Saying this, he charged directly at Wesley.

The scene that followed was brutal. Several of the listeners were struck by the clubs, one of them suffering a broken arm, and Wesley himself was roughly treated. Andrew made no attempt to defend himself and when four large men surrounded him, he calmly said, "It will do you no good to speak against the gospel. Why would you be against Jesus Christ, who loves you?"

"Enough of that! I think he needs to be baptized," one of the obviously drunk men yelled, guffawing. "Grab him and throw him in the brook!"

Andrew was seized and dragged to the rather large brook that curved around the village. Each of his adversaries took one of his limbs, then flung him high into the air. He struck the water headfirst, and then a shock ran through him, a terrible pain, and he knew no more.

After Wesley succeeded in persuading the mob to cease its persecutions and most of the mob had left, Johnson cried out, "They've thrown Reverend Wakefield in the stream!"

Immediately Wesley rushed with a group of others down to the water. "He's drowning! Someone pull him out!" Wesley cried. Instantly Johnson plunged in. Andrew Wakefield was floating facedown and did not move as Johnson grabbed him.

"He ain't movin'!" Johnson cried as he turned the minister over to get his face out of the water. As he moved Andrew to shore, hands reached out to help the unconscious man to the bank. "Is he drowned?" Johnson asked anxiously.

"No, he's breathing, but he's unconscious," Wesley said. They all gathered around and some began praying for the injured man. Finally, Wesley breathed a sigh of relief. "His eyelids are moving. I think he's going to be all right." He waited a few minutes more, then reached down and lifted Andrew's head. "Are you all right, Andrew?"

Andrew came out of unconsciousness. He coughed to clear his lungs and then blinked. As he lifted his hand to wipe the water from his face, his memory came flooding back. "They threw me in," he whispered. "Did I hit my head? It really hurts."

"You'll be all right," Wesley said kindly. "Come now. Let us help you up."

But as they tried to help Andrew Wakefield into a half-standing position, he cried out with astonishment, "My legs! I can't feel them!"

"What's that?" Wesley said.

"I can't feel my legs!" Andrew looked down. "I know they're

there; I can see them, but there's no feeling." His legs buckled; he had no control over them.

"Here. Sit him down here," Wesley said with alarm. They sat Andrew down and Wesley reached out and squeezed Andrew's lower leg. "Can you feel that, Andrew?"

"No. Nothing." And when Wesley tried his thigh, Andrew stared at him. He saw the minister squeezing his leg and he reached out and struck it himself with his fist. "All the way up to my waist," he said. "It's as if it's dead."

Wesley took a deep breath. "He must have a doctor."

Doctor Crowell, a young man of no more than thirty, stood over Andrew Wakefield's bed, with Dorcas on the other side and the twins at the foot. John Wesley had left after obtaining Doctor Crowell's services, promising to return the following day.

Dorcas searched Doctor Crowell's face for a sign of hope. When she saw none, her heart sank. Andrew had not moved the lower part of his body for three days. Doctor Crowell had said that the shock might wear off.

Andrew Wakefield was also studying the physician's face. "It's not good news, is it, Doctor?"

"I wish I could say that it was," Crowell said slowly. He hated this part of being a physician, having to give a bad diagnosis. "I'm afraid that fall injured something in your spinal cord and I fear that only time will improve your condition."

Andrew Wakefield was a very intelligent man. He was hearing Doctor Crowell's words but watching the man's face even more carefully. "You mean, I suppose, that I may never walk again. That I may never get back the use of my legs."

Crowell hesitated. "That's in God's hands," he said finally and got up. "I'll stop by tomorrow, Reverend."

When the doctor was gone, Andrew looked at Dorcas. She

reached out her good hand and caught his. Tears were brimming in her eyes and suddenly they spilled over and ran down her cheek. "Oh, Andrew—!" she said brokenly, then fell on her knees beside him, burying her face on his chest.

"Don't cry, Dorcas. All things are in God's hands. All things work together for good," Andrew said. He looked at the boys and said, "Come here, Paul, and you too, David." The boys stepped toward their father, both of them pale. "I'm sorry you have had to endure this, for when a man has a family, they're hurt by what happens to him."

"You'll be all right, Father," David said stoutly. Paul was quiet, searching his father's face for an answer but finding none.

Andrew Wakefield knew that God was able to perform miracles, so he said now, "We'll trust God to bring the feeling back to my legs. And we'll wait on God. God's will be done."

Silence filled the room and tears came to David's eyes. He wiped them off with his sleeve and accepted his father's encouraging smile. But Paul Wakefield did not weep. Instead, his lips tightened in anger and he thought, *Why does God have to do this to my father? It's not fair!* He did not speak his thoughts, but rebellion was etched on his features. When Dorcas lifted her eyes she saw it. She shook her head slightly, but Paul turned his face away so his father could not see the bitterness in his eyes.

Two

"You Have Been My Life . . . !"

December 1755 – February 1756

Winter struck England like a mailed fist in December 1755. For years afterward it was spoken of as "the bad winter" with no other date or information needed. Trees were split by the cold, cattle were frozen stiff by the temperatures, and the entire country seemed to be more like an island floating in the polar zone. By February 1756 the worst of the terrible weather began to pass. Snow still coated the frozen ground, but at least the temperatures were bearable. The people gave a collective sigh of relief, looking forward to the day when the warm breath of spring would thaw their island and once again green grass would carpet the land.

On February 10, Sir George Wakefield was sitting in his parlor, toasting his feet before a roaring flame. His wife, Caroline, sat across from him reading a book by the light of a whale-oil lamp cleverly made of a blue-colored pewter with a three-printed block pattern. She looked up often, concern creasing her brow, as she studied her husband's portly form. He lay back, his arms folded over his stomach, the only signs of life being the rise and fall of his chest.

The door to the study opened quietly and a tall, cadaverous servant dressed in black entered. He was a pale-faced man of forty who, despite good health, looked much as if he belonged in a coffin. "Sir George . . . ," he whispered and Wakefield stirred, blinking his eyes sleepily. "Yes? What is it, Ives?"

"You have a visitor, sir. A Mr. Gareth Morgan."

"Morgan?" Shaking himself, George Wakefield kicked the stool back. "Well, show him in, Ives."

"Yes, sir."

"What can Gareth be doing out this time of the night?" Wakefield muttered. He heaved himself into an upright position, then stood to his feet, coughing harshly as the blood rushed to his head.

Caroline had put her book down and stood also. She drew her dark maroon robe with white fur trim tightly around her throat. It was late, four hours after the sun had gone down. Very few stirred in this kind of weather. "I'm sure I don't know. Were you expecting him at all, George?"

"Why, no. Haven't heard from him—have you?" There was an odd tone to George's voice, for Gareth Morgan had courted Caroline Barksdale before George had won her. Wakefield had never been absolutely certain of his wife's feelings for Morgan, for despite George's title and wealth, there was no better-looking man in England, indeed no more romantic one, than Gareth Morgan. However, Wakefield was not a suspicious man by nature and the twinge of jealousy that tugged at him quickly faded. He turned toward the heavy oak door and studied the man who entered.

Gareth Morgan had taken off his outer coat and hat, but snow still caked his boots and his face was red as he stepped into the warmth of the spacious room. "A bit cold out, Sir George," he said stiffly. He turned and bowed slightly. "How are you, Lady Wakefield?"

"Why, I'm very well, Gareth," Caroline said. She also had memories of the days when Gareth had courted her. Memories of youthful romance lingered long with some women and Caroline had often wondered what her life would have been like had she married Gareth.

I'm such a spoiled creature, she thought. *I would have been miserable married to a poor Methodist preacher.* However, she still had a fondness for Gareth and his family. Sarah, Gareth's wife, had been a friend of hers for years and the two saw each other on infrequent occasions and exchanged letters. "Is your family well?"

"Yes, very well," Gareth said. He shook hands with George, then said evenly, "I have bad news, Sir George."

George stared at Morgan for a moment, then asked, "What is it, Gareth?"

"It's Andrew, your brother, sir. He's very ill. You know he's never been well since the accident. It's been almost three years and he's never walked a step," Gareth said slowly. He shook his head, his voice tinged with grief. "He doesn't get any exercise staying in bed most of the time—or in that wheelchair I made for him. The inactivity seems to have lowered his resistance. He took a cold about two weeks ago. Many of us did, but his got worse."

"What does the doctor say, Gareth?" Caroline asked quickly.

"He says—well, he said I'd better fetch you, Sir George."

Shock ran across Wakefield's face. He and Andrew were not as close as they might have been, but George had a sincere affection for his younger brother. "I'm sorry to hear that."

"I think it's pneumonia. I rode all the way here to fetch you, Sir George. I think it might be best if we leave at once."

"Is it that serious, Gareth?" George asked with pain in his voice. He was a tall man and considerably overweight. An unhealthy pallor lay over his face, for he had been troubled with poor health for the past two years. "I'll have to go at once, of course."

"In this weather, George?" Caroline protested. "You can't go. You're not well."

"I'm afraid I must, Caroline," Wakefield said firmly. "Gareth, you stay here and rest the night. I'll leave at once and you can catch up with me."

"No," Gareth said firmly. "I'll go back with you, Sir George."

"Well, then—go to the kitchen." Wakefield walked to the door, opened it, and shouted, "Ives, see that Cook makes a good, hot meal for Mr. Morgan and have Haines get the coach ready. Tell him to hitch up the best horses. We've got to go to Cornwall tonight."

"That's good of you, sir," Gareth said as Wakefield stepped to the door. As Gareth left the room, his Welsh eyes glowed with approval and he stepped lightly, despite his fatigue.

Left alone with George, Caroline said, "George, you *can't* go. You know how your heart has been acting up lately. Oh, you don't complain, but I can tell."

"I must go, dear. We're the only help Andrew and his family have. I'll come back as soon as he recovers, but it may be some time."

Caroline hesitated, then asked tentatively, "What if he doesn't recover? It sounds very serious to me."

"I don't know. I can't think right now. I don't want to think about Andrew dying. He's too young—and too good a man. A better man than me."

"No, he's not a better man than you," Caroline replied instantly.

She came over and put her arms around him. He held her, aware his heart was fluttering in that wild erratic way it sometimes did. He ignored it and stood quietly, holding her. "What *will* we do if he dies? Dorcas and the children will be all alone."

"You must bring them here to Wakefield, George."

"Here?" Wakefield was honestly surprised. "Are you sure of that, Caroline? It would be—quite a responsibility and an inconvenience to you."

"Don't speak of that." Caroline reached up to kiss him. "It gets lonely here sometimes."

She said no more, but George knew she was thinking of their three babies who had all died at birth. Wakefield had been a silent place without the voices of children. George was pained by this, but never one word of this pain had he spoken to his wife. He was aware that she wept over it and knew she grieved deeply. Now he said, "I know you want children, but the twins—they're almost fifteen now. They're not babies."

"I know, but we must help them, George. You know how much I've always liked Dorcas. We'll hope and pray that Andrew will recover, but if he doesn't, we'll bring his family here to Wakefield."

"Very well. It will be as you say. Now, come and help me get ready."

An hour later the two men got into the carriage. George Wakefield leaned out to wave at Caroline, who stood in the doorway enduring the cold and waving good-bye. Then as the carriage lurched forward, he settled back with a sigh of relief. He was breathing hard from the exertion of getting to the carriage and climbing up in it and now his eyes closed as he waited for the trip-hammer of his heart to slow down.

Gareth had been aware Sir George Wakefield had been suffering some heart problem, but he had not known how severe it was. *I shouldn't have brought him out in this,* he thought. Glancing toward Wakefield, he saw that the man's color was poor and that his breath puffed his lips out. *It's too late now. I don't suppose I could've talked him out of it.* As the carriage rolled along, Gareth found himself praying not only for Reverend Andrew Wakefield but also for his brother, Sir George Wakefield.

※

The small parlor at the Wakefield cottage was warm, for David had brought in large logs and stoked the fire until the flames roared, sending blazing orange sparks wildly up the chimney. Paul

25

had not helped but had sat watching without expression as his brother built up the fire. He was usually a jocular young man and at almost fifteen was already interested enough in girls to give his parents concern. The shock of his father's illness and the seriousness of it, however, had turned him quiet and now he sat back in the shadows of the room, simply staring down at his hands, lifting them only occasionally to look blankly out the window at the snow that was drifting slowly down.

The Morgan family had all come and Sarah Morgan was sitting with Andrew while Dorcas rested. Bethany, now six, moved at once to sit beside David as he came over and slumped on a couch against the wall. Silently she reached over and took his hand, holding it with both of hers. Looking down at her, David saw that the child was worried and he leaned over and squeezed her. "Don't worry, Bethany. Father will get well."

"But I'm afraid," Bethany whispered, then abruptly turned and threw her arms around David, clinging to him fiercely. She had become very close to Andrew Wakefield, who had filled the role of a grandfather toward her. The Morgans had paid many visits during the long sickness and since Andrew could not carry out the duties of a pastor, Gareth had filled in the gap, serving both parishes as well as he could. Sarah and the children came often and Bethany had grown even closer to David.

Ivor, sitting close to the fire, was whittling nervously on a stick. A tall child of almost eleven with black curly hair and dark eyes, he was the mirror image of his father. He studied his sister covertly and marveled at the affection she had for David Wakefield. Then, hearing the sound of horses approaching, he said, "Someone's coming." He closed the knife quickly and walked to the door. Opening it, he reported, "It's a carriage."

Dorcas, also hearing the hoofbeats, came out of the door that led to the bedroom and moved to stand beside Ivor. She was soon joined by David and Bethany—but Paul Wakefield never moved from where he sat. "It's your father and Sir George," Dorcas said. They stood in the open door until Gareth entered, supporting Sir George. Dorcas, seeing how the older man leaned on Gareth, was shocked at how he looked, but she did not refer to it.

Sir George took his hat off and took Dorcas's hands at once into his. "How is he?"

"Not well, I'm afraid. I'm glad you've come, George. He's been asking to see you. But you shouldn't have made the trip in this awful weather."

"Don't speak of that," George said impatiently. "Let me go to him."

Dorcas led him into the bedroom. Before the door closed, Sarah came out and went at once to Gareth, who put his arms around her and kissed her. "I'm getting you all wet," he said. "It's still snowing. How is he?"

Sarah looked at the children and shook her head slightly. "The doctor was here earlier. He left some new medicine."

Gareth studied his wife carefully, knowing her words meant more than they appeared. He reached over and ruffled Ivor's dark hair. "How are you, Son?"

"Fine, Papa. Come to the fire and get warm."

Gareth nodded and moved to the fireplace on numbed feet. "It was a hard trip. I didn't realize how weak Sir George is. Ordinarily I would not have thought he might make a trip like this, but he insisted on coming."

Gareth looked at Paul, who was sitting in the corner. A stubborn look twisted the boy's face and Gareth read the resentment there. "Perhaps you could fix something to eat," he said quietly. "I'm hungry and Sir George might eat something too, after he's spoken with Andrew."

"Of course," Sarah said. "Ivor, you and Bethany come to the kitchen."

"I want to stay with David," Bethany protested.

"You can be with David later. Come along now," Sarah insisted.

As soon as the Morgans left, Paul spoke up for the first time. "Well, Brother, now we know what God is really like." He stood up suddenly, moving to the window. "First he took Father's legs and now he's going to take his life."

David was shocked at the depth of bitterness that edged Paul's voice. "Maybe not, Paul," he said, joining his brother at the window. He watched the flakes falling for a time and then turned to face Paul. "We'll have to trust God."

"You've been praying for Father to be healed now for nearly three years. Has he walked? No!" Paul spat out bitterly as he answered his own question. Then, staring out into the darkness he asked with a trace of fear, "What will happen to us when Father dies? We'll starve."

"No," David responded at once, shaking his head firmly. "Uncle George wouldn't let us starve!"

"He doesn't care."

"You don't mean that, Paul. You know Uncle George is fond of all of us."

Paul wheeled toward his brother in rage, his eyes dark with pain. There was a hardness that had developed in his spirit over the years that no one could explain. He had none of his mother's gentleness or his father's love for others and he deeply resented their poverty. This hard side of Paul's character had become more evident since his father's accident. At almost fifteen, Paul Wakefield had turned into a very bitter young man indeed.

***

Inside the sick man's room, the brothers exchanged greetings and then George moved to sit beside the bed. George was shocked at the sight of Andrew's once strong and athletic body now so thin. *Why, he's shrunk to nothing,* George thought. The fever and disease had indeed stripped all the excess flesh from Andrew Wakefield. His cheeks were drawn in and his eyes were deeply sunk in their sockets. When he had raised his hand to take that of his brother, it was a skeleton's hand, and the arm itself had little flesh on it.

George had not been able to hide the emotion that had swept over his face and Andrew whispered instantly, "Don't concern yourself, George."

"My dear fellow—my dear chap. . .!" George mumbled. He was not a man who could easily conceal his feelings—at least the few he had. George Wakefield was not given to deep thoughts, to philosophy, to more than the rudiments of religion, but now grief washed over him. Perhaps it was seeing the shriveled body of his only brother and realizing here was a tiny but insistent warning of his own mortality. Death was in the room with him. George had the eerie sensation that if he wheeled and faced the dark corner behind him, he would behold a spectre clothed in black— waiting for the soul of his brother! He tried to throw off the strange feeling, then held on to Andrew's hand, unable to speak.

"You mustn't think I am unfortunate," Andrew said quietly, his voice thin as a reed. It cost him to speak, but a gentle smile stirred his lips and his eyes were filled with affection. "I'm glad you came, George. I wanted to tell you good-bye."

George's lips trembled and he tried to form some words, yet none would come. He was not a sentimental man, but now tears came to his eyes. "My dear Andrew. I—I can't let you go!"

"We all must go, George, sooner or later. It's one journey no man can avoid. Kings must endure their going forth as well as beggars," Andrew said gently. "I have served Jesus faithfully and now it seems I will see him sooner than I expected. That is not a grief to me—indeed, I long to see him who died for me and who has kept me so faithfully. But before I go to him, I wanted to talk to you—as I have before—about your condition before God."

Indeed, Andrew Wakefield had witnessed of his faith in Jesus to his brother many times. He had never received any encouragement, but now as George sat with a grief-stricken countenance, his head bowed, Andrew spoke fervently concerning his brother's soul.

As Sir George Wakefield listened to Andrew's words, he was thinking erratically: *What a selfish swine I've been! And how unselfish this brother of mine! He's going out now to meet God . . . he's safe . . . but what about me?*

"George, I want you to put your trust in Jesus," Andrew said, his voice growing strong and vital. He clasped his brother's hand with desperate strength and looked at him intently. "It would make me so happy to know you have done that. I know you are a member of the church, but I want you to give Jesus all of your heart—everything! That's difficult for a man to do, but now as I stand on the brink of eternity, all I grieve over are those parts of my life that I have not given to God. When you come to die, George, I want you to be able to say that you belong wholly to Jesus!"

Dorcas had slipped into the room and stood listening silently. She knew how burdened Andrew had been for his brother. No one could tell George's condition before God, for though he claimed to be a Christian, his religion was no more than nominal. Now, however, Dorcas saw he was moved greatly.

Finally George uttered a sob. "Don't say any more, dear brother! I *promise* you I will look to my soul, indeed I will. I will give myself to God—my word of honor on it!" He turned, for Dorcas had given a glad cry at his words, and George, with tears running down his face, stared at her for a long moment, then turned back and held his brother's hands tightly. "Andrew," he whispered urgently, his voice breaking. "One thing I beg—don't worry about your family. I'll see to it that they never want, so help me God! They shall be as my own, I promise you."

Andrew's eyes grew warm and he returned the pressure of George's grip. "That's the one thing, aside from your promise to give yourself to God, that would make me most happy. I thank you, dear brother!"

For two days Andrew Wakefield lingered. He spoke several times with George and both benefited from it . . . but the end was near. Each hour, almost, those who tended the sick man could see him sinking and finally the time came when he could take no nourishment. At three o'clock on a Wednesday afternoon in February 1756, the end came. All the family were gathered, including the Morgans, to whom he had already said good-bye.

The small bedroom was crowded, with Dorcas on Andrew's right, his two sons on his left. David had knelt down by his father, but Paul stood erect, his face stiff as wood. They all listened as the breath of the dying man rasped erratically.

"He's going," Dorcas whispered. "Oh, Andrew, can you hear me?" She stroked his face and he opened his eyes at her touch.

"Dorcas—"

"Yes, my love?"

"Do you remember when we were married? How we promised to love each other?"

"Oh, yes, I do remember. . . !" Dorcas's tears fell freely and she made no attempt to stop them. The hot drops fell on Andrew's hand, but he seemed not to notice.

"I remember—so well—that day," Andrew said gently.

A long silence descended on the room, the only sound the ticking of the mantel clock and the faint breathing of the dying man. Finally, Andrew looked over at his two boys and said with a new strength that seemed to lift him up for a moment, "David— love God."

"Yes, Father, I will. I—I love you, Father." David took his

father's hand, bent over and kissed it, then buried his face in the bedclothes.

"Paul?"

Paul bent over and reached his hand out awkwardly, taking his father's. He said nothing, but his father's dimming eyes saw the stern lines on his younger son's face. "Do not ever let my death make you bitter. I love you, my son, and I have prayed that God—will keep you—and will make you a mighty man of God."

Paul listened, his face worked with emotion. He kept the tears back but did whisper, "Papa, I love you so much!"

The words brought a fine smile from Andrew Wakefield. He turned back to Dorcas, studying her face, and said, "I go to the Lord Jesus. . . ."

"Yes, dear . . . but I shall miss you so."

"I will—wait for you. . . ." And then finally in a whisper that only Dorcas heard, "You have been my life!"

He did not speak again and the spirit passed from his body so gently that it was almost impossible to tell at which moment he left this world and joined another. But finally that time did come and Dorcas wiped the tears from her eyes. She reached out, lay her hand over her husband's hair, and whispered, "And so have you been my life and my love. . . !"

The funeral was better attended than any in the memory of the little village. George Wakefield was astounded at how many came even in bad weather. The small church was packed to overflowing and the same large crowd went to the graveside for the brief service there.

When the family gathered back inside the cottage, Sir George shook his head with wonder. "I hadn't dreamed that Andrew had such a host of loving and thoughtful friends."

"He was a loving and thoughtful man," Dorcas said quietly.

George stood with his head bowed, considering this. He did not speak for so long that the twins glanced at each other, wondering why he kept such a long silence.

Finally, George raised his head. "You're coming with me," he said, a strange air of determination on his face. At the look of surprise he saw on every countenance, he quickly added, "I mean, you're coming to Wakefield to live. That will be your home now."

"Why, George, that's impossible," Dorcas exclaimed, her face pale.

"No, you must do it! You have no family except Gareth—and he can't keep you."

"But Caroline would not—"

"Caroline has already spoken of this. It was she who told me that if we lost Andrew I was to bring you to Wakefield."

Dorcas did not know what to say. She had tried to make plans, but she had no life, no family, and now that Andrew was gone, no means of support whatsoever. She looked at George and asked, "Are you sure this is what you want, Brother?"

"I am absolutely certain, my dear! You heard what I promised Andrew, that you would be my family. I will never go back on that promise!" Then Wakefield turned and said, "And since I have no children, the title and the estate will go to you as the oldest son, David."

Shock registered on David Wakefield's face. Such a thing had never occurred to him—and he could only stare at his uncle with amazement.

"We will leave as soon as we can make the arrangements. I will have someone come and get your things. I think we should go tomorrow, Dorcas."

"Very well, George, if you think it wise."

David thought little of what his uncle had said. He was too filled with grief, but as he and Paul were packing their belongings the next morning, preparing to leave, Paul turned to him and said angrily, "It's not fair! You'll have everything and I'll have *nothing* . . . all because you were born a few seconds before I was!"

"It doesn't matter to me. I don't want a title. I'll ask Uncle George to give it to you."

"He can't. The firstborn gets the title. That's the way it is with the Wakefields—you know that."

"Whatever's mine will be yours, Paul," David said. He came over and put his arm around his brother's shoulder. "You'd do the same for me. . . ."

Inside the parlor, Dorcas and George were discussing the same subject. George had commented, "It's strange how little things can make such a big difference." He watched Dorcas walk around the room nervously, seemingly to memorize the setting she had known for so many years. "I mean, if Paul had been born first, he would inherit the title."

Dorcas looked over at him. She had never thought much of these matters, but now she sat down beside George and memory flooded back. "We never thought about such a thing. We thought, of course, you would have children, so it didn't matter."

"Strange about your twins. I never quite understood it—how just a few minutes can determine their fate."

Quick memories of the twins' birth came back to Dorcas. She had never expected to have a husband, much less children, and when God had caused Andrew to take her as his wife and then fall in love with her, nothing on this earth could have made her happier. And when she had become pregnant—and delivered twins—her joy had been complete. "When the twins were born, Dr. Brown was out of town, so Dr. Callendar came. Mrs. Lesley assisted him."

"She was your housekeeper when you first married."

"She didn't like me very much," Dorcas admitted reluctantly.

"She resented my coming to the parsonage. She was very devoted to the previous pastor's wife. I tried to get close to her, but I know she resents me bitterly to this day. But when the birth pains started, she was there. Dr. Callendar was grateful for her assistance. He needed the help because the birth was hard." She smiled and added quietly, "When Andrew came inside the room after the birth, I said, 'God has given us a double blessing, Husband.' Oh, that pleased him so much! I remember he ran right over and looked at the boys. Sarah was holding one of the twins, so he picked the other boy up and held him. When that child cried loudly, I remember Gareth said, 'He'll probably be an evangelist, Mr. Wakefield.'"

"I don't believe I ever knew Dr. Callendar."

"No, his ship left for the Continent a couple hours after the twins were born."

They continued speaking for a while and finally Dorcas said, "I remember that after Gareth and Sarah left, Andrew came over and sat down on the bed. Each of us had a baby and Andrew asked me, 'Which is the oldest?' And I had to tell him I didn't know."

"Naturally you wouldn't."

"No, I was thinking of other things. Since Mrs. Lesley, who'd been there at the birth, was in the room, Andrew asked her which of the boys was born first."

"What did she say?"

"Well, she's a very stern woman, but I remember an odd light appeared in her eyes and she said, 'Why, the one without the birthmark. He was born first. The second-born had a birthmark shaped like a four-leaf clover on his left shoulder blade.' That's how we knew David was the elder. It was only a few moments, of course, but legally I suppose that does matter."

"Yes, it does—it matters greatly."

Soon the coach pulled up outside and the boys filed into the room. George said warmly, "Paul and David, you'll have a new home now. I hope you'll learn to look on me as a father. I'm not the man your father was, but I'll do my best."

"Thank you, Uncle George," David answered quickly. He stepped forward and shook his uncle's hand. "You've done so much for us already."

Paul said stiffly, "We are grateful to you, Uncle George."

They turned then and left the room. George struggled to get into the carriage. The boys helped their mother in, then got in themselves. Leaning out the window, George said, "All right, Haines, take us to Wakefield."

As the carriage lurched forward, the horses straining against the traces, Dorcas looked out the window. When the cottage where she had spent the happiest years of her life with Andrew faded in the distance, she kept her face turned from the others so they would not see the tears.

But David saw them. Reaching over and taking Dorcas's hand, he held it firmly. "It'll be all right, Mother," he whispered. "You'll see."

"Of course it will."

Paul, however, said nothing and did not look back even once—as David did—to see the old home as it faded from view. He kept his eyes fixed on the inside of the carriage, with seemingly no thoughts at all. Only his mother saw the twitching of his lips, but she knew it would be hopeless to speak to him. So she settled back quietly in her seat as the coachman turned the horses toward Wakefield Manor—where a new life awaited Dorcas Wakefield and her two sons.

Three

MISTAKEN IDENTITY

February 1757

As David Wakefield left the bootmaker's shop, he looked down with pleasure at the shiny black boots that now adorned his feet. He had always found it difficult to get shoes and boots that were comfortable, so he wore his footwear until it practically fell to pieces. Finally his mother had insisted a week earlier, "David, those boots are a disgrace!" and had commanded him to go to the village to be fitted for a new pair. He had gone most reluctantly.

The experience had been a strange one for David, for he was not yet accustomed to the lifestyle he and his family had entered after leaving Cornwall and coming to live at Wakefield. All his life he had heard from his father or his mother the words, "We just can't afford it. . . ." Such words were never spoken at Wakefield! Clothes, underwear, boots, shoes, a saddle, or even a horse—all were readily available now.

I can't get used to being rich, I suppose, David thought as he strolled down the street. He nodded pleasantly, speaking to almost everyone he met, for Wakefield was a small place, and during the year he, his mother, and brother had been with Sir George Wakefield and his wife, Caroline, they had met every soul. It was a clear morning and the sun already was beginning to warm up the cobblestones over which David walked. Soon it would be March, and the time of awakening would come to England, with blades of grass piercing the hard earth and wildflowers dotting the meadows and fields with reds, yellows, and myriad other colors.

Taking a deep breath, David looked down again at his boots, alert to the slight creaking sound they made. He felt an absurd rush of pleasure at the perfect fit and gleam of the rich leather. The bootmaker was a good one and now the boots clung to his feet like a second skin. "Lord, it's good to have shoes that fit!" he muttered fervently under his breath, the words both an exclamation of joy and a prayer of thanksgiving. He walked on, feeling certain that everyone was admiring his new boots, then laughed aloud at this notion. The year at Wakefield had brought him and Paul close to their sixteenth year. Back in his old life in Cornwall the clothes he was wearing now would have been considered fine. But at Wakefield they were considered only daily wear: a white cambric shirt with ruffles down the front and at the wrists, tight-fitting breeches made of a lightweight brown wool, heavy, white silk stockings, and a short, tan wool waistcoat worn open.

Halting in front of the delicious smells of the bakery, David stepped inside and addressed the proprietor, a short, thickset man with a ruddy face, white apron, and cap. "Good morning, Mr. Brown. Are those fresh tarts?"

"Indeed they are, Mr.—ah, is it Mr. David or Mr. Paul?"

Accustomed to the confusion by now, David smiled. "Don't try to separate us, Mr. Brown. People never seem to be able to do that. Just Mr. Wakefield will do."

"I never seed two young men more alike," Brown said, shaking his head with wonder, then getting down to business. Picking up a plate covered with a white cloth, he removed it, proudly exhibiting his wares to the young man. "If I do say so myself, they's not a finer tart in all of England."

"I'll take half a dozen, Mr. Brown."

"Half a dozen it is, sir," Mr. Brown said with alacrity, quickly wrapping six of the tarts in a piece of paper. He handed it to David, who gave him a coin, and nodded with satisfaction. "Good day to you, sir."

"Good day, Mr. Brown."

David left the shop and the smell of the tarts was too tempting. He looked around the main street of the village—the *only* street really—and walked over to a bench in front of the tinker's shop. "Mind if I sit on your bench, Mr. Stallings?"

"Of course not, Master Wakefield. Looks like you got a good breakfast there this morning."

"Try one, Mr. Stallings," David said, smiling. He gave the tinker one of the tarts and the two sat down and began nibbling the pastry. It practically melted in their mouths. When Stallings went inside with a customer, David sat there, continuing to eat slowly. He was methodical in this, as he was in all things, taking small bites, thoughtfully chewing, savoring the taste. Paul, he knew, would have bolted his completely by this time, for the two were as different in their eating habits as they were in most things.

With his eyes half closed, David thought of the book he had been reading the night before—a volume of poetry by a minister named John Donne. David had such an excellent memory that he could practically call up before him the exact words of the poem he had stayed up late going over and over again. It was a poem the like of which he had never seen and he had been astonished to find that the writer was a clergyman. He thought of the words, enjoying the phrases and images as much in his mind as he enjoyed the tarts in his mouth and his stomach.

David mulled over each aspect of the poem for some time. The sun was warm and the street pleasantly alive with the noises of an English village at midmorning. When he looked down at the sack, he was astonished to see it was empty. *I've eaten them all!* Shame-faced at being such a glutton, he wadded up the paper, stuck it in his pocket, then arose and started back to where he had left his horse at the farrier's.

"There you are, my pretty man!"

A young woman of some eighteen years appeared and took David by the arm. She was a saucy wench with a mass of honey-colored hair and bewitching green eyes. Her teeth were not the best in the world, but her full figure was displayed to its best advantage by a dress that clung to her curves. Pressing herself against David, who was struck with astonishment, she whispered, "What about it, luv? Shall we meet again out by the river?"

Instantly David understood that whoever the girl was, she had mistaken him for Paul. He himself had practically no dealings with young women, but Paul was like a magnet for them. They sought him out with little effort on his part.

David cleared his throat. The girl was clinging to him in such an intimate fashion that his mind swam and strange sensations began to occur in his body. In a hoarse voice he said, "I–I think you've made a mistake."

"Aw, come on now. You can't fool Molly! My, I never thought I'd have to urge you to come and meet me, luv!"

David remembered Paul's speaking of a local farm girl named Molly Satterfield and he thought, *Why don't I just go with her? She'd never know the difference.*

The temptation grew stronger and as the girl caressed his arm with her strong fingers, he said, "Where by the river?"

Molly Satterfield giggled. "As if you didn't know! You've been there often enough. Don't tell me you forgot now!"

David had wondered often enough what it would be like to love a girl, but except for a few furtive kisses from a young woman back in Cornwall, all of which came to nothing, he had no experience. And now he was stirred to the depth of his soul, for this temptation was as real as anything he had ever felt in life. He was a Christian young man, so he desperately tried to fight off the desire that seemed to be weakening his knees and giving him foreign sensations that were somehow demanding and pleasant at the same time.

He was about to say, "Let's just go together," when a rough hand seized him and he was jerked around to face a hulking young man whose coarse face was red with anger. "I told you to leave my sister alone, Wakefield!" he said with a growl. The young man's hands were massive and rather dirty and he wore the garb of a farmer.

"You leave him alone, Ebon!" the girl snapped. "It ain't none of your business!"

"When a man makes a plaything out of my sister," Ebon said menacingly, "I reckon it *is* my business!"

David was speechless. On one side he was held tightly by Molly; on the other her burly brother towered over him, holding him with an ironlike grip. Ebon was a giant of a man and David was helpless in his grasp.

When Ebon ignored his sister's pleas, she began to grow rougher. But he reached out with his free hand and, as if she were a child, grabbed her arm and tore her away from David. Then without pausing he said, "I told you what you'd get if you kept after her, didn't I? Well, here it is!"

Still holding to David's left hand, the young farmer threw a blow that caught David high on the forehead. It was as if he had been struck by the sledgehammer from the farrier's shop. As he was driven backward, the world seemed to be made of flashing stars and lightning bolts, and the top of his head felt as if it had been taken off. He started to pass out.

Molly screamed, "Now look wot you've done!" She threw herself at her brother and began to pummel him with her fists. He ignored her for a moment, then shoved her away saying, "That's not all he's going to get!" He strode over to David, reached down, and grabbed him by the collar. Jerking him half to his feet, he drew his fist back and struck David again, this time in

41

the mouth. David was just beginning to regain consciousness, so the pain shot through him as blood filled his mouth. When blows rained down upon him, he struggled, covering his head. But he had no chance at all against the brute strength of Ebon Satterfield.

As for Satterfield, his lips were turned upward in a cruel smile. He was enjoying beating the young man. Although Molly struggled and grabbed at his arms to stop him, she could do nothing.

Suddenly Ebon Satterfield's hair was gripped from behind, pulling his neck back with force. He yelled, "What's that—" and cold steel touched his throat! He knew at once it was a knife blade and he cried out in fear, "Don't cut me!"

"I think I'll slit your throat and let you bleed to death right here!"

David, in the meantime, had uncovered his face. The blows had stopped and he looked up in a dazed state to see Paul standing behind Satterfield, holding the man's head back with a knife to his throat. Fear flooded David, for he knew the terrible temper of his twin. "Don't do it, Paul!" he cried out, struggling to his feet.

Paul Wakefield's temper was indeed a frightening thing when it was stirred. When he had seen the brute beating his brother, he had plunged into the fight instantly, drawing the knife he always carried. Even now as he held Satterfield's head back, he put pressure on the knife and with grim satisfaction heard the pleas of the young farmer. He saw the blood running down the man's throat and heard Molly begging him, but a red mist of anger had come over him and he pressed the knife even harder. Then he felt a hand grab his arm, pulling the knife away.

"Let him go, Paul. Let him go! You're killing him!"

David's voice cut through his brother's anger and Paul blinked like a man coming out of sleep. Contemptuously he removed the knife, raised his foot, and kicked Satterfield in the middle of the back. The force of the blow drove the man several steps and he fell on his knees. Paul moved forward quickly and when Satterfield looked up, Paul held the knife right before his eyes. "You ever touch anyone of my name again, I'll cut your heart out! You hear?"

Satterfield, his shirt bloody from a slight cut on his throat, put his hands up. He had thought himself a dead man and now he shakily got to his feet and ran away without a word.

Molly stared at the two. She had seen them often enough, but now at once she realized her mistake. When she gave David a wild look and said, "I didn't know—" Paul began to laugh. He wiped the knife on his handkerchief, stuck it back in the sheath, and said, "It was too bad for you, Brother, but I don't think Satterfield will give you any more trouble. Are you all right?"

David nodded. "Y-yes, I think so."

"Your mouth is bleeding. You better go home and have someone take care of it. You'll have a time explaining how you got it, though. Imagine, the young David Wakefield getting beat up by a jealous brother." Paul laughed again, his anger all gone now. He put his arm around Molly and said, "Come along, sweetheart. You got the wrong man, but you've got the right one now."

As David watched the two walk off, a strange reaction swept through him. He was very glad he had not gone with Molly, for he took the sin of lust as seriously as he took all sins. The second emotion was grief for his brother, who was headed down the wrong way with nothing, it seemed, to stop him. Although Paul never spoke of it, David knew he was still angry that David was the heir of Sir George Wakefield. A barrier like a wall had come between the two, grieving David greatly. He turned slowly and moved toward the farrier's, where he mounted his horse. Then he headed toward home, heavy of spirit, his body in pain from the blows he had taken.

❧

Dorcas and Caroline were seated in the best parlor at Wakefield. The room was the most elaborate in the house, one which always stunned first-time visitors. It was fifteen feet wide by twenty feet long, carpeted with green and crimson, and the walls were painted green, set off by gilded paper and a matching border around the windows and cornices. There were two floor-length windows that allowed the sunlight to filter through, illuminating the elaborately carved mahogany mantel over the fireplace. On it were a pair of brass candleholders and a vase of rolled paper quills. Dorcas sat embroidering in a George I giltwood armchair uphol-stered in crimson silk damask that was placed on one side of a low rosewood table. Across from her on a Louis XIV serpentine upholstered walnut sofa, Caroline was reading a book. The parlor was an ornate room with a harpsichord on the inside wall, looking glasses over the mantel and beside the windows, and a mahogany, quarter-chiming, longcase clock with Roman and Arabic numerals standing just inside the door.

Once, Dorcas looked up and thought: *This room and its furnish-ings probably cost more than our whole house and all that was in it back in Cornwall.* She lowered her eyes quickly as a moment of sadness came to her. Andrew had been dead for a year, but not a day passed that she didn't think of him. Still, life in some ways was much easier. There were no money problems, for one thing. Caroline and George provided for them handsomely. It was good to see her boys clothed in fine suits and getting the best education available through tutors. One day soon they would both go to Oxford; at least that was the plan.

"I'm worried about George." Caroline looked up abruptly, put the book down on her lap, and fingered the silken cushion beside her.

"I know. I didn't want to say anything, but he's not looking well at all."

"The doctor says there's nothing to be done," Caroline said softly. She looked up, sadness in her eyes for a moment, then smiled. "You and the boys have been such a comfort to me."

The two women talked together for a while. Bethany, who was visiting, was engaged in some sort of work with paper and scissors. At the age of seven, she was one of the prettiest—and brightest—girls that anyone at Wakefield had ever seen. She had a sharp, inquisitive mind and had learned to read quickly. David had spent hours reading to her as she clung to him and looked at the book. Early on he had begun moving his finger over the words so that she would learn to recognize them at sight. And as he read the same stories over and over again, pronouncing the words, she had learned.

Hearing a horse approaching, Bethany jumped up and ran to the window. "It's David!"

As she left the room, running to the door, Dorcas shook her head. "It's almost a sin the way that child idolizes David."

"Why shouldn't she? He spoils her every way imaginable. He's just Bethany's big toy! I never heard him refuse her anything."

After a few minutes, Bethany was back. "David's hurt!" she announced, her face twisted with pain as if she herself were hurt.

Startled, both women rose and hurried toward the kitchen, where they found David washing his face in a basin. He turned to face them and they saw that one eye was swollen almost shut and his lower lip was badly cut.

"What happened, David?"

"Oh, just an accident. It's nothing really."

"Here. Let me wash it off," Bethany said, her face pale. She insisted that David sit down and then, dipping the cloth into the water, carefully and gently washed his face. David rather skillfully avoided the issue, managing to put off his mother's and Caroline's questions.

"A little disagreement," he said. "Nothing to worry about. Come along, Bethany. Let's you and I go read for a while."

Instantly Bethany took his hand and led him off to the library, their favorite room in the house.

"Something's wrong," Dorcas said nervously. "David's been in a fight."

"It looks like he took a bad beating. I wouldn't be surprised if it were Paul, but David—you never think such things of him." They said no more, but both women were disturbed about the incident.

Once in the library, Bethany pushed David onto the couch and found a book. "Read this one."

"Why, you wouldn't be interested in this. It's a book of history, Holinshed's *Chronicles*. It's just a story about old kings who have been dead a long time."

"I don't care. I want to hear it."

David shrugged and picked up the book. He had already read it, for it was the book from which Shakespeare's history plays were taken. Most of it was terribly boring. But he began to read, at the same time thinking of the fight and of Paul and Molly Satterfield. Soon, however, his attention was drawn to the young girl beside him, who held to his arm tightly and fired questions at him so fast that it was all he could do to read and answer them. She was a delightful child and David had always been overly partial to her. Looking down at her now, he admired the jet black hair and the blue eyes so dark they were almost black. *She's going to be beautiful,* he thought, and wondered what sort of young woman she would grow up to be. . . .

___

The trouble came as David was certain it would. He and Paul were sent for, the message being brought by Ives, the butler. "Sir George wants you two in his study."

"Wonder what he wants now?" Paul said, smoothing his hair down and admiring his reflection and new suit of clothes in the mirror. "Not a bad fit. What do you think?" Paul had on a coat and knee breeches of a fine burgundy wool, a white silk shirt with ruffles at the wrists, and a quilted, embroidered waistcoat of blue and black, buttoned to the waist. His heavy, white silk stockings had embroidered clocks at the ankles and his shoes were of the finest black leather with huge silver buckles.

But David was not thinking of Paul's clothes and said nervously, "Let's go find out what Uncle George wants with us."

The two young men went down the staircase, made their way down a long hall, and entered the study of the master of Wakefield.

Both of them recognized the sheriff, a thin man named Epps. Paul grew wary and his eyes narrowed.

"One of you two has been accused of assaulting a young man named Ebon Satterfield."

"Ebon Satterfield? Why, I know the fellow. A hulking brute with no good in him," Paul said carelessly.

"His father's bringing charges against you. You pulled a knife and cut his throat."

"Which one of us did that?" Paul asked pleasantly. "Charges against me or against my brother?"

Epps was struck with the identical appearance of the two. He said, "It was against Paul Wakefield."

Paul seemed amused by it all, but David was not. "Come now," Sir George said. "You must have a positive identification. Which one of my nephews is the accused?"

The meeting lasted only ten minutes and at the end Sir George got the story out of David. When he did, he knew it was the truth. "It seems my nephew David was assaulted by Ebon Satterfield. He was battered rather thoroughly and it was my nephew Paul who kept him from being beaten senseless. You go back and tell Mr. Satterfield I'll have him before the judge if he says one more thing of this matter!"

"Aye, sir," Epps said nervously, his Adam's apple bobbing up and down. "I'll tell him that. As a matter of fact, I've already told him. But he's a stubborn man."

"Tell him again," George said. He watched as the sheriff

grabbed his hat and left, then he turned and said, "David, you will excuse us? I want to talk to Paul."

"Yes, Uncle."

As soon as David left the room, George Wakefield sat down heavily at his desk. "Sit down," he said curtly. Paul had learned to read his uncle's moods and this was not a good one. He went over silently and sat down, waiting for his uncle to begin the sermon he knew was coming.

George Wakefield's face was gray, his color not at all good. He had not slept a wink the previous night, for when he lay down it seemed his heart would stop, so he had sat up in a chair until dawn. Now as he looked over at Paul, his voice was raspy with lack of sleep. "I know you're tired of my admonitions and my sermons, Paul, but this is more serious than anything you've done so far."

"Why, Uncle, it was nothing." Paul spread his hands apart in a gesture that was common with him. "He was beating poor David to death. Why, I think he would have killed him!"

"But you cut the man's throat."

"It was not like it sounds," Paul said quickly. "I had to stop the monster. Why, you could cut him in two and have two of me. There was no chance with my fists. I just pulled his head back and put the knife to his throat and told him to stop. In the struggle he got a little slice on his throat, but that's all there was to it."

Paul Wakefield was an artful young man and a quick talker. In this instance he had just enough truth on his side to convince his uncle and when he concluded, Sir George Wakefield nodded. "I believe some of what you say, but you're still headed down the wrong path, Paul. Why can't you be—" He broke off, not able to meet Paul's eyes.

"Why can't I be like David? Is that what you were going to say, Uncle?"

"Well, I just meant that he never seems to get into trouble—and you never seem to get out of it."

"I don't have to stay out of trouble. He's going to be the master of Wakefield. I'm just a poor relation."

"Paul, I wish there was some way I could divide the estate, but only one man can take the title, not two. It can't be divided. I'll care for you as long as I live, and after I die, you know what a good heart David has. He'll always see you're provided for."

"I know that, Uncle. Don't think I'm ungrateful for all you've done for me." Paul did have an affection for his uncle. Beneath all his breezy ways, Paul had a tender spot. Normally he kept it carefully hidden, but now—for one moment—he allowed it to show. He rose and walked over to his uncle, putting his hand on his uncle's shoulder. "You've been good to me and my brother and very good to my mother. My father would have praised you for it."

"Do you think so, Paul?"

"Of course I think so! No man could have treated us better."

George Wakefield drew a sigh. "I've tried to keep my promise to your father." He looked up and said slowly, "I may not be in this world long, Paul, but remember your father. When he died, he prayed you would become a good man. I'm praying that same prayer." He got to his feet then and said, "Don't pull knives on anyone else. Please!"

Paul watched his uncle leave the room and thought, *Why, he's like a dead man. He can't live long in that condition.* His agile mind leaped ahead to what that meant for his family. He knew what it would mean for David. But he wondered, *What will I be when my brother is Sir David Wakefield?*

Four

THE OLD ORDER CHANGES

Nothing seemed quite right.

The sounds had been muted for a time, all the lights had gone out, leaving nothing but a cool silence—and darkness.

From time to time, out of the silence the sounds of voices floated to him, but they seemed very far away—very far, indeed! He could not make them out, what they were saying, although sometimes he thought he heard his name being called and he knew it was his wife. She was begging him to come back to her.

But come back from where? The darkness had swallowed him up and only at rare intervals was there a bright, flashing mass of colors that seemed to come from nowhere. These iridescent lights flickered and then were gone—swallowed up by the blackness.

Nothing was the same and George Wakefield came slowly to recognize that he had reached the end of his life.

So this is what it is to die. . . .

As the thought came, it was accompanied by a dim light. His eyes were shut, but he opened them slightly, barely making out a face illuminated by the lamp to his right. But even as he recognized Caroline, he understood her words. She was whispering his name and he felt her hands holding his and then touching his face.

"Oh, George! Can't you hear me?" Caroline pleaded. George saw tears running down her face and tried to speak. He saw her eyes open as he stirred slightly and managed to whisper, "Caroline . . . !"

As he lay there, slowly the words began to make sense. He remembered walking in the garden, the pain striking his chest a massive blow, and the agonizing struggle to get back on his feet. But he could remember nothing past that.

"Caroline . . . ?" he whispered, his voice a thin, reedy sound. "I've had an attack."

"Yes, George, but you'll be all right. The doctor's been here, and he'll come back. I'll send Gareth to get him."

George studied her face and shook his head slightly. "No need for that," he whispered. "There's nothing he can do."

"Don't say that, George!"

A measure of strength came to George Wakefield then and he managed to move his head. He saw Dorcas standing to his left with the twins beside him. Bethany was standing beside one of them and he knew that must be David. He turned his head again, seeing Gareth and Sarah with Ivor standing just slightly behind them.

"So many times I've been in rooms like this," Wakefield murmured. "Waiting for someone to pass out of this life. It was never comfortable. I'm sorry . . . to be such a bother."

Caroline leaned over, took his face in her hands, and kissed his lips. "George, I love you so much. How could you be a bother?"

"How long have I been here?"

"Two days. Almost three. The doctor—" Caroline broke off, but her meaning was clear. "Is there anything you want done, George?"

George considered the question. His heart felt like a piece of fragile glass. There was no pain, but he felt that one move would shatter it forever. He turned to Dorcas and whispered her name.

When she came close, holding the hands of both boys, he said, "Dorcas, I've tried to keep my promise to Andrew."

"Oh, George!" Dorcas cried, releasing the boys' hands and coming to take his. "You've been a father to the boys and a help to me. Andrew could not have asked for a better brother."

"That pleases me very much. I was not always kind to Andrew. I'm glad I could do this one thing for him." He smiled suddenly and said, "Perhaps I'll be telling him about it soon."

"I think you will," Dorcas said. "I'm so glad you know the Lord Jesus."

George then looked at David. "Wakefield will be in your charge. I pray God that you will have wisdom."

"I feel totally unfitted," David said, biting his lips. He was very fond of his Uncle George, having grown more so in the past few months. He leaned over and touched the dying man's hand, saying with passion, "But I will do my very best, so help me God!"

As David stepped back, George gazed at Paul, who looked pale and troubled. "Paul, do you think I've been unfair to you?"

"No. Indeed, Uncle, you mustn't think that. It's just the way things are. Please, you've been so kind to my mother, my brother, and myself. Don't worry about me. I'll be all right. I know I haven't been what you would have liked and I'm sorry."

George, as weak as he was, spoke for some time to Paul with great kindness and hope. At length he said, "God must have you, my boy. It was your father's prayer. His dying prayer, as it is mine."

George said his good-byes to Gareth and Sarah, then to Ivor and Bethany. And then it was Gareth who said, "Come." He led them all out of the room so George could be alone with Caroline.

She sat on his bedside, holding his hand, and they spoke from time to time. "I'm growing very tired," George said. "It's almost . . . like going to sleep at night."

"I wish I had been a better wife to you."

"A better wife? Why, that could not have been!" Wakefield's

voice was faint and weak. He opened his eyes and for a while talked of his early love for her and asked her forgiveness for his failures as a husband. Then he closed his eyes again. "You must thank Dorcas for doing so much. She and her husband for bringing me to God. And you, most of all, Caroline."

Half an hour passed as the big clock ticked slowly and the family waited outside. No one moved. Bethany sat close beside David, holding his hand tightly. Paul stared out the window while Ivor talked quietly with his parents.

Finally the door opened and Caroline came out. She was not devoid of grief, yet there was strange joy on her countenance. "He's gone," she said simply. "But he went out praising God." Tears did gather then and she dashed them away. "I thank all of you so much for helping to bring my husband to the Lord Jesus. . . ."

⌘

"I just don't have the head for it," David said, staring with a forlorn air at the desk covered with papers and documents of all sizes and shapes. He shook his head in despair. "There's no hope I'll ever be able to administer the estate." Angus McDowell, a slight man of fifty-eight, had an erect posture, bright blue eyes, and sandy hair liberally sprinkled with gray. For years he had served the Wakefields in all legal matters and done well for them. He now studied the young man across from him and thought silently, *I'm vurry glad it's Mr. David who will be head of Wakefield now and not his brother Paul. Paul would ruin the estate before ye could blink an eye.* Aloud he said with a kindly voice, "Now, ye mustn't despair, laddie. After all, ye're vurry young. Ye have years to learn what all these things mean."

But David was not comforted by the Scotsman's words. "It's no use, Mr. McDowell. I'm just not a businessman."

"Weel, naturally ye're not. One could hardly expect it of ye."

McDowell smiled. "When I was almost sixteen, do ye ken what I was doing?"

"What, Mr. McDowell?"

"I was studying for the gallows," the older man said merrily, his blue eyes twinkling. He clapped the trim shoulders of the young man seated at the desk. "Ye're not old enough to take over the responsibility, but that's what I'm here for. Yer aunt and yer mother will guide ye."

"It would be better if Paul had been the heir. He's so much more intelligent than I am."

"I canna believe that's so. He's quicker than ye are," McDowell admitted, rubbing his chin thoughtfully, "but that's not the same thing as being intelligent. Any fule can be quick—and then repent at leisure."

"Isn't there some way that we can let him have a part in running the estate?"

"Why are ye so anxious for that? I know the two of ye are twins and I've always heard twins were closer than other brothers."

"Well, there's that . . . but we're very different, Mr. McDowell."

"Ye may as well call me Angus . . . when we're alone, at least. Perhaps a little respect for these gray hairs when others are around. Ye are vurry different, David; everyone's noticed that the difference lies in that ye are a vurry steady young man and yer brother, I fear, is not."

"But he could learn. He's so quick! He can pick things up in a day that would take me a week to learn."

"Ahh!" McDowell said, nodding wisely. "But a bad decision can be made in a day that probably should take a week. Do ye think yer brother would have the patience to go over these papers? To wait for maybe years until he was able to take his place as the heir of Wakefield?"

"I suppose not, but I'll never learn it. And Paul isn't going to like it."

"Why shouldn't he like it?" Angus asked, although he had had hints already from Sir George before his death and from Lady Caroline.

"Paul—likes to be in charge of things. And I don't want to," David said, lifting his head and gazing at the older man. "I would like to do something else with my life."

"Ahh! Ye have a vocation in mind? What is it? The law?"

"No, sir."

"The church, perhaps? Ye're a very religious young man."

"Oh, no. I wouldn't be fit to be a minister."

"Well, certainly not the army."

"No, I would be a poor soldier."

McDowell stared at him. "Well, what's left for a young man to do?"

"I'd—I'd like to be a writer."

"A writer?" McDowell's eyes flew open. "Why, my boy, ye astonish me! That's no fit profession for one of the aristocracy!"

"It's what I want to do, though. I love to read, I love books, and I believe I could write books. Maybe poetry if I had a chance. But I can't do it if I have to manage Wakefield."

McDowell was so surprised he could not frame an answer, but finally he cleared his throat. "Weel, time will tell. It's entirely possible that ye might do some writing. Other men would rather go hawking or hunting or fishing, but ye can spend yer spare time with books and yer quill. In the meanwhile ye've got to learn what makes the House of Wakefield stay alive! Because as Sir David Wakefield that's yer purpose. To keep the House alive! It will fall if ye do not remain faithful to yer trust. Sir George gave this into yer hands. It's a sacred charge, my boy, and I know ye weel take it as such."

Troubled by the weight of the charge, David picked up one of the papers and tried to focus on it. But before he even spoke of that, he shook his head and muttered, "Paul won't like it!"

"You wanted to speak to me, Mother?" Paul had come to Dorcas when one of the servants had passed the word that she wanted to speak with him in the study. He had gone there at once and saw she was nervous. "Sit down, Paul," she said.

"What have I done this time?" Paul asked. "I feel like I'm called up before the headmaster every time I get this kind of an invitation."

"I wish you didn't feel that way, Son."

"Don't mind me, Mother. I was only jesting. What is it you wanted to talk about?"

"I know it's early, but I've never heard you talk about what you would like to do with your life. Isn't it time you at least think about choosing a profession?"

"Oh, I have a profession."

Dorcas stared at Paul with surprise. Although Dorcas could have worn expensive clothing, she had no desire to do so. Her simple dress of pale patterned linen was worn over wide panniers. Her only adornments were a simple gold chain about her neck, a gift from her husband, Andrew, and her wedding ring. "What profession? Why haven't you told me?"

"Well, I've only recently decided," Paul said. He leaned back, a bland look on his face. "I'm not sure you will approve of it."

"Paul, I'll do anything I can to help. What profession is it?"

Paul laughed. "I intend to be a worthless relative supported by the master of Wakefield, Sir David Wakefield, himself."

"Don't be foolish, Paul!"

"What's foolish about that? Many trifling younger brothers do no different. Some of them, when they get old enough, are even sent overseas. Their family pays them off, in effect saying, 'Go away! If you're going to the devil, do it where we can't see you!'"

Disturbed, Dorcas pleaded, "Please don't talk like that, Paul! I can't bear it!"

Underneath his harsh ways, Paul did have a deep affection for his mother. He rose at once, went to her where she sat on the lounge, then took both her hands. "I didn't mean to upset you. Of course I shall have to have a profession and I have thought of it, Mother. I even talked of it once with Father. He never spoke to you about it?"

"Why, no."

"I expect he was hoping I'd outgrow it."

"What did you tell him?"

Paul held his mother's gaze. "I have been thinking for a long time about going into the army. Oh, I know," he said quickly, "it's not a profession a Methodist family would be proud of for their son. But, Mother, I'm not for the church. You know I'm not fit."

"You might be someday."

"It isn't someday, it's now . . . and anyway, David is more fitted for the ministry than I am." There was a slight hint of envy in his voice, but he added, "And I couldn't be a lawyer. Not one of those pettifoggers! Spending all day cooped up in offices! So, for a long time I just tried to decide between the navy and the army, but since I get terribly seasick every time I even get in a rowboat, that narrowed the choices down."

"Would you really like to be in the army?"

"It's going to be exciting to be a soldier. Great things are happening and the army is going to decide whether England or France will control America."

Dorcas was troubled, but she tried not to let him see it. "I don't really understand what's going on. Your father tried to explain it to me, but I have no head for politics or world affairs."

Paul stood up, his face was alive with interest. "It's very simple, Mother. England has been fighting a long and brutal war with France to see which of them will control the world. Now the struggle is in North America. Sooner or later we must win that battle for England. . . ." For some time Paul spoke of the thrilling events taking place in North America, then said, "I want to do something, Mother, and this is what I would be good at."

"Have you talked to David?"

"About this? No, I haven't."

"I think you should, Paul. He would do anything for you."

Paul hesitated for only an instant, then said with determination, "All right, I will! I'll do it today. Pitt is taking over as prime minister—and he's a man who gets things done!"

Dorcas felt her heart ache for this tall, handsome son of hers. He was so different from David, as he had been different from Andrew. Somehow she knew, as she sat quietly listening to Paul speak of his future, that pain and grief lay before him. She breathed a silent prayer, *Lord—if my son must go to the depths, I pray that you will go with him! Let him be hurt if he must—but bring him safely into the family of God!*

THE PRODIGAL
DEPARTS

ngus McDowell got along very well with the new master
of Wakefield. He found much in David to admire and
had given good reports to his mother and Lady Caroline on the young man's progress. He had added privately, with
some doubt, "It's true enough, the boy's got some sort of foolish
notion of being a poet. Weel, now, he could have worse notions
and I'm sure that, given time, he'll outgrow it. I beg ye both not
to encourage him in this fanciful idea that he has. After all, there
are more important things to be done in the world than scribbling on paper aboot things that never happened!"

Now, however, the lawyer's face was tinged with pink and he
forced himself to hold his rather fiery temper. He had called
David in and had plunged in at once, saying, "Something's got to
be done aboot yer brother! He's ruining himself and bringing
shame to the family!"

McDowell had thought it would be a simple enough meeting.
All he had to do was explain that Paul Wakefield had become
nothing more than a profligate, that he had run up debts all over
town, and that the tradesmen were ready to bring legal action
against him. He had said this, then added, "And he's got to leave
the girls of the village alone! I've bought off two of them already!
I didn't tell ye aboot it, David, because ye're so busy with learning

yer new skills. But I'm afraid yer brother is not a young man to be trusted where young girls are concerned."

David had quickly agreed that Paul must be cautioned about his affairs with the young girls in the villages and on the farms, but he had stubbornly refused to make stringent demands concerning Paul's finances.

McDowell now paced back and forth, his hands behind his back, bent over like a small crane looking for a fish as he stared at the patterned carpet. Finally he turned and, rocking back and forth on his heels, said, "Do ye propose to let the boy do whatever he pleases?"

"I don't think I could do as you suggested, Angus, and cut off his funds altogether."

"And why not? He's got to learn to be responsible with money!"

"I know that, but he needs just a little bit more time."

"Time? He's had time to run up enough bills to bankrupt a small bank! If ye give him more time, what will happen?" McDowell threw his hands up in a hopeless gesture, his eyes glittering with anger. "He will do exactly the same thing over again, David, and ye well know it!"

David was in a poor position. It came as no surprise to him that Paul had run up debts. He had tried once or twice to warn him, but Paul had immediately become defensive and angry, so David had given up. Now he said, "It's very hard on my brother. You just don't understand, Angus. It's not like a father was disciplining him. I'm only a few minutes older than he is. We're the same age, really, and he knows he's brighter and more able than I am. How can he take such a slap in the face from me?"

Angus snapped, "It's not a slap in the face, it's guid business! The boy's got to learn or it's the ruination of him!"

"Well, I just can't do it."

Angus walked over to the table and picked up two sheets of paper. "Perhaps this will change yer mind. Do ye know what this is?"

David took the sheets and tried to read them. They were in legal form and he saw Paul's name on them, but he could not make it out. "What does this mean?"

"It means yer brother will go to jail for debt if these bills are not paid."

"We'll pay them."

"So that he can run up more? David," Angus said in a more gentle fashion, coming over to stand beside the young man, "I know ye love yer brother and I understand a little of how he must feel. But think about it, man. Do ye think ye're doing him a favor? Ye're teaching him to be improvident."

The argument went on for over an hour, but in the last analysis Angus McDowell lost. David finally said, "Pay the bills, Angus. Take them out of my allowance if you please. Take them from somewhere. I can't let my brother go to jail and that's all there is to it!"

A silence fell over the room and for a moment David felt that McDowell was about to launch the argument again. However, the dour little Scotsman knew when he was beaten. "Vurry weel, then, I'll pay the bills. But there'll be more." He slammed the papers down and went and sat in his chair, propping his elbows on the desk and his chin in his hands. "Will ye at least try to talk to him?"

David hesitated. "Yes, I'll try. That would only be right."

"Ye must be firm, my boy!"

David nodded, but there was little assurance in his countenance. When he left the office, McDowell shook his head. "What a shame it is. It's like Cain and Abel all over again. But David's got to learn to handle his brother more firmly. There's no other way out for either of them!"

❦

The scene with Paul was every bit as bad as David had feared. He had waited for two days after making his promise to McDowell to speak to Paul about finances and finally had caught Paul out in the stable, grooming his new horse. It was the one form of work Paul did not seem to mind and now he took great delight in pointing out the animal's fine points to David.

"Did you ever see such a horse?" he crooned, stroking the fine, iron gray hide of the jumper. "Look at those powerful muscles. Why, he could be a steeplechaser. What a hunter he's going to be!"

David, who cared little for horses except as a means of transportation, forced himself to be enthusiastic. "He is a beautiful horse, Paul, and you ride him so well, too. Much better than I ever could."

"You haven't asked how much he cost."

David blinked, for Paul had turned to face him squarely. "Why haven't you?" Paul demanded.

"Well—how much did he cost?"

"You'll be getting the bill. I told them to send it to McDowell."

Actually David *had* seen the bill and knew exactly how much the animal cost. Realizing now was the best opportunity he would ever get, he straightened his shoulders and said, "You paid too much for the horse, I'm afraid. I don't know horses myself, but that's what Eastman said." Eastman was the head stablemaster for Wakefield and knew horses like no other man.

"Eastman doesn't know what he's talking about! This horse is worth every pound you paid for him, Sir David!"

The mocking tone Paul used in pronouncing the name Sir David brought a flush to David's cheeks. Paul continued, "I presume now it's time for you to deliver the lecture. Shall I do it for you?"

"Paul, let me—"

"Paul Wakefield, you've got to stop this reckless spending of yours," Paul said, his face drawn up into a tight mask. "You're a disgrace to your family! You've become nothing more than a wasteful prodigal and if you keep on as you have been, you're going to ruin yourself and bring shame on the family. Furthermore, if you don't stop spending so much, I'm going to stop paying your bills and you will be thrown in jail for debt! Now, that's your choice, Paul Wakefield. What do you say to that?"

David shook his head. "I wish you wouldn't put it like that, Paul."

"Is there any other way to put it?"

David cleared his throat. "You know I don't care anything about money. Actually, Paul, I want to be a writer. I didn't choose to be Sir David Wakefield. I've always wished you were the heir."

"I've wished the same thing myself, but I don't see any way to work it out."

David ignored the ironic light that glinted in his brother's eyes and he plunged in. "Paul, I don't know anything about finances, but Angus McDowell does. And I hate to put the burden on the dear old man, but he says that you've simply got to stop spending so much money."

David talked for five minutes and at the end of that time Paul waved his hand. "You can save the sermon. I knew what you were going to say. Now go ahead and tell me to go to the devil."

"I could never do that. It's not in my heart. I—I wish we could be closer."

Paul grinned sourly. "Give me the title and I think we can be very close. You can write your poetry and I'll run the estate into debt as quick as I can."

There was no arguing with Paul when he was in this mood, so David gave it up. As he walked away, Paul called out after him, "Come and visit me when I get thrown in jail for my debts, Brother!"

David was moody for several hours after this abortive conversation with Paul. He avoided his mother and aunt by going up to a room on the third floor that had become a hiding place for him. It was only a small room, but he had fixed it up with a chair, lamp, table, and a shelf for his books and writing supplies. The most pleasant hours of his life now were those moments when he was able to escape McDowell's instructions or the other duties at home. After the unpleasant scene with Paul, he gave a sigh of relief as he settled down at the desk, picked up a book, and buried himself in it.

He had read for some time when someone cracked open the door. David glanced up, startled. "Who is it?" he demanded. He thought it was a servant at first, but then the door opened all the way and Bethany Morgan came in. "Oh, it's you," he said. "You found me, didn't you?"

"I knew you were here all the time," Bethany said with a precocious manner. She was wearing a new cream-colored silk dress with a white lace apron, elbow-length sleeves with a lace ruffle, and a full floor-length skirt. Her black hair was usually a mass of curls, but now it had been styled in a new fashion. David grinned at her. "You're becoming quite fashionable. Who did your hair?"

"Aunt Caroline did. Do you like it?" Bethany smoothed her hair and looked at him anxiously. "If you don't like it, I'll do it like it was before."

"I think it's very becoming."

"Does that mean it's pretty?"

"Yes, that means it's pretty."

Bethany came over and stood beside him since there was no other chair. "I could bring a chair up and we could both sit at your desk. I could help you with your writing."

The child had the almost magical ability to bring David out of his moods. He laughed aloud and leaned back in the chair. "Indeed, I think we shall do exactly that. You wait here." He left the room and came back with another chair. Soon the two of them were head to head, Bethany propped up with several pillows David had gone back to procure.

"We'll call this our secret room. Mine and yours," Bethany said, nodding with assurance. "And we won't let anybody else in here, will we?"

"No. Nobody else. Just you and me."

"What are we going to write today? A letter?"

"Would you like to write a letter to someone?"

"No. I would like to write a story."

"A story? I knew you liked to hear stories. I didn't know you wrote them."

"This will be my first one," Bethany said. "You write down what I say."

"All right, Miss Storywriter. Go right ahead."

Bethany shut her eyes tight and pinched her lips with her fingers for a moment, deep in thought. Then she said, "Once there was a little girl. She was very pretty, with black hair and very dark eyes. She was a very good little girl who did everything right. She had a friend who was always kind to her. They had a little room upstairs where they would go and write and read books and they lived happily ever after."

Keeping his face straight, David wrote the words out and sprinkled sand over the ink. "Now you must sign it down here to show that you're the author."

Delighted, Bethany signed her name in big, bold strokes. "Now," she said, "you must tell a story, then we will write it down. And you'll have a story and I'll have a story."

"What kind of a story?"

"A story about a little girl," Bethany said. Her stories were always the same and she always wanted to be the heroine. David began improvising and for the next ten minutes told the wildest story he could think of about a little dark-haired girl who fell into all sorts of dangers but at the last was rescued by her friend named David. Finally he said, "And David and Bethany lived happily ever after."

David sighed and leaned back.

"That's a good story. It's almost as good as mine."

"Almost." David suppressed a smile. "Now, I've got to go."

"David?"

"What is it, Bethany?"

The girl gazed at him with a sudden serious look in her large eyes. She was a changeable child. Sometimes the house echoed with her laughter, but oftentimes the Welsh strain she got from her father would come to her and she would remain silent and almost melancholy. Now she had an odd look on her face that David could not identify. He waited and finally she said, "You're my best friend, David."

David leaned over and kissed her on the cheek. "I'm glad of that. You're my best friend, too, Bethany."

She jumped out of the chair. "I'm going outside now and play. We'll come up to our secret room later and write more stories."

"Just let me know. I'll drop whatever I'm doing and come at once," David said solemnly.

"All right," she replied and left the room.

As soon as she was gone, David tossed the quill down and laughed aloud. "What a little minx!" he said, chuckling. "I hate to think what she'll be when she grows up. She'll have some man jumping through hoops!"

❦

"David, I must speak with you."

David looked up from the papers he was working on and saw that his mother was troubled. "What is it, Mother? Is something wrong?"

"Yes, I'm afraid so."

David rose at once and came over and took her hands. "What is it?"

"It's—it's Paul."

"Oh, I see." David bit his lip, his mind exploring the possibilities for disaster. Months had passed since he had spoken with Paul about his bad financial habits and as far as David knew, Paul had paid no attention at all. "Is it about money?"

"No. It's much worse than that."

"What is it?"

"He's going to fight a duel, David."

If his mother had said Paul was going to jump over the moon, David could not have been more shocked. "Fight a duel! I don't believe it!"

"It's true. Gareth found out about it. He's talked to the young man involved and tried to bring about a reconciliation."

"I suppose it was over a woman?"

"Yes, it was. A worthless hussy if there ever was one! But I suppose it was just a matter of time."

"What do you want me to do? He won't listen to a thing I say."

"You remember he talked to you about going into the army?"

"Yes, I do. I thought about it. Is that what you want, Mother?"

"I think it's the only thing."

David was troubled. "I don't like to do it. I'm afraid for him. The army's not a good place for someone like Paul. The bad habits he has will get worse. There'll be others to teach him even worse ideas."

"I know, but he's so unhappy here."

"All right, Mother. Perhaps you're right. I'll talk to Paul. If that's what he wants, I'll see that he gets it."

It was a few days before he found Paul, and David said at once after entering his bedroom, "Paul, what about the duel business? I hope you'll show some judgment and walk away from it."

Paul sneered. "I'm sure that's exactly what you'd do, but he's challenged my honor. I have no choice."

"Every man has a choice. I don't even know the girl, but surely you and this other man can't risk killing each other over her."

Paul was stubborn and for some twenty minutes the two

argued. At last David said, "Paul, I don't want to see you do this thing and I have, perhaps, something that will please you."

"Like what?" Paul demanded suspiciously.

"I've been considering what you said about wanting to go into the army and I spoke to Angus about it. He knows all sorts of people. He has a client who serves General Wolfe."

Instantly Paul's face was transformed. "Do you mean it, David?"

"Yes. And I asked Angus to see if his friend would approach the general and he did. General Wolfe would be willing to take you in his command. There's a commission for sale. You would go as a lieutenant under General Wolfe."

Paul stared at his brother, excitement coursing through him. "David, I know I've been a blackguard, but if you'll just give me this chance, you'll see! I'll make you proud of me."

"You know my feelings, Paul. I'd rather see you in another profession . . . but it's your life. The papers are drawn up. The general has agreed. I can't guarantee that you can please him or that you'll like the life, but at least you'll have your chance."

Paul squeezed David's hand hard. "Thank you, David." Exultant, he began walking around the room, talking about the glory that was to come. David tried to enter into his enthusiasm, but found himself thinking, *He could get killed, and I would never forgive myself!*

⚓

England's fighting men had to be transported to the scene of the battle, and it was the Royal Navy that performed this service. The sailors of the ship *Dominant,* a fast naval vessel, stood ready to cast off and the Wakefields and Morgans were gathered to see young Paul Wakefield off. Paul was wearing his new uniform, a close-fitting justaucorps. The coat of white wool was fastened from the neck to the hem with buttons and had straight sleeves with cuffs of yellow and purple and below-the-waist pockets with flaps. The frilled white sleeves of Paul's shirt extended from the coat cuffs. He also wore a sleeveless, single-breasted waistcoat and woolen knee breeches, both of burnished yellow, with long woolen stockings under black knee-high riding boots. The military black stock was worn, forming a high neck band. The outfit was topped by a broad-brimmed, three-cornered hat that was trimmed with a cockade. Around Paul's waist was a sword belt supporting a military sword.

Ever since the arrangements had been made, Paul's life had been in a whirl. He had met with General Wolfe and found him completely admirable. There had been uniforms to be fitted, gear to be gathered, and through it all David had gone with Paul, seeing that he had the best of everything. Now one of the officers on the ship was crying, "All aboard!"

Paul turned to his mother and kissed her. "Good-bye, Mother. You wait and see. I'll come back covered with glory." He bid the others of the family good-bye, then turned to David. He hesitated, then grinned. "You're Sir David Wakefield, but one day I'll be General Paul Wakefield."

"I hope so, Paul," David said. "I honestly hope the best for you and I'll pray for your safety every day."

The words troubled Paul somehow and he dropped his head, unable to meet his twin's eyes. Then he looked up and deviltry came to him. "The prodigal departs, but I won't go eat with the swine and come back ragged. I'll come back covered with glory. Good-bye, Brother."

"Good-bye, Paul."

The family watched as the *Dominant* sailed out of port, then they turned away. Bethany, sensing David's sadness, took his hand. "Don't be sad, David. Paul will come back."

"Of course he will, Bethany."

"We'll write a story about it up in our room, won't we?"

"If you like."

As they moved to the carriage, David turned to take one last look at the ship, which was a mere speck on the horizon. *I wish I could've kept him here,* he thought. *I wish I hadn't let him go . . . but there was no way to stop him.*

DEATH AT QUEBEC

B y the time Paul Wakefield arrived at the camp of the British army in North America, outside Quebec, it was the summer of 1759. Although he was by far the youngest—really nothing more than an aide with no experience at all—he was such a cheerful and attractive young man and so willing to do whatever he was asked that he was accepted in the lower ranks of the staff. After several months on the ship, Paul had traveled between camps for over a year and a half, setting up tents, storing supplies, then, inevitably, receiving orders to a new camp. And the process would begin again.

The men he commanded were all older than he, with one exception. One private was eighteen—exactly Paul's age. The rest were hard-bitten regulars or soldiers who had been dredged up in England's grim determination to win the Battle of North America.

The camp was humming with activity. Paul was assigned a place in a small tent where he detailed one of the privates, a slender young man named Phelps, who had been a tailor at one time, to take care of his uniforms. Phelps did an excellent job and Paul, who had brought a great supply of uniforms with him, said to Phelps, "I may get killed, but I'll die well dressed."

"Don't say that, sir," Phelps said quickly. "It's not good luck."

Paul simply laughed at him. He went outside and walked over

the camp. He had read of war, armies, and battles all of his life, but now he was seeing the real thing. He was rather disgusted at the poor personal care that the troops took of themselves. Unless they were forced to do so, they took absolutely no sanitary precautions and a stench already hung over the camp. Paul knew little enough about the army, but he knew that this was not a healthy thing and he determined that his men would take better care of themselves.

For a week nothing happened and finally Paul was privileged to sit in at a card game with some of the staff members, including Brigadier Generals Robert Monckton, George Townshend, and James Murray, all sons of peers—and above General Wolfe socially. Paul had plenty of money and was not good at cards, as the others had discovered, so they were happy to let him sit in as long as he was quiet. Paul lost his money as slowly as possible, listening avidly to the discussion of the tactics and of the generals.

"The real enemy," General George Townshend said languidly, "isn't the French army—it's the terrain."

"How is that, sir?" Paul ventured to ask, managing to lose another five pounds to the general.

"Why, look at it, Lieutenant!" Townshend exclaimed. "It's obvious!" Townshend was a cynical man of the world, with excellent political connections. He was a clever and caustic cartoonist, drawing extremely amusing sketches of his commanding officer. He waved toward a map on the wall, saying, "Look—Quebec stands there on the tip of a huge peninsula extending out into the Saint Lawrence. Whoever conquers that blasted city will have to have soldiers who can climb walls like flies!"

General Murray frowned. "There's talk we'll go around and come at the city across the Plains of Abraham."

"And do you think we'll catch a soldier like Montcalm by surprise?" Townshend demanded. "He'll be watching those plains like a hawk."

"We've got nine thousand good soldiers, George," Monckton spoke up. "Surely something can be done with such a fine army!"

But a sour expression swept across Townshend's broad face. "General Wolfe's mission is to capture Quebec. But I do not think he will do it!"

After the card game broke up, Paul left to go to his tent. He was shocked at the attitude of the generals, thinking angrily, *If they were good soldiers, they'd be more supportive of General Wolfe!* But there was nothing a lowly aide could do in such a case, so he kept his own counsel and waited to see what would develop.

❦

When a husky man named Frenchy Doucett became a regular visitor in the camp, Paul asked General Murray why a Frenchman was permitted. "Couldn't he be a spy?" he inquired.

"Frenchy Doucett? He would be if there was enough in it for him. He's just a trapper. I don't think he has any loyalties one way or the other."

Paul hunted and had heard much about the trapping of animals, so he went over at once and introduced himself. "I'm Lieutenant Paul Wakefield," he said. "I understand your name is Doucett?"

"Just call me Frenchy lak' everyone else."

"I'm very interested in the fur business."

"Oh, you have trapped ze animals?"

"Oh, no. I know nothing about it. I've never even seen it—but I'd like very much to know about it. After all," Paul said carefully, "that's what this war is about."

Doucett, a thickset man with lank black hair and dark brown eyes, stared at Paul. The Frenchman wore a short beard that was raggedly clipped and he appeared to be tremendously strong although he was not overly tall. One eye was drawn into a squint caused by a rather fierce scar, giving him a sinister appearance. "I know all about trapping ze beaver, ze animals, Lieutenant. What do you weesh to know?"

"Tell me all about it. Come. I'll treat you to a bottle if you can drink and talk at ze same time."

"I can do anything and drink at ze same time," Doucett boasted.

Frenchy Doucett proved to be a fine storyteller. He drank the wine Paul offered as if it were water and it seemed to have no effect on him. Paul listened with avid attention for over two hours as Doucett described the mountains and the animals that were trapped. "I intend to become reech, Lieutenant."

"Will you sell your furs to the French or to the British?"

"I am a trapper, not a politician and not a soldier. I weel sell ze furs to whoever weeshes to buy them for the mos' money."

Paul laughed. He liked the fellow immensely. "I think that's very wise, Frenchy."

It was the first of several conversations. Paul began to grow more and more interested in the fur business and finally he asked, "Could a man really get rich trapping?"

"*Oui,* eef he ees wise and sells his furs rightly. And sometimes you do not even 'ave to trap them, the furs."

"Why, where do you get them?"

"From ze Indians. They trap them ver' good. You give them a handful of beads that cost maybe ten pence for a beaver hide that weel sell for twenty pounds."

Paul was astonished. "Don't they know any better?"

"They are learning ver' quickly, but a man could go in now with good trade goods and come out weeth a fortune." He studied Paul Wakefield. "Eet ees too bad you are a soldier, Lieutenant. You obviously are a man who has good ideas—lak' me."

Paul did not answer, but he did not forget what Doucett suggested. He pored over it often, becoming obsessed with the idea. But Paul's concern with getting wealthy as a trapper was hastily put aside two days later, for General Wolfe made a desperate move. The army had been near Quebec for a month with nothing to show for it and Wolfe called his staff together to give them a direct order.

"We will attack the enemy, gentlemen," he announced. Without asking for their opinion, he laid out his own plan. "We will land the men upstream and attack the day after tomorrow." He was a short man, but there was an inner force in him, and as he pointed out the movements of the troops on the map, Paul grew excited. *Action at last—and I'll be in it!*

But the three brigadier generals all opposed Wolfe's plan. "It will never succeed, General Wolfe," General Monckton protested. "At this point of contact, the men will have to charge uphill, right into the face of the enemy's fire. They'll be slaughtered, sir!"

Both Townshend and Murray added their protest, but Wolfe was adamant. "The attack will be made—and I expect it to succeed" was his final comment.

"We'll get butchered!" Townshend muttered, his lips white with anger. "Wolfe's a fool!"

On July 31, 1759, Paul was one of the men in the clumsy boats that carried His Majesty's forces up the Saint Lawrence River past the city of Quebec. He was excited—but sitting in the cramped confines of the boat with the sweating soldiers for half a day dampened his spirits. He was amused to see Frenchy Doucett in the boat and asked, "What are you doing here, Frenchy? This isn't your side."

"My side ees *me!*" Doucett announced. "General Wolfe, he pay me to come—to show where to land. I know thees river, by gar!"

When the attack came, Paul was caught off guard. He had slept little and when the flatboats nudged into the shore, it was Frenchy Doucett who shook him awake, whispering, "You bettair come on, Lieutenant—"

Paul awakened instantly and almost fell out of the boat, being saved only by the powerful arm of Doucett. Looking upward, he saw the red coats of his unit advancing and at once moved forward. Captain Monday led the charge, shouting, "Come on, men—for king and country!"

Paul drew his sword and surged up the hill. He didn't get ten feet before steady musketfire broke out, and glancing up the hill, he saw the walls above bristling with guns. Men were falling on each side of him, and amateur that he was, he knew no men on earth could advance into that fire! But he continued with the small group who followed Monday. Then he heard a voice say, "Lieutenant—come down!"

Wheeling around, Paul saw that Doucett was behind him. "Get back, Doucett!" At that same moment, a group of French soldiers launched a counterattack. One of them appeared as if by magic, his bayonet pointed at Doucett's stomach. Without hesitation, Paul leaped in front of Doucett, parried the bayonet with his sword, then drove his blade directly into the heart of the French soldier. The man stopped, dropped his musket, and stared down at the blade that had pierced his chest. He glanced up with sorrowful eyes, seeming to be on the verge of apologizing. Paul withdrew the blade, feeling sick—and looked closer at the face of the young man, who was not more than eighteen. A curtain seemed to fall over the wounded man's eyes and then blood gushed from his lips. He leaned forward slowly, sagged down to the earth, and lay still, looking up at Paul.

"Come on—you weel be keeled!"

Paul was literally dragged down the hill by Doucett. When they reached the safety of the troops, Paul threw up. Doucett covered him from the gaze of the other soldiers. Then when Paul straightened up and stared at him with a face as pale as paste, he said gently, "First man you evair keel?"

"Y-yes!"

"You did ver' good, Paul Wakefield. You save my life—and I don't nevair forget eet!"

⁂

After the battle, Doucett became even more open with Paul. He showed him some beaver pelts and explained the process of turning them into hats. "Who knows what ze fashion weel be next year, or even next month. The trick ees to get in queek, get ze beaver, sell them, and become a reech man. Then let somebody else go trap ze animals. But still, ze best way ees to get them from ze Indians."

"Do you know any Indians?"

A crafty look swept across Frenchy's face. "I am married to the daughter of one of the chiefs of the Ojibway nation. A beeg tribe. They trust me lak' they do no other white man. They know I weel give them good trade goods. Not whiskey and not beads. They do not want much from our point of view. Why, you and me, Lieutenant, we could take some boats in there with trading goods and come out with enough beaver, mink, and fisher to make ourselves reech men! How would you lak' that?"

"I'd like it very well, but I am in the army."

"For how long, Lieutenant?"

"Until I get killed—or sell my commission."

"What ees that? Sell your commission?"

"In the English army we buy our commissions. My brother actually paid for mine. Anytime I want to leave I can sell it to another man who wants to join."

Doucett was quiet for a moment. "You save my life, Lieutenant. Now I weel offer you what I would not offer any other man. I intended to keep it all for myself, but I do not 'ave enough money. Why do you not sell your commission? Put eet into our venture. You 'ave the money. I am married into ze tribe. I can get ze beavers. We could split right down ze meeddle."

79

Paul stared at the Frenchman and listened as Doucett gave him facts and figures. Finally he said, "It will have to wait. I could not leave General Wolfe until after the battle is won."

"Eet may not be. General Montcalm, he ees a ver' great soldier."

"That's very true, and I may be dead. But if I'm not killed, and if we do win, we will talk more of this later, Frenchy."

Wolfe had made a grave mistake and lost the confidence of some of his men, but he was not discouraged. He was a driving, demanding, vain, and secretive man—too secretive. He decided to land his army at Anse de Foulon, two miles above the city. The army would climb the steep cliffs that protected Quebec and catch the French general off guard. His three subordinates asked him for complete details, but Wolfe declined to give them.

Paul was less anxious for this battle, but he was one of those men who climbed the cliffs on the dawn of September 13, 1759. Doucett did not come, but four thousand men did—and they took Quebec!

Paul never remembered clearly the details of the battle. It was all smoke and blood and fire and both the English and the French commanding generals were slain in the fierce fighting. The Plains of Abraham were conquered—and with the fall of Quebec, the war that had drained England and France of money and men was over. The French had lost and would pose no threat to the New World, the colonies along the eastern seaboard. From the date of the fall of Quebec, it was understood that America would be British, not French.

"Weel, so ze British will now rule Canada," Frenchy Doucett said. He took a pull at the bottle that was on the table. He and Paul were sitting in a small tavern on the river in Quebec. Now that the English held the city, it was safe enough.

"It's not all over. There may be other battles."

"No. Montcalm ees dead. The French weel pull back. The French have lost thees country. They weel try to go farther into Canada, but all of thees weel belong to your people."

The two men sat there quietly as Paul drank a considerable quantity. His head, however, was still clear enough so that he said abruptly, "The offer you made about our being partners. Does it still hold?"

"You would leave ze army?"

"I don't really like soldiering," Paul said slowly. "It has moments of glory, but it's mostly long months of drudgery and very boring. It would be more exciting to be very rich." He grinned across the table at Doucett.

"I weel be honest with you. Perhaps I paint ze picture too bright. Many theengs could happen. We could start with our furs down ze rivair and be attacked by another tribe and lose them all. Maybe our lives. It would not be pleasant to fall into ze hands of some of those fellows."

"I don't mind the danger. Tell me how we could go about it."

The candle burned low beside them as the two men continued to drink and talk. Finally Paul made up his mind. "I'll do it, Frenchy! I'll sell my commission and get the cash. You buy the trade goods and we will go get rich."

"We weel drink to that. It ees not Lieutenant then."

"No. Just Paul Wakefield, fur trapper."

The two men drank to that, and Frenchy said, "Time weel see eef ze good God weel make us reech."

"You believe in God?"

"Why, *certainement!* You do not believe in him?"

"I believe in money and I believe in *me.* That's all."

Doucett stared at his new partner. "You weel find out that ees not enough."

"It's enough for me," Paul said doggedly and rose from the table. "I'll get the money as quickly as I can." The two left the tavern and as they left, Paul was thinking. *I may not be a general, but I'll go home rich. That will be enough to show that I am the real master of Wakefield!*

To Have

1 7 6 0 | **Part** | 1 7 6 8
TWO

and to Hold

Seven

FURS

Spring 1760

W‍ell, this looks as likely a place for beaver as any."
The sound of his own voice startled Paul Wakefield,
for he had heard little except the muted cries of birds
and the mournful howling of wolves and coyotes for four days.
He smiled briefly and removed the coonskin cap from his head,
thinking about how different he was from what he had been. *The
making of a fur trapper*, he thought ruefully, *is not a simple thing.*
Memories came flooding back: how when Frenchy Doucett had
first taken him out into the woods, there had been times he had
wanted desperately to throw out the whole thing and go back to
civilization. He had considered himself in good condition, but the
sinewy Frenchman had worn him thin with constant traveling
throughout the deep woods and paddling upstream until his
hands were more like raw meat than anything else.

"I didn't think I'd make it," Paul murmured. Glancing down,
he saw he had filled out so that the muscles on his arms, chest,
and shoulders swelled against the soft deerskin shirt that he wore.
This pleased him, for he took pride in his strength, but he quickly
turned his attention to the scene before him.

He stood before a small tributary that gave signs of being rich
with beaver. Paul's eyes swept the water and he felt his instincts

sharpening. Even as his body had gained strength, he had learned to become part of the woods. The winds, trees, rolling land, sharp mountain peaks—all had become his world and he loved it! He noticed a wedge of ripples close to the bank of the pond. The point of the wedge, formed by a round furry head, came toward him, then turned and went the other way, sending more ripples whispering along the shore. Sweeping the bank with a quick gaze, Paul noticed the cuttings and then his eyes moved toward the little dam made of sticks and mud. Satisfied, he moved along the side of the pond, walking softly in the spring mud, keeping back from the water. Finally he found a spot that pleased him, and he laid his traps down. Leaning his musket against a bush, he cut and sharpened a long, dry stick, cocked the trap, then stepped into the water.

"That's cold," he commented to himself. "Snow fed." Stooping, he put the trap in deep enough so that the surface of the water was a hand higher than the trigger. Next he drew the length of chain out into deeper water until he came to the end of it. Slipping the stick through a ring in the chain, he pushed it firmly into the mud. Taking his hand ax from his belt, he tapped the stick deeper into the mud to be sure it was secure, then waded back to the bank. After cutting a willow twig, he peeled it and took the hollowed antelope horn from his belt.

As he removed the stopper, the strong and gamy odor of the oil assaulted his nose. He dipped the willow twig into the oil, replaced the stopper, and returned the container to his belt before he waded in again to thrust the dry end of the twig into the mud between the jaws of the trap, leaving the baited end sticking four inches above the water's surface. Then he backed out of the water, toeing out the footprints his moccasins had left. Carefully he splashed water on the bank to drown out his own scent.

Glancing out at the pond where he noted several V-shaped ripples, he smiled and nodded thoughtfully. *I'll see you on a stretching board before long.* Then he moved back, picked up his remaining traps, and all morning searched the stream for likely looking spots. There were many beaver dams and he was pleased with his choice. He had left Frenchy four days earlier, the two of them splitting up to cover more territory. Frenchy had been doubtful of the younger man's ability to find his way. "You weel get lost in these beeg woods," he had prophesied, shaking his head doubtfully. "Or maybe ze Indians keel you. You can't catch no beaver when you're dead!"

But Paul had insisted, and after his period of internship under the wily Doucett, he was determined to prove himself able in the woods. After setting the traps, he made himself a shelter out of saplings and covered it with pine boughs. Then, taking his musket, he made his way into the woods. He had not gone more than a quarter of a mile before a large doe stepped out in front of him, not thirty yards away. Quickly he threw the musket to his shoulder, aimed, and pulled the trigger. The explosion rocked the woods and the deer fell to the ground—but leaped up at once and ran into the thickets. Running forward, Paul stopped only long enough to reload his musket, aware of Frenchy's warning never to travel with an unloaded weapon. He found drops of crimson on the pine needles and, following them, soon came to the dead doe. He drew his knife, expertly dressed the animal, and carried it back to camp.

That night, as darkness fell, he feasted on deer steak and fresh spring water that bubbled out of some rocks close to his camp. Leaning back, he looked up at the stars and wondered what his family was doing. He had not communicated with them since he had gone into the woods with Frenchy Doucett, and for a moment nostalgia washed over him. He shook himself, sat up, took another bite of the tasty meat, and said aloud, "I guess David's rich and famous. They'd probably be shocked if they saw me out in the woods like this." Still, he was proud of what he had accomplished. In less than a year, he had learned the basics of trapping. Of course, without Doucett he could not have done such a thing, but the two had made a good combination. Paul was an avid learner and Doucett had been surprised at how quickly the younger man had picked up the ways of the woods.

Pleased with himself, Paul leaned back against a huge oak and savored his accomplishments. He had a streak in him that pushed him on, always wanting to be the best, and ever since throwing his lot in with Doucett he had determined to get rich, like others had before him. Most of the trappers, he was aware, did not get rich. It was the men who bought the furs from the trappers who made the big money. This lay in the back of Paul Wakefield's mind and as he sat there chewing slowly on the succulent meat, adding salt from time to time, he made plans. Somehow far in the future he saw himself going back to England, dressed in expensive clothes, arriving at Wakefield in a fine carriage. The thought of seeing his brother's face and his family's amazement at his success lay deep within him—it was something he did not ever entirely forget.

As the darkness closed in like a dense fog, he watched the sparks from the campfire ascend like miniature stars toward the treetops. The wind blew softly, whispering secrets he could not understand.

Finally he rolled himself in his blanket, wondering how long it would take him to trap enough of the beaver before going back to rendezvous with Doucett.

❦

"You do fine, Paul!"

Frenchy Doucett stood over the pile of beaver pelts Paul had brought back to their main camp and nodded with enthusiasm. "You do bettair than me! How many you 'ave here in thees stack?"

"Nearly thirty," Paul said, basking in the warmth of Doucett's congratulations. After unloading the pelts into the storage room they had built out of poplar logs, they sat down and reviewed their activities. Doucett had gone north and had not succeeded as he had hoped. Nevertheless, between the two they had a good supply of the precious pelts to make a good start for a year's trapping.

Since Paul was exhausted, Frenchy cooked supper, which included fresh baked bread, for the Frenchman knew the trick of sourdough. He had also killed a bear and the rich meat sizzled on sticks as they roasted it over the open fire.

Reaching out, Doucett pulled a chunk of bear steak from the fire and examined it with a critical expression. He was a sinewy man, short and muscular with a swarthy complexion. He ran his free hand through his black hair, then clawed at his beard.

Paul looked over toward the pile of skins and tried to estimate their worth in his mind. "How much do you suppose they'll bring, Frenchy?"

Frenchy tore a chunk of meat off and chewed it thoughtfully. "Eet ees hard to say," he said, shrugging. "It depends on what ze Company decides."

Paul was unhappy with this answer. He hated to be under anyone's control and he was well aware that the trappers were controlled by the fur-trading companies just as the Indians themselves were practically controlled by the fur traders. He rose, went over to the pile of furs, and ran his hand over the smooth pelt of prime beaver. "Fur is what this world out here is built on, isn't it, Frenchy?"

"What do you mean by that?"

"I mean it's fur that makes people live out here. The woods are filled with trappers wanting to get furs. The trappers push the Indians further back and change their way of life. I guess furs are the way the Indians get what they want. The way we get it too, isn't it? It's almost like legal tender."

"What ees thees legal tender?"

"Money," Paul said and grinned. "This is the same as money."

Paul spoke the truth. Hunters and traders invaded the woods, wintering in lonely outposts. They came by the hundreds in their bateaux and canoes, finding the streams and catching the beaver. Then they brought their winter catch in and many of them spent their year's earnings in one wild orgy that lasted only a few days. Then it was back to the woods for another year.

"There's got to be a better way than this," Paul said abruptly. He left the pile of pelts, came back, and sat down close to the flickering flames that reflected the sharp planes of his face and made his gray blue eyes look almost like small flames themselves. His tapered face was mostly covered by a beard that was crisp brown with a touch of red. He stared for a long time into the fire, thinking hard and saying no more.

"What do you mean a bettair way?" Frenchy demanded. He reached beside his feet, picked up a bottle, and took a swallow of the fiery liquor he always carried with him. He offered it to Paul, who shook his head, then he took another swallow. "Look how many beaver we've taken."

"And look how hard we've worked for them! I'm not complaining, Frenchy, because I needed to learn about trapping. But I see now that you and I could trap for the rest of our lives and never do more than make a living. I want more than that."

"You 'ave plenty to eat, and when 'we get back and sell the furs you can buy good clothes. You 'ave women. What more you want?"

"A lot more than that," Paul Wakefield stated flatly. Paul was a proud, stubborn man and was driven in a way Frenchy Doucett could never understand. But Doucett did know this much—Paul Wakefield would never be happy just being a trapper. Now the Frenchman took another swig of the brandy, put the stopper in it, and coughed before saying, "There ees a bettair way."

Instantly Paul Wakefield looked up. "What way?"

"Let ze Indians trap ze beaver, then we buy ze skins."

"You mean join up with the fur company?"

Eloquently Doucett shrugged. "That ees one way. The other way ees to go it alone—but ees ver' hard."

"I hear the fur companies have made it rough on those who tried to work on their own, but it can be done, can't it?"

"Eef a man wants to take a chance, and eef he has money to put into eet—*oui.*"

Quickly Paul reckoned the cash he had left. "I've got enough to make a start. How do we do it, Frenchy?"

"We go buy trading goods. Not from ze trading company. They would make a profit on them. We get them from ze source."

"What kind of goods?"

"Blankets, knives, beads, tomahawks, and whiskey. Theengs lak' that."

"And then what?"

"Then we go to ze Indians and buy ze pelts. When we get enough, we take them and sell them. But I theenk we weel have to sell to ze Company. Eef we get good pelts, we can get a fair price and I'm too old to start a war weeth the American Fur Company or anybody else."

"All right," Paul said eagerly. "Let's do it!"

Frenchy was shocked at the suddenness of Wakefield's decision. "You mean—lak' right now?"

"Why not? We'll take what we've got and sell them, then take the money, and with what I've got we'll have enough to buy plenty of trading goods. Then we go to the Indians. Which tribe should we start with?"

"The Ojibway, I theenk. Some of ze others—weel, they might just take ze goods and our hair instead of giving us pelts. Like ze Huron, for example. Bad people to do business weeth."

"When can we leave?"

Frenchy smiled, his white teeth flashing against his swarthy skin. "We'll leave tomorrow, if you lak'. Me, I always lak'ed to go have a good time in town. Maybe we weel be reech," he said, leaning back and studying his young companion. "That's what you want, eesn't eet?"

Paul Wakefield sobered. He studied his hands for a moment and when he looked up, there was a hard glint in his eyes. "Yes, Frenchy," he said softly. "That's what I want. To be rich!"

⌘

Summer had passed quickly and autumn had turned the maples yellow and scarlet throughout the woods. It was as if a box of paints were passed from one to another and the colors deepened, spreading across the height and setting apart the hardwoods from the evergreens. As Paul and Frenchy rode their horses, Paul looked up at the colors blazoned across the forest and said aloud, "They have a brief time of glory, and then they're gone."

Doucett turned in the saddle, one eyebrow raised quizzically. "What do you mean? Who has a brief time of glory?"

Embarrassed of speaking such a thought aloud, Paul chuckled. "I just meant those leaves, Frenchy." Waving his hand at the glorious hues of the foliage, he shrugged his muscular shoulders. "I mean they're very pretty for a few days and then they turn brown and brittle, fall to the ground, and die."

Frenchy had not gotten completely accustomed to the work-ings of Paul Wakefield's mind. He himself was a simple man, caring for little except the basic essentials of life. Good food, warm clothing, enough liquor for a pleasant drink, a woman for pleasure: These were the things that Frenchy Doucett valued. But he was aware that different kinds of thoughts and desires ran beneath the surface of this young Englishman. Now he studied Wakefield, taking in the set of his shoulders, the strong hands tanned by a year of weathering blistering heat and freezing cold, and admired the look of the man. Still, he was puzzled enough to say, "What will you 'ave them do? Stay red and yellow all year long? The leaves must die or the trees will die. The woods themselves would die. Don't you know that, you foolish fellow?"

"Don't pay any attention to me, Frenchy. I haven't completely recovered from my education yet."

"What do you mean by that?"

"I mean education gives a man notions."

"Them theengs can be dangerous," Frenchy said, nodding wisely. "Get rid of them! They do a man no good."

Laughing, Paul slapped his horse on the haunches and picked up the pace. "I expect you're right," he replied and the two men rode rapidly through the twisting trail. When the ground began to rise, Frenchy said, "There ees the village."

"You've been here before?"

"Oh, yes. Many times. Ze chief ees a good man. His name ees Red Deer. He's not lak' some Indians. Not lak' those blasted Huron! You can believe what he says. He's getting old, though— won't be around too much longer."

Paul had questioned Frenchy extensively about the Indians, knowing he would have to do business with them. He had already begun to learn the rudiments of the Ojibway language and to his surprise had discovered he was able to pick it up rather easily. He had struggled with Greek and Latin as a boy, under a tutor, and had hated it. But this was a living language and he delighted in making sentences with the vocabulary. Once, he had said of the language, "It sounds like a man talking with his mouth full of mush." However, he had discovered that the Indian language, that of the Ojibway at least, was poetic far beyond anything the English language could provide. He had commented to Frenchy, "My brother, David, would love this language. Talk about notions! He's full of them and lives in his imagination. Not a practical bone in his body."

"He would not do well here," Frenchy said. "He would lose his scalp at once. A man must look after himself."

The village they rode into was not what Paul had expected. Somehow there had been planted in his mind a picture of tepees, their conical shapes covered with buffalo hides. He had heard of such villages and even seen illustrations, drawn by an Englishman who had visited the tribes of North America. This village, however, contained no such structures. Instead, rude log cabins, much like those used by the white settlers he had seen, were scattered over a relatively small area. Each cabin had a chimney made of mud and sticks, and from most of them smoke was spiraling lazily into the sky. A pack of lean dogs rushed out to meet them, snarling, exposing white fangs, and Frenchy dismounted, giving the leader a kick under the jaw that turned it in a neat somersault. He cursed the animal in French and the pack slunk away a few feet, still with bared teeth.

"If one of those dogs sinks a fang into me," Paul vowed as he slipped from his horse, holding his musket, "I'll put a bullet in his brain!"

"Then we weel probably 'ave him for supper. Nothing lak' puppy dog soup," Frenchy said, grinning. He shoved his cap back on his head and nodded at the group that was approaching. "Ze leetle one. That ees Chief Red Deer."

As the men advanced, Paul fixed his eyes on the leader. Red Deer was very short but wiry. He had an oversized head, a nose that dominated his face, high cheekbones, and black hair streaked with gray. His sharp black eyes missed nothing. He was the most brilliant of all the Ojibway chiefs, Doucett had told Paul, and when the group stopped, Red Deer held his hand up and spoke to the two in his own language. Frenchy responded at once in kind and then said in English, "Thees ees my partner, Paul Wakefield."

"He is welcome." Red Deer spoke in a pleasant tenor voice in

English. But Paul was sure the Indian's wide lips would give away no secrets. He had found out at least that much about the Indians: They masked whatever was in their minds and hearts with faces that gave nothing away. "I am pleased to meet the great chief, Red Deer," Paul said. He had practiced this speech and saw Red Deer's eyes widen slightly with surprise.

"You speak the language of the People?"

"Very little, but I will learn," Paul said laboriously.

"Come. We will eat, then you will try to cheat us out of our beaver pelts." A glint of humor glowed, Paul thought, in the dark eyes of the chief. This surprised him, for he had thought the Indians humorless. Frenchy had warned him, "They may seem that way to you. They're stiff around strangers. They been pretty cut up by ze whites, but when they're alone sometimes they laugh and giggle lak' girls at a party."

The meal Paul sat down to was better than he expected. There was boiled corn, deer steak, and some sort of stew that he dared not ask about but found very good indeed. During the meal he said nothing but tried to follow the conversation, which was mostly in Ojibway language.

"'Ave you had a good season, Red Deer?" Doucett asked.

"Not good. Many young men were off fighting with the Huron."

"Not good for the Ojibway. The Huron are a bad people."

"Yes, but young men will fight."

"Not me," Frenchy replied.

"You are not a young man. You and I are old enough to have wisdom. Young men—like your friend—they have to prove their courage."

Paul did speak up then. "No fighting for me. All I want is to get many furs."

Red Deer's eyes narrowed and Paul met his gaze. For a moment silence reigned over the group. Then Red Deer picked up a pipe, lit it with a coal from the fire, and puffed it. He handed it to Paul, saying, "I hope you will be a friend to the People. We need friends among the white eyes."

Paul took the pipe and sucked at it, the harsh smoke biting at his tongue. He gave no sign of it, though, but smiled genially. "I hope to be a great friend of the great chief, Red Deer. Our people should be as one."

"That will never be." Red Deer's eyes clouded and he looked over the forest that surrounded the village like an armed fort, the trees rising high in the air. "The white men come like a flood. They do not move like the Indians, but cut down the trees. Soon there will be no room for the Indians."

"That's not for a long time, Chief Red Deer," Doucett said quickly. "Not in our time."

"Quicker than you think. The earth is covered by the white men. There is no stopping them."

Frenchy sat for a moment, considering Red Deer's words. "Someday the English will fight the French. They both want this land. When that comes, who will you join, Red Deer?"

Startled, Paul glanced at Doucett. He knew that the simple Frenchman had hit on the precise truth. The French were filing in from the north, from Canada, moving deeper, past the Great Lakes. The English along the eastern seaboard were moving westward. Both races coveted the rich lands, valleys, mountains, and furs that came out of this part of the world. They had already met with several clashes and soon there would be a more serious one, Paul knew.

"I think with the French," Red Deer said quietly and then looked at Paul. "The French are like us—like you, Doucett. The men come and go but do not take over the forest and strip it for farms. The English will do that. Therefore, we will fight with the French."

Paul spoke up. "I hope that time will never come."

"It will come," Red Deer said prophetically. A sadness washed across his face and his eyes dropped.

Doucett said, "Well, what about a leetle trading?"

"Not now," Red Deer said slowly. The moment—thoughts of what would happen to the Ojibway nation—seemed to have depressed him. Rising, he waved a dismissal and said, "We will talk tomorrow."

Paul and Frenchy rose and went to their horses. They stripped their pack animals and moved toward one of the cabins that a lesser chief had said they might use. Paul remarked, "He's not very anxious to trade."

"That ees ze way of an Indian. Time doesn't mean nothing to them. They don't carry watches. In the meanwhile, just move around and don't get in no trouble. Zese fellows, they don't lak' us too much anyway. But they need the goods we've got. Behave yourself!"

Paul looked up with surprise from where he had dropped the pack on the floor of the cabin. "What do you mean, behave myself?"

Frenchy grinned lewdly. "I mean stay away from these young women. That's a good way to get your hair lifted eef you don't know which one to go after. I know."

"You don't have to worry about that," Paul said shortly. "That's the last thing I want to do, get involved with an Indian woman."

The two men rested the remainder of the day. They ate again, a meal they themselves fixed, and afterward Paul said, "I'm going for a walk." He left the camp and made his way toward a stream that encircled part of the village. When he put his knuckles into the cold white water, it jumped over his hand. "Snow water," Paul murmured, looking up at the mountains that already had ice and snow. After a few minutes, he rose and slowly made his way down the creek. Darkness was falling and as he walked, a sound alerted him. His nerves had become sensitive during his months in the woods. He was conscious of danger all the time, either from wild beasts or men, with the same feral instincts that some lone hunters possessed. He had kept his scalp and now as he whirled toward the sound, he pulled a wicked-looking knife from his belt and held it high, reaching out with his free hand toward the shadowy figure that had suddenly appeared. His hand closed on an arm and he said, "Who are you? What do you want?"

"Let me go!"

Astonished at the softness of the voice, Paul realized it was a woman who stood before him—or perhaps a young girl. He could not tell. He dropped her arm at once, feeling rather foolish standing there with a knife in his hand. Pushing it back in his belt, he said grudgingly, "I'm sorry! You startled me."

"You have good ears for a white man."

Paul studied the young woman, shocked at what he saw. She was taller than most Ojibway women. Caught in the last few rays of sun, her black hair held faint glints of copper. She wore it parted in a braid down her back, and as she looked up at him, he saw that her face was oval shaped instead of square like most Indian women's. But the most startling thing was her blue eyes! *A blue-eyed Indian!* he thought. *Could there have been a white man . . . a trapper . . . an explorer who traveled these forests before?* Then he noticed her full lips and high cheekbones, but her skin was not much darker than some women who had remained out in the sun. She wore a typical Ojibway costume, a short deerskin dress with beads and quills worked in. The sleeves came down only to her elbows and her feet were covered by deerskin half boots that turned over to her ankles.

"Why do you stare at me?"

Paul was embarrassed. "I didn't mean to. I was—well, I was just surprised, that's all."

"My name is Marielle."

"Marielle? That's French. It's not Indian."

"My father gave it to me. He was an Englishman."

The girl's English was good, but at times it was strangely accented with words pronounced differently from what Paul was accustomed to. *A half-breed!* he thought, and at the same time, *What a beauty!*

"What is your name?" Marielle demanded.

"Paul Wakefield."

"Are you from across the water?"

"Yes. From England."

Paul could not decide whether she was a girl or young woman; she could have been anywhere from sixteen to twenty. She reached up and touched her chin gently, then lifted her blue eyes to meet his. "That's where my father came from. He was a big man. Bigger than you."

Curious, Paul asked, "What about your mother?"

"My mother is Wabanang."

Paul tried to say it. "Waban—"

"That means Morning Star in your language."

"She is Ojibway?"

"Yes." The girl's lips tightened; she lowered her head and turned to walk away. Paul, shocked at the abruptness of her movement, watched her disappear down the path. Then he hurried to the village.

"What about this girl Marielle?"

Frenchy was smoking his pipe. He removed it from his lips and his eyes half narrowed. "How do you know about her?"

"I met her when I was walking."

"Stay away from her."

Paul was offended. "I wasn't intending to run off with her!"

"You'd better not!" Frenchy said strictly. "Her mother ees married to Red Deer."

"Oh!" Paul stood there, trying to make this adjustment. "She told me her father was a white man. An Englishman, she said."

"That's right. You can tell, can't you? Never saw blue eyes lak' that in many Indians. She ees a beauty!"

Paul sat down on the blanket spread on a frame, which was his bed. "I wonder what happened to her father?"

"He died of ze smallpox. From what I hear, he was quite a man. Had a reech family over in England, so ze story goes, although there ees no telling about that. Reech to these people could mean anything."

Paul lay down on the bed and pulled the blanket over him. The cabin was growing cool as night fell. He thought for a long time about the girl and finally said, "I wonder why she didn't go back to England after her father died?"

"Huh!" Frenchy's comment was explosive. "I can just see that! Eef he did come from a fine family, they're not lak'ly to take in an Indian girl."

"I suppose not."

After some time, Paul drove the thought of the girl from his mind by beginning to think instead of the furs he had seen. Prime, all of them, and enough to bring in a great deal of money.

"I'll keep my mind on those furs," he said. "Not on any blue-eyed Indian girl!"

A WOMAN TO LOVE

O c t o b e r 1 7 6 1

To Paul Wakefield, Quebec seemed to be a city of bells. He had arrived back at the town in October 1761 and now he sat in the tavern with Frenchy, looking out the window over the rocky heights of the city.

At that moment, the bells of a nearby church began ringing and Paul almost thought he could hear the sounds of chants pouring from the convent windows that seemed to occupy a large part of Quebec.

"What you theenk, my friend?" Doucett said to Paul. "You're not happy."

"I'm fine."

"No. You're not fine. Here we are weethout an Indian to put an arrow in our livers, we're eating *pâté de foie gras* and drinking fine brandy instead of ze rotgut ze Indians 'ave to take. Plenty of women—and yet you're not happy."

"I'm fine," Paul repeated stubbornly. He swirled the amber liquor in his glass and stared at it as if he expected to find some answer there, then looked up with irritation.

But Doucett leaned back in his chair and studied Wakefield. Doucett was wearing new clothes made of linen and silk in the brightest colors he could find. He looked almost like a peacock

101

as he sat there in his finery, but his voice was serious when he said, "I know what eet ees you're thinking."

"You become a mind reader, Frenchy?"

"Eet does not take a mind reader to know about you, Paul."

"What am I thinking then?"

A grin creased the Frenchman's meaty lips. "Marielle."

Startled, Paul looked up and saw that Doucett had fixed him with his crafty gaze. "Don't be a fool!" he snapped. "Why should I be thinking about an Indian woman?"

"Who knows why any man theenks about any woman. To me they're all ze same," Doucett said, shrugging his beefy shoulders. "But you are different, I theenk. You English, you 'ave some foolish ideas about love. You theenk eet ees somewhere in ze heart and one woman ees so different from another that you can only be happy weeth that one."

"I didn't know you were an expert on English love affairs," Paul said with irritation, upset because Frenchy had touched upon what had been gnawing at him ever since they had left the Indian camp and headed for Quebec loaded down with furs. After spending a year in Red Deer's area they had made their way up the Saint Lawrence River, and all throughout the long journey until they left their canoes for a steamer, he had been thinking almost constantly of Marielle. Night after night he would wake, thinking of the startling blue eyes set in her olive face and hearing the sounds of her clear, mellow voice. Now he looked at Frenchy and said, "Don't be an idiot!"

"I weel do my best, but I 'ave a partner who ees an idiot!" Frenchy leaned forward and grasped Paul's arm with vicelike strength. "Forget about that one!"

"Why should I?" Paul shot back, glaring at Frenchy as if he had insulted him. "I can have an Indian woman! You've had hundreds of them, I suppose!"

"Not lak' that one!"

"What's so different about her?"

"For one theeng," Frenchy said, tightening his grip even more, "she ees ze daughter of Red Deer. Eef you offend him, we don't trade weeth them no more. I lak' money, my friend, and so do you!"

"Are you telling me that none of the chiefs allow their daughters to go with men?"

"Marielle ees different," Frenchy said stubbornly. Releasing his grip, he picked up his glass, studied the contents, then drained it off, saying, "She ees a convert of ze black robes."

Paul had heard this before. "So, she's a Christian. She's still an Indian."

"Only half Indian. Ze other half ees English. I 'ave talked weeth Red Deer much about thees woman, and others, too," he said, his voice dropping to a whisper. "She weel nevair go weeth a man unless he marry weeth her and you will nevair do that, weel you?"

Paul did not answer. Instead he stared out the window at the spires that pointed like thin fingers at the sky, listening again to the bells. Then he admitted, "All right. I'm drawn to the girl. She's the most beautiful woman I've ever seen."

"You must not theenk lak' that. She weel nevair go weeth you, Paul. Not unless you weel marry her—and besides, Running Wolf wants her."

"Who's Running Wolf?"

"Son of a ver' powerful chief. Eet weel be a good match. Red Deer has already approved him. Nobody knows why Marielle don't take him."

Paul Wakefield stirred uneasily in his chair. His expression changed abruptly and he said, "I'm going back to Red Deer's camp."

"Eet weel be trouble."

"We've got a lot of goods. We'll give Red Deer a good value for his beaver if he has any more."

"You are not going back for beaver, my friend. You are going back for that woman."

"I don't want to talk about it, Frenchy. When can we go back? I'm tired of this place anyhow."

Doucett glanced toward the painted woman who was waiting for him impatiently, then shrugged. "I guess we can leave in ze morning. We've got plenty of trade goods." He stared at the young man he had grown fond of. Suddenly it seemed to him that a cloud hung over the fate of Paul Wakefield, and Doucett, being a superstitious man, drew his shoulders together tightly but said nothing.

The next morning the two loaded on the steamer *Santa Maria* and as they headed down the Saint Lawrence, Paul said very little. He was caught up with his thoughts of Marielle. It was the first time he had ever felt so strongly about a woman and somehow the mystery of his feelings frightened him. It was as if he were drawn back to her by a powerful magnet and he could not pull himself away from it. Now that riches, comfort, and luxury were in his grasp, why would he be headed back to a woman who was so different that he knew he could never fully understand her? His eyes were on the water as it pearled around the prow of the vessel, but he saw in the intricate patterns of the water nothing to indicate his future.

<hr />

Red Deer's village seemed to have a festive atmosphere as Paul dismounted. It was late October now and the red, gold, and yellow of the trees were bright colors against the gray sky. A chill was in the air and Paul pulled his coat around him as he looked about eagerly, trying to catch a glimpse of Marielle.

"You have come back?"

Paul turned to see Red Deer, who had approached from the opposite direction he'd been looking. "Yes, Red Deer. I have brought many more trading goods for you and your people, and gifts as well."

An enigmatic light appeared in Red Deer's dark eyes. He knew men well and understood, more than most, the heart of the English. Perhaps he had learned it from Marielle's father, Jeremiah Trent. His mind flashed back to the time when the tall Englishman had come and Wabanang, known as "Morning Star," had fallen in love with him. Red Deer had known then that a battle was coming between the English and the French and it grieved him. He knew also that Paul had not come to trade beaver and said quietly, "We have not had time to trap many more beaver. I'm sure you know that."

Unable to endure the steady gaze of the Indian, Paul turned his eyes away. "I thought I might just come on a visit and I do have gifts for you and for your people." He glanced around at the village. "Are you having some kind of a celebration? A religious one perhaps, Red Deer?"

"No. It is time to drain the trees of their sweetness. We have a celebration once a year when this happens." Almost reluctantly, Red Deer nodded. "You are welcome to my people."

Something in Red Deer's tone disturbed Paul, but he smiled and said, "Thank you, Red Deer. I left Frenchy downriver. He'll be here after a time. Perhaps we could rent the same cabin we had before. I would be happy to pay for it."

"You are our guest. There is no pay required."

Paul settled himself into the log cabin—the same one he and Frenchy had shared before—then went out, driven by an anxiety he could not explain. The sun was bright, but snow lay lurking somewhere beyond the mountains. He could hear the sound of an Indian chant and could see a dance going on, something he had never seen before. There was no music, but the rhythm was made plain by the clapping of hands and the syncopated treading of feet upon the hard earth. Paul thought, *White people don't understand Indians. This is a party like we would have back home. They just wear different kinds of clothes, but they like their fun.*

Moving throughout the camp, he stepped into the trees and quickly located the spot where the maple trees were being tapped. Several fires had been built. Heavy iron vessels had been suspended from a pole supported by two forked sticks set in the earth at each side. A woman stood beside each kettle, ladeling away the scum as it formed. At the end of the row, the largest kettle was suspended from a framework attached to a stump about the height of Paul's head. At the same time he saw Marielle standing beside it and he walked toward her at once. She had already noticed him, he realized, and there was a welcome light in her eyes that pleased him. But she only smiled briefly as he said, "Hello, Marielle."

"Hello, Monsieur Wakefield."

"Oh! Don't call me that!" Paul protested. "Just call me Paul."

"Paul, then." Marielle's smile grew warmer and she said, "I'm glad to see you back." As the two stood there talking, Paul was aware of a bird singing in a little grove of evergreens. Overhead a hawk crossed and headed north. But Paul was more conscious of this woman whom he found so enchanting. Once again there was the mystery he could not fathom. Back in England he had seen women in gowns that cost literally hundreds of pounds, yet this young woman wearing a tan deerskin dress with beads and quills captivated him more than any of those.

They were both startled when a voice spoke almost beside Paul in the Ojibway language. Paul turned to see a tall Indian he did not know and Marielle said, "This is Running Wolf."

Instantly Paul remembered Doucett's words and understood well the emotions in this tall brave's eyes. *He wants Marielle, and he doesn't want me around her* was the thought that flickered through him. He gave the standard greeting in his halting Ojibway and saw no warmth in the Indian's eyes. Paul had grown adept at recognizing the attitudes of the Indians and knew at once that Running Wolf was a man who wanted a woman and would kill for her.

Marielle stood almost between the two men as she spoke to Running Wolf rapidly and insistently.

Running Wolf listened and looked once more at Paul. Although he did not speak, his lips drew tight and he stalked away, indignation and anger in every line of his body.

"I hear he wants to marry you," Paul said.

"Yes."

"Are you going to?"

Marielle stirred the potent, boiling contents of the black kettle and did not answer. *If she were going to marry him,* Paul thought, somehow filled with relief, *she would have said so at once.* Aloud he said, "I'm glad to be back. I've missed you."

"You could not think about me while you were away."

"Of course I could." Paul shrugged and said, "I don't understand it, but I have. Every night, almost, I would dream of your eyes. They're very beautiful."

His remark disturbed Marielle. She lowered her eyes and a flush touched her cheeks. "You must not speak that way to me."

"I can't help it. I have to."

"No. You must not. It is not right."

Paul, standing before her in a new pair of soft and pliable buckskins, chuckled.

Marielle thought, *He's so handsome. I've never seen a man more so.* She was accustomed to the rather blunt features of the Ojibways, and the tapering face of Wakefield, the strong cleft chin and a mustache that no Indian would wear, intrigued her. There was a quickness in him that she was unaccustomed to. She knew, with all the intuition of a woman, that he had come back on her account. This pleased—and disturbed—her. Yet, as he stood there, with the sunlight washing over him, bringing out a slight reddish tinge in his dark blond hair, she found herself growing very happy that he had come back to see her.

The party went on for some time and finally a short, stocky brave said, "Come. Get your sugar."

Quickly the crowd lined up with cups of all sorts—anything that would hold liquid. "May I join you?" Paul asked.

"Why, of course. Do you like sugar?"

"I love syrup. It's the sweetest thing in the world. Next to a beautiful woman."

Marielle's cheeks flamed, but she did not rebuke him. Inside, she was pleased at his words, for no man had ever said things like this to her before. It was not the Indian way. The two got their taste of sugar and moved off to one side. Soon they were laughing and talking, unaware that Running Wolf was watching them angrily, ignoring the festivities. He was not alone, for Red Deer stood back in the shadows, his dark eyes troubled by the scene before him. He had known ever since Marielle was a young girl that men would be drawn to her. It had not occurred to him that a white man, an Englishman, would be one of those, and he saw trouble ahead.

"I think you like the Englishman."

Marielle's best friend, Loantha, spoke quickly and there was a light of mischief in her eyes. The two women were working together, sewing hunting coats.

Loantha was almost Marielle's height, the tallest woman of pure Ojibway blood in any of the tribes. The two girls had grown up together, for they were of the same age. But now that Loantha was being courted by at least three young men, her talk was mostly of courtship, marriage, and what was to follow.

Marielle glanced up from her work and shook her head. "It must not be," she said quietly, then looked back down again. The skin she worked on had been soaked in ashes and water for several days. Then she had stretched it on the ground between stakes, scraped it with a bone until it was dry and soft, and then smoked it over a hole in the ground filled with burning, rotten wood. Now as she touched the fabric she knew the coat would be dry and soft, not stiff and hard.

"I can tell you like him more than you like Running Wolf or any other man," Loantha said. She punched a hole in the coat she was making and began to insert a porcupine quill. Her fingers worked rapidly and the quill seemed to go of its own accord into the soft leather. "Will you have him if he makes an offer to your father?"

The question could not be answered quickly. In truth, Marielle had thought of such a thing, for since Paul had returned to the village, she had spent much time with him. The days had passed quickly until November skies frowned over the land where snow had already laid its soft blanket. It was a time of the year that Marielle liked, but she was troubled by her friend's question. "He will never ask," she said softly.

"He likes you. I can see it in his face and he wants to be with you all the time."

"I like to be with him, too," Marielle confessed. "But he will be gone soon."

"I think he will want to take you with him."

"That could never be," Marielle said. "No. I would not go with him."

A wind keened outside and both young women felt the safety and security of the cabin that was Loantha's home. With both her parents gone, she was the only one left. The cabin was comprised of rough logs, and strips of cured meat hung from rafters among drying herbs and ears of corn. Fishing spears, bows, and arrows rested on nails that were driven into one wall. Above the doors and windows were signs to keep evil spirits from entering. Several pelts stretched wrong side out to dry on pointed boards hung above pieces of an old net in one corner. The two women sat on braided mats although there was a bare board table and three chairs in the room. It was a typical middle-class Ojibway hut, but even Chief Red Deer's home differed little from this.

Suddenly Loantha asked, "Have you ever been with a man?"

"No!" Marielle, startled by the question, saw that Loantha was watching her carefully. "Have you?" she asked.

Loantha's cheeks flamed and she lowered her voice, glancing surreptitiously toward the door. "Yes. Twice."

Marielle had thought she knew all about Loantha and discovering she had been with a man shocked her. Loantha was a Christian, as she herself was, and now the other girl said quickly, "It happened a long time ago when I was only fourteen. I wish it hadn't." Then she asked her friend, "Are you afraid?"

"Of being a wife? No. It is what a woman is born for," Marielle said calmly. The facts of life were hard to hide in an Indian village and although she was a virgin, she was well aware of the physical side of marriage. One would learn some of that from animal life if nowhere else. Now, however, she shook her head and said, "I will never give myself to a man unless it is in marriage. That is what we were taught, Loantha." She thought of her father, who had been a Christian, and although he had been dead for years, she still remembered his words as he had sat beside her once and talked about what it would be like when she became a woman. She also remembered that her mother, Wabanang, had once cautioned her never to go with a man as many of the Indian girls did.

The two young women continued working on the hunting coats, neither speaking their thoughts. But Marielle had been more shaken by the conversation than she chose to admit. She did not forget it and wondered what she would say if Paul Wakefield ever attempted to make love to her.

─────────

Time did not seem to run the same among the Ojibways as it did among the English. Paul was conscious of this as the days passed slowly. There were no clocks, no calendars, and the Indians lived by the movement of animals, by the weather, and by their sense of the earth beneath them. It was a time when for Paul Wakefield all that he had known since he was a child seemed shut off. Perhaps this was why Marielle occupied so much of his mind and his thoughts. Day after day he sought her out, almost unconsciously, and the two spent hours walking through the woods when Marielle's work was done. As the cold nights came, Paul spent a lot of time in his cabin with an occasional visit from Frenchy, who often warned him about seeing Marielle. But the words went over Paul's head and dissipated like mist when the sun arose.

The day came when Paul and Marielle had walked through the forest and come to a lake. The first snow had melted and now the grass was dry and brown. The smell of cold weather was evident in the crisp air and as they sat down on a grassy spot beside the lake, Marielle began to speak of things that Paul himself would never have dreamed of uttering. She looked out on the clear blue water and noted a ripple. "Look," she said. "Not a cloud in the sky, Paul. No wind—and yet look. There's a wave."

Paul watched as the wave formed in the center and moved across to the shore. It broke at their feet and he turned to face her. They were sitting close together, his shoulder touching hers, and that very contact went to his head. "What's odd about that? It's just a wave."

Marielle turned to him. Her lips were parted and her skin was beautiful: clear, olive-toned, and smooth, the smoothest thing Paul had ever seen. Her voice was low as she said, "Where did it come from, that wave? There was no wind to make it." She held her hand up in the air as if to feel a breeze, then lowered it. "There's no cause. It formed and disappeared and now look. The water's as smooth as it was before." A sadness came into her tone. "Is that the way it is with us? That's not what I was taught, but my father is gone now. Just like that wave."

"Do you think about things like this a lot, Marielle?"

"Of course. Don't you?"

"Not as much as I should." Paul reached out and took Marielle's hand. "I can't think about anything but you," he confessed. "It's like you put a spell on me." His voice was urgent and when she met his eyes she saw the desire that was in them. He put his arm around her and drew her close. As the soft curves of her body flattened against his chest, he saw alarm rise in her eyes. She started to speak, but his lips covered hers and he held her close. Old hungers rose in him and he held her tighter, aware that she was pushing at him with her hands. But the softness of her lips and the intimacy of the embrace stirred him and he savored the kiss even though she struggled against him.

"You mustn't!" Marielle finally pulled back, drawing her lips together tightly. "You mustn't do such a thing!"

"Why not? It's what a man and a woman do," Paul said quickly. He would have held her close again, but she drew back and stood to her feet. Paul rose to stand beside her and she turned her back to him, gazing out over the stillness of the blue waters. She had been stirred by his caress more than she allowed him to see. Her heart was pounding like a hammer and she had experienced feelings that she knew came from being a woman. Before, she had fought clear of these urges, never allowing men to touch her. But now the feel of his hands seemed to burn into her. Though he stood apart, she knew she would not sleep, that she would remember this caress for days. Turning to him, she took a deep breath. "We can never be—"

"We can never be what?"

"We can never love one another."

"A man can't help that. It comes to a man—and I love you, Marielle." Paul was shocked at his own confession, but as he stood looking into her clear eyes and seeing her vulnerable, soft lips and the trim curves of her body, he knew there was something in this woman that none other had ever held for him. Reaching out, he grasped her shoulders and pulled her slightly forward so they were almost embracing. "I've got to have you, Marielle!"

"No!" Marielle once again pushed him away. "You can never have me!"

"Come with me. We can be happy together. I'll make you love me," Paul insisted, seeing the emotion in her eyes. "You love me already, don't you, Marielle?"

"That doesn't matter. You're English and I am Ojibway."

"Only half Ojibway."

Marielle held up her hand quickly. "I am a woman who believes in God and you are not a man who has faith."

Her answer stopped Paul Wakefield abruptly. He had no response or reply, for what she said was the truth. Perhaps it was this restraint, this purity, that had drawn him to this beautiful, dusky woman in the first place and now he could only stand there and say helplessly, "But—I love you, Marielle."

"You must find another. We can never be one." She turned quickly and walked away, leaving Paul Wakefield feeling as helpless as he had ever felt in his entire life. As another wave rose over the blue water, he thought of her words and realized that somehow a great wind had passed over his life, something he could not understand or control—but he knew what he had to do.

⟡

"But Running Wolf has already come and offered ten horses for my daughter."

Paul had come to Red Deer's cabin and, without hesitation, had said, "I want your daughter to be my woman, Red Deer." He had thought about this for five days, ever since he had held Marielle in his arms beside the lake. He had been restless and miserable and finally had risen early one morning to find the chief alone in his cabin. Now, having received his answer, he replied, "But I will give twenty horses or the equivalent—or the trade goods to pay for them."

Red Deer stared at the tall young man and shook his head. "It would not be a good marriage. Running Wolf would make a good man for her."

For some time Paul pleaded, arguing his case, but finally left, seeing that Red Deer would not change his mind.

At noon when Marielle came in, Red Deer accosted her at once. "Wakefield was here."

Instantly Marielle's hands went to her cheeks. She showed her emotion much more than most full-blooded Indian women and now her cheeks were flushed. She studied her stepfather, saying nothing while she waited for him to speak.

"He will give twenty horses for you. That is a great many."

"I will not have him, Father."

"I told him so, but he is a stubborn man."

"I will never marry him. I will never go with him. It is not what the black book teaches." Marielle had learned to read English and the Bible was almost her only source of reading. Now she said firmly, "You must tell him to find another woman."

"I think you must tell him yourself," Red Deer said. "And quickly, or there will be trouble between him and Running Wolf."

"I will tell him."

As soon as she left the cabin, Red Deer turned to the window. He called out, "Wabanang, come in here!"

As his wife entered, her eyes were wary. "I saw Marielle leaving."

"The white man wants her. He will give twenty horses."

Wabanang shook her head. "It would not be good."

"You were happy with your Englishman."

"He was different. He was a man of God." Wabanang came up and put her hand on Red Deer's arm in an unusual gesture of affection. "You have been a good husband to me, but the Englishman would not be good for her. He wants her, but when he tires of her he will turn aside."

"Perhaps he will marry her."

"Has he said so?"

"No."

"Then she will never have him."

<hr>

Paul had come to Marielle at dusk. "Come outside," he had said, avoiding the eyes of Red Deer and Wabanang.

Quickly Marielle responded, "No, Paul. I will not go with you."

Paul swallowed hard. He had slept but little for the past three days and now he had come with his mind made up. "I've come to ask you to marry me, Marielle."

Both Red Deer and Wabanang revealed their shock by staring first at the white man, then at Marielle.

Marielle herself was taken totally unaware by Paul's words. She had never thought of such a thing and now she could not speak for a moment. She stood there, eyes wide and lips parted with the surprise that held her almost as in a chain.

"I love you, Marielle. I want you to be my wife," Paul said simply. As he said this, he was aware he was cutting himself off from all he had known. Never could he go back to England now—not with an Indian wife. But this did not seem to matter. He had not been happy in England and he thought little of David, although he missed his mother. So he waited quietly and finally asked, "Will you have me?"

Marielle fulfilled the meaning of her name, "Pale Dawn," at that moment, for her cheeks had grown almost ashen. She had dreamed of this but had put it aside with a sadness in her heart, knowing it could never be. But now as she looked at Paul's face under such strain, she knew he was the man she would always love.

"Yes. I will have you if my father and mother agree."

The words brought a flush of joy to Paul. He started toward her but then, remembering her parents, asked, "Will you give your daughter to me, Red Deer and Wabanang?"

Red Deer looked at his wife and saw assent in her eyes. "Yes," he said. "Will you love her and stay with her? Not leave her as other men have left Indian wives?"

"I will have her as my wife forever," Paul said firmly.

⸺ ❧ ⸺

The wedding had been simple. Nothing that Paul could have anticipated, but it was over and he was in the new cabin he had hired built just for him and Marielle. They were alone now for the first time and he looked at her as she stood watching him, her eyes enormous. It was night and the only light was a tallow candle that burned faintly on the table. The bed seemed to dominate the room and Paul, to his astonishment, was nervous and shaken.

"Are you afraid, Marielle? Of being with a man?"

Marielle, too, had known fear, but now she came to him and put her arms around him. She had removed her deerskin wedding dress and was wearing a silk gown Paul had brought back with him to the village to give to Marielle as a surprise gift in case his suit went well. As she pressed against him, she said, "Will you love me forever, Paul?"

For one moment Paul thought almost frantically, *There's still time to leave this. This is forever!* But he smelled her sweetness and pulled her toward him. "Yes," he whispered huskily. "I'll always love you, Marielle."

Her lips came up to meet his as she pulled his head down and said, "Then I am not afraid, Husband. I will be a good wife to you. As good as I know how."

The two clung to each other and there was a hunger in Paul such as he had never known. And later as they held on to one another, he was astonished at the passion he found in Marielle. She clung to him, weeping a little, and yet finally whispering, "You are my husband, and I will love you forever."

At that moment Paul Wakefield knew the door had shut on his past and he could never turn his back on Marielle.

Nine

THE RAID

As Paul approached the cabin, a wave of satisfaction rose in him. The months since their marriage had passed so quickly that it was hard for him to grasp. "Should've gotten married a long time ago," he murmured as he stepped up to the door. "But then, a man who marries the wrong woman is in big trouble." Swiftly he thought of the days and nights and glowed with unusual warmth. Marriage had come as a surprise, for though he had known other women physically, none had ever touched his spirit or brought him the happiness he found with Marielle.

Stealthily he opened the door and stepped inside. Marielle was stirring something in a pottery bowl, her back to him. The sunlight came through the small window on the east side of the room and touched her black hair, revealing the tint of reddish gold—a heritage from her English father. Without making a sound, Paul moved across the dirt floor and threw his arms around her, drawing her close. When she uttered a muted cry, he whirled her around and kissed her soundly on the lips.

"Paul! You mustn't do that!" Marielle protested. But the pleasure in her eyes denied the sharpness of her words and when he pulled her close again, she whispered, "Yes, you can do it again if you want to."

Paul laughed and kissed her once more. "I'm glad to hear you say so. It's what I'd planned on doing every chance I got."

The two stood there in the middle of the simple room, which was unadorned except for a few treasures that Marielle had gathered and one picture Paul had brought with him from England. It was a portrait of the family, including his father, mother, and David. They all sat stiffly, looking at the artist, and Marielle found it fascinating. Even now the eyes of the painting seemed to focus on the young couple as they continued to stand in the middle of the room. Paul kissed Marielle's satiny cheek and then his lips went lower until he nibbled at her neck. Marielle squealed, "Paul, I can't stand that!" But when he continued, she shivered and grabbed his hair, pulling his head back. Her blue eyes sparkled as she said, "I didn't know it was so much fun being married. Nobody ever told me about that."

"None of them ever had me for a husband."

"Oh, you're so proud and vain!" Marielle exclaimed. Then she smiled and her twin dimples, one on each cheek, appeared. She pressed herself against him, her soft form molding itself to his lean, tough body. "I like being married," she said.

"That's good, because you've got me to put up with for the next forty years at least."

Marielle remained in his embrace. As far as she knew, no Indian men treated their wives to such caresses and she had grown to love them. Paul was constantly stroking her hair, rubbing her neck, and now as his hand ran up and down the small of her back, she said, "What did you say this is called?"

"What's *what* called?"

"This time for a while after a man and a woman get married. You told me about it once, but I forgot."

"Oh." Paul smiled and let his hand drop lower. "Oh, it's called a honeymoon."

"I like that. There's nothing sweeter than honey."

"Except you," Paul teased. He continued to caress her until she finally pushed him away and said, "Now behave yourself, Paul."

"I am behaving myself. This is what a husband's supposed to do. Haven't you ever read in the Bible what a man was supposed to do when he got married?"

Suspicious, Marielle cocked an eyebrow and tilted her head to one side. "I don't remember reading anything like that in the Bible."

"Well, it's there. Somewhere in the Old Testament. The book of Deuteronomy or one of those long books."

"What does it say a young man's supposed to do when he marries?"

"He's not supposed to do a lick of work," Paul said, grinning, and reached for her again. Drawing her close, he kissed her thoroughly. "And it says that he's supposed to please his wife for a whole year. I've got a long time to go. I think I'll just quit work entirely. With a woman as lovely as you, it's going to take all my time just to keep you happy and pleased."

Warmth flooded through Marielle. She clung to him tightly. She loved him as she loved life itself and could not imagine being away from him—or life without him. "That's nice," she whispered. Then she pushed him back and said, "Enough of that."

"We'll take this matter up later," Paul said, winking. "You'll get to see my birthmark."

Marielle was still young enough in her married life to blush. "What do your people think that means? That four-leaf clover?"

"Good luck," Paul said. "I hope it comes true. I had luck getting you. Maybe that's what it's for."

"And your brother. The one who is your twin. He doesn't have any mark?"

"Nope! David is just white all over."

Hours later, after they had eaten dinner, Paul had tilted his chair back against the wall. Marielle said shyly, "I have a present for you."

"It's not my birthday."

"No. It's not a birthday present. It's just something I made. I wanted to show how much I honor my husband."

Paul was touched by her simplicity. He watched as she moved gracefully across the room, opened the door to the cabinet fastened to the inner side of the logs, and then returned to him. "Here. These are for you."

"Oh, Marielle!" Paul exclaimed, taking the pair of moccasins from her. "They're much too fine for a hard-nosed man like me." They were of fine deerskin, tanned to a golden brown, with more embroidery than even a chief's usually had. Paul examined the otter-tail pattern running from the puckered seam in front all the way to the plain seam in back. The cuffs were neatly fringed below a wide band of porcupine quills in red and blue. Looking up, Paul smiled, his eyes almost disappearing as they always did. "They're beautiful, Marielle." Then he added slyly, "I'll give you a reward for this tonight." He slipped them on, noting that she giggled at his words just as an English girl might.

Afterward, he sat and talked about his life in England, for Marielle had an insatiable curiosity about that land so far away. She could never hear enough about the country and the people—especially about the masses of people on London's streets.

"Will we ever go there, Paul?"

For one second Paul hesitated, intending to put her off, but honesty forced him to say, "I don't think so, Marielle. You wouldn't like it."

Marielle stared at him and Paul knew that something was going on inside her mind that he could not understand. Sometimes she withdrew to this secret place—perhaps all women did, but he suspected it had something to do with her Indian blood. Indians, he had discovered, were a deeply spiritual people—not just Christian, but believing in the spirits of good and evil in almost everything they saw. They thought about these things a great deal and Marielle, having married this heritage to a Christian belief, sometimes thought things Paul could not discover. "What's wrong?" he asked quietly.

"You'd be ashamed of me in your home, wouldn't you?"

"Of course not!" Paul snapped. "Don't say a thing like that!" There was a sting in her words, however, and he drew her close. "I love you as I've never loved any woman and I'm proud of you. But people are cruel in England. I suppose they're cruel everywhere. When people are different in any way, they make fun of them and I couldn't stand to see that happen to you."

"My people don't make fun of you."

"I think they do a little," Paul said, grinning. "Some of the foolish mistakes I've made. I'm sure they laugh at them."

Some time passed before Paul stirred again, saying, "I've got to make a trip, Marielle."

"Oh no! Where are you going?"

"Frenchy's coming by. He's picked up another load of furs. Along with those I've got, we've got enough for another trip."

"Can I go with you?"

"Not this time. It will be a hard trip. We're going all the way to Mackinac Island. Instead of selling our furs independently in Quebec, I'm going to try to make a deal with the American Fur Company."

"Would they give more money for the furs?"

"No, they'd give less—but if I make a good impression, I'd like to get in with John Jacob Astor. He's the man who started the American Fur Company and the richest man in America, I suppose. One of them at least." A gleam came into Paul's eyes and he seemed lost for a moment. "If I could just get on the inside of the fur company, we'd be rich, Marielle. We could have a fine house."

Marielle looked around, disappointed. She had spent much time and effort making the cabin as attractive as possible. "Don't you like our home, Paul?" she asked quietly.

Paul at once was ashamed of his remark. "I love it," he said. "But young couples have a small place when they first get married and then, as they prosper, they get bigger places. It would be fun building a house and putting the things in it I'd like for you to have." He went on to describe the things that could be available if he were able to get in with the American Fur Company.

But Marielle was unhappy. "I wish you didn't have to go, Paul."

"I'll be back soon. Next time I'll take you with me."

"Do you promise?"

"Certainly. It'll be fun." He kissed her again and held her tightly, saying, "It won't be very long. Then when I come back, I'll bring you a present."

She held up her hand so that the deep blue stone of the ring he had given her caught the sunlight. It seemed almost aquamarine in color as she touched it to her lips. "You don't have to give me anything else. This is so beautiful."

"You like it?"

"Yes," she said simply, kissing him. "Come, it's time for bed."

"For bed? Why, even the chickens haven't gone to bed yet," Paul said with surprise.

The corners of Marielle's lips turned upward. "You've got more sense than a chicken, Paul Wakefield, and besides, you'll have me there."

Paul was taken aback by the almost sensuous look in Marielle's eyes. But he had discovered there were two sides to Marielle: She was virginal and innocent and yet had a deep passion. He grinned then and stood to his feet. "I guess it is bedtime at that. I just didn't understand."

<hr />

Marielle awoke to find Paul already up and pulling his buckskins on. She stretched her arms over her head luxuriously and murmured, "Paul, do you have to go?"

Turning back to the bed, Paul sat down with one hand on either side of her and looked down into her face. "Yes, I have to go." Leaning over, he kissed her and her arms went around his neck.

He held her for a moment, then said, "I'll remember you. How you can make a man happy. I'll drive Frenchy crazy trying to make a quick trip."

This pleased Marielle, for she liked to hear such things. Once again she realized how fortunate she was to have a man who was not afraid to say things like that.

Throwing the cover back, Marielle stood on the floor, slipped her feet into her moccasins, and pulled on a wool robe Paul had bought for her. It was a deep blue, almost the color of her eyes, and she belted it around her. Outside a robin was hopping along the ground and she smiled. "That means a happy summer," she said.

"What—a robin?"

"Oh, yes. When the robin's song is a laughing one, there will be peace and enough to eat. But when it's harsh, there will be trouble and maybe death."

"Do you really believe that?"

Actually, Marielle did not believe too many of the folklore of her tribe, but she knew them all and enjoyed them. "The robin," she said, "is a young girl of our tribe who died from loving a man too much. She asked that her spirit might go into a bird and that she might come back to her people every spring and tell them what the year will hold. She painted her breast red as the promise that she would always come and that we would know her."

Paul, ready to go, donned his coat. "Well, I'm not going to paint my breast red, but I'll come back. You can count on that." He held her for a long time, kissed her, and then left the cabin.

Marielle stood at the cabin door, watching him get his horse and a saddle. He gave her one look, his white teeth flashing against his tanned features, then lifted his hand and said, "Good-bye, sweetheart. I'll be back soon."

"Good-bye, my husband," Marielle called out, then watched as he disappeared into the forest, leading the packhorse. He did not look back again and somehow this saddened her. She turned back to the cabin, stroking the soft wool robe, and sat down for a long time, thinking about what it meant for a woman to pass from girlhood into that mysterious area of being a wife.

Frenchy had found Red Deer waiting as he arrived at the farthest end of the village and stopped to talk to him. "How are ze new husband and wife?" he asked jocularly.

"Very well," Red Deer said with some satisfaction.

"I was worried about them," Frenchy said, shrugging. "But that man, he ees crazy about that girl of yours."

"She loves him very much, too. I've never seen two behave like they do," Red Deer said, but he smiled with a touch of pride.

Frenchy dismounted, saying, "I'm supposed to meet Paul here. We're going to Mackinac to sell ze furs."

"Will you be gone very long?"

"Not if Paul has his way. He'll be flying lak' a pigeon to get back to his bride." The two talked for some time as they walked along the outskirts of the village, but then a cloud crossed Frenchy's face. From far away a loon cried, making its wild, insane sound. "I don't lak' them loons too much. They're funny birds," Frenchy said, shivering. He seemed to be in a philosophical mood and continued, "Melancholy birds, but they 'ave a lot of sense."

"What makes you say so?"

"Well, look at ze loon. He can't walk ver' much, so he don't get on land. You didn't nevair see no loon on land, did you? No, he don't get out of ze water unless he has to." A silence passed as the two men continued walking. Then Frenchy added thoughtfully, "That loon. He stays where he's supposed to. I theenk we ought to take a lesson from him."

Red Deer glanced abruptly at the muscular Frenchman. "You think Marielle is out of her place to marry with an Englishman?"

This was exactly what Frenchy thought, but he did not say as much. "I don't know. Paul ees my good friend. I hope eet works out for him. What about Running Wolf? Do you theenk he weel make trouble?"

"No. He was angry at losing Marielle, but he's found another woman. It's the Huron I worry about."

A scowl crossed Frenchy's face. "They've been on a war party up to the north, I hear. I hope they stay away from here."

"So do I, but who knows about those people. They are a bloody race."

At that moment Paul appeared, leading the packhorse. He pulled up and said, "Hello, Red Deer. Frenchy and I will be gone for a little while, but you'll look out for Marielle?"

"I cannot make her happy as you do, but I will see that she is safe."

The two men said their farewells and left the village. As the cabins faded in the distance, Frenchy looked back over his shoulder and another shiver ran through him.

"What's wrong with you, Frenchy?" Paul said after a half hour of silence, something unusual for the Frenchman.

"Nothing," Frenchy said. But he was a superstitious man and somehow he felt uncomfortable. "I theenk we make thees a queek trip. All right?"

"Yes, the quicker the better," Paul said. He spoke to his horse and the two men made their way at a fast gallop down the trail toward the river.

Loantha and Marielle had been down to the stream where they filled their buckets with the fresh snow water. For a while they had sat on the bank, dabbling their feet in the water, enjoying the spring breeze that ruffled their hair.

"Soon it will be warm enough to come down and bathe in the stream," Loantha said. She leaned back on her hands and glanced at Marielle, who was staring dreamily into the water as it made white bubbles over the rounded rocks. The sound was pleasant and it seemed to have hypnotized her.

"I know what you're thinking," Loantha said and giggled. "You're yearning for that husband of yours to come back. You're lonesome in your bed."

"Oh, Loantha! Don't talk so foolish!"

"It's not so foolish," Loantha said, shrugging. She got to her feet then, dusted her hands off, and picked up the bucket. "Come on. Let's go back. I want to show you the presents that Gray Buffalo brought me."

Rising with her accustomed grace, Marielle smiled at her friend. "Is that who you favor now? Gray Buffalo?"

"I'll never tell that," Loantha said firmly. "Your courtship went too fast. You should have enjoyed it longer."

"The young men weren't lined up in front of my father's lodge as they are in front of yours. They didn't want a white woman."

"Why, you're as much Ojibway as I am, Marielle."

The two young women made their way back into the village and for most of the short trip Loantha spoke of her suitors. When they had put the pails down outside the cabins, Loantha said, "I want my husband to be as nice to me as Paul is to you."

"I don't think you'll find a man as good as he is."

The answer seemed to displease Loantha and she looked down at the ring on her friend's finger. "Let me wear your ring awhile. It's so pretty."

"Paul said it came from across the ocean. A place called Italy." Removing the ring, Marielle handed it reluctantly to Loantha, who slipped it on to her finger crying, "Look! It's just a fit!"

Marielle felt uneasy. She had already grown so used to touching the ring with her free hand that it had almost become a part of her. Many times during the day she would hold it up to the light and admire the beautiful blue tones and the shiny yellow mount that held the stone. Somehow she felt lost without it. But Loantha loved to wear it and Marielle could not deny her the pleasure.

"Come on. Let's go see if we can beg some honey from Yellow Bird. Her husband found a tree yesterday."

"All right."

The two young women started through the village, but they had not gone more than twenty yards when a shrill cry broke out that caused the blood of both young women to freeze. Whirling, Loantha saw a group of warriors break out of the trees. Their faces were painted and they screamed as they raced into the village, waving war clubs and tomahawks.

"It's the Huron!" Marielle cried. "Run, Loantha!"

As the two women started to run, Marielle noticed that several of the Ojibway warriors had grabbed their weapons and now ran to meet the oncoming Huron.

"We've got to hide, Loantha!" Marielle cried.

"Yes, but where?"

"In the woods. Come. There are so many of them."

The Huron were the most fierce warriors among all the tribes and as Marielle ran, her thoughts came quickly. She knew the Huron would have no mercy—and already the screams of the dying rent the morning air. *I can't die. Not now, when I've just found life!* These thoughts flashed through her mind and lent speed to her feet. With Loantha beside her, Marielle headed toward the farthest end of the village. Just as they arrived, however, another group of Huron warriors suddenly appeared, their eyes gleaming and their mouths in merciless grins. One of them called out, "Ha! Two fine young squaws!" and threw himself forward.

Marielle felt the hard, merciless hands of one of the warriors close upon her arm. When she wheeled around, she smelled his breath. The red and yellow paint made him look like a demon from the underworld. She cried out, "Paul—!" and began to fight, but she knew her strength was not enough. Amidst the screams of the wounded and the dying, Marielle fought with all of her strength, but the hands that held her were like eagle talons biting down into the very bone. . . .

Paul and Frenchy arrived on Mackinac Island and saw to the unpacking of their furs. Glancing around, Paul saw that the lodges were built all along the shoreline and that birch canoes nosed in toward them. The island rose high above the water and Frenchy murmured, "They call Mackinac the turtle. Eet looks lak' eet, eh, Paul?"

"Yes, it does." Paul and his companion moved along the beach, where people in rags, buckskins, and bright calico were dashing everywhere among the boats. Canoes of all sizes were scattered the length of the shore.

Paul was not sure of the nationality of the tribes, but he heard the Ojibway language and understood a little of it. They moved along the harbor, which had the shape of a new moon with points reaching out into the water at the east and the west. Following this crescent shape was a long curving road and on it were shops, low white buildings. Here, too, there was activity such as Paul had rarely seen in North America. Some of the Indian women were carrying cloth and finery that their husbands had traded for.

Frenchy swept his muscular arm in a gesture, saying, "There ees ze Company."

Paul glanced up at the huge, boxlike buildings that composed the offices and warehouse of the great fur company of John Jacob Astor. Beyond them he saw the white forked buildings, the blockhouses, and the quarters high up on a cliff above the beach.

To either side, houses were scattered haphazardly. The tops of them gleamed white in the sun and a great cedar palisade surrounded them. "Where do we go now?" Paul asked.

"We go to meet ze manager," Frenchy replied.

As they proceeded along the beach Paul suddenly said, "Who are those fellows?"

Turning to look in the direction Paul indicated, Frenchy saw a large birch canoe, one of the thirty-five-foot *canots du nord* shoving onto the beach. The men were clad in fringed buckskin jackets and they dipped their paddle blades into the water, driving the boat ahead as if it were propelled by a steam engine. They all wore bright headbands or caps of red wool, gray neckerchiefs, and fringes on their arms. A breadth of striped shirt showed where their buckskin jackets hung open in front.

"Those are ze *voyageurs.*"

"They look like pretty tough fellows."

"*Sacre' diable!* They are tough. They stay gone all winter and come in during ze spring to Mackinac to sell their furs. Oh, you weel see some fights tonight!"

Paul listened to the men as they sang a song he had never heard. It was in French and he could understand a little of it:

> Derrier' chez nous, y a-t-un etang
> En roulant ma boule
> Trois beaux canards s'en vont baignant
> En routlant me boule.
> Rouli, roulant, ma boule roulant,
> En roulant ma boule roulant
> En roulant ma boule roulant.

The two then turned and made their way through the maze of canoes, Indians, and French voyageurs up into the white cliffs and the green foliage. Two white spires pointed upward with the flagpole at the fort as if vying for attention. Soon they were passing through a row of shops along the road and when they reached the fort, Frenchy said, "You must make a good impression on ze manager. His name ees Mason. He ees a Scotsman."

John Mason, a short man with ferocious eyebrows, greeted the two men in a friendly fashion. He kept his steady gray eyes fixed on his two visitors. When Frenchy introduced him to Paul, he said, "Ah, ye're from England."

"Yes, but I plan to stay here, Mr. Mason," Paul replied.

Frenchy said eagerly, "He has put in more than two good years here. He knows how to trap ze beaver, but he 'as bigger ambitions than that."

"Weel now, ambition is guid for a mon," Mason said, the rich burr of Scotland on his tongue. "What are your plans?"

"I'd like to work with the American Fur Company," Paul said. He had prepared his speech carefully and for some time he spoke of how he had learned some of the Ojibway tongue and seemed to be good at language. "I get along with Red Deer very well and I think I could do the same with the other tribes. What I would like to do is buy up furs and resell them to the company."

"Weel, that's what Frenchy does."

Paul said audaciously, "I would like to become a part of the American Fur Company and, as Frenchy says, I have ambition."

Mason studied the tall young man and finally he said, "I think there might be room for you. Mr. Astor will be through next month. He's always looking for Englishmen who are guid with the Indians and with the French. We have our troubles, you know. I think he would be interested in your proposition."

"Fine," Paul said, smiling at once. "In the meanwhile, we need to sell our furs and get back."

"He has a new wife, Mr. Mason," Frenchy said, grinning broadly. "He's anxious to get back to her."

"Vurry commendable, I'm sure."

"She's half Ojibway," Paul said. "I think that will help my career."

"Indeed it might. Weel now, you two will have supper with me tonight and we'll talk more about this."

⸙

For the next two days, Paul spent a considerable amount of time with Mason. Soon he was well informed as to the operation of the American Fur Company. He knew John Jacob Astor was little better than a pirate as far as business practices were concerned, but that did not disturb Paul greatly—a fact he imparted to John Mason. The two men got along well and finally, at the end of the second day, Paul said as they lay down on their beds for the night, "I think it's going well, Frenchy."

"*Oui,* I theenk eet go pretty good."

Some gloomy sound in Frenchy's voice caused Paul to look at him. "What's the matter? Did some man beat you out of your sweetheart?"

Frenchy shook his head slowly. "No. That ees not eet." He said no more so Paul shrugged, for he knew the Frenchman, despite his exuberance, to be moody at times.

They rose the next morning and Paul went as planned to spend the morning with the manager. Mason showed him the books and appreciated Paul's quick grasp. "You'll make a fine businessman."

"Glad to hear that. Sir David will be glad to hear it, too."

"Sir David?"

"Yes, my brother. Sir David Wakefield."

"Ah, I didn't know I was dealing with the nobility."

"You're not," Paul said, grinning. "There's only one Lord Wakefield and David's it. I'm the crow in the family and he's the white dove."

Mason raised his bushy eyebrows and smiled. "Did you know that the crow was once as white as snow?"

Aware that the manager was exhibiting his wry brand of humor, Paul shook his head. "I didn't know that. What happened to him?"

"He was caught in a hollow tree and the fire beneath smoked him until he was black."

"Why?"

"Punishment for mischief," was all that Mason replied. "See that you stay out of it. You've got a fine career ahead of you."

The two men spent the morning together and finally at noon Paul said, "I'll be leaving early tomorrow, so this is good-bye."

"But I'll see you again. Remember, in one month Mr. Astor will be here."

"You can count on it."

Paul made his way back to their room and found that Frenchy was gone. He lay down on the bed, thinking mostly of the brilliant future he saw with the American Fur Company. Then his thoughts turned to Marielle and he smiled, dreaming of her until he dozed off.

The bang at the door aroused Paul and he sat up at once. "What's wrong, Frenchy?" Something on the man's face warned him and he leaped to his feet. "Is there trouble?"

"Beeg trouble for you, I'm afraid, my friend."

A fist seemed to close around Paul's heart. He was not a man given to fear and yet if Frenchy was so solemn and had such an odd expression, he knew the situation must be bad.

"Is it trouble with the Company?"

"No. Ees worse than that."

Frenchy seemed to have lost his power of speech. His face worked with emotion and he came over to put his powerful hand on Paul's shoulder, squeezing it. "You must be ver' strong, Paul."

Something ominous and dark rose in Paul. He forgot about the business and at once asked, "Is it Marielle?"

Slowly Frenchy nodded. "Ze Huron. They raided ze village. There are many dead."

Paul swallowed hard. "Marielle——?"

"They burned ze village. Red Deer sent this." Frenchy reached into his pocket and brought out an object. Paul flinched when he saw the gold ring with the blue stone in Frenchy's palm. Numbly Paul picked it up and his eyes filled with pain. A silence fell over the room and neither man spoke for a time.

Finally Frenchy said, "They found her in a cabin that had been burned. They knew it was her only by the ring."

Paul Wakefield stared at the azure stone. He remembered the time he had bought it and he thought of the delight that had leaped into Marielle's eyes when he had placed it on her finger. Even as he stared at it, he could not believe what he heard. *She was so vibrant—so alive!* he thought and then his knees weakened. He sat down stiffly and lowered his head against his clenched fists. His shoulders began to heave and his muted sobs struck Frenchy Doucett's heart.

"I am ver' sorry, my friend. She was one fine woman."

Paul did not seem to hear the words Doucett spoke. Somehow, a wall closed around him. The few brief months of happiness were like nothing he had ever known and now they were gone. The world darkened for him and he knew that wherever he went he would always hear the sound of Marielle's voice. That whenever he closed his eyes, she would be before him. He looked up slowly, his eyes tormented, and said, "I've lost everything, Frenchy."

Doucett could only shake his head. "Weel we go back to ze village?"

Paul Wakefield nodded dumbly. There was nothing he could do. There was nothing left of Marielle except a few ashes, but he would go for the funeral, which meant so much to the Indians, and he would grieve for her in the Indian fashion. He said quietly, "Yes, we will go and do this last thing for my wife. . . !"

Ten

MEN ARE SUCH FOOLS!

April 1766

The year of 1766 was a relatively quiet period for England. True enough, the previous year the Parliament had passed the Stamp Act for taxing the American colonies, thereby laying the groundwork for the explosive events that would culminate in an American Revolution. This, however, was in the future. William Pitt became the Earl of Chatham and formed a ministry that would control England's policies for years. In North America two surveyors, Charles Mason and Jeremiah Dixon, created a "line," later called the Mason-Dixon line, which eventually separated the free and slave regions and foreshadowed a terrible Civil War for that fledgling nation. While Empress Catherine the Great granted freedom of worship in Russia, England's first paved sidewalk was laid in Westminster.

This period was exactly what Sir David Wakefield enjoyed. For more than nine years he had applied himself under the firm hand of Angus McDowell until finally, and to his own surprise, he had done fairly well. The great sorrow in his life was his separation from his brother, who had buried himself in the wilds of North America after leaving the army. Few days passed without Sir David's thinking of Paul with grief and wishing that he could somehow be more of a brother to him.

Now as the April breeze caressed his cheek, David thought of the lines of a poem he had been writing. As he walked over the Wakefield estate toward Mrs. Dossett's farm, he lost himself in the pleasure of creating the lines. They seemed to appear in clear print before his eyes without effort and he longed to get them on paper.

If Wakefield was his duty, then literature was David's joy, and he spent every free moment either reading or writing. On this particular morning he had made his duty rounds to the tenants of Wakefield. There had been a time when he dreaded such a task, for when he had assumed the title he had been a raw young man with no business experience. He had been warned strictly by Angus to take a firm hand and this he had attempted to do. Over the years, however, he had established himself as a fair landowner and his tenants were the envy of those on the surrounding properties.

"There's none like Sir David," his tenants said. "He treats us all fair and when a man needs help, he can go to him."

A trilling overhead broke into David's thoughts as he strolled toward the home of Mrs. Elizabeth Dossett and her daughter, Margaret. Glancing up, he saw a sparrow, its chest puffed out with a running trill of notes that delighted David. "Sing, old fellow. I wish I had your inspiration. It doesn't seem fair," he said, muttering to himself, "that a bird just opens his mouth and the song comes out—but we writers, why, we have to wait until the muse visits us."

His thoughts were interrupted as he approached the house and the door opened. The well-formed woman who came out was slightly plump. Seeing the smile on her face, David greeted her warmly. "Good morning to you, Miss Margaret."

"Good morning, Sir David. Come in. I have a cup of tea all prepared." Margaret Dossett was a woman of some twenty-eight years. Her brown hair was neatly done and there was a pert expression in her sharp-featured face and brown eyes. She was a pretty woman, according to most, and the entire countryside wondered why she had never married, for she had had several offers from yeoman farmers in the vicinity. There were rumors that she had been less than virtuous when she was just out of her teens, but David discounted these. Her father had been a farmer of considerable land, but after his death, somehow the money seemed to flow away so that his widow, Elizabeth, had been reduced to selling it all except the small plot that the house rested on.

"Well, thank you." David smiled and stepped into the cottage.

The room David entered was small but well lit from the rays of sun that came through two large windows. The windows were covered only with a bit of white muslin and the sunlight pouring into the recently whitewashed room made it very inviting. The bare wood floor had been covered with a painted oilcloth in tones of brown, leaving only a narrow border of wood. A pine fireplace dominated the far wall of the room and an astral lamp had been placed on one side of the mantel. David's eyes took in the other furnishings of the room: a well-worn, serpentine-style couch that had been mended meticulously in more than one spot; a red tea table and a pair of Windsor chairs placed between the windows; and an old, longcase clock of beech and softwood that stood in great contrast next to a beautiful desk of Dutch walnut along the opposite wall.

David sat down on one of the Windsor chairs, so highly polished that he thought for a moment he might slide off. He admired Margaret's apricot-colored lawn dress and fichu, which was covered by a white muslin apron and bib and worn over a snow-white, quilted petticoat. He listened as Margaret spoke rapidly. She was interrupted when her mother came in.

"Ah, Sir David. So happy to have you come. I see that Margaret is giving you tea and I made a seed cake. You must try it."

"Your cakes are always delicious, Mrs. Dossett," David said.

The two women made over David considerably and as always he felt flattered by the attention he received. He was really a humble man in spite of his title and unlooked-for position in life and had somehow never learned to be at ease in the company of pretty women.

Perhaps this thought was in Margaret Dossett's mind as she said, "And how is Miss Stella? I presume you will be attending the ball with her next week?"

"I expect so," David said, nodding. "I really take little pleasure in such things, but she does, of course."

"Oh, I wish I could go to that ball," Margaret cried plaintively, running her hand over her smooth brown hair. "It's been so long since I've been to anything like that. I miss it so much."

"I would be happy to see that you get an invitation," David replied. But as soon as he aired these words, he knew that Stella Fairfax would have his head on a platter for it. *Can I ever learn to keep my mouth shut?* he groaned inwardly. *How will I ever explain this to Stella?*

But Margaret and her mother were already exclaiming with delight and planning what Margaret would wear. They were still doing this when David rose to say, "I just stopped by to wish you good morning and to tell you that my gamekeeper will be bringing you a quarter of a deer that I shot recently."

"So kind," Margaret cooed. "Isn't he thoughtful, Mother?"

"Yes, indeed, dear Margaret. And you must come and enjoy a meal with us very soon."

David had done this before, for he felt it part of his responsibility to stay close to his tenants, and because Mr. Dossett was no longer alive, this made the obligation even more real. He was honest enough to admit that Margaret's charms had been at least partly responsible for his visits. She had leaned against him numerous times, her lush figure pressing against him provocatively. Once he had thought she was a flirt but then had decided, *No, she's not aware of what she does to a man.* He stepped through the door, holding his hat in his hand, and bowed. "I will see that the invitation comes from Sir Giles at once."

He made his way back to his horse, mounted, then leaned over and slapped the horse on the shoulder. The animal, a rich chestnut stallion, whinnied with excitement as he felt the touch of David's heel. David was still regretting his invitation to Margaret, not on his own account, but because he knew Stella would never understand it.

He drew up in front of Wakefield Manor and stopped suddenly. He studied the stately buildings with the columns, the panoply of decorations across the frieze, and as happened frequently, wondered, *How in the world did I ever get to be Marquis of Wakefield?* He dismounted and handed the reins of his horse to a servant saying, "Rub him down good, Samuel. He's had a good workout today."

"Yes, sir!"

David entered the house, at once hearing the voices of women talking. He made his way down the hall, tossing his hat and riding crop onto a bench, and once again feeling a tinge of strangeness. It was a rich, ornate hall with black-and-white marble floors. A gilded demi-lune console table with a marble top sat along one wall and on top stood a large, white marble vase filled with fresh honeysuckle. The table was flanked by two carved mahogany chairs covered in a bright blue silk damask. Somehow David had never felt comfortable even after all of his years there.

Turning into the smaller sitting room, he found Sarah Morgan and her daughter, Bethany, talking with his mother, Dorcas, and Lady Caroline Wakefield. The four looked up, but it was Bethany who rose at once and came to him, her eyes glistening with pleasure. She was sixteen now, tall for a young woman, with the blackest possible hair and dark blue eyes that dominated her face.

"David," she said. "Come along. I've got to talk to you about that last story you wrote."

"Now just a minute, Bethany," Dorcas said. "David has more to do now than to read stories to you."

Bethany looked hurt at this and David instantly said, "I'm writing a new one, Bethany. I'll need you to help me with it." He winked over her head at the women and when she looked back, all smiles, he said, "After dinner we'll go up to our room."

"All right, David," Bethany said contentedly and went to sit down beside her mother. After David talked with the four women for a while, he got up to go change his clothes and his mother followed him. When they were down the hall, away from the sitting room, she said, "Come into the library. There's something I want you to hear."

"What is it, Mother?" David said, puzzled, and followed her into the library.

"A letter came this morning from Paul."

Something changed in David Wakefield's face. Usually Dorcas knew exactly what David thought, but this time she could not identify his emotion. There was an unusual relationship between her two sons that she had never grasped. They were so different and yet Dorcas knew David still grieved over Paul's attitude toward him.

"Read it to me, Mother."

Dorcas opened the single sheet of paper and began to read:

Dated March 6, 1766, Quebec
Dear Mother,
You will pardon my failure to write more often, but I have been literally overwhelmed with business. Mr. Astor has put me in charge of more of the Company and it takes more time than I have. The Fur Company has experienced a marvelous spurt in growth and it has been

a great opportunity for me to get in on the ground
floor. . . .

David listened quietly as his mother read the record of his
brother's activities and finally when the letter was over, he said
painfully, "He didn't speak of me at all then?"

Dorcas's heart went out to this son of hers, so gentle and good
in every respect. "No. I'm sorry, David."

"He still resents the fact that I have the title. I wish it weren't
so." David's tone grew bitter. "I'd give it to him in a minute."

"It wouldn't be a good thing. Paul was not made to be the
Marquis of Wakefield. You've done so well," Dorcas said, coming
to stand beside him. She was fifty-one now, but there were only
a few gray streaks in her hair. "You've done well with the tenants
and Angus is pleased with the way you have taken charge." She
waited for David's reply and when none came, she said, "He'll
come around. You'll see. I pray for him every day."

David nodded, but there was pain in his eyes. "So do I."

<hr />

"I'm worried about David." Dorcas had escorted Caroline and
Sarah to the parlor after dinner. Bethany had practically hauled
David up to their secret room where the women knew there was
nothing but talk of literature—poems, histories, novels.

"What's wrong with him? Why are you worried? He looks
fine," Sarah said. The same age as Dorcas, Sarah looked no more
than thirty. She was still tall and shapely, her blonde hair glossy
and rich, and her blue gray eyes dominated her heart-shaped face.
Everything she wore—including her present simple dress—
looked as if it came straight out of the fashion center of Paris.

"I can tell you why," Lady Caroline said. "She's worried about
his attachment to Stella Fairfax."

Sarah asked, "Well, she's quite a catch, isn't she?"

"She's a worldly young woman," Dorcas said. "It's impossible to talk to her about God or religion in general."

"I suppose most young women are that way these days," Lady Caroline said, running her hand over her reddish blonde hair. "But I must admit—" she continued, shaking her head woefully—"she seems more selfish than most."

"I think it's her mother," Dorcas said. "Ever since her husband died, she's been trying to marry Stella off to a rich man." A rare moment of bitterness came to her and she frowned. "I wish she had found one somewhere else and would leave David alone."

"How does David feel about her?" Sarah asked. "Is he in love with her?"

"Oh, you know David!" Dorcas protested. "He doesn't talk about such things. At least not to me."

"He's very shy," Caroline observed. "It's hard to believe that a young nobleman, twenty-five years of age, is so shy, almost backward, in the company of women. I can't imagine how it happened. Paul certainly isn't that way. He wasn't when he was sixteen."

"Are they engaged?" Sarah asked. "I haven't heard about it if they are."

"She won't say. She keeps David dangling," Dorcas said, her lips still pressed tightly together. She wound her fingers together and squeezed them. "He deserves a good woman, but where women are concerned he doesn't know very much."

Sarah had listened to all of this carefully. "You know, I've often thought that he might be attracted to Margaret Dossett."

"Margaret Dossett?" Caroline looked indignant. "I should hope not!"

"Why? What's wrong with her?" Sarah asked with surprise. "She seems like a nice young woman."

"She's not all that young. She's twenty-eight. Older than David," Dorcas said. "And she's respectable enough, I suppose, though she was somewhat wild when she was young—or so I've heard."

"She's not the woman for David," Lady Caroline said. "I've known women like her before. She's plump and pretty, but there's a sharpness to her. She likes to have her own way, that young woman does." She looked glumly at Dorcas. "You're right. Men are such fools where women are concerned."

The conversation turned to other matters, but afterward Caroline asked, "Dorcas, are you really worried that David might be in love with Stella Fairfax?"

"He's so—so innocent. I can't think of any other way to put it," Dorcas said. "He's loved God for most of his life and he needs a godly woman. But he's a man, and a man without experience. I'd hate to see either Margaret Dossett or Stella Fairfax become his wife. Neither of them has any care for God!"

"Stella, aren't you ready yet?" Mrs. Irene Fairfax came into her daughter's bedroom and found her sitting before a mirror applying makeup carefully. Stella was wearing a plum-colored *sacque* of the best silk brocade. Edged around the neckline with pleated ruffles and a dark pink bow, it had a gold satin stomacher, a dark pink overskirt with plum-colored bows, and a flounced light pink satin petticoat trimmed in white lace. It was a dress for a rich woman—and one that flattered Stella's figure. "He'll be here any moment," her mother said. "You've had all afternoon to get ready."

"Don't worry, Mother," Stella said languidly, applying a little more rice powder to her cheeks and examining the result. "He'll wait."

"You're very sure of him."

"Oh, David's a child really. He does whatever I ask him to without complaining."

Irene smiled suddenly. "That's an admirable trait in a husband."

"It is, isn't it, Mother?" Stella stood up and asked, "Do you like my dress?"

"I have to like it, don't I? It cost enough to feed the village for a month. But it is pretty and you look absolutely ravishing. I hope David appreciates you."

A frown crossed Stella Fairfax's face. She was, at the age of nineteen, admittedly the most attractive young woman in the area. Her blonde hair had just a touch of red and her blue eyes were so large and expressive that they seemed to swallow those she looked at. Her figure was neat and trim yet provocative in her dress—an effect that was not accidental.

"I don't think he pays much attention to dresses. He's not very gallant."

"But he *is* Sir David Wakefield," Irene reminded her daughter. "Better to have a man with a title and money than a penniless pauper who spouts poetry."

"He does that, too," Stella said, grimacing. "I don't understand what he means most of the time and then he gets upset—and I get upset because he's upset. All he wants to talk about is poets, writing, and books. He's really not a lot of fun at a ball."

"Well, there will be plenty of other young men there. It will be a good chance for you to meet some of them. That young son of Sir Malcolm Dennis is just back from the Continent, they say. Now *there* would be quite a catch for you, Stella."

"I've never seen him. He's probably skinny and ugly as a frog."

"Not at all. He'll probably look like his father—a handsome man indeed."

The two women stood there talking and finally a diminutive maid stepped in. "Pardon me, ma'am, but Sir David is here."

"Thank you, Marie." Irene went over and stood beside her daughter. She touched up the hair that needed no retouching, then smiled. "Come. Let's go meet Sir David." There was something in the way she pronounced the word *Sir* in such a loving fashion that one could tell she literally doted on anyone who had a title. This was not unusual in her circles and it was the desire of Irene Fairfax's life to present her daughter as *Lady* Stella. It was to this end that she had labored for the past few years, molding her daughter into exactly the sort of woman a young aristocrat might desire.

They descended the curving staircase where David stood waiting for them, decked out for the occasion in a black velvet coat with gold braid trim and rolled-back cuffs that showed the ruffles of his white linen shirt, a short waistcoat of black velvet, white knee breeches, white silk stockings, and black leather shoes with a gold buckle.

"Sir David, so good to see you again!" Mrs. Fairfax said.

David thought, *I wish she wouldn't end every sentence with an exclamation point. She can't say "pass the toast" without trying to sound excited.* But he let none of his feelings show in his face. "Good evening, Mrs. Fairfax. Stella, you look very beautiful. Is that a new dress?"

"Of course it's a new dress," Stella said, knowing full well that David could not tell one dress from another. To spend hours making herself look attractive and then to have her escort not even notice irritated her. But she smiled and said, "I think we have time for a glass of wine before we leave for the ball."

"Of course. There are some things I wanted to speak with you about, Sir David."

Actually David would rather have gone on to the ball, for Mrs. Fairfax bored him intensely. But he was a well-mannered young man who had learned to conceal such attitudes and the three went at once to an ornate sitting room where they were served wine by a manservant.

David gave an account of his doings to Mrs. Fairfax, who seemed terribly interested in them. He mentioned, almost in passing, that he had had a book published. Mrs. Fairfax was most impressed, though her congratulations were cut short when they were interrupted by the maid Marie. She shyly entered the room with an envelope on a silver tray. "A messenger just brought this for you, Sir David." She curtsied as David took it and thanked her, then she left the room.

The two women watched as David opened the envelope and consternation swept across his face.

"Well, what in the world is it?" Mrs. Fairfax asked. "Not bad news, I hope."

"I'm afraid it is. A dear relative of mine has been in an accident."

"Oh, how dreadful!" Stella said. "Is it someone we know?"

"I think not," David said slowly. "It's Mrs. Sarah Morgan, the wife of a Methodist minister, and my aunt. I'm afraid I must go at once."

"But—you surely can't mean you're not going to the ball!" Stella exclaimed.

"I'm afraid I must. She's critically hurt. I must go at once. I'm dreadfully sorry, Stella, but you understand."

As a matter of fact, Stella did not understand, but there was little she could do about it. With full grace she said, "Well, I hope your friend recovers."

Mrs. Fairfax was more genial. "Do let us know how the lady does, Sir David."

"I will certainly do that—and again, my apologies, Stella."

As soon as David was out of the room, Stella stamped her foot, her eyes flashing. "I can't believe he's going to pass up the ball like this! The woman probably isn't hurt all that badly!"

"Well, there'll be other balls."

"I'm going to this ball!" Stella said impetuously.

"By yourself? That's quite impossible."

"You're going with me, Mother. Come along."

"But I can't go in this dress."

"Then change dresses. We are going to the ball!"

<hr />

As soon as David Wakefield entered the Morgans' sitting room, he knew the worst.

"Oh, David!" Bethany had been sitting in a chair with her head down. Now she rose and came flying across the room to him. "She's gone! Mother's gone!"

Shocked beyond words, David held Bethany close while she sobbed. Looking over her shoulder he asked, "Gareth, is it so?"

It was a useless question, as David well knew, but he couldn't believe Sarah was dead. Gareth Morgan stood with his back erect, torment in his eyes. At the age of forty-nine he still had the muscular figure of a coal miner, which he had been in his youth. Although his voice broke only slightly, there was agony in it as he answered, "She went to be with the Lord less than an hour ago." He turned abruptly and faced the window; his voice was hoarse as he said, "How can I live without her?"

Ivor Morgan went to stand beside his father, silently putting his hand on his father's shoulder. As the two stood there together, David realized how very much Ivor, at the age of twenty-one, was like Gareth.

"I'm—I'm sorry I couldn't get here sooner," David faltered, as Bethany clung to him. "I didn't know."

"It was very sudden. The carriage turned over at the bluff by Benson's Park. The horses were frightened by something and ran away. She never regained consciousness," Gareth said, his voice muffled.

When Bethany looked up at David, he said, "You must be brave, Bethany."

"Don't—don't leave me! Please, David! I couldn't stand it!"

"I won't leave you."

Leading Bethany over to the couch, he sat with his arm about her. Because Bethany had such a sensitive nature, the agony of losing her mother, whom she loved most dearly, was tearing her apart. David sat holding her for over an hour. It was one of those times when nothing can be done, when nothing can be said that means anything.

Finally, however, David looked across at Ivor. "I don't need to tell you I am grieved beyond belief."

"Thank you, David," Ivor said, his voice a mere whisper.

"If there's anything I can do—"

"Of course. Thank you, David."

As David continued to sit with his arm around Bethany, thoughts swept through him. *So full of life! A beautiful woman with a fine family. Why did she have to be taken?* Glancing from face to face, he knew this question would surface again and again. *I'll have to do all I can to help,* he said to himself.

For the next two days, David never left the Morgans' household. He discovered that Gareth, for all his strength and faith in God, was lost without Sarah, so David did most of the behind-the-scenes arranging. The funeral was simple but beautiful, held in the church where Gareth was pastor. There were many tributes to Sarah Morgan, and David wept with the family, for Sarah had been a dear aunt to him and he knew he would miss her dreadfully.

After the group returned to the house, Bethany stayed close beside David. He comforted her the best he could, saying, "You must come and stay at Wakefield a great deal of the time. You and I will have a lot to do in our secret room."

Gratitude washed over Bethany's face. Her pallor contrasted vividly with her raven hair, and her wide blue eyes had dark circles under them and were swollen with much weeping. "Can I come, truly, David?"

"Of course. Where else would you go? You and I are the best of friends, aren't we?"

"Yes. The best of friends," was the reply and tears ran down her cheeks again.

Ivor approached David soon after this. "David, I know you are a man who means exactly what he says."

"I hope I am, Ivor. What is it?"

"Well, sir, you've asked so many times if you could do anything for us. There is one thing you could do."

"Anything at all."

"I can't stay here. Would you help me get a commission in the army? It's what I want to do with my life. I always have, you know."

"I know you have. We've talked about it before." David hesitated. "It would mean leaving your father and Bethany."

"I know that and I don't mean right away. But will you help me?"

David nodded, then clapped the young man's sturdy shoulders. "Of course I will, Ivor. As a matter of fact, I can promise you that you will have your chance to be a soldier."

Ivor's eyes grew misty and he swallowed hard. "That's like you, David. And please look after my sister. You always have, but she'll need you more than ever now."

This request was repeated in less than an hour when Gareth spoke privately with David. "You know my life. I'm gone a lot, David, and now Ivor has told me you are going to get him a commission in the army. That's fine of you."

"It's really nothing," David protested.

"That leaves one more problem. Bethany."

"Why, she's a fine young woman. You don't have to worry. She'll grieve, of course."

"She'll grieve more than you can know, David," Gareth said. "Would you consider having her stay with you at Wakefield?"

"You mean permanently?"

"More or less. I'll be gone on my preaching tours. She'll be all alone in this house with Ivor gone, but she loves to stay at Wakefield. I know it's asking a lot, but—"

"It's not asking a lot at all, Gareth. We rattle around in that big old house and you know how much I enjoy having her. So do my mother and Aunt Caroline. Have you talked with her about it?"

"No. I'll leave that to you."

Gareth and David spoke for some time about the arrangements. Later that night, when the others had gone to bed, he drew Bethany aside. "I know it's too soon," he said, "but there's something I want to ask you, Bethany."

"Yes, what is it, David?" Bethany looked up at him with complete trust in her clear eyes and her lips trembled, for her grief could not be contained.

"I've talked to your father. We think it would be best if you came and lived at Wakefield with me and my family." He wondered at first if he had said the wrong thing, if she was offended, for she had immediately lowered her head so he could not see her face. "Ah, Bethany, I didn't mean to hurt you. I thought it would be something you would like."

When she looked up, Bethany's eyes were moist, and her lips were trembling, but she smiled. "I'd like it—better than anything, David," she whispered.

David put his hands on her shoulders. "That's fine." He leaned over and kissed her cheek as he had been accustomed to doing since she was a little girl. "We'll comfort each other and when your brother comes, he will stay with us. And your father will come often, too. We'll be just like brother and sister, you and I."

Something strange crossed the young woman's face at these words, but she was happy. "Do you really want me, David?"

"We're the best of friends, aren't we?"

Bethany Morgan touched David's cheek. "Best of friends always," she said softly. Then he put his arms around her and she leaned against him. He held her for a long time, then finally said, "You must go to bed now. We'll be going to Wakefield soon. It will be all right. You'll see."

"Yes, David." Bethany left him then and when she was gone, David Wakefield thought, *She's a lovely young woman. I've got to see to it that she's cared for.* This was not a burden for him, for he had loved Bethany since she was a child. As he prepared for bed himself, his thoughts were filled with ways to help the Morgan family through their tragedy.

Eleven

"LOVE IS A DANGEROUS THING"

O c t o b e r   1 7 6 7

A mockingbird appeared outside Bethany Morgan's mullioned window and began to sing cheerfully. Bethany, always delighted by a bird of any sort, put down her quill pen and ran to the window. October was mild in England that year and summer had lingered on much longer than usual. Leaning over with her hands braced against the windowsill, the young woman watched the bird, her lips parted slightly, listening as he puffed out his chest, sending his song out over the air.

"Go on," Bethany urged, smiling. "Sing your heart out! I wish I could sing like that myself." Finally the bird flew away and Bethany reluctantly returned to the desk. As she did, she cast her eyes around the room where she had spent most of the last year and a half since her mother had died. It was a midsized room with light blue patterned wallpaper and blue carpet with a white pattern running through it. Along one wall were two small windows with window seats and between them a walnut desk. Along the far wall stood Bethany's large oak bed with a thick feather mattress, its blue-and-white bed curtains matching those at the windows. Beside her bed was a walnut Queen Anne dressing table overspread with a white quilted cover and a large silver candlestick. The fireplace, with two mahogany chairs covered in blue silk damask on either side, dominated the inside wall of her room. On either side of the door stood a George III wardrobe and washstand of mahogany. The washstand held a porcelain bowl and colored bottles of all sizes. Normally Bethany loved the room—and the world in general—but now, for some reason, she was dissatisfied with it and everything else. As she passed a full-length mirror, she turned and stared at herself.

What she saw was a young woman of seventeen, taller than average. Her black hair was fixed in a chignon and her oval face was dominated by wide-spaced blue eyes so dark that at times they seemed almost black. With dissatisfaction she touched her nose and muttered, "Too short!" And then she patted her cheekbones, pronouncing another criticism. "Too high!" She turned around, studying her figure, and was not displeased. She was past the awkward stage of adolescence and now her narrow waist was accented by the generous curves of her upper body. Her new emerald dress, a silk open robe with a plain fitted bodice, full hooped overskirt, and white quilted petticoat, had been a gift from Lady Caroline Wakefield. A fine white linen scarf, held in place by a brooch, draped over her shoulders. The tight-fitting sleeves ended at the elbow in a lace ruffle. After a time of reflection, finally Bethany smiled, then laughed aloud. "There's a funny old girl, you are. Studying yourself in the mirror as if you were going to be queen." She moved swiftly back to the desk, picked up the quill, and began to write firmly with smooth, even strokes. Her handwriting was beautiful and she was proud of it.

October the fifteenth, 1767
 Dear Diary:
 I caught myself just now looking in the mirror and being displeased with everything I saw, which was very wrong of me. I know what Father would say. "God made

you like you are. Whatever you see is what he wanted you to have. So be happy with it."

I am pleased with the dress Lady Caroline bought for me, but who's to see it? As I write this, I know that sounds terribly ungrateful. With Ivor gone away to the army and Father away on his preaching tours, I would be miserable in our cottage in Cornwall. I'm an ungrateful, naughty girl for complaining even a little bit. Lady Caroline and Aunt Dorcas have been so kind to me and, of course, David has done everything he could the past year and a half to make me happy. Why am I so unhappy then? I must be a wicked young woman indeed.

David is busy working on his new book and he won't let me see any of it. I think it's very mean of him. He locks himself up in our secret room and won't let me in at all. Last night I stood outside and banged on the door until he opened it. I told him I was coming in, but he took my wrists and held them together, then smiled at me crookedly. Even his eyes were laughing at me. "You can read it when I'm finished," he told me. Then he simply picked me up like I was a baby, turned me around, and shut the door. I knocked on it again, but he refused to let me in.

For some time the young woman wrote assiduously and finally added a note:

I'm very lonely with Father gone so much, but I know that's what God called him to do and I must be patient. It's hard though, for although life is easy in many ways, David is busy most of the time with the estate and it seems that the time we spend together grows shorter each month.

As she again dipped the quill into the ink bottle, two lines appeared between her slightly arched eyebrows, and her lips grew tight. She wrote with a firm hand in letters twice as large: "I hate Stella Fairfax!"

Startled at what she had written, she reached over and picked up the bottle of fine sand, scattering it over the ink. Sifting it around on the page until it was dry, she dumped the sand into a receptacle. "I'm an even more wicked girl than I thought," she whispered. "But it's true. David thinks she's so wonderful and so beautiful and I just know he's going to marry her. I can't help it—I can't stand her!"

Slowly she closed the diary, carried it to the wardrobe, and carefully concealed it in a box behind her clothes. Going to the window, she sat down, wondering if David would really marry the insufferable Stella Fairfax.

***

"I got another letter from Paul this morning," Dorcas said. She handed it to Caroline, adding, "He seems to be doing so well with his profession."

Lady Caroline read the single page carefully, a puzzled frown passing over her brow. "I really don't understand Paul. Doesn't he have any feeling for family at all?"

Defensively Dorcas said, "He writes me once a month. Very regular."

"I know, but that's not the same thing as coming home." Caroline handed the letter to Dorcas, then leaned back in the silk damask wing chair in the comfortable sitting room where the two women spent most of their time sewing and reading. "He never says a word about himself, except how he's making money selling furs. Doesn't he ever intend to marry?"

"I don't know. He never says a thing about that," Dorcas said quietly. When she looked up, there was pain in her eyes. "I've prayed for Paul since the day he was born. He's always been willful."

"And it seems worse because he was always compared to David." Caroline looked down at the book she had been reading, tracing the edges of the fine leather with her finger. "I think we did Paul a disservice by doing that. David was always so good and never in trouble and I'm afraid we mentioned it too much to Paul."

"I tried not to," Dorcas said quickly. "And so did Andrew." Nervously she touched her hair and then added, "I wondered sometimes about Cain and Abel. One so good and one so evil."

"Don't think like that!" Caroline's voice was sharp as she leaned over to tap Dorcas's hand. "We're all different! You know that! Paul will find himself." But there was not a great deal of conviction in her tone, so she tried to say more enthusiastically, "One day he'll come here and he'll be rich. He'll marry well and you'll see your grandchildren."

"I'd like to have grandchildren," Dorcas said plaintively. "Now that Bethany's all grown up, I miss the sound of children."

"She has grown up, hasn't she? A beautiful young woman, but she doesn't seem to know it. That's rather strange."

"Yes, she is very pretty. But . . ."

"What did you start to say?"

"Oh, just that she's lonely, I think. It's hard on her with her mother dead and Ivor gone. Of course, Gareth comes when he can and she spends time with him, but it's been very hard for her."

"I don't know what she would've done if it hadn't been for David."

Dorcas smiled, her eyes growing bright. "They are a pair, aren't they? Books, books, books! And if it's not books, it's periodicals. I declare, they'd read anything—even Persian poetry if they could understand the language."

Caroline chuckled. "Yes, they would. I was so pleased that David's book was published. He worked so hard on it."

"Well, it didn't sell many copies, but it was encouraging to him after all his attempts. Now he's working hard on another one, but he won't tell anyone what it is."

"I venture that Bethany knows."

"No, she doesn't. I heard her begging David to tell her about it just a few days ago. He just laughed at her and said she could read it when it was finished."

Silence fell on the room and the two women sat occupied with their own thoughts. Finally Caroline asked, "Do you think Gareth will ever marry again?"

"I don't know. I have thought of it, of course. A man as handsome as Gareth would certainly have the opportunity."

"One of his friends told me that every single woman under seventy in the parish had already put her bid in on him. He's going to lose a lot of women friends when he does choose a wife."

"That would be good if he could marry and Bethany could go live with them—although that might be hard, too. Bethany's a grown woman now, but I do worry about her. She does well with her studies. She's such a bright young woman, but somehow she seems unhappy."

Later that evening at dinner, the subject of marriage arose again. Ives, the butler, served oyster soup; roasted venison pie; roasted goose basted in butter; oyster stuffing with minced bacon, nutmeg, and lemon peel; artichoke with toasted cheese; and finally some delicate lemon biscuits accompanied by a fine wine.

Afterward, David leaned back in his chair and said, "That was a fine meal, Ives. Tell Cook I appreciate it."

"Yes, sir. I will do that."

"What have you three been doing all day?" David asked the women.

Bethany said nothing, but listened as the older women told David of their activities. Caroline finally said, "We were talking of your father, Bethany. Wondering if he would ever marry again."

Bethany's eyes flew open. "Why, he never mentioned such a thing." The thought seemed to trouble her. "Have you heard that he might? He's never said a word to me."

"Oh, no," Dorcas said quickly in a reassuring tone. "It's just that I'm sure he gets lonely at times. Of course, it's only been a year and a half since you lost your mother, but I expect some day he'll find a good woman. It's hard to grow old alone."

David glanced at his mother. He knew she missed her husband terribly and although he'd done all he could to be with her and offer her what companionship he could, he knew that this was not the same thing. Quickly he tried to change the subject, but Caroline was not yet through. "And what about you, David?"

"What about me?" David stared at Lady Caroline. "What do you mean?"

"I mean, since we're talking about marriage, when do you think you and Stella will get married?"

"Why, we're not even engaged. At least I don't think so." David Wakefield had the habit of blushing. He had rather fair skin and it infuriated him that he could not conceal those moments when he was embarrassed. Now he dabbed at his lips with the white napkin and said haltingly, "We—we just haven't made, ah—our arrangements yet."

"Seems to me," Caroline said directly, "that a man should know whether or not he's engaged."

Seeing David's intense embarrassment, Dorcas reached over and patted him on the hand. "Don't mind Caroline; she means well."

"Of course," David said, giving her a fragment of a smile. "Stella's so young and, after all, we have plenty of time."

"I would like to have grandchildren," Dorcas said.

Bethany suddenly said angrily, "Well, David can't get married just to give you grandchildren!" and got up abruptly and left the room.

David stared after her. "What's she so angry about?"

"Oh, she's going through a time most young women go through when they're dissatisfied with most things," Caroline said soothingly. Her eyes met Dorcas's and the two women understood as if they had spoken the words. *Bethany is falling in love with David.*

David got up and said, "I'll go talk to her. I haven't spent much time with her lately."

After he had left the room, Caroline said quickly, "She's in for a fall one day. She idolizes David."

"I'm afraid that's true. She wouldn't like anyone that he married, no matter how good a woman she was."

Ascending the stairs, David went to Bethany's room and knocked on the door. There was no response and after a while he tapped again. "Bethany? Are you there?"

The door opened slowly and when Bethany appeared, her face had a tense expression and her eyes were suspiciously red.

"What's wrong, Bethany?" David asked gently. "Did I hurt your feelings? Or did someone else?"

"Oh, no. I'm just silly," Bethany said, embarrassed by the scene she'd created. "Don't pay any attention to me. You know how silly girls are."

"I don't know anything of the sort," David said. "But I know one thing. I want you to come and help me with the book."

Delight leaped into Bethany's eyes. She loved being with David, especially when he talked about books, and at once said, "Right now?"

"Right now. Come along." Taking her hand, he swung it as they moved down the broad hallway and up the next flight of stairs to the third floor. When they reached the room, he unlocked the door, giving her a conspiratorial wink. "I keep it under lock and key. What if some other writer came in and stole my book?"

When they stepped inside, David lit the whale-oil lamp and sat down on the couch, patting the seat beside him. "Come along. I want to tell you what my book's about. You'll have to help me get over a tough spot. I just can't figure it out." When she sat down beside him, he smelled a new fragrance. "What's that scent?"

"It's a perfume Aunt Caroline gave me." She looked at him, anxious for approval. "Don't you like it?"

"Very nice. I think all young women should smell good." He laughed at her and squeezed her hand. "Now, let's get down to business. Here's what the story is about. . . ."

Bethany listened as David outlined the book he had been working on. She was very quick in matters like this and after he had told her the plot, he read her several pages before she interrupted him and said, "Oh, David! That's very good!"

"Do you think so?" he asked. "I didn't think it was as good as it might have been."

"It's better than anything the other novelists have done. Even Fielding never had a better page in his life."

"Well, I'd like to do a little better than Sir Henry Fielding. I didn't really care for his book. Did you read *The History of Tom Jones?*"

"Yes. He was a very ungodly man, wasn't he?"

"Yes, he was." David frowned. "I don't like to see such books appearing. Literature ought to uplift the reader."

"But it also ought to tell the truth about the way things are, don't you think, David?"

"What do you mean, Bethany?"

"In Dr. Johnson's writings on Shakespeare, he said Shakespeare held the mirror up to life. Isn't that what a book's supposed to do?"

David thought hard for a moment. "But life is so awful sometimes. Are we supposed to show those awful things?"

Bethany hesitated. "I suppose it all depends on the way you do it. Do you remember Richardson's book *Sir Charles Grandison?*"

"Yes. Did you like that book?"

"Not really. Sir Charles Grandison didn't have a single fault in the book. He was absolutely perfect."

"That's right, he was. And you don't care for that?"

"I don't think it does us much good to read about people who don't exist," Bethany said.

"But Sir Charles Grandison doesn't exist. He's just a character made up by Samuel Richardson."

"I know. But the characters should be like real people. That's what Dr. Johnson meant. You hold a mirror up to something and look in the mirror. What do you see?"

"You see the reflection of what's in front of it."

"Exactly! And that's what I want your books to do, David. I want them to show people as they are. Oliver Cromwell, the lord protector of England, told the court painter, 'Paint me with all the warts.'" Bethany giggled, making a delightful sound in the stillness of the room. "He wanted people to see him as he was. Not as some painter would show him, with all of his faults erased."

"That's not done in fiction too much. *Sir Charles Grandison* is acclaimed by everyone as a fine novel."

"But there are no men as good as Sir Charles Grandison."

"You don't think so? That there are good men and women?"

"Yes, but not perfect. And part of what fiction has to do is to show how people are. That way when we see them in the books, we can see ourselves. That's what I like about books, David. I see myself in them sometimes."

David was enjoying his time with Bethany thoroughly, as he always did. He was aware of her alert spirit and, at the same time, of all her blooming since she had come to live at Wakefield. At first, she had seemed to him only a child, but now he was aware she was growing into a lovely woman. To take his mind off this he said, "I remember when we read *Gulliver's Travels*. I think that was the first time you told me about seeing yourself in a novel."

"It's a strange book," Bethany said. "There are some ugly things in it. Do you remember the part where Gulliver goes to the land where there are rope dancers?"

"Yes, I remember. The men have to dance on a rope to please their ruler and the higher the rope, the more dangerous it was."

"I remember you told me that Swift wasn't talking just about acrobats—he was showing his readers the foolishness of the English nobility—how they will do anything to please their superiors."

"But do people understand what Swift is doing?"

"Some of them do—others just enjoy the story."

The two talked for over two hours and when Bethany left to go to bed, her last thought was: *I wish David would never marry— that he'd stay here and we could talk about books. . . .*

❦

One week after David's conversation with Bethany, he had one not quite so pleasant with Stella Fairfax. He had gone to her house to spend the evening and all throughout the meal, although Mrs. Fairfax gushed and seemed more talkative than usual, Stella had remained very quiet, merely picking at her food. David, sensitive to her moods, at once began to examine what he might have done to offend her. He knew her loss of appetite usually meant she would give him a hard time soon for some imagined or real offense.

He was right. As soon as her mother left the drawing room to go to bed, Stella turned to David with displeasure. "David, I'm disappointed in you!"

"What have I done, Stella?"

Stella, wearing a dress made of a fine embroidered silk in a light green-and-pink floral pattern, looked beautiful as usual. However, her eyes were almost hard as she said, "I never see you anymore. This is the first time you've been to our house in two weeks."

"Well, I've been trying to finish—"

"I know. You've been working on that old book!" Then, in a voice that was as hard as diamonds, Stella said, "You've got to learn something about women, David."

"I know I'm fairly ignorant in that area, Stella, but—"

"If you're going to court a young woman and try to win her for your wife, everything else has to be put away. With all those books you read, didn't you ever read anything about that?"

As a matter of fact, David had read several silly romances where men did ridiculous things in order to win the love of a woman. He had laughed at them with Bethany but knew he dare not mention such a thing to Stella. "I understand it's hard on you, but once this book is finished, you and I will have plenty of time."

"Before you start your next one?"

"I *will* be writing another one. As a matter of fact," David began eagerly, "I have an idea. Let me tell you about it."

"I don't want to talk about it, David. We're young and this is the time to enjoy life. You realize the last two balls I've had to go to alone because you were locked up in some dusty room scribbling away?"

David's heart sank. "But, Stella, it's my work."

"No, it's not your work! How much money have you made from your book?"

"Well, it hasn't been out very long and it's not the kind of book that many people would buy."

Stella came over, shaking her head despairingly. Knowing how to manipulate men, she put one hand on his arm and the other on his cheek and said sweetly, "David, it's a hobby, and you don't spend day and night on a hobby. It's something you do when there's nothing important to do."

"I see," David said. He was aware of Stella's beauty and her touch excited him. But he said with determination as he took her hand and held it, "I've got to do this, Stella. It's something that's inside of me. I don't know how to explain it." Almost desperately he tried to think of a way to make her understand, but he knew she hated books. She had never read one. She had not even read *his* book. Finally he said, "After we're married, I'll have more time."

Stella pulled her hand back and sniffed with contempt. "I don't see why you think that. Mother says that if a man won't pay attention to a woman before marriage, he certainly won't afterward."

"That's not so."

The conversation sank to a deeper level until it verged on a quarrel with David saying stiffly, "I'm not good company tonight, Stella. I'll come back again soon."

"When you finish your book?"

David's jaw tightened. "Yes, as a matter of fact. But I'll be through this week."

A spoiled young woman accustomed to getting her own way, Stella was angry because she had not been able to manipulate David as she had done in the past. "Good night, David," she said coldly.

When the door closed behind him, David walked swiftly toward his horse. "I didn't handle that well," he said. "But as soon as the book is over . . ."

***

". . . and so you can stop worrying about me in the army. Bethany, I want you to know that I am happier here than I ever imagined possible. My promotion will come through soon and I have written David to tell him about it. But if you receive this letter first, I commission you to tell him that if he never does anything for me again, he has made me a very happy man by establishing me in my profession."

Bethany looked up from the letter in her hands to David, a smile on her face. "Isn't that wonderful? And it's all your doing."

Although a week had passed since David's rough scene with Stella, he had been moody ever since. And now the sight of the young woman's face, so happy and joyful, pleased him greatly. "I'm glad to hear it. Ivor is a fine young man. I wouldn't be surprised but that he rose to be a general."

"I'm so happy he's found his place. Of course, I wish he weren't in the army. It's a dangerous profession."

"It's what he wanted," David said. "A man ought to be able to do what he wants."

The tone of David's voice caught at Bethany. "What's wrong, David?" she asked quietly.

David looked embarrassed. "Nothing really." He tried to say cheerfully, "This is good news. I know your father will be very proud."

But Bethany knew David was not happy. "Let's go for a ride," she said. "Take me with you when you go visit the tenants."

"All right. That would be fine."

The two put on their warm clothes, for November had come in like a lion and now snow lay two feet deep in drifts. "We'd better take the sleigh, Haines," David said. "We may run into deeper drifts than these."

"Yes, Sir David."

As soon as Haines had hitched the team to the sleigh, David helped Bethany in and wrapped a buffalo robe around her, saying, "This came all the way from North America. Paul sent it to Mother."

"I'd like to see a buffalo."

"Awful, hairy beasts, I understand, but the robes are warm. Get up!" he commanded the team.

The wind had died down, but the cold was intense. The sleigh made a hissing noise as it glided over the freshly fallen snow, and the horses' hooves were muffled by the white blanket.

"I've always loved to ride in a sleigh," Bethany said. "I wish it were snowy all year round so we could go this way always."

David laughed. "You are a foolish girl! You'd freeze your nose off!"

She reached over and touched his. "Yours is cold and your hands are, too. Where are your gloves?"

"I don't know. I think I left them at home."

"I know. Put your hands in your pockets and let me drive."

Since David's hands were numb, he handed her the lines. "Don't drive us off into a ditch," he warned, shoving his hands into the warmth of his wool coat. As they thawed out, he watched Bethany carefully. Her cheeks, slightly reddened by the cold, were smooth as alabaster. She wore a fur cap decorated by a burgundy velvet bow, and a hooded and fur-trimmed cape made of deep burgundy velvet. After a while he said, "That's a beautiful cap you've got on."

"Your mother gave it to me for a pre-Christmas present. She knew it was going to be cold, and I needed it." Turning to him she asked, "Can I make them go faster?"

"As fast as you like. Just don't pile us up."

That day's journey was joyful to Bethany. They stopped at half a dozen of the tenants' houses, where she went inside with David and was pleased at how respectful they all were to him. When they walked out the door of one poor family's house, she said, "These people love you, David. Paul could never have done what you've done."

As usual, the mention of Paul brought silence from David. "I'm sure he could have," he said finally as he helped her into the sleigh.

She settled down, waiting until he got in beside her and spoke to the horses. When they started up she said, "I wish you wouldn't feel guilty about Paul. You've done all you could for him. You can't help a person who doesn't want to be helped."

"You don't understand Paul."

"No, I don't!" Bethany said firmly. "I understand he never writes to you. He's never said one word about respecting or loving you."

"He's—upset. You can understand that. I mean, after all, there was only a few minutes' difference in the time of our birth. If he had been born first, he could've been Sir Paul Wakefield and I would have been the poor relation. I wouldn't have taken it well either."

Bethany put both lines in the thick glove of her right hand, then pounded his shoulder. "Yes, you would've!" she said almost fiercely. "If he had been Sir Paul Wakefield, it wouldn't have made a bit of difference to you. You're not like him!"

Shocked at her violence, David pulled his hand from his pocket and grabbed her hand. "Here!" he said with a smile. "Don't beat me to death!"

Bethany let him hold her hand for a while and held the reins with her right. "I won't say anything else," she said. "But I'm right about this."

"I don't think so," David said quietly. He refused to argue with her, however. "One more stop to make. The Dossetts' place."

The visit to the Dossetts was less successful, though Mrs. Elizabeth Dossett was all kindness and her daughter, Margaret, even worse. Bethany watched as the two women made much over David and she said little. They had tea; toast; and plum cake full of spices, dried fruits, and brandy that Margaret had made, apparently especially for David.

During the conversation Margaret asked, "You're having a long visit with the Wakefields, aren't you, Miss Morgan?"

Immediately Bethany understood from the glint in Margaret Dossett's eyes that the woman disliked her. "Yes, they've been very kind to me," she said quietly.

David felt the tension and said quickly, "Actually, I don't look on Miss Morgan as a visitor but as part of the family."

"How nice," Margaret said, then asked at once, "Are you intending to stay there very long? I mean, have you thought of working, or some profession—or perhaps you're engaged?"

"I'm afraid I haven't thought much of any of those, Miss Dossett," Bethany said coolly.

"You're fortunate to have had someone to take you in after your dear mother died," Mrs. Dossett said.

"Yes," Margaret said. "Most young women would have stayed with their father, I think, under the circumstances."

There was no answer Bethany could make to this, for she had reproved herself several times for leaving her father alone. It was true he was gone many weeks out of the year, but still, now that the thing was said out loud, she was hurt.

After the visit was over and they were on their way home, David said, "Are you all right? You look a little pale."

"Oh, yes. I'm fine." But she was thinking, *David doesn't understand that woman or either of them. They make over him because he's Sir David. If he didn't have a title, they wouldn't let him in the front door!*

They arrived home late in the afternoon and went at once to change clothes. Bethany put on a cornflower-colored silk gown and, after a time, went back downstairs. She passed by the library and saw David sitting by the desk staring at a piece of paper. Hesitating for a moment, she almost did not go in. But from the dejection in his manner she knew something was wrong. Going inside, she shut the door behind her and put her hand on his shoulder. "What's wrong, David?"

David's eyes were filled with misery. "You always know when something's wrong. How do you do that?"

"I just know," she said, looking down at the letter. "Is it bad news?"

"Yes." He hesitated only a moment, then handed her the note.

Taking it from his hands, she read the brief note in a woman's handwriting:

David,

It is obvious now, I hope to you as it is to me, that we can never be happy together. We are far too different. If you had any intentions of ever asking me to be your wife, I will ask you to put them aside. I wish you well in your writing, for I see that is where your heart is. It would take a very special kind of woman to be married to a man who devotes all of his time to scribbling. Please do not call and try to change my mind. You will understand my feelings better when I tell you that I have agreed to marry Sir Lionel Frazier.

Sincerely,

Stella Fairfax

"The little vixen!"

David saw the anger written plainly on Bethany's face and she was trembling. "We never would have been happy, I suppose," David said. He took the note and stared at it for a moment. He would have put it in the drawer, but Bethany said, "Don't do that, David."

"What?" Shocked, David looked up at her.

"Don't save that thing. Burn it! Throw it away! Tear it into a thousand pieces!"

"Why in the world do you say that?"

"Because you need to forget her. Put her out of your thoughts. Let me do it."

David hesitated, then slowly handed her the letter. Her face tightened as she tore it into bits, threw the fragments into the fireplace, and then came back to stand beside him. He propped his elbows on the desk and put his chin in his hands. "I suppose I'll get over it," he mumbled.

"You never loved her, David," Bethany said.

"How do you know that?" he questioned. "I certainly thought I did."

"She's beautiful and charming, but how many times did you ever have a single conversation with her on a serious matter?"

Abruptly David stood up and took her hands, managing a smile. "You're right, Bethany."

"I don't want to be," she said. "I hate to see you hurt."

Conscious of the warmth of her hands, he asked, "Will you ever get me raised, do you think?"

She squeezed his hands. "Someday I will!"

Twelve

WEDDING BELLS

Winter 1768

Bethany stared out at the snow that covered the hills, mesmerized by the pristine whiteness. She had come back to Cornwall to be with her father for a month. Now that her mother was gone and Ivor was in the army, the two of them had grown closer than ever. *It's been good for me to be home with Father,* Bethany thought. *He needed me—and I needed him.*

She turned from the window and moved toward the kitchen that was so familiar to her. She determined to fix a good meal for her father and set about it with the energy she always gave to things important to her.

Bethany went over to a long pine worktable that was between two windows and began pulling down a spit and kettles of all sizes. She pushed the spit through a small portion of beef, carried it to the fireplace, and placed it on the tackle to begin slowly roasting over the burning coals. After seeing that the spit and tackle were secure, Bethany returned to the worktable and began the tedious job of plucking a freshly butchered chicken. Feathers flew as Bethany finished the job in record time. She placed the chicken in a kettle with a lid, added some turnips, and put the kettle into the oven. Then she chose a large porcelain bowl from a high shelf, the one her mother used to make bread in, and placed it on the worktable. She quickly went to the pantry and gathered the ingredients needed to make the white wheaten bread her father loved—flour, eggs, yeast, milk, butter, sugar, and salt—then carried them back to the kitchen. She measured the dry ingredients into a smaller bowl, put it aside, and began mixing the eggs, milk, and butter together. She selected a bottle of rosewater to add to the ingredients in the large porcelain bowl. After the mixture was creamy, she began to add the dry mixture. When this mixture formed a large ball of dough, she placed a damp towel over the bowl and set it in the sunlight to rise for the next hour.

Bethany began cleaning the kitchen. She piled her bowls and utensils into a large sink and put the unused ingredients back on the shelves in the pantry. Then she walked across the room to an oak dresser and pulled out a cloth of fine, white linen to cover the round oak table that was in the center of the room. Looking up at the dresser, Bethany decided to make this a special occasion and use her mother's best china. Removing each piece carefully, Bethany carried them to the now clothed table and placed them with care in their proper places. Then she opened a dresser drawer, took out the silverware, and also placed that on the table.

The dough having risen, Bethany punched it down, shaped it into a loaf, and let it rise again on its pan before putting it in the oven. The dinner was almost ready to serve now—another half hour at most.

When she had finished, Bethany prepared the tea for the evening meal, then cut some slipcoat cheese and fresh, juicy apples into slices and arranged them on a porcelain platter in the middle of the table.

Checking the time, Bethany realized her father would be home any minute, so she began pulling the evening's dinner from the oven and off the spit. She put the meat on platters and spooned the turnips into a bowl, placing these on the table. When the bread crusted to a golden brown, she removed the hot loaf from its pan and let it slightly cool, sliced it, and put it on a plate, and then placed it on the table beside the cheese, apples, and Yorkshire pudding. She admired her work, then finished cleaning the kitchen.

By the time the meal was prepared, Gareth appeared, trudging along in the snow. Bethany heard his whistle and ran to look out the window. He saw her and waved, his teeth white against his dark features. When he came in the door, he seemed to fill the tiny kitchen. As Bethany helped him take his coat off, she could not help thinking what a handsome man he was. Even at the age of fifty-one, he showed few signs of aging. His hair was still curly and coal black and his face was smooth and youthful. As she hung up the coat she said cheerfully, "Well, did you meet with the committee?"

"Yes, I did. And I feel like I've been to the headmaster to take a caning."

"Come and sit down. You can tell me all about it while we eat."

As Gareth sat down at the table, he stared at the feast she had prepared. "Well, now. This may soothe my ruffled feelings a little." He said a brief blessing and then plunged in and began to eat heartily, speaking with his mouth full and gesturing with his fork. "The committee," he said, "is unhappy with the way I preach. They say it's not contemporary enough."

"Contemporary?" Bethany said, astonished and somewhat angry. "How can the gospel be contemporary? It's what it is. The way God wrote it in the Book."

"You should have been on the committee. They claim I'm preaching too much damnation and not enough of the love of God." He bit into a piece of the tender bread and chewed it thoughtfully. "You know, I think they may be right."

"Oh, that's foolishness."

"No, it's not." Gareth took another bite of the bread, then turned to face her. "Ever since your mother died, I'm afraid I haven't been as close to God. That's strange, isn't it? It should have brought me closer. I mean, after all, now she's in heaven and every day is another step closer to her and my Savior. But somehow it hasn't worked that way."

"You and Mother were very close."

"Closer than anyone ever knew. Oh, how I miss her, Bethany!"

Bethany was not surprised to see tears come into her father's eyes, for she knew the great love he had for her mother. She wanted to go over and take him in her arms as she would a hurt child, but instead she swallowed hard and said, "I miss her, too, Father."

Gareth blinked the tears away. "Come now, this is no way to act. I mean, after all, here we are, the best-looking father and daughter in all of Cornwall." He winked at her. "I haven't told you what a handsome wench you're getting to be."

"Wench! I like that! What if I called you a poacher?"

The two loved to tease each other and they enjoyed the rest of the meal. Afterward, they had tea in the sitting room as they watched the falling snow. It was a quiet time and a glow of pleasure came over Bethany. "I'm glad I came, Father," she said simply.

"So am I." He grasped her hand and held it for a long time. His hand was still strong from his days in the mines in Wales. Then he looked at her and asked abruptly, "What have you heard from David?"

A change swept across Bethany's face. She removed her hand and smoothed her hair down. When she spoke, her voice was cool. "I'm afraid he's having a reaction against getting thrown over by Stella Fairfax."

"That was a good thing in my thinking. You thought so, too, didn't you?"

"You mean not marrying Stella Fairfax? Yes, it was a good thing." Bethany bit her lip. "But now I'm worried about him."

Gareth sipped his tea and thought, *This young woman I hardly know. The child is almost all gone. I just see a fleeting glimpse of it now and again. Something's troubling her and I think it's David.* Aloud he said, "What's wrong, Bethany?"

Turning to him, Bethany's eyes narrowed. "It's this woman Margaret Dossett. Do you know her, Father?"

"No, I don't believe I do."

"She's the daughter of a farmer who died some time ago. She and her mother live on Wakefield land now and she's after David. I can see it so plain."

"Can you now?"

"Why, anyone could—anyone except David! He's blind as a bat."

"Most men are, where women are concerned. What sort of woman is she?"

"Oh, she's attractive enough. She's two or three years older than David and she flatters him. Heaven's angels above! She pours flattery on him like I pour syrup on a hotcake."

"That bad, is it? And David can't see it?"

For a moment she hesitated, then said, "He is not very wise about women. He doesn't know what a catch he'd be and Margaret Dossett is determined to catch him." Silence filled the room for a time, broken only by the sweep of the wind outside and the gentle ticking of the clock on the mantel. Finally Gareth turned to his daughter, wishing he could help her, but he could only say, "You mustn't be selfish. David's always been partial to you. He's been like a father to you, really. As a little girl you sat for hours on his lap right here in this room, listening to him as he read story after story. But he must marry. You know that, Bethany."

"I know."

"It's hard to turn loose the things we love." Sorrow came to him then as the thought of Sarah flashed in his mind, but he pushed it resolutely aside. "You'll have to find other interests. When David marries, his wife will be the mistress of Wakefield. Things will be very different."

"I know." The answer was gentle enough, but a sudden rebellious light flickered in Bethany's dark blue eyes. "But I couldn't stand it if it was that woman!"

❦

"Ye've done vurry weel, laddie," Angus McDowell said with satisfaction. He was seated beside David at a long rosewood library table littered with papers. "The past year has been the best since ye came to the title and ye've pleased me mightily. I ken yer father would have been pleased, too, and Sir George."

"It's all your doing, Angus," David said. "You taught me everything I know about business."

"Weel now. I wouldn't say that, but I'm glad Wakefield is doing so weel." He studied the face of his young client and saw something there that disturbed him. "I heard about yer broken engagement."

"It wasn't an engagement," David said quickly.

"Do ye tell me that?" McDowell exclaimed with surprise. "Why, I thought it was understood ye would be married to the young lady."

"It never came to that."

The curtness of David's words caught at McDowell. He knew the young man to be the most cheerful of individuals and now he saw unaccustomed gloom. Troubled, McDowell said, "I'll tell ye what. I know a little inn where we can have a bit of haggis. Come along. I'll buy yer dinner."

"What's haggis?" David asked.

"The heart, liver and lungs of a sheep—a little onions and seasoning all boiled in the sheep's stomach. A fine old Scottish dish."

David shuddered. "I'll just have beef or something, if you don't mind."

The two went to a small inn, not at all ornate and in keeping with the Scotsman's penurious ways. The service was good, however, and the food excellent. As David picked at his food and McDowell ate his haggis with enthusiasm, the older man talked about the estate for a while, then said abruptly. "I was dumped once, ye ken."

"You were?" David was surprised. Angus McDowell was a widower and had been much in love with his first wife. He spoke of her often with affection. "I never knew that. I thought Mrs. McDowell was your only love."

"Oh, she was a great woman and I think of her all the time. Much as ye do yer father, I'm sure. But before her, I fell in love like a crazy man with a blonde-headed, green-eyed young woman from Portsmouth. Oh, heaven preserve us. What a fule I made of myself. I walked around like a man out of his senses."

David began to smile as McDowell described his early love affair. He could not imagine McDowell, the sober lawyer, behaving so badly. Finally he said, "Do all men in love behave like that?"

"Every one," McDowell assured him solemnly, a twinkle in his eyes. Then after a time he said, "I hate to see ye suffering, laddie, but ye'll get over it. Ye'll find a woman who will be a guid wife for ye as mine was to me and as yer guid mother was to yer father."

"I hope so, Angus," David said. "But to tell the truth, I'm not very wise about women."

"No man really is. They're a strange breed," McDowell said, stroking his chin thoughtfully. "We can't live without them and we can't live with them. So we take the meat and spit out the bones. Come, laddie. Eat yer dinner. We'll go back to the office and see how ye're going to be even richer next year."

The winter of 1768 passed slowly for David. Despite McDowell's encouragement and the kindness of those at home, he was lonely. He missed Bethany, who had elected to stay over with her father until the middle of summer, and more and more he kept to himself, going for long walks in the woods. Often, however, these walks ended at the Dossetts', where he always found a warm welcome. He did not analyze this, but his mother did. Once as he came in late and she asked where he'd been, he replied, "I stayed late at the Dossetts'. They fixed a fine supper for me."

"Oh? Well, that's fine, I'm sure. Are they well?"

"Oh, yes. Both are well. They're always well." He sat down beside her and seemed to be happy. He spoke of Margaret in glowing terms, saying, "She's a fine cook. I don't know of a better, except you, Mother."

"That's an admirable trait in a woman. Are they having a financial struggle?"

"Oh, I think they always do. Margaret's father didn't leave much and it's all they can do to scrape by."

"I wonder why Margaret hasn't married?"

"So do I," David said earnestly. "She's an attractive woman and very gifted. She plays the harp, you know."

"Yes, I know." Dorcas sat beside her son and they talked about the Dossetts for a while. "Do you think she will ever marry?"

"She should. She could make a man very happy," David said quietly.

Dorcas looked up at that and saw a look of concentration on David's countenance. "Has she had offers?"

"I think she has. A man named Williams from the next county wanted to marry her very badly, her mother said, but she wouldn't have him."

"Why not, I wonder? Was he poor?"

"Oh, he was a farmer much like her father. Margaret wants more than that out of life."

"What more could there be for a woman besides being a wife and mother and doing those two things well?"

David turned to her. "You do them well, Mother. You always have. You made Father, Paul, and me very happy."

Dorcas flushed with pleasure. "It was not difficult with your father, nor with you." Significantly, she did not mention Paul, for the two spoke rarely of him.

But this conversation stayed with Dorcas and she expressed her concern to Caroline later.

"I'm afraid he's getting interested in Margaret Dossett."

"That would be unfortunate. I just can't like the woman," Caroline said. "She's nice enough, well-mannered and all of that, but somehow I just don't take to her."

"I don't think they have many friends, but I don't know why."

"We see them at church and they're faithful enough at that. But somehow there's a reserve in Margaret. Her mother's outgoing— a little bit too much so, I'm afraid."

They said no more, but David continued to visit and bring his reports back to Wakefield. And as the summer wore on, he began bringing Margaret and her mother, from time to time, to have dinner at Wakefield. David enjoyed their visits and more than once asked his mother to go with him to take a meal at the Dossetts' cottage. Dorcas did go with him once, but although the meal was fine and she was cordially received, she did not feel quite comfortable there and found excuses not to go again.

Bethany arrived back at Wakefield in the first week of June. She was greeted with enthusiasm by Dorcas and Lady Caroline and David took her hands, smiling at her warmly. "I'm glad you're back. Now we can talk and get some writing done."

Bethany laughed. The months she had been gone from Wakefield had been good—and yet she now felt that she was back at her second home. "I'm so happy to be back, David," she said. "I can't wait to see what you've been writing."

For a week they would meet every day and talk about the book David was working on. "It's the best thing you've ever done. It'll make you famous," Bethany said after reading the part he had finished.

"I doubt that, but I'm glad you like it. I need your approval, you know."

"You'll always have that."

David had smiled at her then. But Bethany was surprised to find out he was gone a great deal of the time. It was on the sixth day of her return, a Saturday evening, when David came to find Bethany. When she opened her door, he asked, "Are you busy?"

"Why, no. Come in, David." As he entered, she noticed he looked strained and when he turned to her, he placed his hands behind his back, locking them together. He held her eyes for a moment and said, "I have something to tell you."

Apprehensive, Bethany asked, "Has something happened to Paul?"

"Oh, no. It's not bad news," David assured her quickly. He came over and took her hand and said, "I've been very unhappy since you've been gone. You haven't been here and I've been lonely."

"I know," Bethany said. "But now I'm back and—"

David interrupted her. "I have to tell you something." He cleared his throat and looked embarrassed. "I'm engaged, Bethany."

Instantly Bethany knew everything. She turned pale and whispered, "To Margaret Dossett?"

"Why, yes. Did Mother tell you?"

"No. She never said a word, nor did Lady Caroline."

"Well, it's been rather sudden, the engagement itself. Margaret and I have spent a lot of time together. I know you will like her, Bethany. She's a little hard to get to know, but you can get along with anyone if you choose to."

Bethany's throat constricted and her heart cried out, *No, you can't do it, David! She'll make you miserable!* However, there was no way she could say this, so she looked at him and said as cheerfully as she could, "I hope you'll be very happy."

"I will be. We'll have a mistress here now and you two will become great friends."

Bethany managed to endure the conversation, but as soon as David left, she walked over to the window seat and sat down, numbed by what she had heard. Her emotions seemed to be frozen for a time, but the longer she sat there, the more disturbed she became.

At length, she went over, lay facedown on the bed, and tried to suppress the sobs, but they came anyway. She wept freely, muttering between clenched teeth, "She'll never make him happy. She doesn't love him—not like I do!"

***

"Well, I think all the plans have been made for the wedding, don't you, Mother?"

The wedding was now only a week away and Margaret and her mother were at Wakefield every day. The wedding was to be at the chapel and Mrs. Dossett, with Margaret's help, had planned it all. They had asked, out of courtesy, if Lady Caroline or Dorcas had any suggestions, but the two had made none. Bethany, of course, had not been consulted. She had been very quiet during the weeks that had followed David's announcement and more than once he had said anxiously, "Don't you feel well, Bethany? You seem to be so listless and you're pale."

She had assured him she was well and now that the wedding was practically upon them, she kept to herself more than ever.

Margaret spoke to Bethany only one night while she and her mother were there. "And what have you been doing today, Bethany?" she asked.

"Oh, very little. Reading mostly."

"You must get out of that room and exert yourself."

"Yes, indeed," Mrs. Dossett said. "It's not good for a young woman to be cooped up. Why, when I was your age it was one party after another."

Bethany allowed herself a tiny smile. "I suppose I'm not much for parties."

"Well, you should be," Margaret said with authority. "And after the honeymoon, I've made up my mind to help you."

Bethany looked up. "Help me what?"

"Why, help you get into society. There are plenty of young men who need a good wife and I'm going to see to it that you meet them."

"Thank you. I wasn't really thinking of going into society," Bethany said.

Intending to help, David said, "Why, that will be fine. We can have parties right here. Invite young men. We'll find you a husband in no time."

If no one else saw Bethany's pain, Dorcas and Caroline did. Bethany said nothing but simply lowered her head and began to eat. After the meal was over and the guests had gone home, Caroline went to Bethany and said, "She doesn't mean to be unkind."

"I'm sure she doesn't."

Caroline struggled to find some comfort for Bethany. She knew the loss that the young woman was feeling. "It's not as if you were losing David. He'll still be here."

Bethany's eyes narrowed. "You know it won't be the same, Lady Caroline. It can never be the same again." She turned and walked away and Caroline, reporting on this incident to Dorcas, said, "Poor child. David's spoiled her all of her life and now she feels she's losing him."

"She is losing him," Dorcas said quietly. "Margaret will have her out of this house in six months."

Two days before the wedding David went looking for Bethany. He found her out in the garden, sitting on a bench and staring at the sun that was sinking rapidly, throwing a golden glow over the flowers. "What are you doing out here all alone?" he asked, taking a seat beside her. "I've looked everywhere for you."

"I just came out to enjoy the sunset." Bethany's words were quiet and she did not look at David.

He hesitated, then brushed her hand lightly. "I've been thinking a great deal about what's going to happen after the wedding."

"So have I."

Somehow David was taken aback at Bethany's simple response, but he said, "Look, I know you haven't thought much about the future, and I don't want you to."

Bethany turned to look at him, her dark eyes watching him carefully. "What do you mean, David?"

"I mean, we'll go on just as we have been. You and I can have our time up in our secret room. You can help me with my books. You might even write some yourself. It will be wonderful."

For one moment, Bethany considered what he said. She had already thought much about it and now she said softly, "I won't be here, David."

"Won't be here? What do you mean by that?"

"I'll be leaving Wakefield."

"Are you going home to Cornwall to be with your father?"

"No, I'm not."

David could not understand her reticence. She had said almost nothing for days now and he said slowly, "I know you've been thinking of something. Can't you tell me about it?"

"Yes. I've been meaning to talk to you. I've accepted a position as governess to a family in London."

If Bethany had said she was going to the moon, David could

not have been more surprised. "I can't believe it! You can't do it, Bethany!"

"Do you think I'm not qualified to be a governess after all the expensive education you've given me?"

"Oh, no!" David said, shocked. "I didn't mean that at all. You'd be a wonderful governess, but what will I do without you?"

"You'll be married, David. You and your wife will have many interests."

Somehow David felt he had lost something precious and sweet. He pulled her to her feet and the two stood there as the darkness rapidly swept across the land. The shadows were already long and her face was half highlighted by the rays of the dying sun, outlining her high cheekbones and wide, dark blue eyes. He whispered, "You're such a lovely young woman. You've had everything. Please don't go away. I'd be lost without you."

"I must go, David. There's no other way."

"Why must you go?"

But she could not answer. She could not tell him that the woman he was going to marry would not tolerate her presence in the house. He was not ready to receive that. At last she said simply, "It's time for me to get on with my life. You'll be married and I must go find other things."

David started to put his arm around her, as he had always done, but she put her hand on his chest and stepped back. "No, let's say our good-byes here. You'll be busy and I'll be leaving for London immediately after the wedding while you are on your honey-moon."

David, hurt by the way she had stepped back from him, said, "I can't let you leave like this. Somehow I feel things are wrong."

Bethany could not argue with this, for her heart was breaking. She said softly, "Good-bye, David. I hope you have a happy life," and then left him standing there with a feeling of tremendous loss that he could not understand. For a long time, he walked in the garden, trying to think of Wakefield without Bethany, and it proved to be impossible.

⸙

The wedding was what all weddings should be, beautifully done, with everything orchestrated by Margaret and Mrs. Dossett. Margaret made a lovely bride in her white wedding dress, but David could never afterward remember a single thing about the wedding. It was all like a blur or a dream. He was, perhaps, like a man who had been caught in a swift current and was carried away willy-nilly, despite his own desires. His first clear memory afterward was as he and Margaret were getting into the carriage. When he saw Bethany standing back in the crowd, he at once left Margaret's side and approached her. "Will you wish me well, Bethany?"

"I would always do that, David." She reached up and kissed him, then walked away. But David had seen tears in her eyes and the happiness of the day, such as it was, was marred. He felt a hand on his arm and turned around. Margaret had come and was looking up at him almost angrily. "Come, David! The carriage is ready!"

After helping Margaret up, David climbed in and sat down and then the horses started up. The cheers that followed seemed somehow tinny to David. He looked back to see Bethany, but she had disappeared. So he looked straight ahead and tried to think as Margaret took his hand. "Now we're married," she said. "I'm Lady Margaret Wakefield."

David looked at her as the carriage moved on. She was pretty enough in her wedding outfit and he smiled, but he had to swallow before he said, "Yes, my dear, and I will cherish you always."

Far back in the crowd Bethany Morgan stood half-hidden behind a large yew tree. As the carriage disappeared, she knew that part of her life was leaving her. She had cried her tears, however, and now looked ahead. "And now for London," she said. But she could not help whispering, "Good-bye, David—good-bye!"

A Day

1 7 7 2

Part
THREE

1 7 7 3

in Court

Thirteen

PRODIGAL'S RETURN

February 1772

T he hardest part of winter had passed by the time February arrived and, looking outside, Dorcas Wakefield was pleased to see tiny spears of grass piercing the gray earth—the first harbinger of spring. The winter had been long and difficult and her grandchildren had driven her to distraction within the house during the past month. Now she smiled and said, "I think after your birthday party we can go out, Andrew."

At the age of three, Andrew Wakefield resembled his grandfather so much that it was startling: blond hair, blue eyes, and the same neat features, including a broad forehead and small ears. *He looks so much like Andrew,* Dorcas thought, and for a moment the old grief arose in her as she remembered the husband she had loved so dearly. Quickly she said, "It's almost time to go down and see what birthday presents you have."

"I want birthday!" The speaker was the young Susan, whose hair and eyes were as dark as Andrew's were light. She was an energetic child, into everything in the house, and now her lip protruded in a pout.

"You'll have one in June, but today is Andy's birthday, February the twelfth." She put her arm around the boy's sturdy form and gave him a kiss. "You're three years old today!"

"Gran'ma?" he asked, looking up at her. "Will Papa get me a pony?"

"I don't think so—not this year, Andy. You're too little to have your own pony. You'll just have to ride in front of your father for a while yet."

Susan shoved her way between Andy and her grandmother and tugged at the woman's skirt. "I want pony. White pony!"

Laughing, Dorcas reached down, picked the child up, and kissed her soundly. "And you shall have one, Susan. As soon as you're old enough. I promise."

This satisfied Susan and she immediately squirmed to be released. When she was on the floor, she said, "Presents! Open!"

"I'll open them!" Andrew protested, running toward the door with Susan following hard on his heels. As Dorcas listened to their rapid footsteps echoing down the hall, then down the stairs, she took a deep breath. "I hope to get those children raised, but they are a handful." She moved slowly toward the door, for at the age of fifty-seven, her health was not good. The pain in her knees caused her to catch her breath, and she stopped at the door for a moment until it grew bearable. As she made her way down the hall, she held on to the banister thinking, *Very soon now I'll have to have a room downstairs.* The thought grieved her, for she loved her room upstairs where she had put in so many happy years. Since coming to Wakefield, she had been happy—but even as she descended the wide, curving staircase, she frowned. Since David's marriage, she had not been quite so happy. Margaret had been difficult to live with and had become even more impossible since the death of her mother six months earlier. Arriving at the first floor, Dorcas heard the sound of voices in the smaller dining room. Putting aside her thoughts of David's wife, Dorcas entered and found the table covered with a white cloth and several gaily wrapped packages. Caroline was standing beside the window watching the two children with a smile. "Well, Caroline," Dorcas said, "ready for the great celebration?"

"Not much of a celebration." Margaret Wakefield stood stiffly at the end of the table. Since her marriage to David, she had put on weight and there was a sullen look on her thin lips. "What sort of man would forget his only son's birthday?"

"I'm sure he'll be here," Dorcas said quickly. "He had to call on several of the tenants. Old Mrs. Taylor has been very ill and you know how careful David is to—"

"It wouldn't hurt him to pay some attention to the sick people in his own house!" Margaret snapped.

"Can I open my presents now?" Andy spoke up eagerly.

"Not now. You will have to wait until your father comes," Dorcas said quietly. She went over and sat down beside Andy, patting him on the head. "He'll be here soon, I'm sure."

The next half hour was unpleasant for everyone. Margaret complained bitterly about David's absence while Caroline and Dorcas tried their best to smooth the matter over with little success. Andy constantly asked to open his presents, and Susan, impatient as always, began to roam around the room, getting into things and being rebuked by her mother.

Eventually they heard the door close and voices in the hall. "There he is at last, I suppose," Margaret said, sniffing. She waited until David entered and before he could open his mouth said, "Well, you're here at last! Where have you been?"

David stopped short with surprise, not prepared for the assault Margaret had launched at him. He glanced at his mother and saw the warning in her eyes, then at once apologized. "I'm sorry, Margaret. I had more calls to make than usual."

"It doesn't matter that you kept us all sitting here waiting for you for over an hour and that you've neglected your own child for strangers."

Having learned from long experience that arguing with Margaret was fruitless, David quietly said again, "I'm sorry," then walked over to Andy, smiling. "Well, Andy. Three years old today. My, you're getting to be quite a fine young man."

"Can I have pony, Papa?"

Laughing, David picked the boy up and tossed him into the air. "When you're a little bit older. But I'll take you for a ride on Soldier today."

"It's too cold to have the child out!" Margaret said abruptly. "He'll catch his death of cold!"

David gave his wife an irritated glance. *She's a prophet of gloom if there ever was one,* he thought, but mildly said, "I'll wrap him up in furs. He'll be fine."

"I go, Papa?"

David reached down and squeezed Susan. "We'll see. If you are very good, I might take you for a short ride."

"I be good," Susan pronounced and looked around with surprise as her grandmother and Caroline laughed. "I good!"

Kissing her rosy cheek, David answered, "Of course you are, darling. Now, let's get into these presents."

At once Andy began opening the gifts, generously allowing Susan to help him with the little ceremony. He was pleased over the toys David had purchased from London and less interested in the new mittens, boots, and coat.

After the opening of the presents there was a cake and at David's command Andy blew almost all the candles out. Happily Andy said, "Now, I get my wish, don't I?"

"What did you wish for?" Caroline asked, still attractive at the age of fifty-eight. As the small party went on, it was with mixed emotion that she thought of what Wakefield had become. She ostensibly was the head of the family, although David had taken over all the practical side of that. She glanced at Dorcas, thankful again for her friend's companionship and David and Margaret's two children. *If only Margaret were a little more amiable!* she thought. She had been personable enough when she first came to Wakefield. Everything had been new. Margaret had been used to genteel poverty and for the first year of David's marriage, things had gone well. But then the children came and what should have brought more happiness did not. Glancing over at Margaret, Caroline wondered, *Why isn't she happy? She has everything a woman could want. David is a fine husband. She has two beautiful children, all the money she can spend—and yet she doesn't seem to accept all this.* She studied the woman's face and saw that the past four years had aged her somewhat. She still had some attractiveness, but she was insanely jealous of her husband. This, Caroline knew, was part of her problem. She could not allow David to be with a woman of any station below the age of fifty without lashing out at him.

An eruption of this sort occurred when the children had gone to put on their warm clothes for their horse ride with their father. David had been describing his visits and he mentioned, "I stopped by to see Mrs. Cotrell. She's—"

"So that's where you've been!" Margaret's face grew pink. "I knew you would be going to see *her!* You think I don't know how you chase after her?"

"Margaret! The woman's nearly fifty years old and not attractive at all!" Dorcas exclaimed.

"That doesn't matter to David, does it? She's a wench and you go after every woman you see that casts an eye." As Margaret's rage grew, David, as usual, could make no defense.

He did say finally, "She's lost her husband and she has no prospects—and three children to raise. I have an obligation to her as I do to any of my female tenants who suffer this kind of loss."

But Margaret was not to be reconciled and she continued to rail at David until finally, in desperation, he left to take the children for a ride.

After the three were gone, Margaret looked at the other two women coldly. "I suppose you'll defend him. You always do."

Seeing that Dorcas was speechless, Caroline said as gently as she could, "You only make yourself unhappy by doing things like this. David has been entirely faithful to you. You should know that."

"That's what *you* say! You would always defend him. You think he can do no wrong, but I know how he looks at the young women," Margaret said, then left the room.

When she was gone, Dorcas said, "She's so unhappy and she brings it all upon herself."

Half an hour later, Dorcas encountered Leah, one of the maids, taking a bottle of wine upstairs on a tray.

"What's that, Leah?"

"Oh, it's for Mrs. Wakefield, ma'am," Leah said, a knowing look in her eye. She was a smart young girl and, as all servants, very interested in the lords and ladies of Wakefield. "She said for me to bring it up."

Dorcas started to rebuke her, then said, "All right. Do as she tells you, Leah."

"Yes, ma'am."

Margaret's drinking was no secret to anyone at Wakefield; she had begun shortly after the birth of Susan. As Dorcas wearily climbed the steps, pain shooting through her knees, she thought, *Margaret's getting worse. Drinking more all the time and she denies it. No one can talk to her.* She thought of David—how day by day he had to live with Margaret's jealous rages and how he attempted to excuse her drinking—and shook her head. When she finally got to her room, she stretched out with a sigh on her bed, wishing fruitlessly that David had chosen a wife who was more discreet.

———

Two days after Andy's birthday David and Dorcas were sitting in the parlor playing with the children. Though the same warm room with its green-and-crimson color scheme that had always impressed guests, the room had changed in small measures over the years David and his family had lived at Wakefield. The two floor-length windows were now covered with white linen shades and between them was a brass birdcage with a mockingbird. On each side of the large fireplace was a green-and-gilt fauteuil with seventeenth-century needlework, and numerous paintings of Wakefield Estate in gilt frames; in front of the fireplace stood a white settee, covered with red-and-green striped damask, and a maple sewing stand. On one side of the fireplace mantel was a spyglass; on the other were the familiar brass candleholders with green candles; a large oval glass hung above. An array of George III green-and-gilt side chairs were placed along the walls between a mahogany serving table and an oak buffet.

For some time David had been engaged with the children, playing any game they could think up—and usually it was Susan who thought up the most interesting ones. She had finally decided to play horsy, so David had crawled around on all fours while she sat on his back, tugging on his clothes and saying, "Get up! Get up!"

Finally he had risen and said, "That's enough. The horsy's tired." He tweaked Andy's ear playfully. "Why don't you take Susan in and have Cook give you some of that cake you liked so much for dinner last night?"

With a yell that practically shook the windowpanes, Andy and Susan left and David sank into one of the fauteuils, grinning at his mother. "They wear a fellow out."

Dorcas's fingers were twisted with arthritis, but she still worked constantly, doing what she could. Currently she was embroidering a border of delicate flowers on a petticoat for Susan. "You're a fine father, David," she said. "So good to the children."

"No more than they deserve." David straightened his plain brown suit and white shirt, looked down at his boots for a time, and then said, "I'm worried about Paul. It's been a long time."

"Over six months. I'm worried, too."

"It's thoughtless of him not to write."

Dorcas looked up with surprise, for David rarely had any criticism for his brother. "Yes, it is. You wouldn't have done such a thing."

David shrugged this off and the two talked for some time about Paul. A few years prior, Paul had written regularly for a while, always speaking mostly of the fur trade and how well it was going. But a year ago the letters had become more rare and finally had stopped altogether.

"Perhaps I ought to go over and find him. He may need help."

Quickly Dorcas looked up. "Would you do that, David?"

"Of course I would. It would be hard to get away, but Manning is a good manager. He could stand in for me."

"I don't know how you would find him. All we have is an address in Quebec."

"I could try." The past four years had aged David, too, but more in spirit than in appearance. He still was strong and youthful looking. He had taken his duties at Wakefield seriously and spent long hours in the field talking with Manning, the farm manager, or visiting the tenants. He also spent considerable time conferring with his lawyer, Angus McDowell, in London over business matters.

However, Dorcas sensed that David was restless. Although he delighted to be with the children, after a few days of being in the house with Margaret's constant criticism, he often gave more time to outside tasks than was actually necessary. Dorcas studied him as he sat loosely in the chair, his muscles relaxed but a frown creasing his brow.

Margaret entered, a letter in her hand. Given to spending large sums on clothing even though there was no occasion, she was wearing a flattering and expensive open-robe dress of a dove gray satin with an underskirt of dusky rose satin and white lace. Margaret was still an attractive woman, but her voice was tense as she said, "This just came, addressed to you."

"Thank you, Margaret." David stood up, took the letter, and ripped it open. He studied the contents, then looked up and said, "It's from Bethany."

"What does she want?" Margaret demanded.

"She says she needs to see me at once," David murmured. "There is something very urgent."

"Urgent!" Margaret scoffed. "You're not going to go, I trust, at her beck and call?"

David shifted uneasily. He fingered the envelope, then folded it and put it in his pocket. "I think I must," he said. "Bethany's never asked for anything before."

"You run all over the country after every pretty woman and neglect your own family!"

"You're welcome to come to London with me, Margaret. Perhaps you might do some more shopping there."

Margaret shook her head. "I'm sure it would interfere with your philandering." She turned and walked out of the room, her back stiff, and slammed the door behind her.

Dorcas rose and came to stand beside David. She put her hand in his and he held her twisted fingers for a moment, then smiled down at her ruefully. "I don't know why she's so suspicious of me."

"I don't think she knows why herself. She's a very unhappy woman, David."

"Why is she unhappy? I've done everything I can to please her. She spends whatever she wants on clothes, she has whatever she likes, and yet she always suspects I'm unfaithful to her," he said, his voice tinged with sorrow.

Dorcas squeezed his hand. "Go to London. It'll be good for you to get away from here for a while." It was the most she had ever said about David's marital conditions and this was only a hint. Nevertheless, David knew her well and though the two did not speak of it again, he was glad she understood the situation. Leaning over he kissed her and said, "I'll leave at once."

"The children will be after you to take them."

"I'll bring them back a present," he said. "In the meanwhile, we'll think about my going to America to find Paul. I'm worried about him. That's the least I can do."

⁕

Getting out of the carriage in London, David looked up and said, "If you'd wait, driver, I may want you to take me back to the inn. I'll make it worth your while."

"Certainly, sir. I'll be right here."

David moved away from the carriage and ascended the steps of the expensive Georgian-style two-story house.

David sounded the brass knocker and a maid opened the door. "Yes, sir?"

"I would like to see Miss Bethany Morgan, please. My name is Wakefield."

"Come in, sir, out of the cold. I'll find Miss Morgan. I think she's with the children."

David followed her to an ornate parlor, thinking about Bethany's career as a companion for the children of Mr. and Mrs. Clifton Sears. Sears was a wealthy shipowner and paid liberally. David had met Mrs. Sears, an amiable woman, several times during the years Bethany had served in her position. He waited impatiently, then Bethany entered the room. She came to him at once and put out her hands, which he took, a smile leaping to his lips. "Bethany! It's good to see you."

"It's good to see you, too, David."

David studied her carefully. She was twenty-two now, and without thinking he said abruptly, "You don't look much like the little girl who used to sit on my lap and pull my hair until I told you stories."

"I suppose I had to grow up like everyone else."

"You've grown up very well indeed."

Bethany Morgan's cinnamon-colored silk damask dress set off her trim, womanly figure nicely. Its close-fitting bodice was heavily embroidered and had ribbon and lace that ended slightly below the waistline. The open front of the overskirt was edged with short robings and pleats from around the neck to the waist, then down each side, revealing a white silk petticoat. With her black hair done in a chignon and her dark blue eyes dominating her beautifully sculptured face, she was a most attractive young woman.

"Is there some sort of difficulty, Bethany?" David asked anxiously after the two had sat down on a lounge and he had given a report. He had never lost his early affection for Bethany and though she was grown up now, he still saw some of the little girl who had been so dear when he, himself, was but a boy.

For a moment Bethany hesitated, then rose and asked, "Have you eaten?"

"No."

"Come. Let me get my coat and we'll go out and have something to eat. I need to talk to you."

Somewhat mystified, David waited until she came back. Since the weather was still cold, she wore a green wool cloak, silk hat with plumes and ribbons, and tan leather gloves. "I kept the carriage waiting," he said.

"That's fine. I know a place that's not too far."

He escorted Bethany outside, helped her into the carriage, then seated himself after repeating the directions Bethany gave him to the driver.

He waited for her to speak, but on the short ride she merely related some of her activities to him. Her life seemed placid enough and she spoke warmly of Gareth, who had just left London after a prolonged visit. "We had such a good time together."

"I wish I'd seen him. He came to Wakefield two months ago. He stays on the go, doesn't he?"

"Always preaching, always a meeting. Mr. Wesley depends on him a great deal now to help with the younger ministers."

"John Wesley is still setting England on its ear," David said, smiling. "Do you hear him often?"

"Every time I get a chance. He's a marvelous preacher, but you know, I think his brother Charles is better."

"I thought Charles was the hymnwriter?"

"Oh, he does write wonderful hymns and has a beautiful voice. But there's a warmth in him, David, that draws people."

"You don't see that in Mr. John Wesley?"

Bethany hesitated because she admired both Wesleys and then said, "I think he's so burdened down with meetings, classes, and all of the young ministers and the old ones, too, who look to him for guidance. He loves people. I'm sure of that. There's nobody like him."

The two spoke of the Wesleys until the carriage stopped. Soon they were inside, seated at a table beside a window. A fireplace glowed and crackled across the room, casting its warmth on them, and David, after inquiring, ordered a light meal for both of them. As they waited, he spoke of his life at Wakefield and without meaning to do so revealed some of his unhappiness. Never once in all their years of marriage had he ever criticized his wife to anyone, but Bethany had been at Wakefield on visits and had seen for herself what it was like. She knew Margaret was jealous, even of her, and for this reason did not go as often as she might have. She also carried on long correspondences with Caroline and Dorcas, who sometimes spoke of the poor marital situation that existed between David and Margaret. Finally, after they had eaten and were drinking cups of scalding tea, Bethany gave a good report of Ivor and once again thanked David for his support of the young man.

"He's doing so well in the army. I think, really, he'll be a general one day. Well," she said, her dark eyes glowing with a rich beauty, "maybe not a general, but a major at least."

"I'm glad for Ivor. I didn't know if going in the army would be a wise thing, but it has been for him." David then leaned forward and said abruptly, "Something's wrong, Bethany. You didn't call me here just for a visit, although it has been a good one. What's wrong?"

Bethany paused and looked him directly in the face. "Paul's here."

"Paul—in London!"

"Yes, and he's not doing well, I'm afraid."

Shocked, David said, "We haven't heard from him in six months. I talked to Mother just before I came to London about perhaps making a trip to North America to try and find him. What's wrong with him? Why hasn't he come to see us?"

"I think he's ashamed and he's bitter, too, David."

"What's happened, Bethany? How did you know about him?"

"Our pastor, Rev. Jennings, does a lot of work with poor people in London slums. He knew about my connection with you and the Wakefields and he came to me last week, telling me he'd encountered your brother. He was very embarrassed, really, for Paul has gone terribly wrong. He drinks constantly and he was drunk when Rev. Jennings saw him. And he's living in some awful place over in Soho, the worst part of London. He's lost all his money, David, and his place with the company. I—went to see him."

"You did?" David blinked with surprise. "That was good of you, Bethany." He put his hand over hers. "And so like you. Tell me about it."

The memory of her visit was not pleasant, for Paul had not been receptive. He had been dirty, suffering from drink, and surly. Carefully Bethany said, "You must go see him, David—but I want to warn you. He's very angry, and he doesn't want to talk to you at all."

"Why not? What have I done?"

Bethany shook her head slowly. She was an intuitive young

woman with considerable insight into human nature and now as she looked into David's face, she thought, *He'll never understand. He's so good himself. He just can't grasp that there are people in the world who are otherwise.* Aloud she said, "You're a success and he's a failure and he's bitter about that."

David bit his lip. "He's always resented my having the title and I've always wished he could've been the heir."

"Be kind to him, David, but then I know you will." She reached into her reticule, pulled out a slip of paper, and handed it to him. "Here's the address. After you see him, come back and tell me how it went."

"I will," David promised, a sadness coming across his face.

He sat there looking down at the teacup for so long that Bethany said, "He'll be all right. He needs love and acceptance and you have so much of that in you."

"Do you really think so?"

"Why, of course, I do," Bethany said, surprised. "You shouldn't even have to ask. Look how you've babied me ever since I was a child. I don't know what I would've done if it hadn't been for you. Especially after Mother died."

David took her hands again. "My sister," he said, his eyes warm. "It's good to have a sister."

Displeased with this comment and aware of the strength of David's hands, Bethany said almost curtly, "I'm not your sister, David!"

Her shortness surprised him. "Of course not, really. But good friends."

"Always the best of friends, David," she said. "Come. You must go to Paul. . . ."

※

"Well, if it's not the Marquis of Wakefield!"

"Hello, Paul. It's good to see you."

"I'll just bet it is! Nothing would please one of the nobility so much as to have a drunken brother return penniless." Paul was sprawled in a chair, a half-emptied bottle of liquor in front of him and his once-expensive suit now dirty. He was unshaven, his hair lank and unwashed, and his eyes were bloodshot. His lips twisted in a sneer as he said, "Sit down, Brother, and have a drink to the House of Wakefield."

Slipping into a chair, David glanced uneasily around the tavern. It was a low-ceilinged and dark affair and the air was filled with smoke and the odor of alcohol and unwashed bodies. The innkeeper watched him steadily from across the room and David, looking over the clientele, thought, *It looks like you could get your throat cut here without any trouble.* Aloud he said, "You've got to come home, Paul."

"Oh? I don't have any home." Paul's voice was slurred. He sloshed some liquor into a cup, drank it down, then shoved the bottle over and said, "Have a drink, Brother."

Ignoring Paul's offer, David plunged in. "Paul, Mother's worried about you. I've been, too. You haven't written for six months. What happened?"

"I've become a roaring success, can't you tell?" Paul touched his frayed cuff with a dainty motion. "Here I am, back after making my fortune in furs."

David sat there, waiting until Paul was done mocking himself. When Paul finally stopped, David asked, "I take it the venture went bad?"

"Bad? It went broke."

"What happened? You were doing so well."

Paul Wakefield looked up at his brother with red-rimmed eyes. He thought of making up some story about how John Jacob Astor had squeezed out the little fellow. This was partially true, but Paul knew he, himself, could have risen in the company. Astor had favored Paul at first but had soured when Paul's heavy drinking

207

had occasioned some bad business judgments. Paul had tried to pull himself out of it, but he had never been the same since Marielle's death and had not been able to control his bouts with the bottle. Frenchy Doucett had pleaded with him, but Paul had not listened. Now as he stared across at his brother, who sat there looking at him calmly, he asked, "Why did you come here?"

"Bethany sent for me."

"Fine-looking woman. I suppose you and she are still as close as ticks on a dog?"

"We're good friends."

"I'll just bet you are good friends," Paul growled, his lips drawing into a white line. Bitterly he said, "Go away, David! Leave me alone!"

"No, I won't do that. You're coming home with me."

"What for? So I can be a kept man? A poor relation?"

"You're a young man. There are so many things you could do. You were always more able than I. We'll find something."

"Why do you care?"

"You're my brother, Paul. . . . We haven't been close, but I want you to come home. Mother needs you and I need you."

David Wakefield's simple words penetrated the haze of drink that had numbed Paul's brain. Throughout the years he had nursed a grudge against David for his easy life, but now he realized, as drunk as he was, that there was truth in what David was saying. However, he did not give up easily. He argued and shook his head stubbornly, but David persevered.

At length David said, "Look, the first thing is to get you out of this place. We'll find you a nice room and get you some new clothes. You haven't been eating right, I can tell, when you're drinking too much. We can change all that."

"Must be nice to have money to rescue drunken bums."

"You're not a drunken bum. You're my brother. Will you do it, Paul? Mother and I want you to come home."

Paul Wakefield had been miserable for some time. He thought of his past and considered the future, which seemed to be hopeless. Then he looked up at David and silence fell between them. At that point, David did not argue; he knew Paul would have to make up his own mind.

At last Paul said, "All right. We'll try it your way."

"Good," David said, rising. "Let's get your things and we'll find a place right away." As the two left the tavern and went to pick up Paul's things, David thought, *I can help him now if he'll just let me.* He had been shocked at Paul's appearance and his mind was already working on how he could help Paul find a new life.

"Come on, Brother," he said. "We have a lot to do."

Paul Wakefield, staggering slightly but held upright by his brother's strong hands, said nothing. He hated to take charity and this, to him, was what David's offer meant. Still, he was lonely, frustrated, and he longed to see his mother again. As the two made their way down the streets of London, he thought, *I'll try it, but if it doesn't work, I won't stay!*

Fourteen

OUT OF THE PAST

P aul! It's so good to see you!"

As his mother hobbled across the floor toward him, her face lit with joy, Paul Wakefield was struck with two emotions. The first was shock, for age and illness had taken their toll on his mother, and then a sharp pang of grief shot through him as he saw the lines on her worn face and knew that some of them—most, to be honest—were his handiwork. She was frail and her shoulders were stooped, but her eyes were bright as he put his arms around her. The other emotion was shame—that he had been such a grief and a burden to one who loved him so much.

"Mother," he whispered hoarsely, holding her carefully, for her bones seemed fragile enough to break with a single hard squeeze. He could say no more, for his throat was tight and as her frail arms went around his neck, he found himself disgusted with his behavior.

Dorcas held him tightly for a moment, then leaned back. "You're so brown," she exclaimed, "and so strong!"

Paul glanced over her head at Caroline and David, who were witnessing the scene. He searched desperately for something to say, then clearing his throat said, "Well, they say an outdoor life is healthy and I've had that for the past few years." He felt her trembling in his grasp and said quickly, "I'm tired. Let's sit down."

Caroline walked to the door and said, "Leah, make some tea and bring some of the new cake that Cook made last night." She returned and sat on the chair alongside David, across from the lounge where Paul sat with his mother. Paul was different, she saw instantly. David had told her little of Paul's failure in business, but now she saw that the years had brought a hardness to him that she had not noted before. He had always been a carefree, happy youngster, although she had seen a difference in his teen years and after David had assumed charge of the Wakefield family. Now, studying Paul in the fine new clothes David had bought him, she saw he was little changed in appearance. *As handsome, muscular, and strong as ever,* she thought. She caught the little things—the way his eyes crinkled when he laughed and how he frequently turned his head to one side to listen to people. *Just like David. Still, there's a difference in him. He went to the devil, I suppose. He was well on his way before he left home.*

When Margaret entered the room, David said, "Paul, this is my wife. Margaret, my brother, of whom you've heard me speak so often."

Margaret gazed at the newcomer for an instant, then nodded. "I'm happy to see you here, sir."

"It's good of you to have me," Paul said. David had not spoken much of his wife and Paul carefully took in his sister-in-law. Although she was a little plump, she was still shapely, attractive, and well-dressed. At that moment, the children burst into the room and David put a hand on each of them, keeping them calm. "And these are our children. This is Andrew—we just call him Andy—and this is Susan. Children, this is your Uncle Paul."

Both children's eyes flew open and Andrew said, "Did you kill any Indians, Uncle Paul?"

"Andy, what an awful thing to say!" Margaret snapped.

Amused, Paul smiled at the boy. "I'll have to tell you some

stories, but I must warn you that I picked up the Yankee habit of telling whoppers."

"Whopper?" asked Susan. Then, without waiting for an answer, she said, "You look like Papa."

"I told you I had a twin," David said. "You'll have to be polite to your uncle now."

"I polite," Susan said with a smile as she noted the grin on her father's face.

"We'll have a special supper tonight to celebrate your home-coming, Paul."

Indeed, it *was* a special supper. Caroline and the cook came up with a fine meal consisting of roasted venison with a sugared and spiced wine syrup, potted fish, roasted turkey with bread sauce and onions, spinach with cream and butter, cheddar cheese, and a bread-and-butter pudding baked with beaten eggs, currants, and nutmeg.

All afternoon, which Paul spent primarily with his mother, the children pestered their father with questions about the wild Indians. David put them off by saying, "You'll just have to ask your uncle." The meal that night was better than anything Paul had had for years and he complimented Margaret on her table. "A fine dinner, indeed, ma'am."

Margaret shot a glance at Caroline but accepted the praise. "We try to do the best we can," she said. "I understand you've done well in your profession in America."

A flush colored Paul's cheeks. "For a few years it was profitable, but the fur trade will be going downhill now. Animals get trapped out and there's trouble with the Indians. I think the only people who make any money will be John Jacob Astor and a few of the bigwigs."

The supper went on well after that, but Paul observed the lack of affection between David and Margaret. After supper was over and he had spent some time in the parlor with David and the children, he began to find out more about David and Margaret's unhappy marriage, without being obvious. He thought, *There's some kind of a wall between him and his wife.*

After the children went to bed, the two men sat up talking. David spoke of several possibilities in the business world that might be good for Paul. Paul sat back in his chair, drinking a cup of tea, and finally asked, "What about your writing? Are you still at it?"

Paul knew he had touched on a sore spot when David hesitantly said, "I don't have much time for that anymore."

"Doesn't Margaret admire a man of letters?"

David shifted uncomfortably. "Actually, she doesn't. She's not a woman who reads a great deal and she thinks most of my scribblings are worthless. She's probably right."

By the time Paul went to bed, he had spoken enough to his mother, his Aunt Caroline, David, and Margaret, so that he had pretty well figured out how things went in Wakefield Manor.

As he stood at his bedroom window later that night, looking out at the quarter moon that was high in the sky, he murmured, "So David's got himself married to a woman he doesn't love and one who hates writing. That's all he ever wanted to do and now he'll probably never do it again." Turning from the window he slipped into the bed and lay there with his fingers locked behind his head, thinking about the Wakefields. "We're both pretty unhappy fellows," he whispered to the ceiling. "And there's nothing much either one of us can do about it."

***

Bethany came two days after Paul's arrival and everyone was glad to see her—except Margaret. Paul noticed that Bethany loved the children and that they adored her. One day Paul found her alone on the garden path, walking in the snappy breeze. She was wearing a long, hunter green cloak and her face was framed by a fur cap. He looked at the cap and said, "You know, I might have trapped that varmint myself."

"Really? Tell me about it, Paul."

The two strolled slowly, bundled up against the cold, and Paul opened up somewhat to reveal the details of his life in America.

Finally, Bethany asked gently, "Did you never marry, Paul?"

"Yes, I married."

His tone was clipped and almost harsh. Bethany knew immediately there was a tragedy involved. "I didn't mean to pry," she said quietly.

"It's all right. She's dead."

Bethany, seeing the door closed on that subject, changed to another. "The children are wonderful, aren't they? Both of them are so bright and attractive."

Paul grinned. "Susan's like you. Bossy. She bosses David around just as you did when you were a child."

Bethany laughed. "I know. I was so awful, wasn't I? I always had to have his attention."

"I don't imagine that will work anymore. His wife wouldn't like it." Paul watched Bethany's face and saw her expression change. "Now *I'm* prying," he said. "She's very jealous when it comes to matters involving David, isn't she?"

Startled, Bethany looked at the face so much like David's and agreed. "You're very quick. Yes, she's jealous of any woman and it's so ridiculous. David's been completely faithful to her."

"Yes, he'd be that all right." Finally Paul said, "So, are you still in love with him?" He had intended to shock the young woman and he succeeded. Her eyes flew open and she stared at him, her face flushing a delicate pink. He shrugged. "You always were, Bethany. Even when you were twelve or thirteen years old."

"It's—not like that, Paul."

"Oh, I'm sure it's all quite innocent," he said. "I've always rather envied David. Your affection for him. He earned it. He paid attention to you when nobody else did." Abruptly, he took her arm and squeezed it impetuously. "What about you? You're how old now? Twenty-one?"

"I'm twenty-two."

"Old enough to be married. Why aren't you?"

Bethany was flustered and very much aware of his strong grip. "Turn me loose, Paul," she said. When he released her, she turned away from him toward the west, where the sun was going down. "I've never fallen in love with anyone." Getting control of herself, she turned around and forced a smile. Although she was not aware of it, she made an attractive picture as she stood there, her lips soft and her skin alabaster in the dying light. "I've never found a man who suited me. Maybe I never will. I'll be a spinster. An old maid."

"What a waste," Paul said as they continued their stroll then headed back for the house.

"You must never say anything like this to David. It would hurt him terribly."

"Say what?" Paul demanded.

"That I'm—in love with him. I'm not, you know. I'm like a sister to him."

"All right," he said. "No reason I should." She saw he understood how things were with her, but the two said no more about it.

Over the next few days Paul became reacquainted with Wakefield. He rode over the fields, almost always alone, although David went from time to time. Bethany had gone back to London and he tried to make up to his mother by spending long hours with her in the evening. He found Margaret to be pleasant enough, but there was an undercurrent of sharpness that usually vented itself on David.

When a letter came from Frenchy Doucett asking Paul to come back to America to go into the shipping business around

Boston, Paul shook his head, knowing there was nothing for him in America. Since Frenchy himself indicated it would be a risky venture with no big profits in sight, Paul wrote back at once, thanking him but saying he would not be coming back to that country.

During the following weeks he went to London. He looked into several business ventures that David suggested, but nothing piqued his interest. Now that the newness of his return was over, he began to slip into his old ways, drinking more than he should. When David rebuked him for it once, he said, "Why don't you speak to your wife? She's the one you should be worrying about. You know she drinks, don't you?"

David had not been able to answer. He had dropped his head and had not spoken of the matter to Paul again.

Dorcas and Caroline talked often of Paul's future, but Paul himself refused to say anything specific about it. As the days passed, he grew more withdrawn and finally one evening Dorcas said, "What's wrong, Paul? You seem so unhappy."

"Why shouldn't I be, Mother?" Paul was standing at the mantel looking pensive and now he turned to face her. "I've come back home and there's nothing here for me."

"That's not true!" Dorcas protested. "This is your home and you can have anything you want."

"Could I be the Marquis of Wakefield? No!"

"Paul, are you still upset about that? It's been so many years."

"Yes, and nothing has changed. David has everything and I have nothing."

For a long time Dorcas pleaded with Paul to see how much potential his life had, but Paul had fallen into one of the moods that had taken him of late. He refused to argue with his mother and left the house. The next morning he told David in a rather surly fashion, "I've had enough of being a poor relation. I'm going to London. I'll look around there and find a venture."

"Let me help you, Paul," David said. "Here. Come, you'll need money."

"I've got enough!" Paul snapped. Actually he did not, but it grated on his nerves having to take "charity" from his brother. "Don't worry about me. I'll be all right. I'll make my own way."

"You don't have to," David said quietly.

"Yes, I do."

Paul left the next morning for London and, after finding a room, began to pick up his old ways. He spent long hours drinking and managed to pass out each night. Several times he tried to put off his depressing mood, but it only grew worse. Once he got a note from Bethany, asking him to come and see her, but he tore it up and threw it away. "Nothing in that," he muttered. "She's in love with David, he's married, and I'm a poor relation. We've all got our problems."

By his third week in London, he was out of money. His landlord insisted on being paid or he would throw Paul out. As Paul miserably walked the streets of the great city, he even thought of doing away with himself. But he pushed the suggestion away, for he was, if nothing else, not a quitter. Upon returning to his room, he found a note slipped under the door.

Picking it up without interest, he thought, *It must be from David, trying to reform me again.* But when he looked at the writing, he saw that it was a woman's handwriting. He had met several women in London, some not of the best morals, and changed his assumption. He opened the note and glanced down at the signature. "Mrs. Irene Lesley," he read aloud. "I don't know any Mrs. Lesley." The note itself was brief, saying, "If you will come to see me at 120 Hartley Lane, you will hear something that may be to your advantage."

Paul shrugged and tossed the note to one side, intending to ignore it. The next day, however, when the landlord insisted he leave, he packed his things and left. He found a poor room and looked around with distaste. Without volition, he thought of the warm, comfortable, luxurious rooms at Wakefield and this angered him still more. "He's there in all that and this is what I've got," he said angrily, flinging his clothes into a wardrobe. He reached into his pockets to see how much money he had and brought out a thin purse—and the note from Mrs. Lesley. Reading it again, he paused. "What can I lose? Maybe she's a rich heiress who's looking for a man. I guess I could do that. I've done worse." He left the room and, having little money, walked to Hartley Lane. It was not a street where wealthy heiresses lived, he saw, but it was still respectable. It was an old section of London that had once been rather elite but now was chopped up into small houses and boardinghouses.

Finding number 120, a cottage wedged in between two larger houses, he knocked on the door. It opened after a long wait and a woman of the lower class said, "What is it?"

"My name is Wakefield. I have a note here from Mrs. Lesley."

"You'll have to wait," the woman replied and closed the door. Paul stood outside feeling foolish, watching water sellers haul water to the houses that had no wells and men collect night soil. There was an air of genteel poverty over the whole scene. When the door opened again, he turned back to face the woman. "You can come in now."

Because the few windows were covered, the cottage Paul entered was dark and gloomy. The ceiling was so low that he had to duck once to keep from hitting his head on one of the exposed beams. He followed the woman down the short halls until she gestured toward the left and said, "Here he is, ma'am."

Paul looked inside the room, which was filled with mementos and pictures and jammed with furniture. An elderly woman sat on a couch, directly in front of the glowing fire. She looked at him without speaking for a moment, then said in a voice thin with age, "Come in, Mr. Wakefield."

As Paul stepped inside the musty room, three cats eyed him from various positions. All were fat and had luminescent green eyes. As with all cats kept closely confined, they left their odor and the room was stifling. Instead of taking the seat across from the woman, Paul said, "I got your note, Mrs. Lesley. What can I do for you?"

"Nothing." The elderly woman was wearing a long black gown that reached the floor. She was at least eighty, Paul guessed, and age had wrinkled her face and turned her hair white. Her hands were gnarled as she clasped them before her and there was a glint of baleful intelligence in her dark eyes. "Sit down. You'll have time for an old woman."

Against his will, Paul sat down. One of the cats, a striped one with an *M* on his forehead, hissed at him, got up, and moved farther away.

"Miss Dewberry doesn't like you," the old woman said. "But she doesn't like anyone."

Paul shrugged, for he was not a cat lover. "I really haven't much time, Mrs. Lesley," he said shortly. "If you'd just tell me what you want. I can't imagine what business we have."

The old woman looked at him and pulled her shawl more closely about her, although it was hot in the room from the blazing fire. "What have you been doing? It's been a long, long time since I saw you."

"I don't remember our acquaintance."

"You were only four the last time you saw me." The old woman laughed, the sound grating on Paul's nerves. "You don't remember me, of course, but I remember you well."

Paul started to rise. "I really am—"

"Sit down! I told you you'd hear something to your advantage."

Something in the old woman's tone and the glint of her eyes stopped Paul. Searching his memory, he murmured, "Lesley . . .

Mrs. Lesley . . ." Suddenly his eyes widened. "You were a house-keeper for my parents. I don't remember you, but I remember them talking about you."

"Yes, they did talk about me, I venture," Mrs. Lesley said, a cruelty and malevolence in her voice that Paul could not miss.

"If you've called me to ask for money, Mrs. Lesley," he said, "you've asked the wrong one. You need to go to my brother, David."

The old woman leaned forward and the firelight threw its glow across her face, etching the lines that years had left. She had sharp features and her eyes were fixed on him as she whispered, "Are you short of money?"

"I don't have a farthing," he said. "You'll have to see my brother."

Paul rose to leave, but the old woman said, "You have more than you know, Paul Wakefield."

The woman's words sounded an alarm in Paul. He turned suddenly and came to stand over her. "What are you talking about?" he demanded. "I don't have any money!"

"You have all of Wakefield. It's all yours."

"Mine? You've lost your mind, Mrs. Lesley. It all belongs to my brother, David!" With bitterness in his voice, he once again began to leave.

"Let me tell you about the day you were born."

"Why should I want to hear about that?"

"It will be—to your *advantage.*" Mrs. Lesley leaned back in her chair. "How did your brother get to be the Marquis of Wake-field?"

"By being born a few minutes before I was," Paul answered. "You know that, of course."

"Please, sit down. I have been kept informed of your comings and goings. I still have a few friends left at Wakefield. I'm going to tell you about your brother and about yourself. Something that will be to your *advantage.*" As the old woman pronounced the word *advantage* again, her eyes glittered with an unholy humor.

Paul, caught by the drama of it, said curiously, "All right. Go ahead and tell me about this 'advantage' of mine that you talk so freely of."

"Now you're showing judgment," Mrs. Lesley said, and she clasped her gnarled hands together in a sort of ecstasy. "Let me go back and tell you what it was like."

She began to speak and Paul listened. Before she had spoken very long, he realized this old woman had a well of bitterness inside that made his look small. She had been ruler of the rectory before Paul's father, Rev. Andrew Wakefield, and his bride, Dorcas, had come to the church. Mrs. Lesley had ruled the previous minister and his wife with an iron hand. He had been a weak man of feeble will and had allowed her to make every decision. As Paul listened, he could practically feel the malice drip as Mrs. Lesley told how she had been displaced after his father and mother had come.

"Oh, they would have their way! I had no authority at all," Mrs. Lesley said venomously. "It was my place that they took and I hated them for it!"

"They never spoke of you unkindly," Paul offered.

"Oh, they could talk well, but they shoved me out. I was going to spend the rest of my days there with Rev. Milton, but when he left and they moved in, I was left at their mercy. Oh, they had none!"

Paul knew at once this woman's mind was warped, for his parents were incapable of unkindness to anyone. But, knowing this woman was not ready to hear that, he said, "I'm sorry to find you still bitter over something that happened so long ago. But there's nothing to be done for it."

"Just a minute. You haven't heard about your advantage," Mrs. Lesley said. When she saw him pause, she said, "They thought they had their way with me, but I put it on them. Oh, yes, indeed! And nobody knows but me!"

"Knows what?" Paul asked impatiently. The room was so hot he was perspiring freely and he wiped his forehead with a handkerchief. "I really must go, Mrs. Lesley."

"Not until you hear about how I got back at them." The old woman leaned forward again, holding the edge of her chair. "The day you were born, the regular doctor was gone and a new one came. Your mother was in a bad way. I was there all the time with Dr. Callendar."

"All right, I suppose I owe you some thanks for that."

"I can tell you something about yourself," the old woman continued. "You have a birthmark on your left shoulder shaped like a clover, don't you?"

"Yes, I do."

The old woman fastened onto Paul's wrist with her clawlike hand. "Here's what you don't know! I was standing there when both babies came into the world and I tell you this. . . ." She laughed deep in her chest. "The baby with the blue birthmark like a clover—was born first!"

The impact of Mrs. Lesley's statement did not strike Paul for a moment, then he whispered fiercely, grabbing her shoulders, "What are you saying?"

"I'm saying that *you*—not your brother—are the true Marquis of Wakefield! Your brother was born a few minutes later. That few minutes is what kept you from all the riches of Wakefield."

"You're lying," Paul said. "Dr. Callendar—"

"He left right after you and your brother were born," Mrs. Lesley answered. "Your mother didn't know which one of you was born first, so your father asked me. After the way they had treated me, I knew I'd found a way to get my revenge. So I lied. I told them that the baby without the birthmark was born first. That showed them, didn't it?"

Paul Wakefield was not a man of unsteady nerves, but his hands began to tremble. He released the old woman's thin shoulders and sat down abruptly. His head swam and he tried to think clearly. *If she's telling the truth,* he thought, *Wakefield is mine and David is on the outside as I've always been.* Aloud he said, "Why should I believe you?"

"Why should you not? If I'm telling the truth, it makes a difference to you, doesn't it, Mr. Wakefield?"

Paul saw that despite the woman's age and weakness, her mind was keen. He began to question her, trying to trip her in her story, but he failed. She told the same story again and again. The only twisted thing in her, he realized, was her hatred for his parents and the way she had taken her revenge.

"How did you think this would hurt my parents?" he asked. "It's hurt me but not them."

"Didn't it? Now they're going to find out the wrong son has been enjoying all the benefits of the Wakefield family and you've been cheated out of it. If you're the man I think you are, you won't let that stand."

"How do you know about me? How did you get my name?" Paul demanded.

"There's a preacher who comes by, and a young woman."

"Is her name Bethany Morgan?" Paul demanded instantly.

"That's the name! You know her, of course. She brought her preacher by, and he began to tell me about a young man named Wakefield who was going to the devil. I lost track of you for years but found you again. And now, you can claim what's yours!"

"What are you talking about?"

"I'm talking about who you are. You're the Marquis of Wakefield . . . the master. You were born first. I'll swear to that in a court of law and the law will have its way. Your brother will have to step aside and you will be the master and have all that goes with the estate." She lowered her voice to a whine. "You won't forget Irene

Lesley, who brought you all this, will you?" Her eyes grew cat thin. "Oh, I'll see to it that you don't! Before I swear in court, we'll have an agreement, you and me. And I'll be taken care of."

Paul stood to his feet, his knees strangely weak. "I must think about this," he said quietly, making his way to the door.

The old woman's voice followed him. "The Marquis of Wakefield. That's who you'll be. Oh, you'll be back! The preacher told me what a prodigal you were and the young woman did too. Now you'll have a chance to get what's rightfully yours!"

Paul Wakefield whirled, leaving the house. He walked the streets of London for hours, going over and over the conversation he had just had with Irene Lesley.

"She's crazy!" he muttered. "But the clarity of her story seemed to be solid. If she'll swear in court that I was born first, then she's right. I'll be the heir of Wakefield—Sir Paul Wakefield instead of a nobody!"

That night he lay down on the bed without taking off his clothes, his mind swimming with the potential that lay before him. At last he got up to undress. "Tomorrow," he whispered aloud, "we'll see more about who is the rightful heir of Wakefield."

<hr />

Mr. Hartley Small was a tall man, powerfully built, with black eyes and hair. As a lawyer, he never believed what anyone said—only what could be proved. This skepticism had served him well. When the young man had come into his office without an appointment, Small, having a free moment, had agreed to listen to him. Now Small leaned back in his chair and clasped his powerful hands together. "A very remarkable story, Mr. Wakefield."

Paul, who had not slept more than an hour, nervously waited for the lawyer to continue, but Small said nothing. Finally Paul asked, "But what does it mean, Mr. Small? If Mrs. Lesley's telling the truth, what would that mean?"

"According to English law, the firstborn—the eldest son—is the heir to the title, lands, and estates of a nobleman."

"Even if it's only a few minutes?"

"That would make no difference. Your brother has held the title for several years, has he not, on the basis of that few minutes?"

"But will Mrs. Lesley's statement hold up in a court of law?"

"Oh, it's too premature for me to make a judgment," Small said. "You have no money?"

"None of my own, but I will have if I become Sir Paul Wakefield."

"Yes, that's true enough." The lawyer smiled, pleased. He loved dramatic cases and this one, he realized, would be as dramatic as any that had touched England in some time. He saw himself pleading the case, swaying the jury, the judge, and finally said, "The title and the estate are yours if you can prove it."

"I think we can, Mr. Small."

After spending an hour with the lawyer, Paul left the office and began to drink. But the more he drank, the more his conscience began to smart. He thought of David and when the memories of his many kindnesses came, he tried to drown them in more drink.

"He's had it all for years," he muttered into his glass. "Now it's my turn!"

F i f t e e n

THE TRIAL

Angus McDowell stood impatiently in the foyer, waiting for Ives to announce him to the family. As he shifted his weight nervously from one foot to the other, he made unintelligible comments under his breath, his habit when he was distressed. Then he said aloud, "I wish I were a younger man. I'm too old for things like this." He looked around the ornate foyer and the expensive accessories—the red silk chairs, cut glass chandelier, gilt carved looking glass with silver candleholders on each side—and his eyes narrowed. He clamped his lips together, wishing fervently he were any place on earth except at Wakefield Manor.

"Why, Angus—" David came to meet him, surprise in his eyes—"we weren't expecting you. Why didn't you send word? I would've come to London if it was important."

"It's too important for London," Angus said dourly. He shook the hand that David offered, then said, "I'm thinking ye'd best call the family together."

"Call the family?" David Wakefield was accustomed to Angus McDowell's rather strange ways, but this was something new. McDowell had been at Wakefield many times on "social occasions," which generally turned out to be lectures on how to conduct business. Never, had he appeared unannounced and there

227

was a harried look in the Scotsman's eyes that alarmed David. "That sounds ominous."

McDowell shook his head. "There's no sense talking aboot it to ye once and then saying the same thing again. Call the family."

"Very well, Angus. Come along. I think most of them are in the parlor."

Ten minutes later, after assigning the children to the care of the servants, the family sat together, looking at McDowell curiously. Margaret said impatiently, "What in the world is the matter? Can't you do your business in London?"

"Not this time, I'm afraid, Lady Wakefield," McDowell said in clipped tones.

"What's wrong, Mr. McDowell?" Dorcas asked. She liked the solicitor very much and the two had become as well acquainted as their brief visits would permit. Now she tried to soothe over Margaret's abrupt manner. "Won't you sit down?"

"I'll stand if ye don't mind," Angus said firmly. He looked around the room at Lady Caroline Wakefield and remembered her husband, George, with a brief and poignant burst of sadness. He had admired that man more than he admired most and he wished that he had better news for his widow. He had less patience with David's wife, Margaret. He had opposed the marriage but had kept his opinions to himself. He was aware of David's unhappiness and the tense relationship that existed between the two. Oftentimes he had protested to David about the exorbitant sums that Margaret spent on clothes and jewelry, but to no avail. David seemed incapable of checking her.

Now, looking at David, McDowell said, "I have unexpected news."

"And not good news. What is it?" David asked. "Has something happened to Paul?"

"Ye might say that, although as far as I know, he's healthy. Too healthy I might say."

"What's that supposed to mean?" Dorcas demanded. "How can anyone be too healthy?"

"Mrs. Wakefield, I have some news that will bring pain to ye. To all of ye, I'm sure. And it gives me no pleasure to bring it."

"For heaven's sake, Mr. McDowell! What's wrong?" Caroline cried. "It can't be as bad as all that."

"I'm afraid it's worse than you can think." McDowell drew a deep breath. "A suit has been filed in chancellery against ye, David."

"Against me? By whom?"

"By your brother, Paul."

"On what charge?" David asked in amazement.

Angus took out his handkerchief and mopped his brow. "I'm still shocked over this. The papers came to me directly from the court. I went to see your brother, but he refused to see me. I was referred to Mr. Hartley Small, his attorney, and we had quite a session of it."

"What is Paul bringing a suit against David for? What's the charge?" Dorcas asked almost hysterically.

"Do ye recall a woman named Irene Lesley?" he asked, his eyes fixed on Dorcas.

"Mrs. Lesley? Of course I do. She was the housekeeper at the first church where Andrew and I went after we were married. We haven't seen her for years though."

"Was your relationship with Mrs. Lesley happy, Mrs. Wakefield?"

The question seemed to confuse Dorcas. She studied the patterns in the carpet and did not answer for so long that the silence grew almost painful. They were all watching her and finally she lifted her head and met McDowell's gaze. "No, I would not say it was happy. She was very attached to the minister who had been at the church before my husband took over as pastor. She was a very domineering woman and we had quite a clash before I was able to get her to remember her place."

"Would ye say she was a malevolent woman?"

229

"I—think she might be capable of it. We were unable to keep her after we left the large church in London and I never saw her again after that."

McDowell digested all these facts and then asked swiftly, "She was present during the birth of your sons, David and Paul?"

"Yes, she was. What's all this about, Mr. McDowell?"

McDowell took a deep breath and expelled it. "I'll just have to give you the charges, which I know will come as a terrible shock, especially to you, David." He eyed the young man who was sitting beside Margaret, his eyes fixed carefully on the solicitor. "It seems that Paul claims he is the rightful heir to the title and estate of Wakefield."

"What—why, that's impossible!" Caroline exclaimed.

Almost simultaneously Margaret jumped up, her eyes flashing. "What nonsense! What is he thinking about to suggest such a thing?"

David rose and went to his mother, whose hand had gone to her breast in an agitated motion. He knelt beside her where she sat and put his arm around her. "Don't be upset, Mother." Looking up at Angus, he asked, "What evidence does he bring? Does it have to do with Mrs. Lesley?"

"Aye, that it does. Mrs. Lesley is prepared to testify that the child with the clover-shaped birthmark was born a few minutes before the other."

A silence, deep and profound, descended like a blanket so that the monotonous ticking of the clock seemed to fill the room. It was Dorcas who cried, "That can't be true! It can't be!"

"As I understand it, from what Mother's told me," David said slowly, "Mrs. Lesley assisted in the birth." He turned to Dorcas then. "Did you ask her which child was born first?"

"Andrew did and she said the firstborn was the one without the birthmark."

Angus McDowell stood there quietly as the babble of talk went on. Margaret grew hysterical, for she saw at once what this would mean. She began to cry, whereupon David left his mother and went over to put his arm around her. "Now, don't take it so, Margaret. We'll sort it all out."

"Sort it all out! We'll be paupers! We'll be thrown out, he'll be Sir Paul Wakefield, and you'll be nobody!"

"He'll never be a nobody!" Caroline said at once. "This sounds like something out of a very bad novel."

"Aye, madam. That it does," Angus McDowell responded. "But after listening to Mr. Hartley Small, who would not take a case unless there were some meat in it, I'm fearful you may be in for trouble."

"What are the chances of his proving his case?" David asked, holding the pale and sobbing Margaret.

"It depends on whether her testimony can be shaken."

"If she's telling the truth, then Paul is the rightful heir to the family name," David said slowly.

Dorcas looked up at him quickly. She understood at once what this would mean if Paul proved his case. Fear arose then, for she knew that Paul was not the man of honor David was. "We'll have to talk to Paul. Some arrangement can be made."

"That's right, Mother. I'll go to London. It surely won't come to court."

Angus McDowell said nothing, but he remembered the sly look in the eyes of Hartley Small. He knew the man to be a crafty lawyer, rarely taking a case unless he was convinced he could win it. Now as the family sought to comfort Margaret, who seemed to be falling completely to pieces, he thought, *It's a sad day and I fear what will happen to this family. Paul Wakefield would not be an easy man if he were the real master—the true Marquis of Wakefield.*

⁂

The charges of Paul Wakefield could not be kept silent and, indeed, Hartley Small saw to it that the newspapers grasped it.

Any scandal involving a member of the nobility was grist for the mills of the gossipmongers and newspapers of the day. On May the twentieth, 1772, when David arrived in London for the trial along with his mother and Margaret, most people who read the papers were aware that a struggle was about to take place between two young men. The fact that they were identical twins made the mystery of the case even more delectable.

David delivered his mother and Margaret to a set of rooms and then left them to try to find Paul. He was completely unsuccessful, for he had no idea of his brother's whereabouts. When he went to Hartley Small's law offices, he was told by a clerk that Mr. Small would not see him. "But I need to speak with my brother," David protested.

"I'm sorry. We cannot help you," the clerk said, having been instructed to say as much. When David left, he turned to his fellow clerk and said with a smirk, "Sir David Wakefield, but he'll be Dave Wakefield before too long."

After exhausting every attempt to find Paul, David went to see Bethany, hoping she had heard from him. He gained admittance to the house and the two greeted each other briefly in the same parlor where she had entertained him before. Then David asked, "Have you seen Paul recently?"

"No, but of course I've heard all about the trial." Bethany's eyes were large with compassion. "I can't believe he's doing this."

"And you have no idea where he is?"

"No. I sent him a note, but he's moved from his old lodgings."

David sat quietly, holding his hands together and thinking hard. The strain had worn on him, for Margaret had refused to accept the situation. She had drunk so much that he had finally had to assert himself and remove liquor from her grasp. He was aware, however, that not all of the servants were honorable and that she always managed to find whiskey by bribing one of them. She had made life miserable for him and the children, warning them that they would be thrown out on the streets without a farthing to their name. She had frightened the children so badly that David had put them in Caroline's charge and insisted they stay home although they had begged to come. As young as they were, they had been able to pick up on what was happening and it had nearly broken David's heart when Andy had whispered, "Uncle Paul won't throw us out, will he, Papa?"

"Of course not," David had promised. But now as he sat beside Bethany, he said, "It's difficult. Margaret is distraught and the children are upset."

"Do you really think—" Bethany started to speak and then shook her head in self-reproach. Instead she said, "It's difficult, but God is still on the throne, David. I know that sounds trite and easy, but it's true enough."

"I know it is." He looked up at her and managed a wan smile. "It's only money and it will all burn someday, as Rev. Wesley says so often."

"I'm sorry for your family and for you," Bethany said sympathetically and spent the rest of their visit trying to encourage him.

When David finally rose to leave, he kissed her hand and said, "You're a comfort, but I must go now."

After he left, Bethany stood for a long time in the parlor, thinking of the strange case of Paul and David Wakefield. Then she went to her room, fell on her knees, and began to pray for the family she loved so much.

⁂

The courtroom was packed as David escorted his wife and mother into the section reserved for them. He seated them near the front, then went to a table where McDowell sat and took the chair that the solicitor pulled back. Sitting beside McDowell was a barrister hired to defend the case, for solicitors were not allowed to serve as legal counsel in open court.

His name was Elijah Jenkins, and he was, by all reports, a good lawyer.

Jenkins leaned over and whispered, "Your brother has not appeared yet. How do you feel?"

David looked at Jenkins, a short man with brown hair and inoffensive brown eyes. He did not look like a lawyer who could be fierce, but David understood from Angus that the man's looks were deceiving. "I'm fine, Mr. Jenkins," David said. He had no sooner spoken when there was a small stir and he looked up to see Paul enter the courtroom accompanied by Hartley Small.

Paul caught David's glance for a moment and his fine mouth tightened. Then he sat down, keeping his gaze directed at the table and the papers that Small pushed in front of him.

Grieved, David thought, *Surely, if we could have talked, we could have straightened it all out. I know Paul has been jealous of my position, but I didn't think he would do a thing like this.*

The trial itself went amazingly fast. The court reporters who were taking notes in shorthand were prepared for a drawn-out affair, but there was little nonsense about Carter, the judge. He was known to move cases quickly and when he had seated himself, he pushed his wig to one side in an irritated motion and said, "You are for the Crown, Mr. Small?"

"I am, my lord."

"And you are serving the defendant, Mr. Jenkins?"

"Yes, my lord."

"Then we will hear, first of all, the case, and I urge you gentlemen to be brief. There are many cases on the docket and we will not waste time."

Hartley Small stood and said smoothly, "The case will not take much time, my lord. It is a very simple matter."

The judge looked down and said sternly, "I will decide the simplicity or complexity of the case, Mr. Small. You merely present the facts without comment."

"Very good, my lord."

Hartley Small was an excellent speaker. He launched into the case, beginning with his first visit with Paul Wakefield. He said in closing, "A great injustice has been done, but the law has a way of righting injustices. We will prove that the present holder of the title of Marquis of Wakefield is not the legal nor rightful owner of said title. We will also prove that my client, Mr. Paul Wakefield, is by all law and by all legal manners, Sir Paul Wakefield, Marquis of Wakefield."

A stir went over the court. The reporters scribbled furiously and Dorcas stared at her son, Paul, with grief in her eyes. "Why did he have to do this?" she murmured to herself. "However it turns out, my sons are forever separated."

Small, knowing the limited patience of the chief justice, said instantly, "I know this is a serious charge, my lord and members of the jury, so I will present the proof of my client's identity. I call Mrs. Irene Lesley to the stand."

"Mrs. Irene Lesley!"

As the bailiff called the name, a door opened, and Mrs. Lesley came in, leaning heavily on a cane. She was wearing a new black dress and her hair was carefully fixed. She accepted the aid of the bailiff, who assisted her into the dock and swore her in.

"Mrs. Lesley, would you give the court an account of your life insomuch as it bears on the family of Wakefield."

"Yes," Irene Lesley said. She made a good witness as she stood there. Her age did not show so much and she seemed strong and her mind clear. She explained the circumstances under which she had met the Wakefields, and finally Mr. Small said, "So you were a housekeeper at the rectory under the previous minister and then when Andrew Wakefield and his wife, Dorcas, came, you served in that capacity?"

"Yes, sir. That is true."

"Were you happy working under them?"

"No, I was not."

Hartley appeared to be surprised. "You were not happy? May I ask why not, madam?"

"Mrs. Wakefield was a hard mistress. Nothing satisfied her. I finally had to leave because she was so difficult to get along with."

Hartley Small played on this for some time and then said, "You had not left the household when the twins were born to the Wakefields."

"No, I had not, sir."

"Were you active in helping the doctor?"

"Yes, I was in the room all the time with Mrs. Wakefield. The doctor left once, but I stayed the whole time."

"You realize that you are under oath?"

"Yes, sir, I do."

"Then I put the question to you. Were there any differences between the two boys?"

"One of them had a birthmark on his left shoulder blade that was shaped like a four-leaf clover. I've never seen the like of it before."

"Ah, yes—a birthmark." He let silence reign for a moment, then asked, "Mrs. Lesley, which child was born first? The one with or without the birthmark?"

"The one with the birthmark!" Mrs. Lesley said, casting a vengeful look at Dorcas. Seeming to enjoy Dorcas's suffering, she repeated loudly, "The one with the birthmark! He was born first."

"Thank you, Mrs. Lesley."

"My lord, I have here a doctor's statement that gives clear evidence, stating plainly that my client, Mr. Paul Wakefield, has a birthmark such as described by Mrs. Lesley. He is, therefore, the firstborn and as a result, under English law, he is the true Marquis of Wakefield."

Pandemonium erupted across the court. Reporters scribbled

even more rapidly and the murmuring of the spectators brought a rebuke from the judge. "Silence in the court!" he called loudly, banging with his gavel. He waited until quiet reigned and then looked at Hartley Small. "That is your case?"

"That is part of it, my lord. But my learned colleague will want to examine Mrs. Lesley."

Elijah Jenkins rose at once. He took his position and said smoothly, "Mrs. Lesley, was there anyone else in the room besides you and the doctor when the children were born?"

"No, sir! There was not!" Mrs. Lesley was defensive. She stared at Jenkins with glittering eyes, as wary as a fox avoiding a trap.

"The doctor and yourself then were the only ones who knew which child was born first."

"That's correct!"

"But the doctor left very early, I understand, Mrs. Lesley, so that after he left you were the only one."

"Yes."

"And Mr. or Mrs. Wakefield, did they ever ask you which child was born first?"

Mrs. Lesley stared at the floor. "Yes, Mr. Wakefield asked me."

"And what did you tell him?"

"I told him which one was born first."

"Would you repeat your own words, as well as you can remember?"

Hartley Small's voice shook the court. "I object, my lord! That's a long time for a woman to remember."

"But, my lord," Elijah Jenkins said gently, "the whole case is built upon this woman's testimony. If she cannot remember what she said, how could her memory be trusted for anything else?"

"Objection overruled! You will answer the question, Mrs. Lesley."

Mrs. Lesley looked up and said clearly, "I told her the one without the birthmark was born first."

Again the crowd stirred and Jenkins said, "The one *without* the birthmark. But now you come to this court and swear under oath that the child *with* the birthmark was born first? How do you explain that?"

"I lied! I didn't tell the truth."

Jenkins's voice swelled. "You *lied?* Are you aware that one who lies is a liar?!" He waited for Mrs. Lesley to reply, then said, "Why did you lie?"

"Because they treated me shamefully!"

"So you decided to get your revenge?" Jenkins said, eyeing her like a hungry shark. "So now you come to this courtroom saying that you lied? Mrs. Lesley, you've taken an oath that you are now telling the truth. The question is, did you lie then when Mrs. Wakefield asked you or are you lying to this court now?"

"It's the truth! The child with the birthmark was born first!"

"Are you aware of the penalties for lying under oath?"

For some time Jenkins continued to hammer at the witness. Finally Hartley Small said, "He is badgering the witness, my lord. Mrs. Lesley has sworn to what she saw. That should be enough for my colleague, as it should be enough for the jury."

Jenkins waved his hand, saying, "Oh, I think the chief justice knows how much weight to put on Mrs. Lesley's testimony. No more questions."

Sitting down he whispered, "They lost. The jury will never bring a verdict in their favor on that woman's testimony."

However, Hartley Small said, "I call to the stand Dr. Howard Callendar."

Jenkins flinched. "I didn't know that doctor was still living."

"I thought he had died," Angus said. "That was the report I got." He looked stunned as a short, portly man came out of the waiting room and was sworn in by the bailiff. "If he bears her story out, we're lost, Jenkins."

"Dr. Callendar," Small said firmly, "you were in attendance on Mrs. Dorcas Wakefield at the birth of twins in the year 1741."

"That is correct, sir." Callendar was in his seventies now and his figure had thickened, but his brown eyes were still sharp. Although Dorcas had seen him only that one time, thirty-one years ago, she recognized him instantly. Her heart sank, for she knew that he would not be here if he were not prepared to testify for Paul.

"You were the family physician for the Wakefields thirty-one years ago?"

"No, sir, I was not. Dr. Barnabas Brown was their physician, I believe."

"Then why were you, Dr. Callendar, attending during the birth of the twins?"

"Dr. Brown was called away. I, myself, was on my way out of the country at the time, but I stepped in to do what I could at Dr. Brown's request."

"I see. And so you can testify to this court that you brought the two babies, Paul and David Wakefield, into the world?"

"Yes, sir."

"Was there anything unusual in the birth of the babies?"

"It was a hard birth," Callendar said. "Her first children, but all went well."

"Did you have help in this particular birth?"

"Yes. The housekeeper was there. She assisted me since I had no help of my own to bring."

"Mrs. Irene Lesley?"

"Yes, that was her name."

Smiling contentedly, Hartley Small let this fact settle over the court for a minute, until the judge began to frown. Then Small asked, "Do you recall any differences between the two babies?"

"One of them had a birthmark. Otherwise, they seemed to be completely identical."

Hartley paused, then said, "I ask you to think carefully, Dr.

Callendar. It is the basis of a most important decision this court must make. Which baby was born first? The one with the birthmark or the one without the birthmark?"

Callendar said instantly, "The one with the birthmark."

A sob went out that was heard by everyone in the courtroom and every eye turned to Dorcas. She had bent over, her face hidden, but her cries were audible.

Paul Wakefield's face contorted and he was about to rise when he was fixed by Small's hard gaze and Small's assistant pulled him back into his chair.

"I would ask you, Doctor Callendar, to repeat what you've just said." Callendar willingly repeated it.

"How long ago was it you delivered these babies, Dr. Callendar?"

After Callendar specified the month, day, and year, Small asked, "How can you be so sure after all these years? Do you remember all your cases so clearly?"

"I have a fairly good memory, sir."

"But this was thirty-one years ago. How can you be certain?"

"I can be certain because I record the history of every case. I have it written in one of my early journals." Callendar reached into his pocket and pulled out a small black book.

"Please turn to the date mentioned and read your entry," the Chief Justice instructed.

Callendar turned to a page in the book and read, " 'Delivered Mrs. Dorcas Wakefield of twins at 9:26 and 9:29 in the morning. They were both healthy and exactly identical except for a small birthmark shaped like a four-leaf clover on the left shoulderblade of the child who was born first."

When the Chief Justice received the notebook, he looked at the entry and nodded.

"That is the case, Your Honor," Small said smoothly. "Obviously Mrs. Lesley lied, which is indeed regrettable. It is, perhaps, more regrettable that there is nothing this court or anyone else except God can do to punish her for that. But the truth has now come out and it is clearly the court's responsibility under English law to restore to Mr. Paul Wakefield his rights and privileges and estates."

Paul Wakefield seemed to be half asleep. He kept his eyes down during the procedures that followed Dr. Callendar's testimony. When he took the stand, he gave a brief statement of his life, explained how Mrs. Lesley had contacted him, and told how she had revealed the secret of his birth, of which he had been unaware.

David listened quietly, his eyes fixed on Paul's face. He knew that all hope was gone and he longed to leave the box and go to his mother, who was weeping constantly.

Then it was over. The judge said, "I find this a very simple case. The testimonies of the two witnesses agree and there has been no evidence brought forth by Mr. David Wakefield or his counsel to prove any different." Silence followed this statement and then the judge looked directly at David Wakefield. "Mr. David Wakefield, this is a difficult moment for you. The court does not believe for an instant that there was any wrongdoing on your part. But a terrible miscarriage of justice occurred and you must now accept it." Then, turning to Paul, he said, "Will you stand to your feet, Mr. Paul Wakefield?" When Paul was standing, the justice said in a clear tone, "It is clear that you, Paul Wakefield, are the elder son of Andrew Wakefield. By due process of law, I now pronounce you to be Sir Paul Wakefield, Marquis of Wakefield and all it entails. . . ."

Sixteen

A Poor Man's Way

As Gareth Morgan dismounted, the dying rays of the sun caught him squarely in the face. The low-lying hills to the west caught the reddish globe, pulling it downward into the darkness that would soon become night. The evening stillness had already begun creeping over the land, and somewhere close by a rising chorus of crickets began.

As Gareth's feet touched the ground, his legs seemed weak and he looked down at them as one might look at a pair of traitors who had betrayed the cause. *Getting old,* he thought. *There was a time when I could've gone on a trip without my legs giving way on me.* This was true, in a sense, for though Gareth was now in his middle fifties, he had traversed the kingdom of Britain from Scotland to Wales to Ireland many times during the past thirty-plus years. Although still strong for his age, he found himself weary, so much so that he said softly, "I'll have to give up some of these preaching journeys. Leave that to the younger men."

"Well, now. Hello, Rev. Morgan."

A short, muscular servant with flaming red hair approached and held out his hands for the mare's reins. "Let me take your horse, sir."

"Give her a good rub down, if you will, Silas, and grain her. She's had a hard journey."

"That's the truth, and you, yourself, look a little weak." The strain of Old Wales was in Silas Evans's voice and he looked at the minister, cocking his head to one side and raising an eyebrow quizzically. "In truth, sir, you look worn down to a fine point. Have you been out preaching the Word?"

"What else, Silas?" Gareth smiled faintly. "And how about you? Are you still walking with the Lord Jesus?"

"To whom else shall I go, sir? He has the words of life." Silas was one of Morgan's converts and was always eager to see the minister. "You'll be staying the night, won't you, Reverend?"

"I think I will."

"Then perhaps you'll have a bit of time for me." Silas reached up and plowed his flaming hair with stubby fingers. "It's a little problem I'm having with the book of Daniel."

Amusement glinted in Gareth's eyes. "What problem is that? Still having trouble with the prophecy?"

"That I am, sir. To tell the truth, it's the antichrist. I can't quite get him pinned down."

With a rush of irritation, Gareth thought, *If people stopped worrying so much about the antichrist and worried more about living for God in this world now, it'd be better off. I've seen many a good Christian almost ruined by getting carried away with what Daniel means.* But he was fond of the stocky hostler. "What seems to be the problem, Silas?"

"I thought I had him all pinned down. I thought he was the pope. But the pope, he up and died on me last month." Again Silas scratched his long carroty locks. "Every time I think I got the rascal pinned down, he up and dies on me!"

Unable to restrain a laugh, Morgan slapped the young man on the shoulders. "Well, that's a subject that's troubled scholars for quite a while, but we'll talk about it before I leave."

"That will be mighty fine, sir. Perhaps I could get a few folks together and you could preach us a sermon."

"I'll do the best I can, Silas."

"Thank you, sir. I'll see that you get a good crowd and if any of them get rowdy," he said, lifting a massive fist and winking broadly, "I'll see to it that they quiet down."

Leaving the hostler to his problems with the antichrist, Morgan trudged across the yard and ascended the steps, casting a look up at the towering battlements of Wakefield. Although it was not as old or as imposing as many residences in England, Wakefield had a grace, dignity, and strength of its own. By the time he reached the top, the door opened and Ives greeted him solemnly. "Good day, Rev. Morgan."

"Hello, Ives. How are you?"

"I suppose I will not pass away anytime within the next twenty-four hours."

"You're the gloomiest chap I ever saw, Ives." Gareth Morgan slipped out of his coat and handed it to the butler, then said, "Is my sister in?"

"Yes, sir." Ives's face took on a sepulchral cast. "I'm afraid Lady Caroline is ill. I wouldn't be surprised if . . ." He left his gloomy prophecy unspoken. "I'll take you to Mrs. Wakefield at once, sir."

Ives led the minister to a large room down the broad hall and gestured with his thin hand, saying, "Mrs. Wakefield, your brother is here." He turned and disappeared like a wraith.

Entering the room, Gareth took the hand of his sister, who had risen and come to greet him with a smile on her face. "You look tired, Sister," he said. "What's this about Caroline?"

"Oh, she's been ill, but she's better now."

"To hear Ives tell it, we were getting ready to have the funeral."

"Oh, that man!" Dorcas exclaimed. "But underneath it all, do you know he actually has a rather cheerful spirit?"

"Hides it pretty well." Morgan studied the face of his sister who at the age of fifty-seven seemed rather frail. "You've worn yourself out nursing Caroline, I'll be bound. Come and sit down."

"Let me get you something to eat."

"I could do with a bite. It's been a long journey."

Gareth sat down in a horsehair chair and for the next hour let the weariness seep out of his bones. He let the servants pamper him, bringing him a tray in the room, and hungrily enjoyed the mutton and fresh vegetables.

"This is good cider," he said. "You always did make the best cider, Dorcas. Even back home in Wales."

"That was a long time ago."

"Yes, it was. Do you think of those days often?"

"Yes, I do. It seems sometimes, as we get older, those things that took place forty or fifty years ago are clearer than the things that took place the day before."

Gareth chuckled. "That's true. I wonder why that is?"

The two sat there talking and then Gareth stretched and stood to his feet. "I've heard from Bethany."

"Has she been to Cornwall, Gareth?"

"No. She stays pretty much in London, but I hear from her often and she's coming next month to stay with me. I'm going to take a little vacation from preaching."

"That'll be the day I'd like to see, but you never will!" Dorcas smiled fondly at this broad-shouldered brother of hers, thinking of how far he had come since he was a hot-tempered young man in Wales. He had grown in grace and she could never, somehow, properly express her pride in him. Now she leaned back in her chair, her fingers busy with the embroidery that seemed to be a part of her. Although her fingers were getting stiff now, she could not be still and do nothing. "How is she doing, Gareth?"

"Very well. I worry about her sometimes. Here she is, practically an old maid and no sign of ever getting married!"

"An old maid? Don't be ridiculous! As pretty as she is and as smart?"

"Men don't want smart wives, I don't think."

"That's just one of your foolish ideas. Any man would be proud to have her."

Pacing the floor nervously, Gareth said nothing for a time. When he turned to her, she saw that he had two parallel creases between his eyebrows, a sure sign that he was bothered. "Why hasn't she married then? She's twenty-two!"

"That's not old!"

"I suppose not. It's just that . . . well, I'd like to have grandchildren and she and Ivor aren't doing their duty, it seems."

"What about Ivor?"

"Oh, he's doing very well. First lieutenant of a fine regiment. He's coming in September for a leave. I miss that boy."

"Not a boy any longer, is he?"

"No, a full-grown man now and a fine soldier. It wasn't a career I would have chosen for him, but he seems to be made for it. Shouldn't doubt but what he'd be a general someday."

They talked for a while about Ivor and Bethany and finally Gareth clasped his hands together and sat down, facing his sister. "I brought news of David and it's not good."

Dorcas looked up from the embroidery. She was a woman of deep emotions and not especially good at hiding them. She had always been plain, simple, and honest, and now her pain over the distance of her two sons leaped out at Gareth. "What's the matter with him?"

"He's living in a poor section of town and barely eking out a living with his writing, I think. He does some scribbling for some of the periodicals, but that doesn't pay anything. Bethany, I think, has been buying things for the children."

"I miss them so much!"

Gareth looked over at his sister, sympathy flowing through him. "I know you do. Why don't you go see them?"

"Me? You mean in London?"

"That's where they are."

"It would be very expensive."

"Well, you've got the money, Sister, and Caroline would help, I'm sure."

For a while Dorcas protested, but the longer she thought of it, the more the idea appealed to her. "All right. I will!" she said firmly.

"Good! I really came down to get you. I'll rest up tonight and we'll leave early in the morning. You can be in London by evening." Gareth rose, saying, "Get a good night's sleep and do all your packing. We'll leave early. It's a long trip."

"I'm glad Caroline is better. I really think, with Mrs. Beard, she'll be fine." Mrs. Beard, Wakefield's housekeeper, was as good as a nurse. "I'll go tell her now so I can make all the arrangements. I'll be ready when you are in the morning, Gareth."

Dorcas had never liked London and now as she and Bethany made their way along its gritty streets, she said, "I'm glad I don't have to live here, Bethany."

"It's not for everyone," Bethany replied. She glanced over at Dorcas. *She looks so tired and weary and she's worried about David. And so am I.*

There was a jaded aspect to the streets, for most of the mills had left off grinding for the day. The very pavements had a weary appearance, worn by the tread of millions of feet. And yet, even as the echoes of the busy city lingered in the air, the quiet was more like the prostration of a spent giant than anything else. "I'd forgotten how bad the fog is in London," Dorcas remarked, looking out at the yellowish brown haze that covered the city and caused its citizens to dab at their smarting eyes as they blinked, wheezed, and choked along the streets. Gaslights were already flaring in the shops although it was only midafternoon. They had a haggard air, as if knowing themselves to be night creatures that had no business abroad under the sun, which only broke through the fog from time to time.

In the Holloway region in the north of London, between Battle

Bridge and this district where the two women traveled, a tract of homes littered the landscape. Dorcas saw with displeasure that tiles and bricks were burnt and that rubbish, including old bones and carpets, was thrown out in the street where dogs fought.

"What an awful place!" Dorcas exclaimed. "Is this the best David could do?"

"I'm afraid so. Rent is so dear in the city itself." Bethany had tried to get David to accept a loan, but he had adamantly refused. She had made the trip out to this area several times and each time was appalled by the marks of poverty that were evident in the dilapidated houses and the air of the inhabitants.

"Do you think he will ever do well enough in his writing to make a decent living?"

"It's very difficult. There are probably twenty thousand men in London who want to be writers, most of them as poor as David. It's like a school of sharks fighting and devouring each other for the few crumbs that are tossed to them by publishers who pay only a pittance."

"But some writers make a great deal of money, don't they?"

"Oh, yes! The successful ones, but it's not a good way to amass a fortune." Bethany's lips were drawn into a tight line, for she had thought much about this. Now, however, she tried to cheer Dorcas up and soon she said, "There's where he lives!" Leaning out, she said, "Driver, pull over to that house there—the yellow one."

The house in front of which the carriage stopped was an ancient building marked by the grime of passing years and fog. It was three stories and the steep-pitched roof boasted six dormer windows, all with grimy panes little better than the opaque surface of the timbers themselves. The oak timbers of the house had grown black with age as the years had rolled on.

As the two women descended, Bethany said, "We may be an hour. If you'll come back for us then, I'll make it worth your while."

"Aye, miss. I'll do that."

Dorcas accompanied Bethany as the young woman walked up to the door and opened it without knocking. When Dorcas looked surprised, Bethany said, "The house has been chopped up into private living quarters. There are three families on the first floor. David and Margaret and the children are on the second. The third floor is simply storage space—an unfinished attic for the most part." She led the way down a broad hallway, turned, and began climbing a dark, twisting stairway. When they emerged on the second floor, light filtered through the grimy windows at the end of the hall. "It's right over here," Bethany said, walking confidently to the door. She knocked and it opened almost at once. "Bethany—!" David exclaimed.

"I brought you a visitor," Bethany said, smiling, and she pulled Dorcas forward. "A surprise for you, I think."

"Mother!" David's face lit up and he stepped forward and took her in his arms.

Dorcas hugged him hard and had to squeeze back the tears as his strong arms went around her. She dashed them away unobtrusively and then said, "Well, now. Where are those grandchildren of mine?"

For a moment there was confusion, for the children, on hearing voices, came running in from another room.

"Andrew—Susan!"

Dorcas leaned down and hugged the two, kissing them thoroughly, then said, "My! You seem to have grown in just a few months!"

"Are there presents?" Susan asked in her high, demanding voice. For a young child, she had learned quickly enough that Dorcas was usually good for something. Since the trial, both children had lost weight and their clothes were dirty and unpressed.

"I believe I did!" she said. She turned to the bag she had

brought, having filled it with things to eat, including sweets, and soon the two children were arguing over the division of the spoils.

"Sit down, Mother. It's so good to see you. Let me get you a cup of tea."

As David moved across the room and began to fix tea on a small wood-burning stove, Dorcas glanced around at the tiny, low-ceilinged room with grimy wallpaper and only one small window. The odor of tallow candles hung in the air and Dorcas well remembered when she, herself, had used the ill-smelling tallow as a means of economy. The furniture was ancient, worn, and mismatched and there was a general air of bad housekeeping and dirt that appalled her. She caught Bethany's eyes, seeing that she agreed, then asked, "Margaret's not home, David?"

David had just returned with the pewter tea tray and the pot of tea and he faltered for a moment. "No—no, not right at the moment, but perhaps she'll be home soon."

Immediately Bethany spoke up. "Perhaps I ought to leave your mother here to visit with you alone."

"Oh, don't do that!" David said quickly. He set the tea down and laughed halfheartedly. "I wish I had something good to offer you to eat, but I'm afraid we're a little low right now."

Dorcas made a mental note to bring food, for she realized that David's purse did not include feeding tea and cakes to visitors. "Tell me about your writing, Son," she said.

David allowed Bethany to pour the tea, then, taking a cup, he leaned back, discouragement in his voice and shadows of fatigue under his eyes. He was wearing brown breeches with white stockings and a white shirt, open at the neck. He had always been fastidious, but the grime around his collar gave evidence that he was losing the struggle in this place. He began to speak of what he was doing.

"It's very hard. I go out every day and take my manuscripts to different publishers. There are quite a few of them in London, but none of them seem to be interested in what I've written."

"They will be," Dorcas said. "You must be patient."

David smiled at her and began to speak more cheerfully. "I don't know what we'd do," he said finally, "if it weren't for Bethany. The children look forward to her coming and so do I."

Dorcas noticed that he did not mention Margaret. There was something strange about the situation and she did not know what it was until half an hour later when the door opened and Margaret entered the room.

"We have visitors, dear!" David said, moving over to her instantly. "Bethany and my mother have come for a visit."

Margaret Wakefield was wearing a rather ornate dress for an afternoon of shopping, if that was where she was. The blue-and-green silk dress had a low, square neck and a tight bodice with lace insets. The underskirt was also made of white lace. Dorcas saw that she had put on weight and she noted also that Margaret's cheeks were flushed. Dorcas knew she had been drinking. Rising, she went over and kissed Margaret. "It's so good to see you, my dear," she said quietly.

Margaret laughed and waved her hand around the poor room. "We've got to entertain you!" she said, a hard look coming into her eyes. "We're not as fancy here as we were at Wakefield."

"This is fine, Margaret," Dorcas answered. "Why don't you sit down and we'll have tea? You can tell us what you've been doing."

Suspicion flared in Margaret's eyes as she studied Dorcas for a moment, then seemed to relax. "Oh, I've just been out buying a few things. Not that we've got money to buy much." She shifted her eyes toward David and said, "I don't suppose any of your publishers came offering you a fortune for your book?"

There was such sharpness and unkindness in the woman's voice that Dorcas cringed. She saw how David dropped his eyes and could not find the words to answer his wife. There was such misery in his face and dejection in his slightly stooped shoulders that Dorcas cried out in her heart, *Oh, God, why does it have to come to this?*

Bethany said quickly, "We were passing by the store and the butcher had these chops on sale. I thought you might need them, Margaret."

A sharp retort flew to Margaret's lips, but she restrained it and said shortly, "Thank you, Bethany." Then her glance shifted to Dorcas. "If it weren't for charity, I suppose we'd all starve to death. We probably will anyway!"

During their visit, Bethany and Dorcas tried hard to cover up their discomfort by talking to the children. The hour passed quickly and when the two rose to leave, Dorcas said, "I'll be in London for a while. I hope we can see a great deal of each other."

"Where will you be staying, Mother?"

"Oh, I have plenty of room. An extra one, as a matter of fact," Bethany said. Somehow her simple green dress with small rows of black ribbon on the bodice and a full, plain skirt gave her an air of grace. David thought fleetingly of how lovely her cheeks were but quickly drove this from his mind.

Bethany said, "I've brought your manuscript back. It's very good, David."

"I've got a new one. Perhaps you'd go over that with me, Bethany."

Dorcas's eyes flew to Margaret, seeing unhappiness written on the woman's face. She had gone over to a rickety lounge and sat down with her arms folded, removing herself from the conversation.

"Perhaps you can come over for dinner some evening, Mother, and you, too, Bethany."

"If they do, they'll have to bring the dinner themselves," Margaret said bitterly. She rose and stood stiffly, obviously waiting for the visitors to leave.

When Dorcas and Bethany had said their good-byes, kissed the children, and made their way outside and into the coach, Dorcas said, "My dear, it's so pitiful!"

"Yes, it is. It's hard on the children especially."

"Margaret seems so—so unhappy."

"She's very dissatisfied, but then I think she always was."

Dorcas nodded slowly. "You're right. She had everything once, but she was never really happy on the inside."

Silence prevailed, with only the sound of the horses hooves breaking it. Then Bethany said, "I'm afraid for David."

Dorcas looked at the young woman, knowing exactly what was in her heart. "I'm afraid, too," she said. As the carriage made its way out of the section where David Wakefield had fallen to such low estate, both women were occupied with their own thoughts.

***

Sir Paul Wakefield was surprised to see Gareth Morgan. The minister had appeared without warning as Paul had come in from a ride on a new horse. Throwing the reins to Silas, he said, "Rub him down good, Silas!"

"Yes, sir."

"Well, Uncle Gareth," Paul said, strolling over to put his hand out and greet the minister. "Did you come to preach a sermon to the prodigal?"

Gareth Morgan took in the figure of Sir Paul Wakefield. He had seen his nephew only once since the tides of fortune had brought Paul to the height and his brother, David, to the depths of their social world. Now he saw that Paul had taken advantage of his wealth. He was wearing a dark blue double-breasted serge riding coat that was triple caped, a short gray waistcoat, a gray blue shirt with ruffles at the neck and wrists, dark blue knee breeches, and black leather top boots. "I do want to talk to you seriously, Sir Paul."

"Oh, never mind the sir! Paul's been good enough for years, Uncle Gareth. Come along to the study." He led the way, walking energetically, and soon the two were sitting in the study surrounded by the hundreds of leather-bound books that had been the pride of Paul's father, Andrew Wakefield. He poured himself a glass of wine, offered it to the minister, knowing he would refuse, then gestured with the glass toward the books. As the sunlight shone through a high mullioned window, catching the rich red of the beverage, Paul studied it and then his eyes went back to the books. "All these books. A man couldn't read them in a lifetime."

"I suppose your father did."

"Yes, he did. He was a great reader, wasn't he?"

"He was a great man. Truly a humble spirit."

Paul drank the wine down, refilled the glass, then stared at the sturdy figure of the minister. "Rather too bad that all of his humility went to David and I got none of it!"

"I want to talk to you about David."

"I thought that might be the subject of your visit." Paul leaned back in the cherry-wood chair. "You did come to preach a sermon, I see."

"A little sermon would do you no harm, Paul." Squaring his shoulders, Gareth Morgan lifted his head and said, "It's a shame the way you're letting your brother live in poverty! He would not have done the same for you!"

"If he wants anything, all he has to do is come and ask me for it."

"He'll never do that."

"Ah," Paul said, his eyes brightening. He looked very handsome—lean and muscular—with his eyes exactly matching his ruffled shirt. "So he's not so humble after all."

"I don't blame him. He shouldn't have to come. Family is family and you should offer to help him—as he so often offered to help you."

"Oh, he was always quick to hand out charity and I'll do the same."

Gareth had a temper that he had managed to keep under control for the most part. Now, however, it flared out. "You're no good, Paul! If you had an ounce of decency in you, you'd think of your nephew and your niece, if not your brother! It's no man you are!"

Paul had a temper, too, and his cheeks flushed. He straightened up and said, "Get out, Gareth! Don't come back until you've learned better manners!"

"Aye! I'll get out!" Gareth said. "But I'll tell you this. Sooner or later you're going to be broken, Paul!"

"The prophet of gloom makes his statement! Now, leave Wakefield and don't bother to come back unless you have learned to speak more politely!"

As Gareth left Wakefield, his anger boiled over and he growled to his mare, "I'd like to take him and teach him a lesson with my fists!" Then, after he had ridden a mile, he cooled off. Speaking to the mare as he often did on their long, lonely journeys, he said, "You can't change a man by beating him. God has to do something in his heart." He began to pray for Paul Wakefield, but he found it very difficult going. After struggling for some time, he said aloud, "God, you know I don't even have faith for this man. All his life he's been tied up with himself, but I pray that whatever you have to do to make Paul Wakefield a good man, even if you have to break him in two, you'll do it."

⁂

"Ivor! Look at you now!" Bethany had been surprised when her brother appeared at her quarters in a beautifully cut dark blue uniform. His knee-length coat had a red lining and black braid trim on the cuffs and down the front and his white knee breeches were tucked into black top boots. But if her eyes were taken by her brother's handsome appearance, she was even more taken by the young woman he had brought with him, a Miss Lydia Owen.

"This young lady will be your sister-in-law very soon now," Ivor had said proudly, putting his arm around the young woman. "Pure Welsh, she is, and proud it is I am to have her! And I hope you'll take her to your heart as I know you will."

Lydia Owen was a petite, well-shaped woman with large brown eyes and sleek brown hair that had a tendency to curl. She touched the curls nervously now and giggled in a half-embarrassed fashion. "Ivor, you shouldn't say such things as that!"

"And why not? It's the truth!" Bethany said. She went at once, gave the girl a hug and a kiss, and said, "Welcome to the Morgan family! You're the sister I've been needing. Now you two come in and tell me all about the romance. Don't you leave out a word, Ivor! I know you men. You want to tell the big story, but I want to hear all the little things. Lydia, you tell me how this ugly brother of mine ever managed to persuade a pretty thing like you to marry him."

The three had a fine time together and Bethany could tell Ivor was proud of his bride-to-be. Love shone in his eyes and he spoke longingly of the time when they would be married.

"When will that be? The wedding, I mean," Bethany asked.

"We can't quite decide. There's trouble over in America and my regiment's going to be sent over there. Some of the officers are taking their wives with them."

"I don't know that I'd like to spend my honeymoon with the red Indians pulling my scalp off!" Lydia said good-humoredly. She was a fun-loving girl and now she held possessively to Ivor's arm. "But I'll love you in America just as I do here in England."

The visit was a success and as Ivor and Lydia left to go back to Lydia's home and obtain the final permission of her parents, he said, "What about you, Sister? You haven't been able to catch a man yet?"

"Oh, it's no man I'd have that I'd have to catch."

"Why, of course! You catch him and he catches you," Ivor said, his eyes going fondly to Lydia. "What about that young man— what was his name—Davis, who was underfoot for so long?"

"Oh, he's already married. I let him get away from me, but there's no sorrow to that. He cracked his knuckles."

"You wouldn't have a man because he cracked his knuckles?" Ivor said, laughing. "Faith now. You've got to stop looking for a perfect man!" He grew sober then and said, "You need a companion. I worry about you here all alone. When we're gone to America, it'll be just you."

"Oh, I have friends. I see Dorcas, Caroline, and David quite often."

"That's not going well, is it? David, I mean. From what you've told me he's in poor condition." He had picked up a little bit, mostly about how Bethany had not spoken of Margaret. He was a wise young man, this Ivor Morgan, and knew this sister of his. He knew that she, for years, had clung to David Wakefield and now a thought came to him. He tried it for a while in his mind, but finally decided to ignore it. "You find a fine Christian young man, get married, and have a house full of children. That'll keep you busy! And that's exactly my plan!" he said, reaching over to squeeze Lydia again.

After the two had left, Bethany thought, *He knows I love David, but he wouldn't say anything. Ivor could always see my heart, but I'm glad he didn't speak. There's no help for it.*

Thinking about David, however, she could not get away from the idea that had come to her for the past day or two that she needed to make a visit. She timed her visits carefully, for Margaret, she knew, did not welcome her. However, it had been a week since Dorcas had gone back to Wakefield and Bethany thought it might be appropriate to go and take some things for the children and somehow smuggle in some food. This would not be difficult if Margaret was not there, but she knew the woman's jealousy so she had to plan carefully.

Leaning forward in the murky light of the hallway, Bethany knocked on the door. She could hear voices inside, children's voices she thought, but she had to knock several times, more loudly each time, before finally the door opened.

"Auntie Bethany!" Susan's tear-streaked face was scored with fear as she threw herself into Bethany's arms. "I 'fraid!"

"Afraid? What are you afraid of, darling?" Holding the child's slight, trembling form in her arms, Bethany stepped inside. "Where's your father?"

"He gone." Andy had come out of the other room. His eyes were wide with relief as he took Bethany's free hand. "I'm scared."

"But where're your parents? Your mother. Is she here?"

"She gone," Andy said, "Mrs. Stems is here."

"Mrs. Stems? Who's that?"

"She come when Papa not here," Andy said. Susan was still clinging to Bethany with such a fierce possessiveness that the young woman knew something was terribly wrong.

"Well, now," she said. "Let me get my coat off. It's getting a little cold out there. Don't you have any fire?"

"It went out. There not anything to burn." Andy was a sturdy young fellow for three and a half, but Bethany saw he had been more frightened than he wanted to admit.

"We'll just have to get some coal, start a fire, and make us some tea and cakes," Bethany said. "Won't that be fun?"

Bethany stepped outside, for she knew that a coal seller lived three doors down. When she knocked on the door, the man stepped outside saying, "What can I do for you, mum?"

"My name is Bethany Morgan. I want to buy some coal for Mr. Wakefield's house. They're out."

Embarrassment scored the man's face. He was a thin, undersized man of some fifty years with salt-and-pepper hair and sad-looking blue eyes. "I hate to be hard on him, but they owe me so much I couldn't afford to leave them no more, miss."

"Oh, I've got the money. If you'd just bring it over, I'd be so thankful."

Immediately the man's countenance grew brighter. "Yes, ma'am! Right away! Be glad to do it!"

Forty-five minutes later a cheerful fire was glowing in the stove, the teakettle was piping away a little tune, and the smell of the fresh-cooked meat Bethany had brought with her filled the room. "We'll have a regular picnic," Bethany said, sitting the children down, heartsick to see how eagerly they ate their food. *Why, they're starving!* she thought, indignant. But she knew she had to be very careful. As an outsider, she had no rights at all here and she knew well that Margaret's temper was a fearful thing when aroused. "When did your mother say she would be back?"

"Late," Andy said, chewing happily on a bite of meat and washing it down with the milk that Bethany had brought with her. "This is good, Aunt Bethany."

"Well, old man, eat all you can. There's plenty more."

"I want Papa."

Slowly Bethany sorted out the problem. According to what the children said, David had gone to the city to work, having obtained some sort of employment that they did not quite understand. Their mother had stayed only an hour after he was gone, then had gone to fetch old Mrs. Stems, who had apparently agreed to sit with the children.

"Where did Mrs. Stems go?"

"I don't know," Andy said.

I'd like to dig my fingernails into Mrs. Stems and pull her hair out! Bethany thought angrily. She let none of this show on her face, however, and settled in to wait for the return of either Margaret or David.

It was a long wait, for night had come before the door opened and David entered, giving a surprised look at the visitor. "Why, Bethany!" he said. "I didn't expect to find you here!"

"I just came by for a visit, David. But I did some cooking while I was here. Sit down and eat while it's hot."

"But where's Margaret? She's not here?"

"No. The children said she had to go out."

"And she left the children with you?" David said with surprise. His black suit badly needed pressing, and as he sat down and began to eat hungrily, he seemed to be troubled. "I don't understand," he said, frowning.

"Mrs. Stems was here, Papa," Andy said, busy with a piece of cake that Bethany had brought. Then he looked up at his father guiltily. "We were scared."

Pain washed over David Wakefield's face. "How long were you alone, Son?"

"Long time," Susan said. She stuffed the last of her cake in her mouth and came over, pulling herself up into her father's lap. She held on to his vest, saying, "Mrs. Stems mean. I cry."

"We'll have to do better than that," David said comfortingly. He lifted his head, his eyes meeting Bethany's. The two did not speak, but a look of understanding passed between them.

"I'm glad you were here, Bethany."

"So am I." She innately understood the gratitude in David's words, although he said no more about it. "It was a treat for me to come and sit with the children."

After the meal the four of them sat at the table and, at Susan's insistence, played drafts. She had just learned how to play, and although she did not understand the rules, she liked to move the round markers. The room soon was ringing with laughter and David leaned back with a relaxed air. "I haven't had this much fun in a long time."

"I'm glad," Bethany said, letting her eyes rest on him. "You look tired. Exhausted really." She knew that the struggle to merely stay alive was wearing him down. Neither of them spoke of Margaret until finally the children grew sleepy.

"Bethany, put me to bed," Susan demanded.

"Why, that would be just what I would like," Bethany said. She heated water in a pan and then washed the girl, admiring her long dark locks. "You're the prettiest girl I know."

The young girl beamed.

"Honestly! The very prettiest!"

This pleased the child greatly and Bethany realized she did not get many compliments. Probably none except from David.

Finally the two children were in bed and for a moment there was an embarrassed silence between Bethany and David as they stood in the center of the room. When Bethany got her coat, preparing to leave, David put out his hands and she took them without thought. They were strong and warm and when she looked up, she saw he was struggling to express his gratitude.

"I don't know what would've happened if you hadn't come. God must have sent you here."

Secretly Bethany thought the same thing. She had had this strange urgency about coming, but now she said only, "I'm glad I was here to help." She wanted to ask about the future, but realized she had no right to do that. "Good night, David."

"Good night, Bethany, and God bless you."

As Bethany left the house and walked down the street, she was saddened by the visit. *They're caught in a trap*, she thought. *David and the children. And Margaret—if she doesn't change, she's headed straight for a tragedy*. There was an inn down the street, so she stopped inside to ask the innkeeper about a carriage. He sent his young son to get one of his friends who drove. "A little late for a young lady to be out," the innkeeper said.

"I've been visiting my friends the Wakefields."

"The Wakefields?" A strange light leaped into the innkeeper's eyes, although he said no more. But when he left the room, his wife, who had been listening, came and said, "Be you a friend of Mr. David Wakefield?"

"Yes, I am."

"Tell him to mind his house then!"

"What do you mean?"

The woman, tall and dark featured, with piercing black eyes, was silent for a moment. "That wife of his. She's no good!"

"Why—"

"She's taken up with men! Right here in this very tavern! If you want the proof of it, just stay long enough and you'll see it! She's seein' men all right! You'd better tell her husband to keep her home!"

Shocked, Bethany could only stare at the woman. Finally, when the young boy came back and announced, "Your carriage is here, miss," she thanked him and left. Getting into the carriage, her mind rejected what she had heard, but her experience of the day whispered to her that there was truth in the innkeeper's wife's words.

"Poor David," she whispered into the darkness. "Oh, my poor David!"

Seventeen

An Old Flame

Winter 1773

The home of Sir Lionel Frazier was built for pleasure. As Paul Wakefield moved around the gigantic ballroom that was ornate enough for Versailles, he could not help but be impressed with the magnitude and opulence of it. The oval room's walls and ceiling were white with gilt carvings and one wall had six floor-length windows covered with red velvet drapes. Two handcut-crystal chandeliers hung toward the center of the large room. As the dancers glided smoothly over the black-and-white marble floor, polished to a high shine, the pink, red, blue, green, and yellow dresses caught the flickering of the many candles that were placed in sconces between the windows and in the insets around the room. On the inside wall, two white marble fireplaces were lit, adding to the atmosphere, and above the mantel hung large gilt looking glasses with sconces on either side. Numerous walnut sidechairs were placed along the outside walls of the room. The eight large William IV mahogany dining tables covered with white damask cloths held an array of food in silver bowls and platters, silver plates, and cut crystal glasses.

The weather outside was bad, so Paul had almost elected to remain in the warmth and comfort of Wakefield. However, the winter of 1773 had been boring for him and he was discontent with himself for some reason. Now, as he moved around the room, the feeling stirred in him again and he was puzzled. If he had put his thoughts into words they would have been, *I don't know why I'm unhappy. I'm Sir Paul Wakefield, master of the family estate. I can have all the money I can spend, all the horses I can ride. I've got everything I've always wanted.*

Paul moved into the shadows at one corner of the large room and watched the dancers carry out the ornate steps of the quadrille. How long he had stood there he could not have said, but he was startled when a voice spoke close to his side.

"You're not having a very good time, Sir Paul."

The woman who faced him was strikingly beautiful and Paul racked his memory, trying to bring to mind when he had seen her. She was not a tall woman but had a poise and a presence that went only with the aristocracy. Her hair was blonde with a touch of red and her eyes a pure blue. Her dress—a sheer pink silk with lace and embroidery inset on the bodice, around the neckline, and following down the edges of the robed skirt, and a white silk embroidered petticoat—had cost enough to feed Wakefield Village for a month, Paul estimated. Regathering his thoughts, he said quickly, "Why, that's not so, my lady! I'm having a fine time!"

"You don't remember me, do you?"

"I—am embarrassed to say that I do not."

"I knew you as soon as you came in the door. I'm Stella Frazier, but you knew me as Stella Fairfax."

Instantly, Paul's memory came to his aid. This was the woman who had broken David's heart and driven him into an overhasty marriage with Margaret Dossett. He had met her several times, but she had matured since those days. *She must be about twenty-six, I suppose,* he thought. *But she doesn't look it.* "Of course! Now I remember. It's been a long time, Lady Frazier."

"Oh, Stella will do, and you're Paul!" Stella's azure eyes were lit with interest as she looked at the tall figure of the man before her.

"I remember. I could never tell you from David. I suppose I still couldn't."

"You haven't seen him, I suppose?"

"No, I understand he's married and has a family."

"You won't pretend that you are unaware of the change in the situation," Paul said, a grimness in his gray blue eyes.

"No, it was fairly well publicized in the papers. And so you are now Sir Paul Wakefield."

"Yes, I'm the villain who threw his brother to the wolves."

Stella's eyes opened wide. She was almost shocked at the bitterness in Paul's words. She studied him even more carefully, caught again by the resemblance between him and his brother. Since she had married Sir Lionel, her life had been complete in one sense—and empty in another. All that she had wanted in the way of clothes, carriages, perfumes, and jewelry were hers for the asking, for Sir Lionel was a generous man. It had been a pleasure during the earlier days of her marriage to be introduced to the sovereign and to the lords that Sir Lionel moved among. All this had been gratifying—for a time.

But as she stood looking at the virile young man before her, quick thoughts of what she was missing in life came to her mind. Sir Lionel had been an elderly man when she married him. He had carefully explained to her before marriage, "My dear, you must not expect romance or even any sort of sexual comfort from me. I am past all that and cannot give it to you. If you can be satisfied with those things that money can buy, then I will be happy to have you as my wife. But you must understand that it is a marriage of . . . well . . . the type they call December to May. Being a young woman, you would be wise to reject me."

Stella, however, had not been wise enough for that. She was a passionate young woman and since her marriage had been strongly tempted by several fine-looking and wealthy young men who moved in her circle. Somehow she had found it possible to resist their advances, but now, looking at the lean strength of Paul Wakefield, she felt a sudden nostalgia and almost pain, knowing that she did not have what other women had from their husbands.

"I hope that your new situation," Stella said quickly to change the subject, "has been an improvement for you."

Paul smiled. "Why, it's wonderful having a great deal of money. Every day I open the mail and forty-seven churches, I find, are to be erected with half crowns, forty-two parsonage houses need to be repaired with shillings, and there are over thirty organs to be built with halfpence, and twelve hundred children to be brought up on postage stamps. That's not to mention," he said, shrugging, "the letters that come saying, 'My dear, Sir Paul. Having consented to become the chairman of the annual dinner of the family party fund, I have undertaken to ask you to be a steward. Soliciting your favor or reply, I am your faithful servant. The steward's fee is limited to three guineas.'"

Despite herself, Stella laughed and agreed. "I know. Sir Lionel gets practically baptized by requests for help constantly. I don't know how he puts up with it."

"Oh, indeed, it becomes quite a task. If I answered all the requests I got for help," Paul said, "I'd be bankrupt in a month. But those are just corporate beggars." He moved closer to the woman, inhaling the subtle fragrance of her perfume and noticing how her dress clung to her figure. There was an aura of sexuality that hung about Stella Frazier that Paul, as always, was drawn to. "There are individual beggars and some are utterly ruined. Some among them are daughters of general officers accustomed to every luxury of life—except spelling, I might add—who little thought, since their gallant fathers wage war for the nation, that they would ever have to appeal to those whom Providence in its inscrutable wisdom has blessed with untold gold. . . ."

Paul went on for some time. Finding him amusing, Stella said, "Are you a married man, Sir Paul?"

A change passed over Paul Wakefield's face. "No," he said, "but since I've come into my fortune, I think the opportunity is there."

Stella smiled. "I would think so. For a good-looking man with a title and money, the opportunities must be endless."

"I think sometimes my tailor puts on the back of my suit a large sign: 'Eligible! On view! One English lord seeking wife.'"

"It's almost that bad, isn't it?"

The music started again and Paul said, "Are you engaged for this dance?"

"Why, no, I'm not."

"May I ask you to have favor upon me then?"

As the two moved around the floor, Paul became even more conscious of Stella's intense attractiveness. He remembered how she had completely dominated David's thoughts and now he understood why. Later, after the dance, they had refreshments and Paul noticed that a very tall man with blond hair and light blue eyes was glaring at him. "Is that your husband giving me that jealous look?"

Glancing in the direction of Paul's nod, Stella laughed. "No, that's Keith Valentine. You'll be meeting him, now that you're moving among the nobility."

"Is he a lord of some sort?"

"Oh, yes! His father was a very wealthy man indeed. He died last year and since Keith is a second son, he didn't come in for the title. Oh," Stella said, looking up, "I suppose I shouldn't have said that. I know how you must've felt the same way."

"It's not easy being a younger son. But why is the fellow glaring at me? Only husbands have that right."

He glanced down at Stella, who looked somewhat confused. "My husband is an older man," she said. "I don't suppose you met him."

"No, I haven't, but I've heard of him, of course."

"He's been an invalid. Our married life has been rather— quiet."

He remembered hearing then that Frazier was an elderly man indeed and suddenly he understood more about Stella Frazier than he had. "You must allow me to call, Stella," he said.

She looked up quickly, for there was an inviting tone in his voice. "Why, of course. I'll see that you're invited the next time we have dinner guests."

Paul left the ball that night, his thoughts on Stella Frazier.

During the weeks that followed, Paul saw Stella Frazier several times. He called at their home upon her invitation and found that Sir Lionel Frazier was a frail man, obviously in very bad health. He had gone to bed early on Paul's first visit, which had given Stella an opportunity to show Paul the portraits in the large gallery. The two had walked along, and then, at the end of the hall, Paul had reached out and kissed Stella thoroughly. She had responded, as he had known she would, but then had pushed him away. "Please!" she said. "You mustn't do that ever again!"

"I probably will," Paul had said—and so he had. He had no intention of anything serious, but Stella, he had to admit, was a tempting woman and he was a young man, restless and uncertain as to what to do with himself.

David trimmed the tallow candle, then picked up the quill that he had put down and began writing again. As the point moved across the paper it made a faint scratching sound, but he was unconscious of it. When he wrote, something seemed to possess him so that he was unconscious of his surroundings, thinking only of the words that went on the paper. Now he was fervently engrossed in the work that he loved. He had met none other than Dr. Samuel Johnson, who had promised to look at his next manuscript. Dr. Johnson was the lion of the London literary world along with Mr. Boswell, Mr. Goldsmith, and a few others. David had been encouraged enough to tell Margaret that he thought Dr. Johnson could be a great help to him. She had responded merely with a shrug, for long ago she had given up on his making any money by writing.

As his pen moved across the paper, David was startled when a knock came at the door. He sat upright and blinked sleepily, for the hour was late. "Who could that be?" he said softly, putting the quill down. The children were asleep and Margaret had come in after what appeared to be a night of heavy drinking. David knew by now that she was unfaithful to him, but he was caught in the trap of his own marriage. He had given her all he had, but it had not been enough. Now as he moved toward the door, he glanced toward the bedroom, half expecting her to appear, but he knew that when she drank she slept like the dead. Opening the door, he stood there for a moment in shock, then swallowed hard. "Paul!" he finally managed to say.

"Hello, David. May I come in?"

"Of course. I'm sorry." David stepped back and when Paul entered the room, he waved at the chair. "Sit down. I wasn't expecting anyone. I'm afraid I don't have anything to offer you."

"I didn't come for anything," Paul said, sitting down and taking in the poor quality of the room. There were signs of poverty everywhere he looked. "I suppose Margaret and the children are in bed?"

"Yes. I was writing."

Paul pulled off one glove, then the other. He had not seen David since that day in court when he had been declared the Marquis of Wakefield, but he had thought of him every day. Now he studied his twin's face, looking for signs of anger, bitterness, jealousy—but he found none of that. Somehow this irritated him, for it would have helped to find his brother of the same mind as he, himself, was.

"I have been expecting you to call on me."

"I suppose I should've done that, Paul, but it's a little difficult when you have a regular job."

"Bethany tells me you're working for a newspaper now. Tell me about it."

"There's not much to tell. I go to trials. I learned to write shorthand some time ago, as you remember." His face turned grim. "I cover executions of important people, something I could do without."

"I should imagine so. I don't know why people want to read about that."

"Read about it? They want to *be* there. I can't imagine anyone going deliberately to see a man hanged, drawn, and quartered, but the streets are always full every time there's an execution."

"It would be easier on me than on you, I suppose. I could always take that sort of thing best."

"Yes, you could." David felt at a loss for words. He was glad that Margaret was in bed, for she hated Paul passionately and David knew she would have been screaming and perhaps even trying to hit him. Keeping his voice down, he said, "How have things been for you?"

"Very well. Better than for you I would imagine."

"I can't complain."

"Can't complain?" Paul's irritation grew. "Why can't you complain? If you had any sense you would!"

"I don't know what you mean."

"Why, man, I expect you to come to me and ask for help! And I would give it, too! All you have to do is ask."

"Why, I never thought of it. It's your property, Paul. I had the use of it for a long time, but now it's yours."

The simplicity of David's words struck Paul a hard blow. He blinked, not imagining anyone behaving as this brother of his did. "You're a fool, David!" he said caustically. "I just wanted you to have a taste of what I had to go through for so many years, but there's no point in your living like this."

David shifted uneasily in his chair. He ran his fingers through his hair and tried to put into words what he was feeling. "I just didn't feel that I could come to you and ask for anything. A man ought to be able to make it on his own and I will, Paul." Eagerly he began to explain how Dr. Johnson had agreed to read his next manuscript. "If he likes it, he'll help me find a good publisher. And once that happens, why, things will be much better. I'll tell you—"

The door opened and Margaret came out. Her hair fell about her shoulders in a unkempt fashion and the robe she clutched about her had not been washed recently. "What are you doing here?" she demanded.

Paul felt much more comfortable with Margaret's obvious hatred. "I just stopped by to offer my help to my brother, Margaret. But he tells me he can't take it."

Margaret stared at Paul, then turned to David. "You fool!" she said. "Take what you can get!"

"Really, Margaret, I don't think—"

"If you were any man, you would provide for your family! Here it's being thrown in your lap and you're too blind to see it!" Her voice rose as she excoriated David.

Paul sat there, wondering why a man would stand for such a thing. He would have slapped her in the face and walked out. *It's the children, I suppose. He can't walk away and leave them.* Paul finally interrupted Margaret. "I've come at a bad time. Just remember. There's no point in your living like this, David. I'll be glad to help. Come and see me soon."

As soon as the door closed behind Paul, Margaret glared at her husband. She came up and stood before him, her eyes almost wild, the smell of liquor still on her breath. "You're not going to do it, are you?"

"I really can't, my dear."

Margaret's hand lashed out and caught David a resounding slap on the jaw. She cursed him and David stood there, unable to speak for a moment. Then he said, "Please, Margaret, you'll wake the children."

It took some time before he got her quiet. When she finally went back to bed, David slumped down at the table and tried to continue his writing, but his thoughts were gone. "Maybe I *should* have done that, but I just can't do it. I just can't." He thought of how miserable his life had become. The only joy in it was his writing, his children, and an occasional visit from Bethany Morgan, and even these were rare now.

I've got to do something, he thought desperately. *I've got to hire somebody to take care of the children.* Margaret had become worse about leaving the children alone so it took every penny David could scrape together to be sure they were cared for while he was at work. "I've got to do something," he murmured.

The something David did meant taking another job. From then on he worked eighteen hours a day and it was all his strength could endure. The winter had been harsh and he had been ill more than once. He was terrified lest the children become ill. He had not gone back to see Doctor Johnson, for just the struggle to keep his family intact was all he had the strength for. Finally, one day, in the middle of March, he was so weak he could scarcely carry on. Whatever sickness he had had given him a fever and he was afraid to go home lest the children catch it. He had pleaded with Margaret to stay with them and had left her enough money to hire the young woman who had proved to be fairly reliable.

He found a bed that night and got up the next morning with a raging fever. He had been too sick to go to work and late that afternoon, in desperation, knew he had to go home.

"We'll just have to pray the children will be kept safe." He walked through the streets of London, his eyes bloodshot and his limbs trembling, since he had no money for a cab. It was a long walk and by the time he had reached his house, he was shaking like a man with ague.

When he knocked on the door, it was answered almost at once—by the two children. He looked over their heads and his heart sank. "Is your mother here, children?" he whispered.

"No!"

"What about Loreen?" This was the young woman he had left money to hire.

"I don't know, Papa," Andy said, his face drawn. "Are you sick?"

"Yes. I am a little." David moved in the door and the two children hung onto him closely. He slumped on the divan with the broken springs and listened as they told him that their mother had been gone for a long time. David finally pieced it together. *She took the money I gave her to hire Loreen and spent it on drink!* he thought in despair.

Trying to be cheerful, he said, "You'll have to take care of Papa. I don't feel very well." He got up and stumbled into the bedroom. He fell into a fever-ridden sleep and the next morning was not able to get out of bed. He heard vague voices from the other room and tried to make himself understand, but his fever was so high he could not think clearly.

"Papa?"

David looked up to see Andy standing over him. "Here's a letter from Mama."

Desperately, David ignored his pounding head and the fever that burned like fire within. He managed to sit up, then whispered, "Bring me the candle over there, Son." When Andrew brought the candle and stood beside him, he unfolded the note, but the letters seemed to run together. He shook his head, which was a mistake, for it felt like hammers beating spikes into his brain. He blinked his eyes until the letters swam into position and read, "'You'll never be anything, David. I found a man who can give me everything I want. Don't try to find me. You're better for the children than I am. Good-bye.'" She hadn't even signed her name at the bottom of the note.

"Papa?" Susan had come in and had crawled up in the bed with him. Tears came to David Wakefield's eyes, something that had not happened since he was a boy. Andy moved in on the other side, saying, "What's wrong, Papa?" His voice was filled with fear.

"Nothing. It will be all right. Your mother—has gone on a little visit—so we'll just have to take care of each other—until she comes back."

The words sounded hollow in David Wakefield's ears and he could see no hope at all. The fever caught him again and he lay back down, saying softly, "I'll be all right tomorrow." But as the fever mounted, he felt frantic with fear. *What will happen to Susan and Andy?* he thought. *Who will take care of them if I die? I've got to get out of this bed. I've got to get help.*

But his mind was stronger than his body, for his limbs would not obey the commands. He felt himself slipping into the oblivion of fever and the last thing he remembered was praying for God to help him.

BETHANY TAKES OVER

David's fever was like a fire that swept over him, burning his whole body. At times there would be almost no consciousness, just the sense of death and the burning. But then there would come the feeling of cool dampness. He was vaguely aware of someone placing wet cloths over his body to bring the fever down. When his mind surfaced enough to be logical, he tried to think about who he was and what was wrong with him, but all he knew was that he was terribly sick. Most of the time he lay quietly when the fever was gone and then again he was conscious of hands, gentle and tender, touching his face, and of someone whispering that he must eat.

It was a timeless state, for there were no yesterdays, todays, or tomorrows. There was only the burning heat of the fever, the coolness that came, and the soft, encouraging voice.

Then one day he awoke, coming out of his feverish stupor to realize that the fever was gone. He was so weak that, for a moment, he could not even move his head. But when a movement to his right fell across the yellow light of the lamp he managed to turn his head and blink his eyes several times to clear the blurriness. Then the face appeared over him and the voice said, "David, you're awake!"

Bethany! Her features came into view, and David, for all of his weakness, managed to raise his hand and touch her cheek. "Bethany!" he whispered but could say no more.

Bethany looked down at the sick man, joyful that the fever was gone. She put her hand on his forehead, which had felt dry and cool the night before and now was regaining some of its natural color. "Can you sit up?"

"I—think so." David struggled to an upright position, conscious of her strong arms helping him. Aware that his lips were dry as toast and that his tongue felt large and coarse in his mouth, he whispered, "Water, please."

"Here." Bethany poured water into a tumbler and held it to his lips. She watched as he grasped the glass desperately and began choking the water down. "Not so fast! You can have all you want, but take it in tiny sips, David."

"All right." He longed for more of the water but obeyed. From time to time, he would take a tiny sip. It was better than anything he had ever had in his life, he thought. "That's good," he said. Then he looked around the room and tried to remember. "How long have I been here?" he asked.

"You've been unconscious for almost three days. The doctor was here. He'll be back soon."

"I don't remember him."

"No. You were too sick."

"The children—where are Andy and Susan?"

"They're well taken care of. I hired a woman to keep them. She lives not too far away and comes well recommended. Her name is Rebecca Hayes. She's fine with the children. They love her. She looks a little bit like your mother," Bethany said. She took the glass, refilled it, and watched as he drank in slow sips. She dipped a white cloth into the basin, wrung the excess water out, and then began to bathe his face. "How do you feel?"

"Terrible!"

"You'll feel better after a while."

"That's good. I'd hate to think I'd feel this bad for the rest of my life," he said with humor.

Bethany smiled, pushing his hair back. It was lank and needed washing and she made a mental note to do that. "You're getting better if you can make jokes."

David took another sip of water. "I can't seem to remember anything."

"You were very sick. The man who sells coal remembered my name. One of the children went down and told him you were sick and their mother was gone, so he managed to get in touch with me. I arranged to take a leave from the Searses' and came at once. Then I got the doctor and we've been taking care of you ever since."

"I feel so helpless." David held his hand up and it trembled slightly. "I never have been really sick. This is the first time. I don't like it."

"Most people don't," Bethany said dryly. She pulled a chair closer and sat down. Seeing he was still confused, she continued, "David, I found the note that Margaret left."

Instantly it all rushed back and his lips twisted in a tortured fashion. "She left me and the children. How can a woman do that, Bethany?"

"I don't know."

David sat quietly in the bed, holding the tumbler of water. He looked up at the young woman across from him and saw her eyes had circles under them. "You've worn yourself out taking care of me," he said. He wanted to touch her, but sudden weakness hit him very hard. "I'm so tired."

"You must eat something before you go to sleep. You'll be getting better now. I have some broth made. Don't go to sleep now!"

David managed to stay awake until he had gulped down a delicious bowl of soup. Then, almost as if he were struck in the head, he fell into a deep sleep. But it was, Bethany saw, a normal sleep, and when the doctor came she told him, "The fever's all gone. He's sleeping very normally."

Dr. Sawyer leaned over and examined the sick man. "I think you're right, Miss Morgan," he said. His gray eyes considered her with interest. "You'd make a fine nurse, if you ever have that inclination."

"No. I don't think so. He is going to be all right, isn't he, Doctor?"

"He's going to be sick for a long time. Very weak, I'm afraid." Again the doctor looked at her. "Is he a relative of yours?"

"Yes, he's my cousin," she said, "and I love his children very much. I'll stay with him and see that they're taken care of. His mother isn't too well. She lives outside of London, but she'll want to come as soon as she's able."

"Well, he'll need a lot of care."

"I can do it, Doctor." There was such assurance in the young woman's dark eyes that Dr. Sawyer felt there was more to this case than met the eye.

"I'll stop in tomorrow. He ought to be eating solid food by then."

After the doctor left, Bethany went and stood over David's bed. She had left the note from Margaret out on the table beside the bed and her first instinct was to destroy it. But then she thought, *It's not my note. He'll have to live with it. He can't get rid of it by destroying a piece of paper.* She sat down then and studied the profile of this man she had loved so long. Slowly she reached out and stroked his hair. He was safe now. He was asleep. She longed to take him in her arms and more than once she had done that while he was unconscious and his mind was wandering. But now that could not be. She rose, hopeless, realizing that this man she loved so much had a wife and that he would never, never leave her, even if she left him.

Dorcas and Caroline were reading the letter that had come from Bethany. Dorcas looked up from the line, saying, "He's better. Bethany said he's going to be all right."

"I don't know what would've happened to him," Caroline remarked, "if Bethany hadn't gone."

"How could Margaret have done it? She's an unnatural mother!"

"She's an unnatural wife!" Caroline said sharply. "He's better off without her!"

The two women sat there speaking of the sick man, and Dorcas said, "I urged Paul to go see David, to at least pay for his care. I think he probably will."

"I should hope so. David is his only brother. He owes him that much." She hesitated. "From what I hear, he's seeing a lot of Stella Frazier now that her husband's died."

Dorcas said nothing. Both women had been aware that Paul had been seeing Stella Frazier even before her husband's death the previous month. "I wonder if he'll marry her?"

"I wouldn't be surprised. She's got a fortune now and Paul's an attractive man."

"I wonder what David will feel like. He was very much in love with her once, or thought he was."

Caroline shook her head. "I'm not sure David was really in love with Stella. He was fascinated by her. David was so young and inexperienced in the ways of women that naturally he was dazzled by her."

"Well, Paul isn't that easily dazzled," Dorcas said almost bitterly.

The two women sat there until Dorcas finally rose. "He'll be miserable if he marries her, but I'm not worried about him. It's David I'm concerned about."

At that moment, the subject of the women's conversation, Paul

Wakefield, was sitting across from Stella, the widow of the late Sir Lionel Frazier. He had not seen her since the funeral but had received a note asking him to come. Now he sat in the large, ornate drawing room. Stella was not particularly marked by grief, but he had not expected her to be. "Well," he said, "now you're free to marry."

"It's still too soon to think about that. But I can't be a hypocrite, Paul," she said, looking him in the eye. "I was never in love with Lionel, nor he with me. I was an ornament for him. He needed a wife to take care of his house, but there was never love between us. You know that."

Paul could not help but admire the woman's poise. "You're a cool one, Stella," he said. He bent down and kissed her. "I can't be a hypocrite either. I don't know whether or not I will ever love a woman as she should be loved, but you've got into my blood."

"Have I, Paul?" Stella pulled him close to her. She clung to him. When he finally released her, she flushed. "As I say, I can't pretend that I loved Lionel. I've been a lonely woman."

"You don't have to be any longer."

She looked up quickly. "You mean that, Paul?"

"Well, why not? I don't have a wife. You don't have a husband. We both have plenty of money and we can go anywhere we want. We could have a fine life together."

She came to him again, holding him tightly. "I've been lonely, Paul," she said again. "You'll never know how lonely a woman gets without a man."

"I imagine about like a man without a woman." There was such a strange note in his voice that Stella leaned back and said slowly, "There was a woman, wasn't there?" When he didn't answer she said, "An attractive man like you? There must have been."

"You don't have to think about her. That's all in the past."

"Did you love her?"

"Yes. But she's dead."

Stella blinked at the harshness of his words, then her lips softened. "I'm sorry, Paul."

The two stood there holding one another and Paul Wakefield thought, *I can at least get something out of this money. I could've never had Stella if I didn't have the title. I guess we're both made for each other. Selfish to the bone.*

"We'll have to wait for a while. At least six months. Maybe a year," she said.

"The marriage can wait," he said, sweeping her into his arms again.

⟡

As the months passed, Paul found himself more and more satisfied with Stella Frazier. She was a lovely woman. As far as the world was concerned, Stella Frazier was a woman lately widowed who would one day marry again and Sir Paul Wakefield was the man she would most likely favor. London society accepted new widows looking out for husbands, for it was difficult for a woman to make it on her own in England during that period. Keith Valentine was bitter, for he had felt that he might marry her himself. He made himself so obnoxious that Paul showed great restraint in not calling him to account, but Stella had begged him, saying, "He'll get over it. He's in love with me, or thinks he is."

Paul had managed to survive Valentine's slurs. He had also become more interested in his brother's well-being and had actually gone to see him several times to offer his condolences.

It was late in May when Paul visited his brother again and he was not too surprised to find Bethany there. The two of them were sitting at the table going over a manuscript and David had jumped up to greet him. *He's gotten over his sickness,* Paul observed, *and looks healthier than he has in months. It helped him to get rid of that*

283

shrew of a wife of his, Paul thought, but said only, "What are you two up to?"

"We're writing a great book," Bethany said, smiling at him. Paul and Bethany had managed to work the finances out, keeping it a secret from David. Paul had supplied her the money that David was reluctant to take, and Bethany had managed to keep the house going with Mrs. Rebecca Hayes's help. In the process Bethany had come to feel more charitable toward Paul Wakefield. Even now she saw that, despite his wealth and the title, he had a sadness and emptiness that nothing would ever fill. *Nothing but God,* she had said to herself numerous times. Now she said, "We're almost through with the novel. Sit down and help us read the last chapter."

"Not me," Paul said, laughing. "I don't believe in romances."

"Well, I do," Bethany said. "I just love them. David writes better than anyone about love."

Interested, Paul arched an eyebrow. "How do you account for that, Brother?"

"Oh, I don't know!" David said. "Bethany's always overstating my ability to write."

It was a pleasant visit, and after Paul left, he thought, *Well, there's one good deed I've done. If the blasted fool won't take help directly, the woman's got more sense.* He thought about the pair, aware that Bethany had been in love with his brother for a long time. *She'll never do anything about it, though. She's too good for that.* He tried to think hateful thoughts, but he knew there was a goodness in Bethany Morgan that he had seen in few women. For a while he was tempted to go by and visit Stella, but instead he chose to go home. He went to bed early and slept well, but at dawn the next morning a servant came to him, a worried look on his face. "Sir, there's a gentleman to see you!"

"A gentleman here? Who is it?"

"He says his name is Angus McDowell."

"McDowell?" Paul got up at once and began to dress. "Did he say what he wanted? No, of course, he wouldn't."

Quickly Paul dressed and went out to meet McDowell, who did not return his smile or his greeting. "Sir Paul," he said, "I've got something vurry difficult to tell ye."

"What is it? Have we gone bankrupt, Angus?"

"No, it's not that. Not a matter of money." Angus twisted his hat in his hand. "I don't know how to tell ye this, but ye better come with me, sir."

"Come? Where should I come with you?"

"Down to the docks, sir. There's someone there asking for ye."

Paul tried to get the dour Scotsman to say more, but McDowell said, "I feel like it's yer business, sir. And the quicker ye tend to it, the better."

"All right. If you won't open your mouth, I'll have to go, I suppose," Paul grumbled. The two made the trip down to the London docks in silence. Paul made no attempt to discover McDowell's closely guarded secret. Nevertheless, he was filled with curiosity.

When they got to the docks, the two men disembarked from the carriage, and McDowell said, "Over here, sir. In the house of Jennings and Company. I've asked them to meet ye there."

"Who is *them?*" Paul asked with considerable irritation. "What are you talking about, Angus? You can tell me now."

"Only a moment, sir."

McDowell led the way to the large, flat-roofed building and opened the door for Paul, who stepped inside. A clerk met them and greeted them pleasantly enough, but McDowell ignored him as did Paul. "Down this way, Sir Paul," he said.

Paul could only imagine that something had gone wrong with the business, but he did not see why McDowell was so secretive about it. He followed the man down a corridor and McDowell stopped in front of a door. "In there, sir. I'll wait out here."

"All right, Angus."

Paul opened the door and stepped inside. He turned quickly, for the large room was empty except for two figures to his right. It was a bright, sunshiny morning and the light was behind their back. Paul blinked, asking, "Who are you? What do you want with me?"

And then a voice came out of the grave. "Hello, Paul."

The world seemed to stop for Paul Wakefield, for one of the figures stepped out of the blinding sunlight—someone he had never expected to see again on this earth.

"Marielle—!"

She came right up to him and though she looked older, she was still as lovely as she had been the first day he had met her. She reached up and touched his chest. "You thought I was dead."

"Yes! Of course I did! We found the body with the ring on that I gave you!"

"It was my friend, Loantha. I had given her the ring to wear and when the Huron came they killed her and burned all the bodies. But me they took north."

Paul's head was swimming. He reached up and rubbed his brow. "I can't believe it," he whispered. "All these years. You've been a captive?"

"Yes. But Frenchy Doucett saw me there. He bought my freedom and my passage to England."

Paul Wakefield felt like a man in a dream. He remembered clearly the days of their youth and their love. Now Marielle was older—mature, tall, and proud. She was wearing the dress of the Huron and as he stared at her, trying to form words, she turned suddenly and said, "Come here, Honor."

Paul Wakefield saw a young boy approach, no more than ten or eleven. One look at his face and he knew the truth, but he heard it from Marielle as she said quietly, "This is your son. His name is Honor Wakefield. . . ."

A House

1 7 7 3 **Part** 1 7 7 5
——
FOUR

Divided

Nineteen

A Matter of Blood

Marielle had been exhausted by the long, tiring voyage. Seasickness had laid her low and for the first half of the journey she could eat nothing. Eventually the sickness passed, but she had lost weight. And now the strain of making such a trip and not knowing how she would be received had made her sleepless. Frenchy Doucett had been delighted to find her and Honor and had taken great care in bringing them out of the camp of the Huron to the coast. It had been Doucett who had convinced her to go to England and find her husband.

"That man—he loves you lak' I nevair see a man love a woman!" Doucett had declared. "When he theenk you die, I was afraid that he would keel himself." When Marielle had protested that too much had happened, that for all she knew Paul would be married, Doucett had assured her, "No! I hear from him now and then. He nevair marry weeth no one. You go and take ze boy. Eet ees what you must do, Marielle."

As Paul Wakefield stood before her, Marielle felt weak and for one moment was afraid that her legs would not hold her up. Honor stood beside her and her arm went around his shoulders. Nearly eleven, he was a strong, wiry child and Marielle took her eyes from Paul to look at Honor's face. He was staring across the room at the tall man who had entered and Marielle could not read his features. Although only one-quarter Ojibway, he had inherited some of the stoicism that went with the race. Turning back, she tried to speak but found she could not. Paul had not changed, except to grow a little heavier than she remembered. Every day during her captivity and every night she had thought of him and had prayed to God that somehow she and Honor would be delivered and would find their way back to him. As the years had passed, her faith had remained strong and she had carefully instructed Honor in the ways of God. Although the boy had never seen his father, he had heard much about him.

"Marielle. . . !" Paul stammered, then stepped forward. Since he appeared to be stunned, Marielle whispered, "I don't suppose you got the letter from Doucett?"

"No . . . nothing," Paul said quietly. His eyes were wide and he shook his head in disbelief. "I can't believe it's you!" Then his eyes went to the boy and he swallowed hard. "When—?"

"Honor was born seven months after I was captured."

Paul Wakefield was a man of great inner resources. His life had built a strength in him that enabled him to handle most situations. But as his eyes locked with those of the boy who stood before him, so straight and so proud, all of his self-reliance deserted him. He came forward awkwardly and put out his hand. "Well, Honor," he said haltingly, "this is a little hard on both of us."

Paul waited for Honor to speak, but the boy said nothing. Studying the youth's face, Paul saw that many of his own features had been passed on to the boy—especially the gray blue eyes, which no Indian had ever had, and the same widow's peak that marked Paul's and David's foreheads. He noted that Honor's hair was auburn and remembered that Marielle had told him that her father, Jeremiah Trent, had had auburn hair. There was no doubt of his heritage.

Marielle said, "You did not get the letter, so you could not know that I was alive—or that you had a son."

"No," Paul said, clearing his throat and trying to think. "I still have your ring. . . . Why didn't you try to escape?"

"I tried many times, but they watched me too closely. It's been a long time, Paul—over eleven years. . . . You haven't changed much."

Paul was growing calmer now. He noticed that her deerskin dress had porcupine quill insets and that her hair was still black with glints of copper. Even the startling blue eyes in the oval-shaped face, the full lips, high cheekbones, and black braids that hung down her back were still the same. "You've changed very little, Marielle. We're both a little older, but I can't believe what's happening."

Marielle waited for Paul to come to her, to embrace her, but he did not. Her heart sank and she wanted to flee when she saw she was a stranger in his eyes. She had been afraid of this moment since the time Doucett had brought her out of the camp, but somehow she'd hoped Paul would still be the same. She had not changed. Her love for him was as it had been before, but now she saw he could not take in everything that was happening.

Shaking his head abruptly, Paul said, "Well, we can't stand here. Come along, we'll go find a place." Turning, he led them out of the room and found Angus McDowell waiting, a question in his eyes. "Angus, we've got to find some place for—" He hesitated and almost said "my wife," but instead changed it to "Marielle and Honor."

"Will you be taking them to Wakefield?"

"Oh, no, I don't think so. That's too far," Paul spoke quickly. "We'll find a good inn here in London. They can rest up and we can—have time to talk."

Honor was watching his father carefully. He was an astute boy and, having been ripped out of his world, was frightened and at the same time defiant. His mother had tried to prepare him for what sort of man his father was, but after years spent in the company of the Huron, he had imbibed some of their hatred and distrust of the white race. His life had been hard, for he had not been accepted into the tribe because of his white blood. He had been an alien among them and his mother had been the only stable thing in his existence. Now as they made the short trip from the docks, he looked out of the windows at the busy streets, dazzled and confused by the multitudes and the huge buildings. After a lifetime of nothing but small cabins or deerskin huts, the city of London was a frightening place to him. He got out of the carriage when it stopped, watching with interest when his father reached up to help his mother out. His eyes brightened a little and he kept very close to Marielle as the party moved inside under a sign with a lion blazoned in red.

Marielle clung to Honor's hand as Paul spoke to the innkeeper, a tall, burly man with a shock of coarse black hair. "I'd like to have a set of rooms," Paul said.

"How many will be staying, sir?"

"Just this lady and this young man."

Both Marielle and Honor felt the weight of the innkeeper's gaze. Although he seemed pleasant enough, each of them had seen enough hostility during their captivity to recognize it. Marielle felt Honor's hand tighten on hers and she leaned close to encourage him.

Paul eyed the innkeeper steadily until the man's eyes dropped. "I want the best rooms you have and their meals will be served there. And I'll want the best of that, too."

"Yes, sir! What name shall I say?"

"My name is Sir Paul Wakefield." Paul reached into his pocket, pulled out a sheaf of bills, took several of them, and handed them to the innkeeper, whose eyes grew large.

"Certainly, Sir Paul! You can depend on it!"

Turning to the couple, Paul said quickly, "You must be exhausted after your trip, Marielle, you and Honor both. I'll leave

292

you here so you can bathe, get a good meal, and be refreshed. I'll come early tomorrow and we'll have time to talk about all this."

"All right, Paul."

Marielle watched as Paul turned and walked away. She looked at McDowell, who said in a friendly fashion, "Ye'll be weel taken care of here, ma'am, ye and yer son." He hesitated, then put out his hand. "Welcome to England."

"Thank you, Mr. McDowell." Even this gesture of friendliness warmed Marielle's heart as the innkeeper led them up to their room. Stepping inside, she saw it was large and airy, with two full-sized mullioned windows that allowed the sunlight and air to come in. "I'll be sending a meal up as soon as me wife has cooked it, ma'am." The innkeeper nodded, then closed the door. Going down the steps, he went behind the bar, pulled out a piece of paper, and, dipping a quill into an inkwell, began to write. When he had finished, he looked up and called, "James! Take this note over to Mr. Keith Valentine!"

The servant, a tall, angular man with close-set pale blue eyes took the paper and asked, "Take it to where?"

"His house, you fool! You know the Valentine place over on the Thames! You took him home more than once!"

"Oh, yes! I remember now." The servant left and the innkeeper leaned his elbows on the bar. Placing his chin on his fist, he murmured, "So, Sir Paul Wakefield has got him a squaw and a papoose! Keith will be glad to hear that. It'll be worth a bit of change, I think, for him to find out about his rival."

When Paul and McDowell entered the carriage, the Scotsman said nothing until the carriage rumbled over the cobblestones. Finally he spoke. "Paul, I've tried to be an honest steward of yer family's resources for years."

"Why, you've been that, Angus," Paul said, startled out of his thoughts. "No one could have been a better lawyer for the family than you."

Shifting slightly on the leather cushions, Angus formed his words carefully. "I'd like to think I could be more than just a lawyer, an employee. I'd like fer ye to think of me as a friend." When Paul did not answer but looked with surprise at him, McDowell continued, "I think ye need a friend at this time. Would ye care to tell me anything aboot what's happened?"

"I haven't been able to talk about it," Paul said slowly, looking down at his polished boots, then back up to the Scotsman's eyes. He began to speak of how he had met Marielle, fallen in love with her, and married her. He traced the whole story and finally ended with an account of what seemed to be her death. "Nothing ever hit me that hard, Angus," he said. "I loved her so much that I guess I just withdrew from the world. Threw myself into making money."

"Ye never thought of marrying again?"

"Oh, I thought of it, but I never seemed to find the right woman."

"She seems to be vurry fine. And the boy—ye knew nothing of him?"

"Nothing." Paul clasped his hands together and squeezed them hard. "It's a bit of a shock, Angus. I don't know what to do. Things have changed. It's been eleven years!"

"Weel now. It'll take a bit of thinking, but to my mind it's not a bad thing for a man to have a beautiful wife and a fine-looking son like I've just seen."

"But they're Indians. You know what that means."

Angus McDowell was a traditionalist. If anyone had come to him earlier and suggested that Sir Paul Wakefield marry an Indian woman, he would have been shocked and would have fought against the idea. But the brief encounter he had had with Marielle had somehow changed his mind. "Do ye still love her?" he inquired quietly.

Paul Wakefield did not answer. His mind was swimming with the enormity of what had happened to him. He remained silent and McDowell did not repeat the question. *He'll have to fight this battle for himself,* McDowell thought and said no more until he got out of the carriage. Paul did not even bid him farewell and the carriage rumbled off. Angus McDowell shook his head sadly, saying to himself, "It can be a good thing for him, but I doubt that Sir Paul Wakefield will know how to handle it."

As soon as Paul entered the room, Dorcas knew that something was wrong. "Where have you been, Paul?" she asked, coming up to take his hand. As usual, she held her crippled hand behind her back because a lifetime had not broken her of this habit. But she held onto Paul and repeated her question, as he seemed unable to reply. "I've been so worried about you."

"I'm sorry, Mother," Paul said. His halting manner was unusual and it troubled Dorcas. He walked over to the window and looked out. The early June air was warm and a breeze swayed the tops of the chestnut trees while large white clouds drifted across the azure sky. The faint sounds of mourning doves floated through the window, along with the muted voices of servants outside in the garden. For a time Paul simply stood there. Then he turned, his eyes filled with something Dorcas could not imagine or understand.

"What is it, Paul? Something awful has happened."

"I—don't know if you could say that, Mother." Paul came over and stood next to her. Despite his misspent life, he knew that this woman loved him and he knew also that he had given her no reason for doing so. When she looked up at him, he noticed her fragility and thought of his father, wishing fleetingly that he were there. Then he realized he had never given his father any reason to be proud. "I don't know how you're going to take this, Mother, but when I was in America, I married an Ojibway woman named Marielle." Paul explained how he had fallen in love with her and married her, then told about the raid and the pain of receiving her ring and finding out it had been discovered on a body burned during the raid. All these years he had thought she was dead.

For a second Paul hesitated in his story, then said tightly, "But she's here, Mother. She's not dead at all." Seeing the startled light in his mother's eyes, he continued to trace the story of how she had been captured by the Huron and taken deep into Canada for these many years. "And she has a son—my son. His name is Honor. He is almost eleven years old."

The shock of Paul's announcement made Dorcas's knees weak. Seeing this, Paul helped her to the sofa. "You remember Frenchy Doucett, my old friend in the trapping business? He found her and bought her out of slavery. He wrote, but I didn't get the letter, so as you can imagine," he said wryly, "it came as quite a shock when I walked in and saw Marielle and the boy."

"Why didn't you come to me at once, Paul?"

"I didn't know what to do. My head's whirling like a hive of bees." Paul got up and began to pace the floor. "I never heard of such a thing before."

"But is she all right?"

"She looks very well, but I don't see how. To be a slave among an enemy tribe—that's not the best life in the world."

"But why didn't you bring her here?"

Paul stopped abruptly and came over to sit down beside her again. "Mother, I can't do that."

"You can't do it? Why can't you do it? She's your wife—and the boy—he's your son!"

Paul had been half drunk for the three days since Marielle and Honor had showed up. At first he had taken refuge in just a few drinks, but the more he had thought about his situation, the more confused he had grown. The liquor had not helped him to think more clearly, and it had also been unable to blot out the problem. However, he had come to one conclusion and now he spoke it to his mother. "I can't accept her here as my wife. You know what it's like in England."

Dorcas Wakefield was a mild, generous woman, warmhearted and filled with love for her sons. Now, however, righteous anger rose in her. In a voice colder than Paul had ever heard, she said, "And why can't you do it? Are you too good? You're so holy that you can't have a wife with Indian blood? And your son? Are you going to throw him out?" She continued to speak harshly and Paul's eyes fell, unable to meet his mother's gaze.

"Mother, you don't understand. Why, I'd be thrown out of society. No one would accept us."

"So you want to marry Stella Frazier with all her money and her society connections! Will that make you more of a man?"

"Mother, I—"

"Oh, Son! Haven't you ever read Scripture? 'What shall it profit a man, if he shall gain the whole world, and lose his own soul?'" Tears appeared in Dorcas Wakefield's eyes and she grabbed Paul's arm with amazing strength. "Paul, you've thrown your soul away all of your life and now God has given you a chance. He's restored to you that which the locusts have eaten. You think I haven't seen the bitterness that's been in you? The unhappiness? And you think to find it by marrying a rich woman? You have more money now than you can spend!"

As Paul Wakefield listened, the words his mother spoke from Scripture somehow burned into him. *What shall it profit a man if he shall gain the world, and lose his own soul?*

Paul felt something he hadn't really felt before—fear. Now, confused and filled with this new emotion, he said, "Mother, you—have to give me time."

"God *has* given you time, Son," Dorcas said. "I want to see my daughter-in-law and I want to see my grandson."

Paul swallowed hard, for his mother had never spoken so harshly to him before. "All right, Mother. I'll take you to see her."

"Paul," Dorcas whispered, touching his cheek. "Don't throw your life away! Your soul belongs to God and now he's given you a precious gift. Don't put your honor in the dust." Then suddenly she said, "The boy's name is Honor?"

"Yes. Marielle calls him that."

"Honor Wakefield," Dorcas said, her dark blue eyes warm. "What a wonderful name for a child! He's of our blood, Paul, the Wakefield line. He comes from noble and good men and women and now you have a son to carry on for you."

Paul Wakefield listened numbly. He left the house finally, agreeing to come back and get his mother, but first he knew he had an unpleasant task. Setting his jaw, he got into the carriage and said, "Henry, drive to the Frazier home."

<hr />

As Paul entered the opulent drawing room, he was shocked to find Keith Valentine standing beside Stella. "Hello, Valentine," he said and stood waiting, his eyes fixed on Valentine.

"Well, I'm surprised to see you here, Wakefield," Valentine said, a glint in his eye. "I'm surprised you would have time to leave your dusky Indian maiden and her papoose."

Fury rose like a wave over Paul Wakefield, almost blotting out his surroundings. He had a terrible desire to throw himself across the room and smash the grin from Valentine's face. Somehow he managed to get a grip on himself and said, "You're well informed. I suppose your spy system works better than most."

"Oh, I don't begrudge a man a little entertainment. I understand those Indian women are rather easy."

He's trying to make me lose my temper, Paul thought. *And he's doing a good job, but I've got to put up with him.* He turned to Stella and said, "I need to speak with you, Stella—alone."

"I was just leaving," Valentine said. He took Stella's hand and kissed it. "I suppose you do have things to talk about, but I'll be seeing you later."

"All right, Keith."

Stella was dressed for the occasion, as always. She was, Paul thought abruptly, like an actress who played many roles. Her dress, made of the finest, apricot-colored silk, suited her, but there was a sober expression on her face. "What's this all about, Paul?"

"What did Valentine tell you?"

"One of his friends saw you, the woman, and the boy at the Red Lion Inn. He sent word to Keith and Keith came to ask me about it."

"He takes a great interest in my affairs, doesn't he?"

Stella shook her head. "I don't understand, Paul. Who is this woman? Did you have her brought here from America? Was she your mistress there? Is the boy yours?"

Paul said in a steady tone, "I told you once that I was married but that she had died." He told the tale of Marielle's last eleven years simply and boldly, ending by saying, "And so, until I saw her in that room, Stella, I thought Marielle was dead. And I certainly never dreamed that I had a son."

Stella listened carefully. Keith had made a joke out of it, saying, "If you marry Wakefield, you'll have to put up with his Indian mistress. I will admit he has good taste. I never saw a more beautiful woman."

Now jealousy burned in Stella Frazier and she came up and whispered, "Paul, I can understand. You were young and she was available. Everyone knows how easy native women are. I can understand a man's desires."

Paul shook his head. "It was more than that, Stella. It's true enough that white men have used the Indian women callously, but I never did. I saw her and fell in love with her, knowing all the time it would mean cutting myself off from England." He tried his best to explain to Stella how it was, but he saw that it made no impression on her. Finally he said, "In any case, she's alive and the boy is my son."

Stella turned and walked around the room quickly. She loved Paul Wakefield and their uniting would mean two fortunes rather than one.

"Paul," she pleaded, her eyes fixed on his face, "you can't have it both ways. You can have your Indian woman and all that she can bring you, but you know what troubles that will be. You'll never be accepted. I love you, Paul. We can have all that a man and woman can have." She came to him then and kissed him, her lips lingering on his. As she felt him stir beneath her embrace, she pressed herself more closely and began kissing his neck. "Paul, we love each other."

Paul was stirred by this woman and her sexuality, as he always was, but this time he drew back. "Stella, I've got to be fair to Marielle and the boy."

"I know. I'm glad you feel responsible, but all that takes is money, Paul. And you have plenty of that. All you have to do is give her money. She'd be very unhappy here in England. She needs to go back to her own people, and the boy, too. They would never fit in. . . ." Then, pressing against him again, she said softly, "We've got each other, Paul. We can't lose that."

After Paul left, he wandered in despair around the streets of London. He had never been so confused, but out of the many voices, one seemed to rise above all the rest—his mother's. He spoke her words aloud as he moved along the foggy streets. "'What shall it profit a man if he shall gain the whole world, and lose his own soul?'"

He thought of Marielle's face and the time they had spent together, loving each other. "She's still lovely," he said to himself.

"She's still the same despite all the horrors of slavery in a Huron camp. She hasn't changed, I can tell. And the boy, I can see myself in him. He's my blood!"

As he finally turned and moved toward the Red Lion Inn, he spoke aloud, startling a bypasser. "I've been a fool all my life—but I'll pay the bill for this if it costs every penny I have!"

Twenty

A TIME FOR HONOR

After four days in their rooms, Marielle felt she had to get out. "Come, Honor," she said finally.

"Where are we going, Mother?" Honor asked with some alarm.

"I can't stand these rooms any longer. I've got to get outside."

Quickly Honor rose from the chair where he had been staring out of the window and followed his mother downstairs. The innkeeper looked at them with a squint, as he always did. Honor met the big man's eyes evenly, then followed his mother as she left the Red Lion Inn.

"How will we ever find this place again?" Honor asked, casting a worried look about the twisted streets that interwove everywhere he looked.

"We know it's the Red Lion Inn. We can ask if we get lost." Marielle smiled and said, "You could find your way home through a forest. This isn't too different."

However, as the two made their way somewhat fearfully through London, they discovered it *was* different. The world seemed to be on wheels, with carts and coaches thundering by. They passed by men, women, and children at every corner— some in the sooty rags of chimney sweeps—but they also encountered the aristocracy, gazing languidly out of their sedans borne by lackeys with thick legs. As they moved slowly along, Honor watched porters sweating under their burdens and trades- men scurrying around like ants. "Be careful, Mother!" Honor reached over and pulled his mother back just in time to avoid a deluge of slop that someone threw out of one of the upper windows that overhung the narrow street.

"It's like living in an anthill!" Marielle exclaimed in a low voice. "Don't get far away, Honor."

The two finally found themselves in front of a shop with glass windows. Stopping for a moment, Marielle looked down at her deerskin dress, then glanced at Honor's buckskin trousers and jacket. She made up her mind instantly. "Come along. We're going to buy some English clothes."

The next hour was difficult for both of them. The clerk, fortunately, was a young man who was able to hide his astonishment at seeing two American Indians enter his shop. Politely he advanced and said, "Yes, madam. May I help you?"

"I want to buy an English dress and shoes and my son needs English clothes also."

"Certainly. I think we have just what you need. Come this way, madam."

An hour later the two emerged and Marielle stopped to look at their reflection in the glass windows. She marveled at the difference in what she saw. She was wearing a light brown-and- blue printed dress with an off-white lace ruffle around the neckline and elbow-length sleeves. The full skirt, of the same print, had a small ruffle of lace along the edges. Long ribbons hung down her back from a small straw hat that was trimmed with flowers. Honor wore a light brown knee-length coat, a tan waistcoat, a white, ruffled shirt, tan knee breeches, white stock- ings, and black leather boots.

Honor looked down at his feet. "These shoes hurt!"

"You'll get used to them," Marielle said. "My! Don't you look handsome though! A fine young gentleman."

Marielle walked along, holding to Honor's arm, and the two of them found their way back to the Red Lion Inn. They smelled cooking meat and ordered kidney pie, both finding it very good. As they sat there drinking cider, a new experience for both of them, Honor looked across at his mother with a strange expression on his face. "I want to go home!"

Marielle could not answer for a moment, for she had some of the same inclinations. Paul had come back twice, both times for short visits, and there had been great constraint between the three of them. Marielle looked at her son. "I feel the same," she murmured heavily. "But where can we go?"

"Back to our people."

"Our people are gone. Frenchy said that only Red Deer is left and he is an old man and will not live long. The Ojibway were wiped out in the attack."

"We can find someplace, Mother. I hate all of this."

Marielle started to answer, but before she could speak, a shadow fell across her face. She looked up, startled to see a tall man with blond hair staring at them curiously. Immediately Marielle was cautious. She turned away, ignoring the man.

"Welcome to England!" The man, Keith Valentine, smiled at them. "I suppose you're suspicious of strangers. My name is Valentine. I'm a friend of Paul's."

Instantly both Marielle and Honor looked up. "You know my husband?"

"Oh, yes. Quite well. I understand you've just come from America to be with him."

"That is so," Marielle said carefully. There was something about the man that troubled her, a boldness in his eyes that she had learned to associate with men who were in pursuit of her. During all of her years with the Huron, she had seen it and had managed to keep away from danger whenever it approached. She rose, wanting to get away, and said, "Come, Honor."

Valentine, however, reached out and seized her arm with a powerful grasp. "Now, just a minute. Don't run away like that. You and I are going to be good friends."

"Let her go!"

Valentine turned with amusement to see the boy's gray blue eyes fixed on him murderously.

"Well, now, my young savage! I'm just going to have a talk with your mother. Why don't you run along!"

"Let her go!"

Valentine laughed and turned back, increasing his grip so tightly that pain showed in Marielle's face, although she said nothing. "Let me go!" she said.

"After we've had a little talk. Now we'll just—" A cry of pain burst from Valentine's lips, for a streak of fire seemed to have run down his right forearm. He looked down and saw that his sleeve was slashed and blood stained his white cuff. Releasing Marielle, he whirled, his face filled with fury. He stared at the Indian boy who held a knife in one hand. As the gray blue eyes glared up at him fiercely, Valentine snarled. "Cut me, will you? I'll teach you!" Valentine's eyes fell on a pair of fencing foils fastened to the wall to his left. He sprang to them, ripped one of them off, and advanced, saying, "Drop that knife or I'll run you through!"

Marielle moved forward, putting her body between the advancing Valentine and her son. But she had no time to do more than that, for a voice suddenly sliced through the room. "Drop that sword, Valentine, or I'll ram it down your throat!"

Valentine turned to see Paul Wakefield, who had entered and was now striding across the room with murder on his face. Relieved to see the man had no weapon, Valentine cried, "What will you do, Wakefield? Your whelp there has cut me and I'll have—"

There was no time for him to say anything else, for Paul had picked up a chair and brought it crashing down on Valentine's head. Valentine only had time to raise his hands to fend off the blow, and the rungs struck the sword from his hand. He fell to the floor gasping, but before he could arise he felt the point of a sword at his throat.

"I'd love to ram this through your throat! It's what you deserve!" Paul Wakefield's face was dark with anger. He expertly swept the sword across Valentine's chest, cutting through the coat, shirt, and cravat. "Get out! Or I'll cut you up into little bits!"

Valentine rose to his feet, a murderous light in his eyes. "You'll pay for this, Wakefield! You'll pay!"

"Get out!"

Wakefield waited until Valentine had left, then turned to the innkeeper, who was frozen in place after watching the entire thing. "If that swine comes in here again, throw him out!"

The innkeeper did not answer, could not, for there was something inherently dangerous in Paul Wakefield's manner.

"Come along," Paul said. "Get your things. You can't stay here."

"Where are we going?" Marielle asked, her heart still fluttering.

Looking at the two who stood before him, Paul Wakefield made a quick decision. "You can't stay here," he repeated. "You're coming with me."

Suddenly Honor spoke up. "You don't want us! Send us back to our home across the sea!"

A sudden flush tinged Paul Wakefield's cheeks. He stared at the boy, his face so much like his own, and seemed to see himself as he was when he was eleven years of age. He said slowly, "I'm glad that you protected your mother, Honor. It was a gallant thing to do."

Her face pale, Marielle managed to say, "Paul, send us back home. We can't stay here."

For one moment there was silence and both Honor and Marielle thought that the tall man meant to agree. But then his lips closed with determination. He shook his head with an almost angry motion and his voice was even and quiet as he said, "I'm taking you to Wakefield."

"I don't think we need to bother with dinner tonight, Caroline," Dorcas said. The two women had come to the kitchen to talk with the cook. "There's no point in cooking a lot for just the two of us."

"I suppose not. Anything will do, Cook. You decide."

"Yes, ma'am."

As they left the kitchen and were on their way down the hall to the small parlor, Dorcas, whose hearing was better than Caroline's, said, "That was a carriage driving up, I think."

"I can't imagine who that would be," Caroline said. "It's getting late. Come along. I want to show you something that was in last week's *Spectator.*"

The two women had no more than entered the parlor and sat down when Ives, the butler, came in with a strange look on his face. "It's Sir Paul, Lady Caroline. He's here with—"

Seeing shock in the normally unexpressive butler's eyes, Dorcas rose. "What's the matter? Tell Paul to come in." She turned with Caroline toward the door and waited as Ives disappeared. "What's wrong with Ives? I've never seen him so shaken."

Caroline had no time to answer, for at that moment Paul entered, his face pale. He stepped back and, with a gesture of his arm, indicated the two who had accompanied him. "Mother, I want you to meet Marielle. And this is Honor." To the frightened pair, he said, "This is my mother and this is Lady Caroline Wakefield."

After her talk with Paul, Dorcas had been praying for exactly this sort of thing. She took a deep breath and moved forward at once. Going to Honor, she held her hand out and said, "Honor, I'm your grandmother and I'm very glad to see you." To Honor's complete amazement, the older woman with the maimed hand leaned forward and kissed him on the cheek. So shocked was the boy that he could not say a word, but he lifted startled eyes to face the woman.

"You're very like your father," Dorcas said. "The same eyes." She touched the widow's peak on his forehead, "And he always had this." Her hand lingered on his cheek as she said, "I'm so glad to meet you, my boy." Then she turned and went to Marielle and, without asking permission, kissed her also on the cheek. "My dear, I'm so very glad that you've come. I've been praying that you and Honor would come to be with us."

Marielle was unable to speak. The unexpected kindness of the elderly woman went straight to her heart, for ever since she had known Paul she had had an inherent fear of meeting his family. He had told her that they were very wealthy and leaders in English society and she had expected them to be arrogant and haughty. But there was such gentleness in Dorcas's face that Marielle could not resist her. She looked at Honor and saw that he was as surprised and taken aback as she was. "Thank you, Mrs. Wakefield," she whispered.

Lady Caroline came forward and offered her hand, both to Honor and to Marielle, greeting them warmly. "Welcome to Wakefield. I'm so glad you've come, but I must go to the cook. This is cause for a celebration!"

As Lady Caroline left the room, Dorcas's heart began to beat faster, almost fluttering as it had from time to time over the past few months. For a moment the room seemed to swim and Paul came forward anxiously. "Are you all right, Mother?"

"Oh, yes—quite all right. I'm just so happy to see your family."

Paul hugged his mother and said, "I brought them to Wakefield. I know that's what you wanted."

"It is." Dorcas turned to her son with pride in her eyes. "You did well, Paul," she whispered and saw that her words touched him. Then she said, "Why don't you take Honor up and give him your old room? He can stay there. I imagine some of your old things are still there. And I'll take Marielle to her room. We'll put her in the guest room on the second floor."

"All right, Mother." Paul and Marielle's eyes locked for a moment and he saw that some of the fear that had been with her since they had begun their journey to Wakefield had faded. "You go along with Mother, Marielle," he said. "Honor and I will be all right."

After a nod of approval from his mother, Honor followed his father out of the parlor, leaving the two women alone.

"I'm so excited I don't know what to do! Imagine! My daughter-in-law. A brand-new daughter-in-law—at least brand-new to me." She came closer, and since her sight was not as keen as it once was, she leaned forward. "How lovely you are, my dear. I can understand how Paul fell in love with you."

Marielle's cheeks were tinged with color. "That—was a long time ago."

"It doesn't matter. Love never changes."

Startled, Marielle looked at the older woman. "Do you believe that?"

"Yes, I do."

Marielle dropped her eyes. "I wish I did, but things happen."

"Come along, my dear. We'll have lots of time to talk. I want to tell you all the things Paul did when he was a boy and you must tell me all about how he courted and won you. I know that was an exciting time."

"Yes, it was," Marielle said, blinking away the tears brimming in her eyes. The warmth of Dorcas Wakefield's love enveloped her and as she followed the older woman up the stairs, she breathed a prayer. *Thank you, God, for bringing us this far.* She had prayed for years to be restored to her husband, and all that had seemed lost from the moment she saw Paul at the docks. But now at Wakefield, through Paul's mother's love, hope came to her afresh.

The two women entered the room and Dorcas said, "This will be yours, my dear. I hope you like it."

Marielle looked around the large room, which was more beautiful than she could have imagined. The room had two large windows but now was lit by a large astral lamp that had been placed on a bedside table. The walls were covered with a blue-and-green patterned wallpaper and the floors with a blue and white carpet. Her eyes took in the large oak bed, canopy, bed-curtains, and the ornate fireplace. There was a beautiful mahogany bookcase filled with many leather-bound books, and a washstand with a porcelain bowl and pitcher.

"I'm going to have the servants bring hot water up, and a sweet young girl named Phoebe will help you dress for dinner."

"But I don't have any other clothes—except my Indian dress."

"That's no problem. I'm sure you are about the same size as my dear niece, Bethany Morgan. She stayed here so much that she left some of her clothes here. This was her room and in this wardrobe I'm sure you can find something. Phoebe will help you. She's very good with things like that. Maybe she can help you with your hair as well."

"I—thank you, Mrs. Wakefield."

"Don't thank me. This is your home, my dear." Using even her twisted hand, Dorcas once again embraced the young woman, holding her tightly.

Tentatively Marielle put her arms around the old woman. She had not caressed anyone for years and it was very strange to her. There was a fragility about Dorcas Wakefield and she held her carefully, but when she stepped back she saw that Dorcas was weeping. "It's so good to see my new daughter and my new grandson!"

Marielle did not move for a moment after Dorcas left. But then the tears welled over and she leaned against the wall sobbing.

By the time Phoebe, a plump, pink-cheeked young girl no more than sixteen, came in, Marielle had gained control of herself.

"And now, ma'am, I get to help you bathe and pick your clothes out. Won't that be fine, ma'am? I'll make you look like a queen."

"Will you, Phoebe?"

"Oh, yes, ma'am! You'll see!"

Down the hall Paul was showing Honor his room. It brought back old memories. He ran his fingers across some of the books in the bookshelf, pulled one out, and opened it. Looking up, he said, "I read these books when I was about your age." Getting no answer, he put the book back and walked around, touching the treasures that had meant so much to him when he had first come to Wakefield. Suddenly he turned and said, "I wasn't born here, you know, Honor."

"Where were you born?"

"In a very poor house not awfully far from here. It was very strange to me and my brother when we first came here. I know it's strange to you now, but I hope you'll let me be your friend. There are all sorts of things," Paul said, "that we might do. There are horses to ride. I can teach you to hunt. I'm sure you already know how to fish, but perhaps you could teach me a few things."

Honor stood stiffly in front of the tall man. He distrusted him, as he distrusted practically everyone except his mother. Some of his resistance had been broken down by the kiss that the elderly woman had given him, but still it was this man with whom he must deal. Since he had been mistreated all of his life by his captors, he had fought his fights and carried his scars alone—except for his mother. Now, after the terrible journey into this strange place, he looked up and asked, "We're going to stay here?"

"Why, yes," Paul answered, puzzled by the remark.

"For how long? For a long time?"

Paul made the mistake of letting doubt show in his face. Then, seeing that the boy read his expression, he said quickly, "Yes, I hope for a very long time."

But Honor shook his head. "You wouldn't want us. I've seen how the whites look at us because we're different! We're Ojibway."

"Yes, but your mother is only half Ojibway and you're only one-quarter. You have more English blood in you than Indian."

"The Huron never would accept me because I was white and now your people will never accept me because I'm Indian!"

Paul sat down carefully and began to talk to the boy. Slowly he tried to express himself, but he found himself in difficulty almost at once. He tried to encourage Honor by saying, "You'll be whatever man you make of yourself—with the help of others."

Honor didn't answer but instead looked him straight in the eye and asked, "What about my mother? Do you care for her?"

The direct question caught Paul Wakefield off guard. He blinked and lowered his head, unable to meet the direct gaze from eyes so much like his own. Long thoughts raced through his mind, but he could find no words to give to the young boy who stood watching him.

Finally Paul raised his eyes. "I did once," he said quietly, knowing he could say no more than this. Then he left the room, saying, "I'll come back and we can talk later."

Honor watched as the door closed and then he sat down abruptly. He was weary, confused, and, most of all, afraid. He had come to an alien place where he had found no acceptance except from the woman called Dorcas. Now as he looked around the room, he felt more alone than he ever had in his life.

Twenty-One

CLOUDS OVER
BOSTON

When Ivor Morgan had entered the army it was with great hopes that he would one day rise in the ranks. His greatest opportunity came when he was sent with his regiment to America. Ivor still intended on bringing his fiancée to America, but money was so very short. They had agreed to wait for a more auspicious time. On the surface, his regiment's being here did not seem like a propitious assignment. The Americans had been giving the Crown trouble and General Thomas Gage had been assigned to settle the unruly rebels down. Better men than he had failed, but always the Crown was insistent that the Colonies should come under the iron hand of England.

Perhaps it was pure fortune, but afterward Ivor always called it God's providence that he met General Gage. A kindly, gentlemanly fellow, Gage favored officers who had ambition and talent like Ivor Morgan. Shortly after the young lieutenant arrived in America, Gage had singled him out and it became well known among the officers that young Morgan was due for rapid promotion.

Ivor did not like America, but duty was duty and the opportunity to serve as an aide to a ranking, commanding general was much to his liking. He found his quarters acceptable, his fellow officers amiable, and his duties light. He did not, however, understand the politics of England concerning the Colonies in North America. Keeping his eyes open and his counsel to himself, he filed information rapidly. The one thing that was abundantly clear was that the Americans hated their English cousins. Almost three weeks after his arrival and assignment to General Gage's staff, he received a lesson in English governing power. He had attended a staff meeting and afterward General Gage had called out, "Oh, Lieutenant. Stay awhile. I have some letters and my adjutant is absent. I'd be obliged if you would write them for me."

"Of course, sir. It would be my pleasure."

For over two hours Ivor obliged, thanking the Lord that his strong suit was good handwriting, learned under a hard headmaster. He wrote quickly and legibly, pleasing the general. When the last letter was completed and they were relaxing, Gage asked, "Well, Lieutenant, what do you think of life in America?"

"To be truthful, General, I really don't understand our position here. Obviously the colonists hate us. Their citizens throw rocks at our soldiers and call them lobsterbacks."

"You don't understand it, eh? Well, it's no wonder. I'm not sure anybody does," Thomas Gage remarked, leaning back in his chair. "I think a little history lesson, combined with diplomacy, might be in order." Gage loved to lecture and began to speak rapidly, outlining the history that had brought tension between the Colonies and the mother country. "I think it began when England imported her kings from Germany—the Hanoverian line. The first was George I, who despised England so much he never bothered to learn English. He loved pleasure and was not delicate in his choice of it. No woman came to him amiss if she was willing and very fat. He was a stubborn, ignorant man, not fit to rule England."

"Was George II an improvement, sir?"

"No, not a whit! He was as greedy as Satan, and Lord Chesterfield said he never knew of him performing a charitable deed. He had the puffy, gargoylelike features of all the Hanoverians, but he did have courage. He was the last English king to lead troops into battle—that was at Dettingen against the French. But what a miser! He gave Queen Caroline a team of horses—then used them himself and charged her for the fodder they ate!"

"Not my idea of a noble ruler, General."

"Noble! He hated his son, the Prince of Wales. George said, 'My dear firstborn is the greatest beast in the world and I most heartily wish he were out of it!'"

"I trust his mother felt more for her son."

"Less, Lieutenant, less! She said, 'Fred is a nauseous beast and he cares for nobody but his nauseous little self.' He was not much, but he left a son named George before he died."

"Our present sovereign, George III."

"Yes—and I must say he's a better man than either of the others. He's a weak man, however. He was brought up to believe that God put him on the throne of England to make her a great nation, but he's not the man to do it."

"He's a good family man and rather handsome, from all I hear," Ivor said.

"Yes, I must admit that. Fourteen children—can you imagine?" Gage grinned and yawned hugely. "If it hadn't been for the war, George might have done well—but he's making a mistake about America."

"What mistake, sir?"

"He thinks the colonists ought to pay for the freedom that His Majesty's troops won for them in Canada. And he's right, but he'll never make them do it. These colonists are as stubborn as mules and they've got their minds made up they'll fight before they pay taxes imposed by England."

"But they couldn't win such a war!" Ivor protested. "England has the biggest army in the world!"

"And where is it? All over the world," Gage snapped. "Mark my words, if we go to war with the Colonies, we'll lose!"

By now Gage had finished four glasses of port and was a little drunk. Grinning foolishly, he said, "Well, get to bed. But you see, my young friend, we can't win this war. Good night, Lieutenant."

Ivor went to his quarters puzzled, and somewhat shocked, by General Gage's analysis of the political and military situation. Never once in all his thinking had it occurred to him that England might lose her possessions in North America. He refused to believe it. And as he pulled the blankets up, he muttered, "The general's been drinking a little too much. I'm sure he wouldn't want any of this repeated. We can't lose here. A bunch of unruly, rude farmers against the power of the British Empire! Impossible!"

General Gage never mentioned his history lesson or his political philosophy to Ivor again after that night. He did, however, remark the next day, "Men say odd things when they've drunk one glass too many, eh, Lieutenant?"

"Certainly, sir."

"Well, let's get on with our business then."

Ivor filed the lecture and the general's attitude in his mind and set about to be the best soldier he could. It was very difficult for him because he could not walk down the streets of Boston without enduring the jeers and taunts of the citizens. They were a bold lot, stirred up, he understood, by Samuel Adams, who kept the political pot boiling. He had learned to feel compassion for the common soldiers whose circumstances were so hard that many of them had to work at whatever jobs they could find during their off hours just to make ends meet. He made up his mind that if he ever had any influence in the world of the military, he would see that the men were better paid and better cared for.

One bright spot of his duty was that there were, surprisingly, many social occasions. The royalist citizens, people loyal to the Crown, saw to it that there were parties, balls, breakfasts, suppers, and entertainment of all kinds. Several dramas were given, which, though rather amateurish, were welcome enough to the bored troops of His Majesty's service.

Ivor had attended one of these on the behalf of the major of his company, Major Stephens. The major liked young Morgan and as the two stood at a table partaking of the refreshments, Major Stephens commented on various civilians, seeming to know them all. He had been in Boston longer than most of the troops, knew the situation well, and was good friends with many of the loyal subjects of King George.

As the two men stood talking, a curvaceous woman with flaming red hair came up and leaned against Ivor. "I don't believe I've met this young man, Major."

Major Stephens covered a grin with his hand, then quickly introduced the two. "No. He's new to our service here. This is Miss Lena Miller, one of the local beauties, as you can see, Lieutenant Morgan."

Miss Miller was very attractive but a little overblown. She wore too much makeup and was rather forward, pressing herself against young Morgan at every opportunity.

Ivor finally managed to separate himself from the young woman and upon encountering the major asked, "What sort of a woman is that?"

"A man-hungry woman! There are quite a few of them here in Boston. You don't mean you resisted her advances?"

"Yes," Ivor said and added nothing else.

"Well, you're a long way from home. No one will know what you do over here. Miss Miller would certainly make a willing companion, I can tell you from personal experience. It's a long way from England," he added, encouraging the young lieutenant.

"But it's not a long way from God."

His remark caught Major Stephens off guard and then he remembered that Ivor Morgan was a religious young man. "Well, it's good to see there's one officer in His Majesty's forces who has a moral fiber. Although, I must say, that America is about as far away from heaven as one can get."

Ivor smiled at that remark and the two went on talking. Stephens commented on the lack of morality in Boston, then shrugged. "I suppose it's no worse than it is in London or Lancaster."

"I suppose not."

"Look! You see that fellow over there? The one standing by Colonel Ames?"

"Yes. What about him?"

"His name is Charles Jaspers. A good friend of the Crown. We need his sort over here. There are so many of the other kind. But the thing is, he's got a wife in New Hampshire and three children."

"What's so unusual about that?"

"I was just pointing out that all the immorality doesn't exist on the army's side. Jasper's brought a woman back from England with him. He introduces her as his wife, but everyone knows that's not so. She's already had affairs that I know of with two officers in our regiment. He can't keep her."

Ivor was not very interested, although such things were common enough, he supposed. Five minutes later, his whole attitude changed when Mr. Jaspers and his companion walked up to Major Stephens. After greeting Mr. Jasper, Major Stephens turned to him and said, "Mr. Jaspers, may I introduce Lieutenant Morgan?"

"Happy to know you, Lieutenant." Jaspers extended a limp hand, which Ivor shook, and then said, "This is my wife, Margaret." The woman, who'd been facing away from him, turned on hearing her name called and Ivor caught his breath—for the woman he faced was Margaret Wakefield, David's wife!

The two stared at each other speechlessly for a moment. Ivor could not think of a thing to say. Finally when he saw that Margaret was staring at him, also in shock, he said merely, "My pleasure."

"Lieutenant," Margaret said. She looked older than he remembered. He had not seen her for several years and knew, of course, that she had left David for another man. But the shock at finding her here was so great that he made his excuses and moved out of the house. He walked woodenly back to his quarters and for a long time sat at his desk, wondering what to do. At length he said, "Something's got to be done." Picking up a quill and a sheet of paper, he began writing: "My dear sister Bethany, I have the most unfortunate news for you. . . ."

***

"Susan, you can't have all of Andy's things!" Bethany reached over and picked up the toy camel that Susan had snatched out of Andy's grasp. The two children were playing with a set of carved animals that she had brought them and Susan, as usual, had tried to appropriate them all for herself.

When Susan began to cry, Bethany said, "It's late. You've got to go to bed. Both of you." This, of course, brought protests, but ignoring them, she washed the children, put their nightclothes on them, and put them in bed. As usual, she said a prayer for them, then kissed them.

"Auntie Bethany," Susan said, "I sorry I mean to Andy."

"I know you are, darling. You won't do it again."

"Maybe," Susan said blandly. "But you love me anyway."

Bethany had to restrain a grin. "Yes, I will. Now, go to sleep." At that moment David came in and leaned over to kiss both children.

"Did you have a good time?" he asked. And when they affirmed that they did, he said, "Say good-night."

"Auntie Bethany, you stay with us? You be our mummy."

Andy was sleepy, but he nodded, adding, "Yes, that would be good."

Bethany's face burned and she said quickly, "Go to sleep now."

She turned and left the room, with David following after her. He shut the door and said quietly, "Children say odd things, don't they?"

"Yes, they do," Bethany said, glancing at the clock on the mantel. "It's late. I'd better go."

"Oh, stay just a little while. We've had hardly any chance to work together. The children take all your time."

"That's what I come for. To take care of them."

David blinked and then came over to her. He was tired, for he was still putting in long hours on his newspaper work, then trying to write his book. "I know you do," he said, "and I don't know what I would have done without you."

Bethany was very conscious of his presence. She had come often to help with the children, for David had little money to pay someone to stay with them. Lately she had come when he was gone, but tonight he had come home early. The four of them had enjoyed the supper that she had fixed and then had played together until the children had grown weary. Now, however, she was nervous. "I must go."

"Bethany, wait!" David came up to her and to her surprise, took her arms. He had never touched her, not in all these weeks that she had been coming to his little house. Now there was something in his eyes that she could not read and, very conscious of his hands on her shoulders, she said, "What is it, David? You look so odd."

"I've found a publisher for my novel."

Joy surged through Bethany. It was what she had prayed for and they had hoped for and dreamed of. Without thinking, she threw her arms around him and hugged him. "Oh, David, that's *wonderful!*"

David, shocked by the pressure of her trim figure as she clung to him, put his arms around her and held her, his lips against her fragrant hair. "I couldn't have done it without you. You've been so wonderful."

Bethany lifted her face to say how glad she was and, before she realized what was happening, David lowered his head and kissed her. She knew she should pull away, but she had been lonely for a long time and now his strong arms drew her closer, enfolding her, and the pressure of his lips on hers was sweet. Powerless to stop herself, her arms went around his neck and she pulled him ever closer, lost in the moment, forgetful of everything except his caress.

David held her tightly, savoring the touch of her smooth lips, her fragrance, and her womanliness. Then suddenly she pulled away, her lips barely framing the words, "David! We must never do this again! You have a wife!"

David's joy fled. "I'm sorry. It was all my fault, Bethany. I don't know what came over me. It's just that—well, you're so good to me and the children and I'm so grateful to you."

"David!" Bethany said, her lips trembling. "That wasn't gratitude!"

David flushed. "No, you're more honest than I am. It was more than that. You're such a lovely young woman—and so sweet and generous."

Reaching up, Bethany put her hand over his lips. "You mustn't say such things to me! You mustn't!"

David removed her hand. "I'm sorry. I will be very careful, but you must know you've always been very precious to me. And now—more than ever."

Bethany was shaken. They were still in a half embrace and she felt the impulse to throw herself into his arms again. Everything that was within her as a woman cried out for him, for she needed his love. She needed to be told that she was sweet and precious and that she was lovely. As the hunger she had suppressed for years rose in her, she pulled herself back, whispering, "I—I must go!" Grabbing her coat and hat, she fled the house. Hearing the door close behind her, she paused for a moment outside. "I love him so much, but I can't let it ever happen again. I can't get close to him! It wouldn't be right! It wouldn't be right!"

The next day the letter came from Ivor and her instinct was to go to David at once, but Ivor had written: "I cannot tell David what his wife has become. He already knows, but I must tell someone. Perhaps it would be wise for you to tell him. You two have always been so close. I'll leave it with you, my dear sister. You have wisdom beyond your years and I know that you will do the right thing."

Bethany lowered the letter and as she thought of David, her heart seemed to break. She loved him and she knew what a terrible thing it must be for him to be rejected.

"I can't go to him with this! I can't!"

Slowly she folded the letter and gazed across her room staring blankly at the wall. For a long time she stood there in thought, then she said, "I could never love another man! Never as long as I live!"

Twenty - Two

Two Women

November arrived with icy blasts that paralyzed the land. The ground around Wakefield was layered with thick, fluffy snow that blinded the eyes when the sun struck the crystals. The house itself was transformed into a fairyland and Marielle never tired of putting on her heavy winter clothes, going outside, and climbing the rise to the west to look down on it. The circular tower and spire were like nothing she had ever seen and the steep roofs were punctuated by the chimneys that broke the symmetry of the crystalline surface. Heavy rolls of smoke poured out of the chimneys, rose slowly as if reluctant to leave the earth, and then were caught by powerful gusts that disseminated them before they had reached a hundred feet.

Paul had taken Honor out early one Thursday morning for another hunting lesson. They had eaten a hearty breakfast and then Paul had seen to it that Honor had bundled up in warm clothing. He had taken the boy to the bootmaker and bought him an excellent pair of leather boots that fit better than the first ones Marielle had bought for him. Now, wearing thick gray trousers and a heavy blue shirt, both made of wool, and a sleek fur jacket that buttoned up around his neck, Honor's eyes gleamed as the two of them left the house.

"Better put on your hat," Paul advised. "Your ears will freeze."

He reached out and playfully tweaked Honor's ear lightly, then grinned when the boy said, "Ow!"

"Hurts, doesn't it? I always hated it when people did that to me."

Honor turned quickly to look at his father. There was still a wall between them, but they had spent much time together, and true to his promise, Paul had taught the boy to shoot. He had even purchased him a fine hunting rifle of German make and had been pleased to see that the boy could strip it down and reassemble it before he had had the weapon for two days. The youngster was also a fine shot and Paul commented now, as they walked along through the deep drifts, "I wish we could get a nice, tender doe today."

"We'll get one." Honor nodded confidently. He glanced at Paul Wakefield, this man who was his father yet in many ways a stranger, admiring his tall strength. Honor had been forced to accept strength as the measure of a man rather than wisdom or kindness or generosity. The Huron had these characteristics, but the warrior, the hunter, the killer was the one the tribe looked to. Now Honor took in the easy strides and the constant surveillance of the gray blue eyes as they marched along and thought, *He would have been a great man among the Huron.*

They had gone more than a mile through the heavy snow when Paul said, "I'm a bit winded. Are you all right, Honor?"

"Yes, I'm all right." Honor had never referred to Paul by the name "Father" and this pained Paul. He had become, to his surprise, very attached to the boy and now as he looked at him he thought, *No wonder he can't accept me as his father. I've known him only a few weeks and he's had to grow up alone in a hostile environment. Marielle has told me what a hard time he had being an alien, really, among the Huron.* A grim resolve grew in him and he thought, *Somehow I'm going to make it different here.* Although he continued to be confused about the social situation, Paul knew there were many men who had illegitimate sons and had raised them to high rank in the navy, the army, or even sent them to Oxford. *Money is the answer to all things,* Paul thought as the two trudged along, their eyes sweeping the ground for signs. *I'll buy him a good life! By George, I will!*

Suddenly Honor halted. "Look!" he said, pointing at the ground, his eyes glowing with excitement. "A buck! A big one!"

Paul saw the tracks in the snow and smiled warmly. "You've got good eyesight. You're a good tracker. Better than I am."

The compliment pleased Honor, but he merely ducked his head and Paul said, "Come along. I think we might start one up over in that thicket by the creek."

When they reached the thicket, tracks were thick, for the ground was frozen and the brook itself was skimmed with ice. It had been broken at several places and Honor said, "They've been drinking. They'll come back if we hide and are very quiet."

"I think you're right," Paul agreed. The two of them took station behind some brush and waited for thirty minutes. Paul's face grew cold and his hands numb. He noticed that Honor did not seem to be affected by it and thought, *I could do that when I was in America. I've gotten soft.* Even as he thought this, Honor stiffened and Paul saw a buck and a doe step out of a copse and advance cautiously toward the water. The wind was blowing away from the deer and toward Honor and Paul so Paul risked whispering, "You take the buck. Shoot first."

Honor nodded and his heart seemed to swell. He had never killed a buck, for the Huron would never take him on their hunting expeditions. He had killed smaller animals with a bow and arrow, but this was different. Trying to remember all the instructions Paul had given him, he slowly raised the rifle. When it was dead center on the buck's heart, he pulled the trigger. The rifle kicked his shoulder and threw the muzzle up, but immediately he heard another shot and cried with excitement. "We got both of them! Look, Father!"

Paul lowered his rifle and eyed the boy. "Yes, we did," he said. The title the boy had given him in his excitement had made him realize that there was something about blood ties that he had never known. He'd had ill will toward his brother for years and now he knew suddenly that this boy, who was his own flesh and blood, was what he would leave on this earth when he himself passed from the scene, his signature on time. He reached over and put his hand on the boy's shoulder. "You did well, Honor."

Honor pulled away automatically, but then he stopped. He forgot about the deer, excited as he was, and looked up at the tall man.

"Can't we be friends, Honor?" Paul asked quietly.

Honor considered these words, his eyes never leaving Paul's. "If you are my father, we must be more than friends."

Struck by the wisdom of the youth's words, Paul nodded slowly, not knowing how to answer. He had not yet made up his mind to publicly acknowledge Marielle as his wife and Honor as his son. Constantly he struggled against the words that were captured within his skull. *What shall it profit a man, if he shall gain the whole world, and lose his own soul?* They seemed to be burned into the back of his eyelids, for when he closed his eyes he could see the words. They had affected him as no words from Scripture ever had and now he saw the choice was very clear. He could either have the world—or he could turn and acknowledge Marielle as his wife and this tall, lean youth with the gray blue eyes so much like his own, as his son.

Honor wanted to reach out to his father, but such a gesture of affection was not in his nature. He had never been touched affectionately by a man. He had had only his mother's love. Now he saw that the man was thinking of his words.

Finally Paul said simply, "You're right. We must be more than that." Then Paul shook his shoulders and continued, "Come, Son. We'll have to bring packhorses out to haul these deer in, but we'll eat well." He paused again and asked, "Is it your first kill?"

"Yes."

"Isn't there a custom among the Indians that a young man must be marked with the blood of his first kill?" Paul asked. Honor's eyes widened with surprise at this white man's knowledge. "Come," Paul said. He led the boy over to the buck, who was now completely still. He reached down, dipped his finger in the rich blood that had pumped from the animal, straightened up, and marked Honor's brow with it. "Now," he said with a smile, "you're a hunter and a man."

<hr>

"You've done so well with Honor," Dorcas said. She looked up at Paul, who sat across from her in front of the fire, studying the flames as they leaped from the chestnut logs. "You've become very close to him."

Paul shifted uneasily, then turned to face his mother. "I don't know, Mother," he said. "It's not going to be easy. He's absorbed all the Indian ways. That was all he knew. It's going to be difficult for him."

"God will help him. And you," Dorcas said with quiet conviction. She had observed Paul's deliberate life change in turning his attention toward the boy and had been grateful to God, for it had been her prayer. However, she knew that he was not close to Marielle. There was a barrier between them. She knew that they did not share the same room at night, that Paul went to his own room. Although they were polite and talked sometimes of unimportant things, still they were like strangers.

Paul had never been an easy man to advise. Dorcas knew that he was in the greatest struggle in his life, that God was dealing with him, and that he was still caught up with Stella Frazier. And yet, the appearance of Marielle and Honor had changed all of that. *He's got to come to his senses,* Dorcas thought. She prayed for wisdom and then said, "Do you know what I think, Paul?"

"What's that, Mother?" Paul looked with affection at the woman, noticing she had been more cheerful and had even seemed to feel better since the arrival of Marielle and Honor. He had watched with amazement as she had grown close to Marielle, but he realized that the two of them were Christians with a deep, spiritual bent to their nature. Of course she had loved Honor, for she loved her grandchildren. He had watched carefully to see if she acted differently toward his son than she did toward David's children, but he could see no changes whatsoever. Now he studied her face and asked curiously, "What is it?"

"I think," Dorcas said slowly, "it would be a good thing if you would take Marielle on a trip."

"A trip? Where would we go—and why?"

Dorcas lifted her eyes and held her son's gaze. "I think you should take her somewhere. Just the two of you. Leave Honor here with me. We'll find many things for him to do. Silas is a good hunter. He'd be safe to take Honor hunting every day. But you need to get away. You and your wife."

Paul flushed slightly at the use of the term *wife*. He felt uncomfortable with it. Things were so different in England. Still, he knew his mother was wise. "I don't think we'll ever get back to where we were."

"You loved her when you first knew her, didn't you, Paul?"

"Yes, of course I did. She's the only woman I ever loved but—"

"Time changes many things, but I don't think it changes true love."

Paul was well aware of his mother's insistence that real love was unchanging. He wished to believe it, but his experience had proven otherwise. He saw around him, in English society, men who seemed to love their wives for a time but then turned from them to other women. It had become almost epidemic in the circles in which he moved.

However, the emptiness, longing, and confusion in him made him say suddenly, "All right, Mother. I don't know what good it will do and I don't know if she will go."

"Ask her. I believe she will."

Later Dorcas spoke to Caroline about what she had engineered and Caroline patted her cheek. "You're just a matchmaker, Dorcas," she said, smiling. "But I think it's a wise thing to do."

Marielle had been reading in her bedroom when a knock sounded. Rising from the chair, she went to open the door. She was wearing a sky blue dressing gown that picked up the color of her eyes. It had been a gift from Paul and she treasured it for that reason. When she saw him at the door, she was surprised, for he rarely sought her out. "Come in," she said, standing back. He entered and closed the door behind him, then walked over to the fire that sputtered and snapped as the logs were consumed. "Cold outside," he said awkwardly, for want of anything else to say. He could not help noticing that, despite the years, Marielle still had the figure of a young woman. The blue robe belted around her waist revealed the swell of her upper body and he turned his eyes away, flushing slightly. "Honor and I have had quite a bit of time together," he said. Shifting his weight uneasily he continued, "I thought—"

Marielle was puzzled. "You thought what, Paul?" She moved toward him, trying to understand his hesitancy.

"I thought," Paul said, facing her and simultaneously admiring the smoothness of her cheeks and her heavy lashes that would be the envy of many English women, "that you and I might take a trip together."

"A trip? Where?" Marielle asked, astonished.

"Oh, no place in particular. It's hard weather, so we'd have to go on a sleigh. We'd take the wheels off one of the light carriages, put runners on it, and then hitch up a good team to it. I've always enjoyed sleigh rides."

"But where would we go?"

"Oh, I don't know," Paul said. "I'd like to show you some of the countryside."

A quick strain of joy rose in Marielle's breast. It was the first time Paul had suggested anything like this and she said quickly, "I'd like it very much, Paul." She looked very beautiful as she stood there, with her warm eyes, perfect teeth, and slightly parted lips. "When will we go?" she asked.

"Why not today? As a matter of fact, I was hoping you'd go, so I've already had the buggy converted to a sleigh."

"It would be fun, I think," Marielle said. "I've never ridden in a sleigh."

"Well, pack a bag. We may be gone for several days. We'll have to stop at some wayside inns," Paul said, fighting down the sudden impulse to touch her. Marielle saw it in his eyes, but he blinked and swallowed, saying, "I'll go down and get a lunch to take with us. Wear your heaviest clothes and don't forget your gloves."

"I won't, Paul," Marielle said. As soon as the door closed, her hands went to her breast. She had loved Paul deeply as a young woman and now she realized she loved him more than ever. Maybe Dorcas's words, "Real love never changes," *were* true.

"It's so quiet!" Marielle exclaimed. She was sitting beside Paul, bundled up in her fur coat and the heavy blankets he'd brought along to pull over them. It was a small carriage and the two of them sat close together, so that she was aware of his body pressing against hers.

Paul loved to drive over snow and now he spoke to the horses, who broke into a faster gait. "You can't even hear their hooves striking in the snow!" he said excitedly. "It's like living in another world, isn't it?" He grinned at her and she smiled back.

"It's beautiful," she said. "Look at those trees all covered with ice!"

"Are you glad you came?"

"Yes, it's been like nothing I've ever seen."

They had stopped the night before at an inn and Paul had gotten two rooms. Marielle had not commented on it, but Paul was awkward enough as he said good-night after they had had their evening meal and talked for a long time beside the fire in the large dining room of the inn.

For the next three days they traveled toward London and on the fourth day they were in the city itself. They arrived at a large inn called the Blue Duck, and Paul, once again, got two rooms for them.

"I think we could go to the theater tonight. You've never seen a play, have you, Marielle?"

"No, I haven't."

Paul made the arrangements and that night they went to see a production at Eve's Theater. He had seen many plays, but it pleased him greatly to see how Marielle's eyes glowed and how she threw herself into the action. Once she got so excited she grabbed his arm unconsciously and he leaned over and whispered, "It's just a play, Marielle. It's not real."

"I know," she said, "but it seems real."

Afterward, as the two left the theater, Paul was shocked to see Stella Frazier, accompanied by Keith Valentine. They met in such an abrupt fashion that something had to be said. "Good evening, Paul," Stella said, her eyes fixed on Marielle. She was surprised at the beauty of the woman. Paul had seen to it that Marielle had suitable clothes and the gown she wore was, he thought, one that flattered her the most: a royal blue velvet petenlair, a short jacket with a sacque back, square neckline, long sleeves, and a bow at the waistline. Delicate embroidery bordered the bottom edges of the jacket and the long matching skirt. Marielle's hair was pulled back and piled high on her head in a large coiffure with curls and small ribbons flowing down her back.

Finding the situation amusing, Valentine greeted Paul Wakefield carelessly but kept his eyes fixed on Marielle. "A little bit different from your tepee in America, I would guess. What is it—Marielle?"

Instantly Paul grew alert. He knew that Valentine would do anything to hurt or embarrass Marielle as a way of getting at him, so he took Marielle's arm firmly and said, "We have an appointment. Good to see you both."

Later, when they were back at the inn, they had a late supper. But as the candles threw their amber light over Marielle's face, Paul only picked at his food.

"The tall man hates you," Marielle said suddenly.

Surprised, Paul looked up. "Yes, he does."

"Is it because of the woman?"

There's no way to fool a woman, Indian or not, Paul thought desperately, knowing that Marielle must have heard about Stella, although he had never mentioned her. He sat there quietly for a moment, then said, "Yes."

"Is she in love with you?" Marielle asked simply.

For a moment, Paul could not meet Marielle's eyes, then he looked up and admitted, "Yes. When I thought you were dead, I didn't have much to do with women for a long time. Then last year Stella's husband died and we've seen quite a bit of each other."

"Are you her lover?" Marielle asked quietly.

Paul swallowed, unable to meet her gaze again. At last he whispered hoarsely, "Yes, I was."

"Do you love her, Paul?"

Paul Wakefield had never felt so awkward. "I don't know what I think anymore. She's rich and the man who marries her will gain a lot of money."

"That's not what I asked you. Do you love her, Paul?" Marielle asked again. Her lips were tense and her eyes glowed as she watched his face. She had always admired his rough, handsome features and now she knew her own life was in the balance as she waited for him to reply. *He can have any woman he wants,* she thought. *Why would he want an Indian wife?*

Finally Paul said, "Let's walk awhile."

They got their coats and left the inn, walking down the streets together but saying little. It was late and the city was sleeping, except for a few candles in windows. Outside, lanterns hung at regular intervals cast their yellow gleam over the snow that had fallen lightly.

When they completed their walk and got to Marielle's room, Paul asked suddenly, "Do you ever think of the days when we first loved?"

Marielle gently whispered, "Of course I do, Paul. That's what I thought of all those years I was a captive. I can remember everything about them." When she began to speak of their early days together, he was astonished how she remembered every detail: how he came home and greeted her, how passionate they had been in their love. As she spoke of memories they shared, she looked so lovely that Paul Wakefield forgot the present. Now, in the quietness of the hallway as the two stood there, he slowly reached out and put his arms around Marielle. "Do you remember how I used to tease you about being so passionate?" he asked.

Marielle lifted her face to meet his gaze. Her cheeks glowed for a moment as she smiled. "I remember. I liked it, Paul, when you teased me like that. And I was so in love with you that I shocked myself. I knew nothing about men. You taught me what it was to love."

Paul pulled her forward and she came into his embrace. As his lips fell on hers, her arms went around his neck. There was a sweetness, and yet a wildness, in her lips that stirred memories that had lain dormant for years. She put herself against him with a hunger she made no attempt to hide. Paul savored the taste of her lips, the softness of her form as she lay against his breast, and time seemed to stop.

Marielle had dreamed of this moment. She knew somehow that Paul Wakefield still cared for her. He had known other women, she knew that, but somehow now as he kissed her, she knew that the love they had known so long ago was not dead and when he lifted his lips a glad cry came from her own. "Oh, Paul, I love you so much!"

Paul could not answer. He was shocked at the power of emotion that had flooded him at Marielle's embrace. It was like going back in time. He remembered when they had first loved, how it had always been like this—wild and free.

After he left Marielle, he hardly slept that night. He could think only of what it was like to hold Marielle in his arms again. The soft touch of her lips seemed to linger on his and the gentleness and the abandon of her love would not leave his mind.

When he rose early the next morning, the innkeeper delivered a letter. It was from Stella. She had a servant search the inn near where she had seen him. She knew he had few other choices of lodging. He opened it at once, and read:

Paul,

You can't go on like this. People are talking. We're going to lose everything if you don't come to your senses! You know the way out. You have money enough to provide for her, but don't throw your life away like this. I beg you!

With all my love,
Stella

When Paul saw Marielle coming down the stairs into the dining area, he crumpled the note quickly and shoved it into his pocket. He seated Marielle, then started to sit down when a voice called, "Paul Wakefield!"

Turning, Paul saw that Keith Valentine had been lounging at the bar. Paul had not noticed him, but now Valentine approached, extremely drunk.

"I don't think we have anything to say to each other, Valentine."

"I've got this to say to you!" Valentine slapped Paul across the cheek. "Are you a coward as well as a squaw man?"

His face dulled from the blow, Paul said nothing for a moment. Then, in a fierce undertone, he answered, "My friend, I will call on you."

"Fine. I understand I'll get the choice of the weapons."

"Anything you want," Paul Wakefield said. "Now, get out!"

Valentine glared at him, then left.

As soon as Valentine was gone, Paul sat down and stared at his hands, which he folded in front of him.

"What does it mean, Paul? Are you going to fight him?"

"I must," he said. "If I don't, I'll be branded a coward."

"Don't fight him, Paul. You don't want me. That's what he's angry about, isn't it?"

Paul looked up and said wearily, "I have to fight him."

Marielle understood then that the fight was not over her but over Stella Frazier. A great sadness overtook her, for the hope that had been in her heart the night before, when he had kissed her, left and in its place a heaviness settled.

"You must love her, Paul, if you're willing to risk your life for her." Marielle stood up. "I must get back." Paul rose and started to speak, then saw that her face was set. "Just take me back," she said. "I have much to think about."

Paul agreed and murmured, "I'll get the sleigh, if you'll get your things together."

"All right. It won't take long."

The trip back to Wakefield, almost two days, was marked with long periods of near total silence. Paul's mind was on the duel that was to come and yet he somehow felt a tremendous loss. At the end of the second day, when they were almost home, he turned and said, "About the other night, Marielle . . ."

"It was a mistake, Paul," Marielle said quietly. "You're a man and you wanted a woman. There is no need to apologize. That's all it was."

Paul knew suddenly that that was not all it was, but he could not answer the sternness that was in her eyes. So he spoke to the horses and they moved faster over the white snow, carrying two miserable people back to Wakefield.

Twenty-Three

DUEL AT DAWN

T he world into which Honor had stepped was far more strange to him than the forest would have been to an inhabitant of London. Life among the Indians had been hard but relatively simple. There had been the need to obtain food and shelter, to escape danger from wild beasts or from the savage enemies of the Huron. Day after day had gone by, leaving no more of a trace than water did when it rose over stones in a stream. Time had meant little and Honor had grown from infancy to boyhood immersed in the life of the Huron.

But England was a far different matter and since his arrival in his father's native country, the boy had found it difficult. At first there had been an impenetrable wall between Honor and his father because of Honor's fixed determination to dislike anything English, even the man who was his father by blood. He had acted withdrawn and had refused all of Paul's advances for a time until his mother counseled him earnestly and gently, saying, "He's your father, Honor. He thought I was dead and he didn't know you existed. You can't hold him accountable for that." Her warm eyes glowed as she whispered, "Give him a chance, Honor. He will love you. I can already see it in him and I know you can learn to love him, too."

These words from his mother had been important to Honor and he had, from that moment on, begun to open his heart, mind, and life to the tall man who seemed to care for him. For Honor, the days that followed were marked by those times he spent with his father. They fished in the streams and ponds and hunted large and small game in the forest. These days were much like the life Honor had known with the Huron warriors, except that his father was eager to teach him. For the first time in his life, Honor had a man to look up to, to learn from. He had always loved his mother, but still, as with every boy, Honor yearned for another male to pattern himself after.

And so, the two had grown closer, but Honor was still shy, almost reluctant, to trust Paul. Perhaps it was because all his life he had been forced to defend himself against hurt, physical and emotional, and he did not think he could bear to be hurt again.

Since his father had leaped to his defense against Keith Valentine, Honor had been strangely silent. He had spoken to no one about the fight, even to his mother, but it had left a deep impression upon him. One morning, as he and his father walked toward the stable, preparing to go for their early morning ride, Honor glanced at Paul several times, trying to read what was behind the older man's expression.

After saddling the horses, they rode out toward the south over the low-lying hills. The sun, a pale disk, offered little warmth and the wind was sharp.

"You've learned to ride well, Honor."

Honor looked at his father, his face burning with pleasure. He was unaccustomed to compliments on his achievements, having known almost none during his years with the Huron. "It's easy with a good horse," he said and patted the sleek roan on the shoulder. The horse had been a gift from his father and he had named it Thunder after the sound a stallion's hooves made as he raced across the downs and the plains.

"I'm glad you like him. He's a fine animal."

The two rode on, Honor silent for the most part, with Paul

doing most of the talking. But when they flushed a covey of grouse, Honor said, "I wish I had a gun."

"We'll come back and get them later," Paul replied.

Honor suddenly pulled his horse up and Paul, surprised, did the same. "What's the matter?" he said, seeing the tense look on his son's face.

"Are you going to fight Valentine?" Honor asked tersely, his shoulders stiff. There was an odd look in his eyes as he waited for Paul's reply.

"There's no way out. I'll have to fight him."

"One of you may get killed."

"That's the way it is with a duel," Paul said, then remarked, "You must've been around death quite a bit with the Huron. They're a warrior race."

"Yes, there were many times after raids when warriors would come back wounded to the death so that they died later. Others didn't come back at all. They were there one day and gone the next."

Paul twisted in his saddle, studying the boy's countenance. The handsomeness in the boy's features pleased Paul. "It's something we all have to face," he said. "Death comes for everyone. Your mother's taught you that."

"I've always known that," Honor said, stroking the sleek, muscular shoulder of the horse. He let the coarse mane fall between his fingers, then tugged at it for a moment until the animal lifted his head in protest and snorted. Then Honor continued, "I—I wouldn't like it if you were killed."

"Neither would I." Paul grinned wryly. "Let's hope I won't be."

"Why are you doing this? Fighting that man?"

"He dishonored your mother."

"You don't have to."

"Yes, I do. Do you know what your name means in English? Your English name, Honor?"

"My mother told me when I was very young that honor meant doing what was right."

"She's right and it's right for me to defend your mother. That's what a man does for his family."

At the word *family* Honor looked up quickly. It was an oblique reference to Paul's relationship to his mother, but the boy caught it instantly and was pleased. After a moment's pause, he said, "You're a man of honor."

"I hope so, Son. I've done things I shouldn't have, but as far as you and your mother are concerned, I want to do what's right by you. You understand that, don't you?"

A silence fell on the young boy. His auburn hair caught the pale rays of the winter sun as his honest, gray blue eyes examined the man before him. Finally he said, "You are a man of honor and I'm glad you're my father."

Paul Wakefield, at that moment, felt he had crossed some kind of river in his life. He moved his horse closer, clapping the boy on the shoulder. "I'm proud of you, Son. You've had a hard time and you've come through it. Your mother named you well."

As the animals broke into a brisk gallop, Paul thought, *There's never been anything like this in my life. I never wanted children, but now that I see this boy with so much of me in him—and so much of Marielle—I understand what it means to have pride in the family. David's always had it. He's always been proud to be a Wakefield and now for the first time I see I'm just one in a line. There was Andrew before and here I am with Honor following me.*

⁓

"I'm so glad to know you, Marielle," David said, smiling and advancing across the room. He had brought the children, along with Bethany, for a visit to Wakefield at Paul's invitation. Now he bowed and said, "I've always wanted a sister."

Marielle stared at David thinking, *He's so much like Paul.* Pleased at David's words, she said, "And this is my son, Honor."

"I'm very happy to know you, Honor," David said. He put out his hand and with a certain amount of awkwardness, the young man took it. David held it for a moment and, squeezing it hard, said, "I'm glad you're here. Your cousins need someone in the family to look up to and now they have you." He turned and said, "Susan, Andy, this is your cousin, Honor."

For once, the irrepressible Susan was taken aback. She had been told she would meet Uncle Paul's wife and son but had not been prepared for their appearance. "Your skin is so dark!" she blurted out.

"Susan!" David cried, shrugging helplessly. "You're impossible!"

Marielle, however, was not offended. She smiled and said, "We both have Indian blood, Susan. That's why we're darker than you are."

"Can you shoot a bow and arrow?" Andy asked, his eyes fixed on Honor.

"Of course I can," Honor said. He had been apprehensive about meeting more of the family, but when he saw open admiration in Andy's eyes, he couldn't help but say, "I'll teach you how, if you'd like."

"Would you?" Andy cried out. "Yes! Yes! Now!"

Honor laughed aloud, something Paul had heard very rarely. "We'll have to make a bow and arrows. That'll take some time."

Paul Wakefield stood slightly to one side, relieved to see the warmth and welcome on David's face. "I got to be a pretty good shot with a bow myself. Not as good as Honor, I wouldn't think," he said, "but maybe he could give us all lessons."

Honor's face flushed with pleasure, but he said nothing. Susan came over at once and held her arms up. "Pick me up!" she commanded.

"That's what I like about you, Susan. You're so bashful!" Paul said, grinning. He winked at Bethany, who stood on David's left. "Bethany, this is Marielle and my son, Honor. This is Bethany Morgan."

Bethany came forward, looking pretty in a navy blue wool dress with long sleeves and a full overskirt, both decorated with green ribbon, and a white quilted and embroidered underskirt. She hesitated, not knowing how to address the woman, for Paul had not referred to her as his wife, although she knew she was. Then Bethany said quickly, "I'm so glad to meet you. Dorcas has told me so much about you. She's thrilled to death to have a daughter-in-law and another grandson."

Marielle warmed to the young woman and later in the day the two went off together, leaving Honor to watch the children.

Paul and David stood at a window, watching as Honor participated in the games of the two smaller children. "I was worried about how your children would take to having Indians in the family."

David said, "They're very excited, Paul, and so am I."

"Not everyone will be."

When David saw the tense look around his brother's mouth, he admitted, "Some will be unkind, but we're family now. We Wakefields have to hang together."

Noting that David had gained weight and that he also dressed more carefully than he had in the past, Paul thought, *Bethany's had something to do with that. She's cleaned him up and made him buy some better clothes. David never cared about anything he wore.* Aloud he said, "How's your work going?"

David's face brightened. "Very well. Very well, indeed! Mr. Mongomery, the publisher, tells me that there'll be another edition coming out very soon."

"So you are making money."

"Yes, some, and Mr. Montgomery wants me to do another

novel. A sequel to the first one. I'm already halfway through it."
He turned to Paul saying, "I appreciate the financial help you've
been giving me."

"You never asked for anything," Paul said.

David laughed sheepishly. "I suppose that's just pride. I wanted
to do it myself." Then he changed the subject, worry furrowing
his brow. "What about this duel with Valentine? You're not really
going to fight him, are you?"

"No choice."

"Certainly there's a choice!" David protested. "Dueling's an
archaic practice anyway! What does it prove?"

Paul shrugged his trim shoulders. "It proves that one man's a
better shot than the other, I suppose."

"But it doesn't prove that the one who's the better shot is in
the right. Might doesn't make right, you know."

"I'll leave that to the ministers and the philosophers," Paul said.
"Valentine challenged me and if I'm going to stay in England I'll
have to fight him."

"I wish you wouldn't." David came closer and, with an unexpected gesture, laid a hand on his brother's arm. "I wouldn't want
to lose you, Paul."

As the warmth of David's hand burned into Paul Wakefield's
arm, he stood very still, conscious of how he had wronged his
twin. He did not know how to say it, but somehow he wanted to
grow closer to David, the man he knew so well and yet so little.
Although he wanted to ask David's forgiveness, Paul Wakefield's
pride had not yet been broken. All he could say was, "I'm glad
you're doing well, Brother."

"And you won't give up on this duel?"

"I can't." Paul bit his lip thoughtfully, then stared into his
brother's eyes. "I could never face Honor again if I didn't do this
thing. Don't try to talk me out of it, David," he added quickly.
"It's something I've got to do."

On the second day of their visit Bethany and Marielle were walking through the garden when Marielle touched a dead bloom and murmured, "This must be a beautiful place in the summer."

"It is in the spring. See? I planted a special kind of rose over here, Marielle." Bethany walked over to the bush and touched one of the thorns, making a slight grimace. "They are a beautiful peach color with just a tiny touch of crimson right in the center." She looked at the thorns and mused, "It's strange how beautiful things like roses have thorns to hurt you."

Marielle looked down at the vine, which appeared to be dead and lifeless, and touched the stem. Then, in a quiet voice she said, "I think most things we love have the power to hurt us."

Touched by Marielle's words, Bethany knew the Indian woman had an innate wisdom from her years of suffering.

"That's true, isn't it, Marielle? Strangers can't hurt us as much as those we're close to."

"Yes."

There was such a poignant tone to Marielle's voice that Bethany felt a surge of sympathy. Moving closer, she touched Marielle's arm lightly. "You've had a hard time—but you're home now."

"Am I home?"

"Why, of course."

"I do not think so." When Marielle faced Bethany, there was deep sadness in her startling blue eyes. "Paul has gotten close to Honor. He wants a son. But . . ." When Marielle lapsed into silence, they heard a dog howl far away. Overhead in the gray skies, a flight of geese made their way steadily southward in a V formation. Marielle was not a woman who revealed herself to anyone. She had built a wall of protection, living within her own spirit, her own heart, during her years of captivity. But now, almost involuntarily, the words poured forth. "Honor has a father—but I have no husband!"

For a moment Bethany was speechless. Then, moved with compassion, she put her arm around the woman. She had seen how stiff and unnatural Paul had been with Marielle and had noted how he never referred to her as his wife. "It will come, Marielle. You will see."

"I do not think so."

"Yes, it will. You are a believer. You must've asked God to restore your husband to you. Now I will join with you, my sister. We will both pray for this."

Marielle's eyes began to burn. Although she had ceased crying over her misfortunes years ago, Bethany's kindness touched a deep spring in her. In a quivering voice she asked, "Do you really believe that it can happen?"

"With God, all things are possible," Bethany said.

Marielle embraced the younger woman, holding her tightly and the two knew a bond had been formed between them. When Marielle drew back, she said quietly, "And I will pray for you. Like me, you love one who cannot be yours."

Bethany's face turned pale and her hands flew to her breast in a gesture of confusion. "How—how can you say that, Marielle?"

"It is plain that you love my husband's brother."

"He already has a wife."

"She's gone. She has left him."

"In our world that does not matter. You know what Scripture teaches. A man and a woman are married until death parts them."

"That is true—and that is why I grieve for you, Bethany. I do not know how to pray for God to give you happiness, but I know that he can."

Bethany had been shocked by the knowledge that Marielle had seen her love for David because she thought she had kept it covered as much as possible. But Marielle had a deeper intuition than most women and now she bowed her head, saying, "We will pray for each other."

❦

John Gunther, a tall young man with reddish hair, looked across at Lesley Dumont, Paul's Second, saying, "My principal is ready, sir."

Lesley Dumont, a short muscular man with intense blue eyes and blond hair, who had known Paul for years, had been shocked when Paul had asked him to serve as his Second in the duel. Now Dumont looked at Paul, who stood silently in the gray late November dawn. The wind was cold and all present, including a physician named Summers, were wearing heavy wool cloaks.

"My principal asked me to inform you that an apology would be acceptable," Dumont stated.

Gunther did not even look at Valentine, who was glaring at Paul Wakefield from ten feet away. "That is out of the question, I'm afraid."

Dumont shrugged, saying, "In that case, we must proceed." He opened the leather case under his left arm, revealing a beautifully crafted set of dueling pistols. "I trust these will serve?"

John Gunther moved forward and examined the pistols.

"Very fine. Shall I put the charges in?"

"If you please, sir."

Throughout the preliminaries, Paul seemed to be almost uninterested. His mind was filled with what had happened in the darkness of the early morning just before he had left the house to meet Dumont. He had had the hostler saddle his horse and was preparing to mount when he heard a voice so close that it startled him. "Paul . . ."

Paul had turned instantly to find Marielle, wearing a long gray cloak and a hood that shielded her face, standing beside him in the darkness. She had begged him not to fight the duel, but he had said only, "I'm sorry, Marielle. There's no choice."

But now, as he watched the two Seconds arm the pistols, he wished he had said more. Her presence had shaken him and when she put her hand out in a pleading gesture, he had taken it and found it strong and warm. She had squeezed his hand and looked up at him saying, "You don't have to do this for my sake."

"Yes, I do, Marielle," Paul said. "You're my wife and a man must protect his wife."

Paul remembered sharply how his expression, "You're my wife" had brought tears to Marielle's eyes. It was the first time he had addressed her in that way and now he wished he had done more—that he had embraced her and assured her. But he had done none of these things, merely said, "Don't worry. I'm a good shot," then had swung into the saddle and ridden away.

Now Dr. Summers, a large man, said, "If you two gentlemen will come, we will begin." As the two men approached, he asked, "Is there anything that might be done to change you gentlemen's minds?"

Valentine shook his head, his lips pale in the sharp breeze, his eyes glittering. An accomplished shot who had survived two duels already, he was filled with confidence.

Paul saw the hopelessness of talk and also remained silent.

"Very well," Dr. Summers pronounced, his voice loud in the silence of the glen where the small group had gathered. He gave them their instructions, which were simple enough. "You will stand here back to back and as I count, you will march ten paces. On the count of ten you may turn and fire." He pulled a pistol from his own belt and said bluntly, "If either of you fires before the count of ten, I will shoot that man down."

Both Paul and Valentine understood that Summers meant what he said. They nodded and then took their positions.

The count began—"One . . . two . . . three"—and as Paul

stepped in time to the cadence, his boots crushing the frost that was underfoot, he seemed to hear his mother saying, *What shall it profit a man, if he shall gain the whole world, and lose his own soul?* So clearly did the words come that Paul hesitated, losing the timing, and thought suddenly, *I may be dead in a few seconds and there's nothing I can point to in my life and say, "This is what I've done that was right."*

"Five . . . six . . . seven." The count went on inexorably as Paul Wakefield's mind flashed over the events of his life. He saw it now as being wasted, useless, with no meaning, and then he seemed to see the faces of Marielle and Honor as clearly as if he were looking at a painting.

This is what I will not be able to do if I'm killed, he thought. *I'll never be able to make it up to Marielle. To tell her that I love her as I always have.*

"Eight . . . nine . . . ten—"

Paul whirled, pointing his weapon at Valentine. There was no time to think, but regret flooded his soul. Even as he heard the sound of Valentine's weapon exploding, he had thrown his pistol up. But he was one fraction of a second slower and a red-hot pain stung his neck.

Missed! He missed! Paul thought. He was still standing with the weapon upright, turned sideways in the classic position. Valentine's face had turned as pale as paste and his lips were trembling. Death was staring at him in the muzzle of Paul Wakefield's pistol and Valentine could do no more than stand there and wait to die.

What shall it profit a man, if he shall gain the whole world, and lose his own soul?"

Paul Wakefield's finger tightened on the trigger. He could not miss at this distance and both he and Valentine knew it. For one long second that seemed to last for an eternity—especially to Valentine—the field was a place of imminent death. Paul's neck was burning and blood was running down to his shoulder, but he paid no heed. As he studied Valentine's face, he saw pain and fear, but the man did not flinch. *He does have courage after all,* Paul thought.

Suddenly Paul Wakefield lowered his pistol and pulled the trigger. The shot rang out and the bullet plowed into the dirt, kicking up a clod. Paul stood there silently, then called out, "You can have her, Valentine!" Then he turned and walked away, not seeing the Seconds, the doctor, or Valentine's look of anguished relief. But he could still hear humming in his mind the words that his mother had spoken: *What shall it profit a man . . . ?*

Twenty-Four

NO WAY OUT

A wintry blast caught Bethany squarely as she opened the door. Catching her breath, she blinked and then, recognizing the man who stood there, stepped back, saying, "Come in, David."

Entering and removing his hat, David shivered. "It's cold today. The coldest November I've ever seen, I believe."

"Let me take your coat." Bethany took the dark blue wool overcoat, hung it on a clothes rack, then took David's arm and led him across the room. "Come over to the fire," she said. "Your hands look like ice! Where are your gloves?"

"I—forgot them."

His tone caught Bethany's attention and she stood across from the fire crackling in the grate to study him for a moment. He seemed anxious, even nervous, and that was unusual. The two of them had spent so much time together that Bethany knew his ways and how his mind worked. She knew that sooner or later he would tell her what the problem was. But he remained silent for so long that she said, "Is it the children? Are they sick?"

"Oh, no!" David spoke up quickly, running his hand through his hair, then holding his fingers out to the fire again. "I'm just worried about Paul."

"No word of him yet?"

"No. Not a trace. Not a sign—and it's been three days since that duel."

"He must be all right if what we heard was true. Nobody actually got shot, did they?"

"No, Paul's neck just got nicked. I went to Valentine myself. I think he's a little shocked. He told me all about it. He said that Paul had a perfect chance to kill him but he lowered his pistol and fired into the ground." David shifted his weight, clasped his hands together, and then added thoughtfully, "I think it puzzled him a great deal. He told me if *he* had had that chance he would have killed Paul instantly."

"Did he know anything about where Paul might be?"

"Not a thing. Neither does anyone else. I've gone to all the places I can think of where he might be and he's not there. But I've got to find him. Something must be terribly wrong."

"Here. Sit down. I made some crumpets today and the tea is almost ready."

"I don't think—"

"You mind me now, David!" Bethany commanded with a maternal insistence. She took him to the settee in front of the fire, practically pushed him into it, and for the next few minutes busied herself making up the tray with fresh crumpets and strong, hot tea. "There. Now you eat these and there are plenty more."

David grinned and said, "I feel as if I'm about five years old, being chastised by my mother."

"Well, you need a keeper! Going out without your gloves and look, you have on those lightweight shoes! They're no good for snow! You've got to learn to take care of yourself!"

"I was never very good at that," David confessed.

"No, you weren't. But you're not too old to change."

Across the room the walnut clock, a large George II quarter-chiming longcase, kept up its solitary, rhythmic motion. The monotonous sound calmed David and, glancing up, he said, "I've always liked that clock."

"Have you? It's one of my favorites, too." Bethany talked about the clock for some time and then finally asked, "What is it, David? What do you want?"

Shaking his head, David said ruefully, "I never could fool you, Bethany. Even when you were a little girl you always seemed to look right into my head and know what I was thinking."

"You're not difficult to read. Everything you think shows on your face."

"I guess that's why I'm such a rotten card player."

Bethany smiled gently but refused to be put off. "You're troubled. What is it? You can tell me."

"I'd trust you with anything, Bethany. Well, the fact is, I've got to find Paul and I need someone to come and take care of the children."

"Is that all?" Bethany said. "You had me thinking something awful. Of course I'll take care of the children. I suppose it's so that you can look for Paul full-time?"

"Yes."

"Of course I'll do that." She hesitated, then asked, "How are Marielle and Honor?"

David shifted uncomfortably. "It's hard to say. I guess it all depends on Paul."

"She's a beautiful woman and he's a wonderful boy. Any man would be glad to have him for a son."

"I can't understand Paul," David said. "He told me once that he loved Marielle as no man ever loved a woman. Can all that be gone?"

"No."

Glancing at her with amusement, David said, "Just *no?* You mean you really think that love lasts forever, just like in the storybooks?"

"Just like in the stories, David."

David studied Bethany's warm dark blue eyes and oval face, thinking of how great a part this young woman had played in his life. Words rose to his lips, but he realized, *I can't say these things. Not with a wife.* So he rose from the settee and said, "The children will be glad to see you. Our neighbor is taking care of them right now, but they're always glad to see you."

"And I'm always glad to see them. Shall I come with you now?"

"Could you, Bethany? It would mean a lot to me. I've simply got to find Paul. I'm sure he's in London—that's where he's gone before to disappear!"

"You'll find him. We'll pray for it."

"That's always your answer, isn't it? Well, it's a good one. Get what you need and I'll see to a carriage."

For two days after David brought Bethany to his home to take care of the children, he searched the streets of London diligently. He knew the town fairly well and had spent a great deal of time there, but he quickly discovered that if a man wished to disappear, London was the place to do it. There were countless streets, inns too numerous to mention, taverns beyond adding, and all in all, by the end of the second day he had exhausted all of his resources.

I might as well give up and go home, he thought dejectedly. *I've looked everywhere I can think of.* He was in the Blackmoor district on a poor street composed mostly of taverns and shops, but none of his inquiries there had brought any fruit. He was sharply conscious of his failure when he encountered a short, rotund man with a tall hat and bright, inquiring eyes.

"Well now, Mr. Wakefield."

"What? Oh, hello, Jarvis. How are you?"

"Fine. Fine." Jarvis said. He was employed by the firm that had printed David's books and the two had become quite fond of each other. Jarvis laughed abruptly, saying, "I made quite a mistake. I took another fellow for you just this morning."

David's senses sharpened. "How was that, Jarvis? Was it someone who looked like me?"

"I should say. The spittin' image, David."

"Where did you see him?"

"Where? It was over at the White Hind."

"What is that," David inquired anxiously, "a tavern?"

"Right. A tavern it is. It's over in the Soho district. Down past the monument. You know it?"

"Yes, I do. The White Hind, you say? Thank you, Jarvis."

Jarvis opened his mouth to say more, but David wheeled and ran for a carriage. The horses reared as he approached, waving his hands, and the cabby looked down with a stern expression of disapproval. "'Ere now, don't be scarin' me 'orses!"

"Take me to the White Hind Tavern. Do you know it?"

"Over in Soho? Yes, I knows it."

"Get me there as quick as you can. There'll be a half crown in it for you!"

"Righto, guv'nor! Get up there!" He commanded his horses and their hooves began to clatter along the cobblestones. As the carriage wheeled toward Soho, David found himself praying that Paul was the man Jarvis had seen and that he would be all right. For some reason, he had had a sharp impression that something terrible had happened to Paul. At first his fear was that he would be killed in the duel. That had not happened, but something else was wrong. There was no other reason for his brother to disappear.

"'Ere we are, guv'nor!"

David got out, handed the man a crown, and said, "You may keep the rest."

"Oh, thank you now. Shall I wait?"

"I don't think so, but come back in an hour, if you will, and then I'll pay you for your time if I don't want to go anywhere."

"Righto, guv'nor." The cab man pocketed the coin, clucked to the horses, and then moved away.

David turned and glanced at the sign The White Hind painted on a board that swung in the wind. The frosty temperature bit at his ears and hands and he quickly entered the tavern. Inside there was the aroma of whiskey, bodies, and food. David approached the innkeeper and said, "I'm looking for Mr. Paul Wakefield."

The burly man with a half-bald head glowered at him under fierce, bushy eyebrows. "He's up on the second floor. You can tell him from me that I'll be needing his room."

"Something wrong?"

"I don't like it. People think he's a loony up there! They say, and I've heard him myself, that he's talking to himself. Tell him I need the room. That's all."

David stared at the innkeeper, then nodded slightly before he turned and moved toward the stairs. On the second floor, he went to the room indicated by the innkeeper and paused. *Something's wrong with him,* he thought and breathed a quick prayer, then raised his fist and tapped on the door. He received no answer, although he knocked strongly three or four times. Finally he called out, "Paul—Paul, are you in there?"

There was a long silence and then the door opened, with Paul Wakefield clinging to it with one hand. He looked terrible. His eyes were darkly circled, his clothes dirty and wrinkled, and as soon as he spoke, it was obvious he had been drinking.

"Oh, it's you, David. What do you want?"

"I want to talk to you, Paul."

At first David thought Paul would refuse, but then he shrugged and turned back into the room. "Come in."

Stepping inside, David closed the door, removing his coat and hat. There being no other place, he tossed them on the floor. "Everyone's been worried about you, Paul," he said at once.

"Well, they shouldn't be." Paul Wakefield had always been stubborn, but now David saw something else. Something akin to fear. As far as David knew, Paul Wakefield had never feared anything on earth or in heaven. But now his eyes revealed an uncertainty and his lips were pale as he kept them clamped together.

"What's wrong, Paul?"

"Nothing's wrong."

"Of course there is! Do you think I wouldn't know? I know you too well, Paul." He almost reached out to touch Paul's shoulder but realized that would be too much. "I heard about the duel. I'm glad you didn't get killed—and that you didn't kill Valentine."

At the mention of the duel, Paul lowered his head, picked up a glass, then a bottle. He tried to pour, but his hand trembled and the alcohol sloshed over his other hand. Angry, Paul slammed both vessels down, then stared at David. "Have you ever been almost killed?"

"No, not really."

"I've had some close calls, Brother, but this was different."

"Can you tell me about it? Maybe it will do you good to talk."

Paul put his elbows on the table, pressing his forehead against his hands. He began to speak slowly, incoherently, sometimes drawing a choking breath. He revealed to David all the details of the duel and then whispered, "And that bullet Valentine sent at me was just an inch away from killing me—just one inch, David!"

"It must've been terrible."

"I've—never been afraid of death, but I was this time. Of course, I could've killed Valentine. It was my right. I pointed the pistol right at his head, my hand was tightening on the trigger, and then . . ."

"And then what, Paul? What happened?"

"I couldn't do it. I began to tremble." Paul's face was drawn with anguish. "You know, all I could think of was what Mother said to me: 'What shall it profit a man, if he shall gain the whole world, and lose his own soul?' I couldn't get away from that. I could almost see the words in great black letters on a white page, *'Lose his own soul.'* Look at that!" Paul demanded, holding his right hand up, the trembling evident. "I didn't think anything in the world would make me lose my nerve!"

David recognized that his brother was finally broken. Paul Wakefield had always been strong, hard, and self-assured, but now all that was gone. The man David saw before him was almost cringing, his manhood shattered, his confidence gone. David breathed another quick prayer, *Lord, help me to say the right thing.* Then he said, "Paul, you've never wanted to hear me talk about the Lord, but I'm going to now. The only way you can stop me is to throw me out. I want to tell you what it's like to be in the hands of God."

David thought Paul would rise up, for anger flared in his eyes. But he abruptly lowered his head and clasped his hands tightly, turning the knuckles white. The room was silent for a moment and then Paul said, "All right. Tell me. I'm no good, David, and never have been."

"You're a sinner, Paul; all men are sinners. But there's one good thing about that—Jesus is the friend of sinners. He loves you, Paul, and he wants to give you the best thing that can come into a man's life. You have all that the world can offer. You have a good wife and a fine son if you can just come to yourself. But it's going to take God to do it."

Paul slowly lowered his hands and his head lifted. There was a twitch in his right eye as he said in a tone David had never heard from his brother before, "All right, David—tell me about God."

The candles flickered in their sconces on the wall, throwing a yellow illumination over the two men as David began to speak. For a long time he went on, until the candles guttered lower in their holders. There were no witnesses, but somehow heaven was aware and as the night wore on, David grew stronger and more persuasive in presenting God's demands. He quoted many Scriptures and each one struck like an arrow into Paul's heart.

Dorcas knocked gently on Marielle's door, which opened almost at once. "Are you busy, Marielle?"

Marielle looked tense and her eyes were tired. In fact, she looked exhausted and her shoulders were slumped in defeat. Dorcas stepped inside and looked over on the bed at the valise Marielle had brought with her from London. Quickly Dorcas turned to Marielle. "You're packing?"

"Yes." Marielle drew herself up very straight. There was a regal quality about this woman and pride burned strong in her. But rejection showed in her eyes as she explained, "I've got to get away from here."

"You can't leave now!" Dorcas said. "Just wait until we find Paul. Talk to him."

"It wouldn't do any good. I've done everything I know how, but he doesn't love me."

Dorcas took Marielle's arm with her good hand. "Don't give up. The Bible tells us we are to keep on praying and asking. The minister always tells me to ask, seek, and knock not once but many times."

"I have prayed and I have sought God," Marielle said sadly. "But it hasn't done any good. Paul loved me once, but no longer."

"He loves Honor."

"I think so, but he doesn't love me."

Dorcas drew the younger woman over to a couch and the two sat down. For a long time Dorcas pleaded with the woman, offering every word of encouragement she could give, but Marielle was adamant. "No, he wants an English wife, if he wants a wife at all."

"I think you are wrong, Marielle. I think Paul is going through a difficult time and if you will just wait, I think you will see God's will done. Please! Just stay until Paul is found."

Marielle hesitated, then agreed reluctantly. "Very well, but it will do no good."

"It will if we pray. Prayer changes things. You know that, Marielle."

"I thought I did, but my faith," Marielle said helplessly, "has grown weak."

"We all know times like that," Dorcas said. "I've had many of them and every time I do, I pray what the man with the ill son prayed: 'Lord, I believe. Help thou mine unbelief.'"

Marielle looked up, a glimmer of hope in her blue eyes. During her years of captivity, her one dream had been to be restored to her husband and that had not happened. Now heartsick, weary of the strain, she wanted nothing more than to flee from it all. But with Dorcas's loving eyes fixed on her, she could not do that, so she stayed.

Two days later the sun came out, driving away the dark clouds that had threatened more snow. Marielle welcomed it, for the days had been gloomy. She thought of her earlier conversation with Dorcas and shook her head with doubt. "I promised to stay and I will," she said softly to herself. "Besides, Honor loves his father. How can I tear him away from Paul now?"

All that morning she had kept to her room, eating little and praying much. When she happened to glance out the window midafternoon, she saw a carriage approaching.

I wonder who that could be, she thought. And then as the man stepped out, she exclaimed, "Paul!" She watched eagerly as he entered the house and then she paced the room nervously. She had not long to wait before a knock sounded at her door. "Come in," she called softly.

The door opened and Paul came in. He was thinner, she could see that, and his face was lined with care and strain. But he looked different, and his eyes were clear. "Marielle." Paul strode across the room, reached for her hands, and then to her astonishment, kissed both of them.

"Paul!" Marielle gasped. "What's happened to you?"

"Something I never dreamed would happen to me," Paul said. "Can I tell you about it?"

"Of course." He was still holding her hands and she did not pull them back. As he continued to speak, she was very conscious of the new spirit that was in him and the feeling of release that had not been there previously. When he told her of how David had found him and presented the gospel to him, her eyes opened wide with surprise.

Paul dropped her hands, but put his arms around her. "Two things happened, Marielle. I did exactly what David has been trying to get me to do for years. I turned away from my life as it was and called on Jesus Christ—and he saved me."

"Oh, Paul, I'm so happy!"

Paul held her tightly, his eyes brilliant, and his new joy overflowing. "And so I'm a Christian now. I don't know what that means. It won't be easy for me, but I've determined to serve God for the rest of my days."

Happy beyond words, Marielle said, "What's the other thing?"

"Well, David said I was a new man in Christ and I know one thing. You're my wife, Marielle," he said intensely. "My own true wife." He pulled her close and as her head tilted back, he looked in her eyes, long and tenderly. Marielle felt his strong arms and knew this was not the old Paul Wakefield. Perhaps there was a little of the early love that he had had, but now he was a mature man and his caress was even sweeter.

"Will you have me as your husband, Marielle?" Paul asked.

"Oh, yes, Paul!"

Paul Wakefield smiled, kissed her for a dozen heartbeats, then straightened up and took a deep breath. "Come along."

"Where are we going?"

"We're going to tell our son that we're a family."

Twenty - Five

BLOOD WILL TELL

December 1774

Many of the aristocratic Englishmen's houses were more imposing than Trentwood, the home of Sir Edgar Trent and his wife, Mary, but none was more comfortable on the inside than their three-hundred-year-old home. The Trent family had prospered, but rather than build a new home, which was the custom of the day, they had furnished Trentwood with the most comfortable and attractive fixtures.

The room most used at Trentwood was the large parlor. Its size could have been intimidating, but because the Trents had so carefully selected the furnishings, there was a warmth and an attractiveness to the room that immediately made one feel comfortable. The walls were covered with a warm brown-and-green-flocked wallpaper and the floor with a wall-to-wall, brown-and-white patterned carpet. Just inside the door to the parlor was a cherry-wood, Queen Anne tallcase clock. Across the room were four large, mullioned windows, covered with a light brown moreen pulled back with fabric bows to let in the bright sunshine of the day. Spaced between the windows were silver candle sconces with two candles in each. A fire crackled in the elaborately carved, white marble fireplace, sending sparks flying up the chimney. The mantel above the fireplace had a crystal vase of paper spills, two sets of silver candle holders, each holding four white candles, and a large looking glass with an oak frame. Flanking the fireplace were two George II mahogany wing chairs in tan horsehair fabric.

Lady Mary Trent sat beside the window knitting, as usual. A petite woman with silver hair, Lady Mary had a fair complexion that contained traces of her former beauty. She had been a belle in her youth, sought after by many, but had given her heart to the young aristocrat who had stormed into her life and taken her love captive. Her many years at Trentwood had been good, but now as she looked out over the crystal blanket of snow that covered the lawns and foothills and turned the trees into fluffy shapes, she turned to Edgar, saying, "Christmas should be a happy time, but it isn't, is it?"

Sir Edgar Trent was standing at the enormous bookcase that reached from floor to ceiling, holding a brown leather-bound book in his hand. At her words, he turned, a strange expression in his eyes. Sir Edgar was a rather large man, not heavy or over-weight, but tall, with some of his earlier athletic grace and strength. His dark green coat fell to the knees and his tan waistcoat was buttoned from top to bottom with only the ruffles of his white silk shirt showing at the neck and at the end of the sleeves. He also wore brown velvet breeches, white silk stockings, and black leather shoes with silver buckles. Sir Edgar knew his wife well, for their life together had been good. They had seen many apparently happy marriages break up and love depart and Sir Edgar was constantly amazed and grateful that his and Mary's love had lasted so long.

"Christmas is the time to rejoice in the birth of the Savior," he said gently, putting his hand on his wife's shoulder. Then he sat down across from her, noting that, although she was usually a cheerful woman, she was not so now. "What's the matter, dear?" he asked gently.

"Oh, I've just been thinking of the earlier days," she said. Her fingers ceased to be engaged with the knitting as she looked up at him, trying to smile. "Remember how noisy it was when all the children were here? Right here in this room—right there. We always had the big tree."

"Yes, and we always had quite a row over who would get to help me trim it. Then after we trimmed the tree we'd have eggnog, apple cider, and cakes of all kinds. And the Christmas pudding. Oh, those were the most wonderful meals!"

"I think about them a lot."

"So do I. I suppose that's what's sad about Christmas. You think of days that are gone that you can't bring back again."

Mary did not answer but dropped her head and picked up her knitting needles. Outside the wind was sighing gently in the cold, but inside the parlor, the fire in the huge fireplace warmed the pair and sent a glow throughout the whole room.

Trent got up and walked across the room. He paused underneath a large painting and stared at it. It was a painting of a family, his own, and he studied the faces there as if he were trying to find some meaning in them. His eyes passed from his own features to Mary's and he realized again how beautiful she had been—and still was—in his eyes. Then his gaze lingered on their three children and as he looked at the tallest of the two boys, he felt a stab of grief. When he saw Mary watching him, he turned away from it.

At that moment a tall thin servant, dressed in black, entered. "A gentleman to see you, Sir Edgar."

Edgar was surprised, for it was the time of year when people stayed indoors except in emergencies. Taking the card that the servant held out on a silver tray, Edgar Trent read it aloud. "Sir Paul Wakefield." He frowned slightly. "I've never met him."

"I think I did once—or perhaps it was his father. I'm not sure," Mary said. "Wasn't there some sort of trouble in the family?"

Then Trent remembered and nodded. "Yes. Strange affair. Twins were involved, I believe. I can't remember the names now, but evidently this is the one who wound up with the title and with the estate. I wonder what he can be doing here? Bring the gentleman in, John."

"Yes, sir."

The Trents waited, filled with curiosity, and when a tall, well-dressed man wearing a brown wool cape and chestnut-colored coat with brocade trim stepped inside, they were ready to greet him. With the addition of a brown waistcoat and knee breeches, white silk stockings, and black leather boots, Paul Wakefield seemed to be a very prosperous gentleman. "I apologize, Sir Edgar and Lady Mary, for interrupting your Christmas season."

"Not at all, sir. Come and take a seat." As their guest sat down, Sir Edgar had a flash of memory. "I knew your grandfather, Sir John Wakefield. We were at Oxford together. For a time we were very close, but we got separated in the course."

"That's very gratifying to hear a good word about my grandfather."

"I'm afraid we've not kept up with your family," Lady Mary said, admiring the tall young man with the gray blue eyes who sat easily in the chair before her. "What about your father?"

"He became a minister in the Anglican church, my lady."

"Oh, indeed? That sounds like a worthy occupation. And the rest of your family?"

Paul Wakefield smiled. "I expect you must have read about our family turnabout a couple of years ago?"

"I did read something about it," Trent admitted, "but I can't remember the details."

"It was like something out of a romance novel," Paul said. He went on to trace the history of the mystery of his birth and how he had taken his brother's place with the title and the estate. "And so," he concluded, "it's rather strange that a few minutes, at the most, could make such a difference."

"And how is your brother taking this? He must be very bitter," Sir Edgar said, fascinated by the story.

"That's the miracle of it, Sir Edgar, for my brother, David, is not in the least envious. He is probably the least ambitious man I know and I on the other hand, would probably have reacted quite violently if someone had stripped me of my title."

"What is your brother doing now?"

"He's become a writer," Paul said with satisfaction. "And doing well, I'm glad to say. He has two books out now that are doing exceptionally and, according to his publisher, his future is made."

After a little more talk about Paul's history, silence fell across the room. Paul shifted in his chair uncertainly, then stood up and walked to the fireplace. He stared into the fire as if trying to make up his mind how to speak, then said, "Sir Edgar, I've come to give you some news about your family."

"My family?" Sir Edgar said, surprised. "Really, sir, our family is very small. Is it about our daughter?"

"No, sir. I'm not acquainted with your daughter."

"We had two sons, Sir Paul, but they both died. Our only living child lives in Scotland now, an invalid."

Paul then said softly, "Your son, Jeremiah, emigrated to America."

"Yes, it broke our hearts," Lady Mary said, stiffening as if the memory had brought another pang.

"He was a wild lad," Sir Edgar said. "No holding him down and I didn't handle him well, I'm afraid, Sir Paul. I was just a young man myself and did not know how to speak to a son. We had words and I insisted on his going into the law. He said he hated the law and would not follow my dictates." The older man shook his head sadly. "So many times we have regrets that linger for a lifetime and I suppose that's the greatest regret of my life. He might have done great things, for he was a promising young man, if I do say so myself. He ran away to America."

Lady Mary asked, "Why do you speak of Jeremiah, Sir Paul?"

Paul hesitated, not knowing how to break such momentous news. He finally said, "Your son married when he was in America."

"Yes," Sir Edgar said, "We heard he had an Indian squaw."

"It's true enough that there was a great deal of immorality between the white settlers and the Indian women, but in the case of your son, it was quite different."

The older couple's attention was riveted on Paul Wakefield. "How was it different?" Lady Mary inquired. She had forgotten her knitting now and leaned forward with anticipation.

"The woman he married was an Ojibway—a fine woman."

"You knew her?"

"Yes, I did."

"How did that occur?"

"I was somewhat like your son, Jeremiah. I more or less ran away to America and in the course of time I became a trapper. While I was there, I met a young woman. She was half Ojibway and half English."

This information stunned Sir Edgar Trent. His mind worked slowly for a time and he said, "Sir, do you imply that . . ."

He could not go on and it was Lady Mary who said, "Who was the woman, Sir Paul?"

"She was the daughter of your son, Jeremiah."

Lady Mary rose, her hands fluttering at her breast with agitation. "Can this be true?"

"Yes, it is true. I know, because I married her in America. Her name is Marielle. She is your granddaughter, Lady Mary."

Sir Edgar seemed to have trouble with his breathing. Emotion overcame him and he came to stand next to Mary. Both stared at Paul with unbelieving eyes until Sir Edgar stammered, "But—why—how is it that you're here?"

"We have a son, Marielle and I," Paul said, keeping his eyes fixed on the couple. "His name is Honor."

"My great-grandson," Lady Mary whispered.

"Yes, your great-grandson. He's a fine boy. One any man would be proud of, or any woman either."

"Did you just come from America? Did you see them there?"

"No, they're here," Paul said quietly.

"Here—you mean in England?"

"I mean they're waiting outside in the coach. I brought them with me in case you would like to meet them."

Edgar Trent could not believe what he had heard. Conscious of his wife's hand on his arm, squeezing him fiercely, he could not think for a moment. But Mary looked up at Paul and said, "Bring them in, sir. We would very much like to see our granddaughter and great-grandson."

Relief washed over Paul, for he was very much aware of the prejudice against Indians in English society. Now he was glad he had persuaded Marielle to come. She had been reluctant, but he had insisted.

"I'll bring them right in," he said, then turned and left the room, walking rapidly.

"Come, my dear, don't be distressed," Sir Edgar murmured.

"Can it be true, Edgar?"

"I don't know. It's all too sudden." He passed a hand across his forehead in dismay. "I—I just can't take it all in."

The two stood there for what seemed like a long time. At length the sound of footsteps echoed in the corridor outside, the door swung open, and Paul stepped in. Holding the door open, he admitted a woman and a young boy.

"This is my wife, Marielle, and my son, Honor. Marielle and Honor, may I introduce you to Sir Edgar Trent and Lady Mary Trent?"

Marielle had been frightened when Paul had introduced the idea of going to her father's family, but now she saw nothing to fear. The elderly couple were obviously more disturbed than she, so she put her arm over Honor's shoulder and said softly, "I am very happy to know you. My father was such a good, kind man. I think of him so often."

Lady Mary moved across the room in short steps, her eyes fixed upon the young woman. She put out her hand and when Marielle took it, Lady Mary whispered, "I'm so glad to see you, my dear." Then her eyes turned to the boy and she said, "And this is Honor?"

"Yes. My name is Honor."

Sir Edgar studied the pair. The woman wore a scarlet and pearl gray dress of a heavy, embroidered material. And the boy wore a gray wool coat and red waistcoat, both with black brocade trim, a white silk shirt and stockings, black velvet breeches, and black leather boots.

Sir Edgar had been expecting them to come dressed in deerskin and feathers as in the pictures he had seen, so he was shocked that they looked more English than Indian. He shook himself out of his daze and came forward to offer his hand to the woman, who took it and returned the pressure, then turned to the young man. "Well, sir. It appears I have a great-grandson." He managed a smile and looked down at the young man, saying, "Do you suppose you could give your great-grandfather a handshake?"

"Yes, sir."

Then Lady Mary, who was staring at Marielle, said, "Look, Edgar—she has Jeremiah's eyes!"

"She does," Trent said. "And you, my boy, you're very like Jeremiah. Come, let me show you." Trent led the way to the picture and Marielle and Honor stood, looking up at it.

"That's Jeremiah, my father. He was older and I didn't know him for long, but I would know that picture anywhere," Marielle said.

After they had taken in the picture of Jeremiah Trent, Lady Mary said, "Let's sit down. Edgar, have John bring some tea. We've got so much to talk about."

They did talk, slowly and haltingly at first, for there was an awkwardness over the group. But as they grew more easy in each other's presence, Marielle began to speak of her father. "I never had a picture, but I remember him so well. I loved him so much. He was always so kind and gentle with me and with everyone."

The Trents drank all this in, their eyes locked onto the young woman and the boy who had appeared in their lives with no warning whatsoever. Their grief for their son had been keen and lasting. Scarcely a day passed without both of them thinking of the young man who had left so abruptly, never to be seen again. Now as Trent stared at Honor's face, he felt, somehow, that a second chance had been given him and he went to sit beside the boy. Drawing him out, he found that the boy was rather shy. But when he said, "I don't suppose you like horses, do you, Honor?"

Instantly Honor turned, his eyes bright. "Yes, sir. I love horses!"

"I've got one or two out in the stable that need riding. Do you suppose you and I might take that little task on? I'll have to warn you, though, the one I have in mind for you is a bit of a handful."

Honor's head turned quickly toward Marielle and Paul. They both smiled and nodded, so Honor said, "Yes, sir! I would love to ride!"

The visit lasted all day. Honor rode with his great-grandfather and what they said neither ever revealed. But they were firm friends by the end of the ride, that was easy to see. Honor was calling him Grandfather as easily as if he had been doing it all his life. Meanwhile Lady Mary was greatly pleased with the sweetness she had found in Marielle Wakefield. "You've made this a very good Christmas season for us, Sir Paul."

"And for all of us," Paul said softly.

"I hope you will share Honor and your wife with us. I've

longed for a granddaughter and great-grandchildren all my life and now God has given them to me in my old age."

"It would be our great happiness to spend as much time with you as you choose. I think Honor and Sir Edgar are going to be great friends."

Marielle took the old woman's hand. "And you and I, we'll have much to talk about, too. I want to know all about my father when he was a boy."

When the visit came to an end, the older couple walked with them all the way out to the carriage. They extracted promises to visit and accepted Paul's invitation to take Christmas dinner with the family at Wakefield. Marielle embraced Lady Mary, kissing her on the cheek, then put out her hand to Sir Edgar. But he shook his head, smiling. "I'm afraid you'll have to give me a kiss, too, Granddaughter." He took her kiss on his cheek, then shook hands firmly with Honor, slapping him on the back with his free hand. "Now, sir, we'll be there for Christmas. And you and I will do some of those things we've talked about."

When the Wakefields were inside the carriage, they waved farewell and Honor said, "Are they really my great-grandparents?"

"Yes. They really are," Paul said, "and I don't think you could've gotten any better ones. As a matter of fact, someday you may be called Honor Wakefield-Trent. They're both fine names."

As the carriage rolled along, Honor Wakefield leaned back in the leather seat, aware of a fullness to life that he had never known before.

Twenty-Six

A Time for Bethany

W akefield had not known a more jovial Christmas than the one that came in 1774. As the house echoed with the sound of Honor's voice, the servants smiled at each other. The weather was perfect, the ground was white with snow, but the warming winds cut the chill of the air, and by the time the annual Christmas feast arrived, all the preparations had been made.

The house was decorated from front door to back with holly and mistletoe, some of the holly woven into wreaths by the servants and hung from the ceiling by fine threads. The red berries of the holly lent a cheerful, holiday air to the festivities and the house was filled with the delicious baking smells emanating from the kitchen.

The Trents arrived and stayed for three days prior to the Christmas dinner. Marielle had gotten very close to Lady Mary and the two of them spent much time together. It was a joy to the older woman to see her son's features in the beautiful young woman's face and more than once she would touch Marielle's hand, saying, "It's like having Jeremiah back again."

Marielle was pleased. After her long, hard years in captivity, it was strange but exhilarating to feel herself a part of a family. "I suppose that's what children are. Part of ourselves. A legacy for the future," she said quietly.

"And Honor!" Lady Mary exclaimed. "He's Jeremiah all over again! When Jeremiah was his age, he was exactly like Honor. So full of life, so intelligent!"

Marielle sat talking with the older woman for a while, then got up and went to the kitchen for more tea. She had just stepped into the foyer when strong hands seized her, wrapping around her and pulling her back. She squealed and then felt lips nibbling at her neck.

"Paul! You stop that!"

"I can't," Paul said and proceeded to kiss her neck with a resounding smack. He released her enough so that she could turn and when she faced him, he put his arms around her and held her tightly. He looked up and said, "Hmm. There's some mistletoe."

Marielle looked up involuntarily and could not help but smile. "Well, what are you going to do about it?"

"What I'm supposed to do!" Paul kissed her firmly and then gave her an extra squeeze. "It's downright distracting to live with such a beautiful woman! I'll never get anything done with you around!"

Marielle loved it when he teased her like this. She always had and she thought back to the old days when he had caught her off guard. "You'll have to let me go. I've got to take great-grand-mother some tea."

"Lady Mary can wait for her tea."

"No, she can't! Let me go, Paul!"

"All right!" Paul said, releasing her reluctantly, then winked pointedly. "We'll take this matter up later, Mrs. Wakefield."

Marielle slapped him playfully and said, "You!" then went to get the tea.

Paul turned to the right down the hall and went to the library where he knew David would be working. Entering the library, he greeted his brother saying, "Don't you ever stop writing?"

Laying aside his quill, David grinned ruefully. "It's just a habit, I guess."

"Well, break it. It's time for us to talk for a bit."

David sat down across from the fire and faced Paul, who was resting one elbow on the mantelpiece.

"You know, I never much believed in storybooks, David," he said slowly, "but our lives are almost like that."

"It has been a twisted tale, hasn't it?"

"Very much so and up until recently I would have said it was not going to have a happy ending."

"I've had those thoughts myself, but I've always reminded myself that whatever happens to us comes through God's hands."

Paul had been studying the Bible steadfastly under the tutelage of his brother. Now he said earnestly, "I can believe that now, but for most of my life I couldn't. And God has been so good to me in spite of my bad ways." He laughed shortly, then picked up the poker to shift the logs. As they moved and sputtered, sending myriad sparks up the chimney, Paul continued, "I'm like the Prodigal Son in the parable. I couldn't believe that God would be willing to take me after all I'd said about him and all the sins I had let stack up in my life."

David replied, "It's hard for any of us to believe God could really love us, but I think that it's not that God *has* love. The Bible says God *is* love. That's his nature. He can't change because he's God."

The two men spoke for some time until Paul said abruptly, "David, aren't you even a *little* resentful?"

David's eyes flew open in surprise. "Resentful? About what?"

"Oh, don't be so obtuse!" Paul exclaimed with exasperation. "I mean, that I've taken the title and the estate and left you with nothing."

David shook his head slowly. He had gained weight since his sickness and once again the two men looked interchangeable. "I suppose there may have been a few times when I resented what happened, but God's given me peace about it. I don't think about it anymore. I don't want to be Sir David Wakefield. I just want to be David Wakefield, author."

"And from what I hear that's going along in a swimming fashion," Paul said. "What's the latest news from your publisher?"

"Good news." David went on to tell Paul the details of his literary career and when the two men left the library to go for a ride, David said, "It's good to be close, Paul."

"Yes, it is. I didn't know what I was missing when I was so cut off from everyone."

***

Bethany was in her room, staring out the window at the whiteness of the snow, when a gray fox appeared. They were usually such shy and nocturnal creatures that one rarely saw them in the daytime, but this one was a huge fellow with a fluffy gray tail and an alert face.

"What are you doing out there?" Bethany murmured. "You'd better get going. If the groundsman sees you, he'll shoot you for stealing the chickens."

Sensing her eyes, the fox glanced up, then trotted away without the least bit of alarm. "I've never seen a fox in daylight come that close," Bethany said, the sound of her own voice startling her. When someone knocked at the door, she opened it. "Why, hello, David."

"May I come in, Bethany?"

"Of course."

David stepped inside, admiring Bethany in her hunter green velvet dress with the white velvet stomacher that ended in a V at the waist. Underneath the green overskirt was a white velvet petticoat with small green velvet bows sprinkled at random. When David looked at Bethany, he saw a sweetness and goodness that he found in no other. Her beauty existed not just in his eyes but in reality. As he took in her hair and eyes, he couldn't say what he wanted to say and said instead, "You're all grown up, Bethany. It's hard to believe you used to be that little girl with a runny nose who sat on my lap."

"I didn't have a runny nose!"

He grinned at her quick retort and said, "Yes, you did. I had to give you my handkerchief many times. As a matter of fact, I think some of the bad colds I got came from you! You were always right in my face!"

Thinking of those times with sweet poignancy, Bethany said quietly, "Those were the best years, David."

"They were good, weren't they?" Seeing her expression he asked, "Is something wrong? You seem sad."

"No, nothing's wrong. What's that you have?"

"Good news." David held a letter out. "It's from Montgomery, my publisher. Look what he says."

Bethany took the letter and read it. "David, this is wonderful news!" she exclaimed, her face suffused with happiness.

"Yes, it is. According to Montgomery, he will publish as many books as I care to write. All my books are doing so well that they're saying I might be the next Henry Fielding."

"You're better than Fielding."

David laughed and reached for her hand. "I think you're a little prejudiced, but I'm glad of it." Then he looked into her face. "Every word I write is partly yours, Bethany. I couldn't have done it without your support and without your care."

Bethany, very aware of his hand holding hers, nervously pulled it back. "I'm happy for you."

"Well, it'll mean one thing. I can take care of my family now and I'm going to buy a house very close to you. You can visit all the time and we can visit you."

Bethany shook her head slightly. "I'm afraid that's not going to be possible, David."

"What did you say?" David blinked with surprise. "What are you talking about?"

"I'm going away, David."

"Going where? What do you mean? You can't go away." Astonished, David reached up and took her arms. "What are you talking about, Bethany?"

Bethany had foreseen this scene for some time and had prepared exactly what she wanted to say. Looking at him steadfastly, she said, "I can't live any longer as I have been, David."

Nothing could have stunned David more, for he had been so happy with the news of his writing success that it had not occurred to him Bethany might have problems. To his mind, her life had always been perfectly arranged and so serene that the idea of her leaving was foreign to him. Suddenly the world seemed not so bright and cheerful and he said, "Come and sit down, Bethany. Tell me about it."

Bethany allowed him to lead her to the settee and when they were seated she said, "David, you know that I love you. It's not something I planned, but it's there. I think ever since I was a little girl I loved you. You were always the kindest, most gentle, caring person I ever met and that was fine when I was a child." Then she looked at him with an odd expression in her dark eyes and added, "But I'm not a child anymore, David. I'm a woman and a woman wants all of a man. I can't bear not to have all of you. It's a torment for me to be around you, David. So I'm leaving."

Speechless, David Wakefield looked down at his hands, as if hoping they held some answer, but he knew there was none. The matter of his wife was never far from his mind and he muttered miserably, "I can't stand the thought of living without seeing you. I love you, too—"

"You mustn't talk like that. You have a wife and that ends the matter. I'm going to Ireland to be a governess for a family there."

"Ireland's so far away."

"That's as it must be." Bethany stood up, her voice breaking. "I wish you'd go now, David. I—I want to be alone."

David had risen with her. He wanted to put his arms around her, to tell her he loved her, but he knew he could not. It was all so useless and futile. He had a thousand times repented of his marriage and realized his mistake. He loved his children, but he struggled with his memories of Margaret because they were bitter. And he felt he was missing the real life he wanted because of his hasty decision. Still, he knew Bethany was right: He had a wife and that ended the matter.

"When will you be leaving?" he asked resignedly.

"Next week. Now, please go, David."

David left the room, moving like a man in a trance. All throughout the festivities that followed he acted out a role, for one glance at Bethany made him realize that when she left he would be losing part of his life. *It's like someone has ripped the sun out of the sky,* he thought miserably on the last day she would be at Wakefield. And when the time came for her to go to her London home to begin packing, she barely lifted her eyes and whispered almost inaudibly, "Good-bye, David."

His throat full and tight, he could not answer her. As he watched the carriage disappear, he turned blindly away, not able to foresee a future without Bethany Morgan in it.

The *Marybelle* pulled into the dock in London in January 1775 and as soon as the gangplank was down, Ivor Morgan was the first passenger to depart. Handsome in his dark blue uniform, Ivor drew several women's eyes as he marched erectly down the street. He hailed a cab and gave an address, saying jovially, "Hurry up, driver! I've come all the way from America!"

"Have you now, sir? Well, then, we'll see what we can do!"

Ivor leaned back in the cab, his eyes going quickly from the people who crowded the thronging streets to the buildings he had known all of his life and thought, *London hasn't changed. I don't suppose it ever will.* Then he thought of the struggle that was taking place in Boston and shook his head angrily. *They're fools to think the Americans will give up their liberties. They'll all die fighting before they'll do that, but I don't suppose King George III has any idea what Americans are really like.*

He tried to put these troubling thoughts out of his mind and let images of his fiancée fill his heart. He was gladdened that would see her soon. His thoughts were interrupted when the carriage lurched to a halt and Ivor dismounted. Standing on the icy pavement, he handed the driver a coin, took his thanks, and then bounded up the steps to the house. He knocked on the door vigorously and when it opened, he said, "Hello, Mr. Wakefield, a New Year's surprise for you."

"Ivor!" David's eyes glowed and he pulled the young officer inside. "Come into the house! Let me look at you! What a sight you are!"

Ivor laughed at David but ignored his praise. "I've come a long way."

"What are you doing in England? I thought you were in America."

"I've come to bring dispatches for the Crown from General Howe. I think he's asking for more help, which he probably won't get, but even if he does, it won't do any good."

"Tell me about it." The two men went into the small sitting room and while Ivor thawed out by the fire and was served tea and cakes by his host, he told David the sad plight of England's misguided actions in America.

"If King George would only see that Americans *will* have their own country. It's inevitable," Ivor said firmly. "Together England and America could form a strong union—the strongest in the world. But the colonists will not be servants. They'll have their own government and they'll die to get it."

"But they can't stand against the army."

"Have you looked at a map lately?" Ivor grimaced. "The king's forces are scattered all over the world. The navy, too. If it were only the Colonies that were giving trouble, it'd be no difficulty clinching a revolution. But America's an enormous land and the colonists will refuse to fight like Europeans. King George thinks they'll all line up in nice, neat rows and allow themselves to be shot, but they won't. They'll fight like Indians, sniping from trees and behind rock walls. If we beat them in one place, they'll just retreat and go somewhere else." He went on speaking for some time about his feelings about America.

David listened carefully, then said, "I think your sympathy is with the colonists."

"I think they deserve better than the king has given them. Some of them demand too much, but with a little consideration, they would be good, loyal Englishmen." He spread his hands wide. "But that'll never happen now."

David took all this in, then asked, "Have you seen Bethany? She's leaving, you know, for Ireland soon."

"No. I hadn't heard. I must've missed the mail. Why is she going to Ireland?"

David could not answer, could not tell Bethany's brother the truth, so he said weakly, "I—suppose she just wants the change."

But Ivor knew the real reason—his sister loved David Wakefield. He also knew that neither Bethany nor David would consider anything but marriage, which was impossible as long as David had a wife.

Ivor leaned forward, his eyes almost electric. "I have something to tell you. It may come as a shock, David. . . ."

⌁

Back in London, Bethany heard a carriage drive up but paid little heed to it. She continued packing, her mind on the future, which was not a pleasure to her. She had visited Ireland once and thought it a beautiful country, but now just the thought of leaving England and all that it had been to her was abhorrent. She set her teeth, saying, "You can't think about it, Bethany. Don't think about anything but today and today you have to do some packing."

A knock on her bedroom door interrupted her reverie and she straightened to open it, then gasped slightly. "David!"

David Wakefield entered without her permission. "I've got to talk to you, Bethany."

"David, no!" She grasped his arm, attempting to stop him. "There's no point in talking! It's hopeless!"

But David seized her arm and pulled her out of the bedroom, saying, "Come into the sitting room and listen to me."

Bethany saw a vehemence in his eye that she had never seen before, but also an air of happiness. *The least he could do is be as miserable as I am,* she thought almost indignantly. But she allowed herself to be escorted to the sitting room, then said at once, "David, please. I wish you hadn't come. I don't want to talk. Nothing can be settled that way."

But David seemed not to have heard her. As he stood there studying her, he was pleased with what he saw. Then he realized she was highly disturbed and his compassion grew. "I wouldn't have come, Bethany, but something has happened."

"Are the children sick?" she asked, fear coloring her voice.

"No, no. They're fine."

"What is it, then? There's no point trying to talk me out of going to Ireland."

David Wakefield did a strange thing then. He smiled. "I believe I can," he said confidently.

"No! Don't even try! What happiness is there for us? We can never have each other. Please go away, David!" She would have turned away, but he grabbed her arms. She struggled, but he held her until she ceased and when she looked up at him with tears in her eyes, he said, "Don't be grieved, Bethany. I want to tell you something that will change everything."

"What is it?" Bethany could not imagine anything that could change their lives. But at the same time she was thinking, *This may be the last time he'll ever touch me.*

"Ivor came to my house two hours ago."

"Ivor? He's here in England?"

"Yes. He wanted to come, but I had to see you first, to tell you what he told me."

An intuition came to Bethany and she grew very still. "What is it, David?" she asked quietly.

"There's been an epidemic in America. Hundreds are terribly sick, and many have died."

Bethany waited for him to continue and when he did not, she asked, "Was one of them Margaret?"

"Yes. She had a hard time, I'm afraid." David bit his lip. "I wish I could've been there to help. Ivor saw her when she was very ill and he did what he could. She had been forsaken by the man who took her from England and Ivor saw to her comfort as much as possible. He said she died asking forgiveness for what she had done."

"I'm glad of that and that she made her peace with God."

As silence built up between them, David pulled her forward. She did not resist him and when she lifted her face, he kissed her on the lips. He held her soft womanly form as a man holds a very precious gift. "We'll have to wait for a while so that it will be proper. But I love you, Bethany Morgan, and I want you for my wife and as a mother to my children."

Bethany's heart filled with joy. She kissed him firmly, then stepped back. "You'll have to do more courting than that, Mr. David Wakefield!"

David stared at her with bewilderment. "What do you mean?"

"I mean I'll expect to be courted."

David could not believe his ears. "I've known you since you were a child and held you in my lap. We've known each other for—"

"I don't care how long we've known each other. You'll come courting me and everyone will see that David Wakefield is a man in love. And I'll not be easy to win either! I'll expect love poems and we'll have a lover's quarrel." Her eyes sparkled then and she laughed aloud. Reaching up, she tugged his hair. "And I'll pull your hair like I did when I was a little girl."

David grinned broadly. "Love poems?"

"If you can write novels, you can write love poems."

David loved the sight of her eyes dancing with life. She had been so sad and downcast and now she was the old Bethany.

"All right," he said. "I suppose a man in love will do anything to please. So, love poems it is."

Bethany leaned on him then and they embraced again. Then Bethany said, "Can you believe it's going to be you, me, and the children? A family?"

"Yes, I believe it, Bethany. You're the woman God has for me."

"And you're the man God has for me."

As the two stood there in each other's arms, enjoying the quietness of the room and their shared love, Bethany cried, "Oh, David—we're going to have such a life!"

THE END